Darrell started⸱⸱⸱⸱⸱⸱ We—"

Erin's side wi⸱⸱⸱⸱⸱⸱ slivers across the ⸱⸱⸱⸱⸱⸱ ⸱⸱⸱⸱ The sound of an explosion followed a beat behind. Erin screamed. Something stung Darrell's right arm. He grabbed a cut on his skin and then looked across the seat. Damn. Erin's arm was bleeding, bad.

He couldn't breathe. "Erin?" He stared at her for a second and then jerked his gaze back to the road and straightened the car.

Something hit the rear window. Luis yelped. The glass shattered and a second later, another crack followed. Luis fell forward. Was he hit? Darrell's gaze jumped from the road to Erin to the back seat. Luis had fallen to the floor. Darrell couldn't see him.

"Luis?" Erin called.

No answer.

Dragging his eyes from the road, Darrell shot another glance at Erin. Her entire arm was now turning red, the edge of her short sleeve wicking up the scarlet. The fingers of her left hand gripped tight around her right arm, the knuckles turning white. The blood still seeped through.

Dragging his eyes from Erin for a second, he turned in his seat to try to look into the back. He screamed, "Luis!"

Darrell wrenched farther around to look, and his leg bumped the steering wheel. He heard an ugly thump. Too late, he jerked back around to see the car careen over the berm. In three seconds, it slammed into a tree. He heard another explosion and was slammed back against the seat.

Everything went dark.

"A fascinating mystery and I was pulled in with trying to solve it."

"An exciting paranormal mystery I couldn't put down... A great read, especially for this time of the year. Highly recommend!"

"I loved everything about this book. As a ghost story combined with a mystery, a romance, a social injustice and stunning historical details, *Crimson at Cape May* has something for everyone."

"Masterly spooky adventure ...an accomplished work of haunting mystery fiction that fans of the genre won't want to miss out on. Highly Recommend."

"The plot is so engrossing it had me hooked from the very first page."

"A haunting yet fast paced whodunit that captures the readers' attention from page one. A wonderful book!"

BLOOD ON THE CHESAPEAKE:

"An amazingly complex, detailed novel that offers well-developed characters, a stunning backdrop and an unpredictable story line."

"A thrilling whodunit with a supernatural edge. Delightful and engrossing."

~Futures Mostly Mystery Magazine

"A tale to be savored in a darkened room, with an eye to all the possibilities lurking just out of sight."

~William Kent Krueger, NY Times bestselling author

"An absolutely chilling ghost story wrapped around an even scarier piece of history—or perhaps the other way around. Recommended. BEST BOOK"

"Timely and original, this contemporary ghost story is genuinely entertaining …a terrific one-sitting read."

~Hank Phillippi Ryan, bestselling author

"A standout novel of suspense…a spellbinding tale of what happens when past and present collide."

~Mystery Tribune Magazine

"The novel is compelling, a gripping story filled with twists and turns. Realistic and entertaining."

Scarlet at Crystal River

by

Randy Overbeck

Scarlet at Crystal River

COPYRIGHT © 2021 by Randy Overbeck

Cover Art by *The Wild Rose Press, Inc.*

The Wild Rose Press, Inc.
PO Box 708
Adams Basin, NY 14410-0708
Visit us at www.thewildrosepress.com

Publishing History
First Edition, 2021
Trade Paperback ISBN 978-1-5092-3787-6
Digital ISBN 978-1-5092-3788-3

Published in the United States of America

Acknowledgments

Even though writing is often portrayed as a solitary act—one man or woman with a computer—the actual process of bringing to life a narrative like Scarlet at Crystal River has been anything but. First, I want to thank my wife and supportive family, who have been my biggest fans. Again, I asked a group of dependable beta readers to review early versions of the manuscript, and they came through with several great suggestions. Also, I'm confident this novel would not be near as strong without the critiques of the Tuesday Dayton Writing Group, who continued to meet virtually to support me and each other even through the pandemic. Finally, I'm especially grateful to the invaluable advice and recommendations of my two skilled editors, Jaden Terrell and Dianne Rich.

I also want to acknowledge and thank the fine folks of Crystal River, Florida, who welcomed me and supported my story idea for their town. When we visited, we found the merchants and businesspeople friendly and as warm as the sunshine in this charming Gulf Coast town. I'm particularly indebted to Ardath Pendergast of the Citrus County Chamber of Commerce for her help in navigating a town new to me and her coordination with the other fine people of the county. Most of the places, locations, and businesses depicted in and around Citrus County and Crystal River are real and, I hope, accurately portrayed.

Finally, I want to thank Jared Emerson, the very real, very talented artist whom I depict in these pages. I had the pleasure of meeting Jared several years ago and was immediately impressed with the person and the talent. My admiration for his work has only grown since then. Today, Jared Emerson is a renowned performance artist who was gracious enough to allow me to use his real person (at a much younger age) in this fictional account to provide a touch of added authenticity to the work. You can check out his bona fides on the accompanying page.

Chapter 1

December 1999
When we're together, will it always be Christmas?

The honeymoon started with such promise Darrell Henshaw would never have guessed it could've gone off the rails so badly.

Shortly after the jet had reached cruising speed, a flight attendant announced over the loudspeaker, "Congratulations to our newlyweds aboard in seats 13E and D," and the entire plane erupted in applause. Since he hadn't arranged it, Darrell figured Al McClure, his friend and chief tormentor at Wilshire High School, must have given them up. Still, he really enjoyed hearing "Mr. and Mrs. Henshaw" coming through the speakers. And the slightly embarrassed smile Erin wore made it that much sweeter.

As they boarded, the flight steward announced, "We have a completely full flight today. We need to get everyone where they want to go for Christmas." The plane was packed.

He glanced around the cramped space inside jammed with bodies and swallowed the lump in his throat. He willed himself to get smaller—not easy at two hundred ten pounds—but found it hard to fold his six-foot-plus frame into what passed for seat 13E. Thank God the flight lasted only two hours. He could make it. He could do this for Erin, his new wife.

He still wasn't sure that had sunk in completely. Less than two years ago, he was cheated on, heartbroken, and dumped at the altar, not sure he'd ever find anyone again. Hell, he'd moved six hundred miles simply to get away from it all. Now, he had this great job teaching and coaching at Wilshire, *and* he found the most captivating, enchanting, and intelligent girl. Best of all, when he asked her to marry him, she'd said yes!

Since the night sixteen months ago when Erin had stepped into the McClures' family room after her shift as an OB nurse, Darrell had fallen hard. When he first saw that tired but beautiful face, dotted with a few freckles and framed by the lustrous red hair, he'd been hooked. Her gorgeous smile, which she gave him often, made his day. And he soon learned her heart was even more beautiful than her looks. She tended to her patients, young mothers and their new babies, like he cared for his students. And she didn't seem to mind his OCD tendencies—though she sometimes kidded him about them—and even appreciated his special *gift*.

Had his proposal been five months ago? The time had flown by in a heartbeat. Between teaching his classes and coaching another season of football at Wilshire and Erin's schedule at the hospital, they used almost every moment together to plan the ceremony and reception. Deciding on the guest list had taken almost two weeks. And Erin spent at least that long searching for the right wedding dress. But, like he told his student athletes, good prep was time well spent.

Man and wife. He took another deep breath.

Images of their wedding day flashed by in his head, welcomed distractions inside the crowded cabin.

The church decked out in its finest holiday decor; gorgeous blooming poinsettias overflowing down the steps and into the aisles. The three bridesmaids in deep crimson gowns, strolling down the center between pews adorned with pine garlands; the entire church smelling like an old growth forest. Then the whole crowd standing as Erin entered in that dazzling white gown with the high neckline; the beautiful sight of her taking his breath away. Across the length of the nave, thirty rows away, she flashed a crooked smile at him, and his heart had done a flip.

Behind him, someone coughed, shattering his daydream. His gaze drifted across the rows and rows of people stuffed like sardines—sweaty, germy sardines— into the too tight seats. Sweat trickled across his hairline.

He snatched his personal bottle of hand sanitizer out of the seatback pocket and squirted some onto his palm, rubbing his hands together vigorously. It was already the third time he'd used the stuff during the flight. Thinking of the germs accumulated on the cushions, the armrests, the seatbacks, not to mention those dumb plastic trays that folded down, he shuddered and rubbed harder.

As he massaged, his strokes so hard his palms heated up, he caught his wife's grin. He shrugged, then chuckled. Her expression reminded him of the same grin at their reception yesterday.

The traditional dances under a banner emblazoned with their theme: "When we're together, it'll always be Christmas." Erin and her dad swishing across the floor in the customary father and bride dance; a proud smile across his leathered face and Erin giggling at something he said. The relaxed and easy dance with his own mom, their steps measured and rhythmic.

The wedding toasts. His dad surprised Darrell with a terse, insightful dedication about love and forgiveness. Even Al hadn't embarrassed them, offering a lame pun, barely humorous, but in good taste. When his older brother Craig limped up to the microphone and uttered his stirring toast, Darrell couldn't hold it in anymore. He broke down in tears and wrapped him in a bear hug.

Erin had even been kind to him and *not* smashed the delicious wedding cake all over his face—as she'd threatened more than once—the entire crowd applauding. And she wore that same grin. The whole thing had been damn near perfect.

Two or three rows ahead—he couldn't really tell— another person gave a loud sneeze, and Darrell reached for the sanitizer again.

"Hey, if you look down, you can just see the coastline. And look at the incredible blue of the water." Erin's whispered words carried her excitement.

From the tight middle seat, Darrell leaned across and glanced out the window but couldn't get the right angle to locate the shoreline, seeing only an endless expanse of azure. When he pulled back, the small glass pane reflected Erin's face, exhilaration evident in those shining emerald eyes. So he nodded and smiled back.

He stared at his lovely wife—it felt great simply to think that—and worked to tamp down his OCD. He focused on that beautiful face, the freckles popping with her excitement, and he breathed slowly in and out. She sported a long sleeve shirt in a sky blue, top two buttons open and collar turned up, barely brushing the

4

tresses of lustrous red that hung down. The top was the perfect complement to her flowered jeans, the denim also a lighter blue. She needed the warmth when they left the Eastern Shore, but the outfit would soon be too warm for the Florida climate.

"Can't wait to see Crystal River." Erin broke into his reverie. "From what I've heard, it sounds delightful."

"When your doctor friend suggested it—" Darrell started.

"Dr. Simmons," supplied Erin. "When we get back, he gets the first thank you note."

"Yeah, Dr. Simmons. I still can't believe he lent you his house—right on the water," Darrell said. "He must be some nice guy. Or he owes you, big time."

Erin wrinkled her nose. "I'm not telling, but he's old enough to be my father."

"Anyway, I don't think I'd ever heard of Crystal River before. But when I checked it out, it looked like a really neat place. A small, quaint town with an interesting history built on some beautiful freshwater springs. Supposed to have a nice sandy beach and some great running trails."

"Don't forget about the manatees," she added. "Doc Simmons usually comes down at Christmas simply to see the manatees, only this year his wife wanted to go to Colorado for the holidays. That's why he let us have his house. Well, that and because I'm his favorite nurse." Her green eyes sparkled.

"And won't it be terrible to have to suffer through temps in the seventies the whole Christmas break?" Darrell teased.

A serious look crossed her face. "You sure you

won't miss the usual Christmas atmosphere? Your mom told me it often snowed at Christmastime in Michigan. She said they already had four inches on the ground up north. You don't think you'll miss a white Christmas?"

"Maybe a little. I used to love going outside on Christmas morning and having a snowball fight with Craig and the other kids on our street." Darrell grew wistful. "But it will be hard to miss that when I have my own Christmas Queen." His eyebrows did a dance up and down, and he lowered his voice. "Naked in bed beside me."

Erin said, "Shhh," but there was no conviction in it. She glanced over to their row mate, who sat on the aisle, headphones still on both ears, apparently oblivious to their whisperings. She smirked.

A flight attendant stopped at their row and leaned in. "I hope you two have a fun and exciting time on your honeymoon."

"We're really looking forward to it," Erin bubbled and glanced at him.

"We certainly are," Darrell said, but thought not *too* exciting.

Exciting.

That single word conjured up a memory of the past week he'd been trying to forget. The bachelor party thrown by Al, his best man, with way too much drinking and male adolescent antics. He'd expected most of it—the ridiculous toasts, the ribbing from his friends and family about the ball and chain, the bad puns, even the striptease act. But he hadn't anticipated the huge cake with a surprise guest inside, popping out in a skimpy bikini. The raven-haired, dark-skinned young woman with generous proportions and ruby-red lips drew nimble limbs out of the fake cake, all the while leering at Darrell.

He even recalled Al's taunt, "In another two days, you'll no longer be a free man. The knot'll be tied. Better take advantage while you can."

Al maneuvered them both into a private booth he'd arranged, cordoned off from the group. It was all in good fun until…until his addled brain recognized the woman was Natalia. The medium with other less savory *talents.* He hoped she'd do some exotic lap dance or something, and he'd be done with it. Instead, alone with him, away from prying eyes, she grasped both his hands and, like the times before, electricity shot up his arms. It hurt like hell. He started to pull back and yell something when her eyes rolled back in her head. Same as before. Even drunk, that freaked him out again. Her words, whispered in that strange Slavic accent, burned into his beer-soaked brain.

"Ve do not have much time. Ven you go to Crystal River, you vill have…two visitors from the other side, two visitors vaiting for you. The earth shudders vith their veeping, vith their silent cries of anguish. But you must be careful. I see a malevolence, a great danger lurking nearby. There are those who do not vant them found. These two are the forgotten ones, insignificant and ignored. No one knows or cares. *You* must care, Darrell Henshaw. *You* must help."

Now, ten thousand feet in the air and dead sober, he wondered whether he should tell Erin about Natalia's prediction. *That* would be trouble. Erin couldn't stand Natalia.

He glanced at his wife, her face beaming with excitement, eyes shining with anticipation. He didn't want to do anything to mess this up. He realized if things went sideways, he could use her help. She kept her calm and sometimes saw things he'd miss. Not to mention having her beside him made him braver, gave him courage.

But come on, they were on their honeymoon. And the last thing he wanted to do was to spoil it. *If* he ran into two ghosts, two victims, he'd figure out a way to manage the whole thing. He could always clue Erin in later.

"This is your captain," a deep male voice announced over the intercom. "We're beginning our approach to Tampa International Airport. Please return your seatbacks to their upright positions and stow any tray tables." There was a pause, and then he came back on. "Thank you for flying with us, and we hope you have a great holiday. Oh, and don't get caught in the air on Y2K, when all the computers are going to seize up and stop." A chuckle came through the loudspeakers followed by, "Only kidding, folks."

Just what he needed, one more thing to worry about.

Chapter 2

Not quite home for Christmas

"*This* is your doc friend's vacation home?" Darrell turned toward Erin who studied a paper in her hand.

Her gaze went from the sheet to the house and back to Darrell. "It's the address they gave us."

Following the directions from the real estate office, they'd taken US 19 to the edge of the small town and turned onto a road with a Native American name Darrell had trouble pronouncing. The street turned out to be a two-lane bordered on both sides by towering palm trees, with deciduous trees, shrubs, and bushes crowding every space. As he drove, windows open in the delightfully warm Florida air, the earthy and mossy smells floated in. Making their way on the long and winding road, they'd passed only a few driveways and never sighted a single dwelling through vegetation so thick it seemed impenetrable. Then, after several very slow miles, as if on cue, the woods opened into a huge natural clearing that edged a half mile of rugged shoreline. And beyond lay the river or bay. Several houses dotted the shore, their backs to the water and cement driveways jutting out to meet the paved road like bright white tongues. Checking the numbers on the mailboxes, Darrell had steered the rental into the third driveway, which curved in a semicircle in front of the house, stopping behind a bright red SUV.

Before they were even out of the car, the oversized front door burst open, and a tall, attractive woman in a sleek, jade pantsuit strode out. She hollered at them, her voice with a warm, southern inflection, "You must be Erin and Darrell. I'm Bonnie Bradford, and I handle this property for Dr. Simmons. He called and told me to make you feel at home."

She reached the car, and Darrell and Erin hustled around the front to shake hands with the woman, who continued, "Welcome. I'm sorry I couldn't meet ya at the office when ya picked up the key, but I had a few things to take care of and wanted to give the house a final check."

"Nice place," Darrell said, indicating the tall ranch house.

It was not new. In fact, much of the front of the house was covered with hundreds of small, flat fieldstone rocks fitted together—very old style—as if some nineteenth century artisan had crafted a masterpiece. The generous wood trim edging the fieldstone was painted a very Floridian teal, which set off the scrubbed white and gold of the stone. A huge pine wreath hung suspended in the middle of the fieldstone.

"Very nice." Bonnie pointed to the front door. "Come on in and I'll show you around."

She led the way, holding open an ornate door with beautiful inlaid glass etchings as they crossed the small porch and entered. "Dr. Simmons, Harold, told me you're on your honeymoon. Congratulations!" She practically gushed and patted Erin's arm.

Darrell studied the agent's face—bright brown

eyes over a small nose and mouth, all framed with brunette hair, cut pageboy style—and decided she looked sincere. He laced an arm around Erin's middle. "Yeah, I got really lucky and won her heart. Way out of my league, but she said yes anyway."

"Lucky man." Bonnie turned and winked at Erin. "It's nice to be appreciated. Right?"

Nodding, Erin flashed a smile, a slight blush on her cheeks.

Darrell asked, "We know Crystal River is in Citrus County, but when we drove here from the airport, we didn't see any citrus groves. Did we miss them, or are they not located near the highway?"

"No, you didn't miss any groves. There's an interesting story behind that." Bonnie grinned. "Part of our history here you might be interested in. Harold mentioned you were into history. A history teacher, right?"

Darrell shrugged. "Guilty as charged."

Bonnie took a breath. "You see, early settlers here found citrus trees growing in abundance, thanks mostly to the Spanish explorers who'd brought oranges with them to fight scurvy and then simply discarded the seeds here. Then, following the Civil War, people from the North started arriving, attracted by our great climate and the chance to get into the citrus farming business. And things went pretty well for a while, earning the name of Citrus County."

Darrell was intrigued. "But—"

The real estate agent continued, and Darrell could tell she'd given this spiel before. "Things were going well until the harsh winter of 1894-95. The area had a major freeze, and it wiped out almost all the citrus trees.

11

The serious farmers moved their business farther south, but the county name stuck."

Erin came up alongside her husband. "Thanks. Darrell is always interested in the history of places."

Darrell waved one hand to indicate the house. "Now, what can you tell about this place?"

Bonnie took the hint and launched into her realtor mode. "This is known as the Franklin Place, a really old homestead with great bones, and has sat on this land for almost a hundred years." She went over and patted the drywall. "Built with twelve-inch-thick concrete walls, it's withstood three hurricanes with barely a scratch. But when Dr. Simmons bought it back in '96, he had it completely renovated. He brought all the plumbing and the wiring up to code and updated the bathrooms and the kitchen." She pointed down the small hallway. "Com'on. I'll show ya the place."

Bonnie led them to the center of the house, and the first thing they noticed was an eight-foot Christmas tree in the family room, fully decorated, its gold ball ornaments sparkling in the sunlight. The room radiated a delightful pine scent.

Erin beamed and squeezed Darrell's arm, her eyes scanning the tree. "It's gorgeous."

The Christmas tree was tucked neatly into the corner of the spacious family room, snug against wide French doors that afforded a wide view of the water. On the left wall beside the tree sat an oversized fireplace, its hearth constructed of fieldstone that matched the design on the exterior. Atop the fireplace hung a wood mantel, stained a deep brown to match the hardwood floors. Two stockings hung on the mantel, one with a needle-pointed Santa and another with Mrs. Claus.

Erin pointed and squeaked, "Look, Darrell. Mr. and Mrs. Claus."

Darrell grinned. "Almost as good as Mr. and Mrs. Henshaw."

Erin snapped her fingers. "Hey. Got an idea. Wait a sec." She reached into her large purse and pulled out a small, black disposable camera. To Bonnie she said, "We had these at all the tables at our reception. Afterward, we collected them, and most of them still have photos left. Brought a few along to finish off the pictures." She handed the camera to the agent. "I'd love to have a photo of us next to that great tree. Would you do the honors?"

Darrell and Erin posed, arms around each other's waists as the agent clicked.

After the quick photo session, Bonnie led them down a short hallway. "Here's what you're really going to love." She opened double doors to reveal a huge master bedroom, complete with a large four-poster, king-size bed. The room faced the water, and another set of French doors opened onto a screened-in porch with his and her chaise lounges. She led them to the right, and they found an equally impressive master bath, with a large, glass-enclosed shower for two and a double Jacuzzi.

Darrell slid his hand along the Jacuzzi tile and did a Groucho Marx thing with his eyebrows. "This Dr. Simmons must be a real romantic. We'll have to do our best to live up to his amorous aspirations."

Erin's cheeks bloomed red again, and she smacked Darrell lightly on the arm.

"You two." Bonnie chuckled. "Oh, one more thing. I don't know how many meals you'll be making in—we have some really great restaurants here in Citrus County—but you're going to love the kitchen. It's been completely redone, and it's fabulous. Dr. Simmons installed a commercial fridge and freezer combination and a gorgeous granite-topped island—"

The doorbell rang, cutting her off, and she turned to the two of them. "Are you expecting any deliveries?"

Darrell and Erin shook their heads.

Bonnie hustled to the front door, opening it. "It's probably Luis. I asked him to bring some stuff by." As Darrell and Erin followed, they heard a rapid, though pleasant exchange in Spanish. The realtor swung the door wide open and gestured in. "Darrell and Erin, this is Luis Alvarez, my executive assistant."

A short young man with tan skin, a wide smile, and bright hazel eyes stood in the doorway holding two large bags, one from a local grocery and one with the logo of an Italian restaurant. The young man looked as if he was bursting with energy and joy, his features lighting up at Bonnie's acknowledgement. Though a little under six feet tall, he carried a slender frame with small, rounded shoulders. He set the bags on the floor, stepped forward, and reached out to shake Darrell's hand, his grip firmer than his build suggested. He nodded to Erin and said, "*Mucho gusto. Bienvenidos a Florida.*"

Bonnie probably saw their puzzled looks because she said, "You must not speak much Spanish. You'll hear a lot of that down here. Luis said he was pleased to meet you and offered his welcome."

They both nodded, and Darrell said, "*Gracias.*"

The young man said, "*Sí,*" and nodded, smiling. Bonnie made a few more comments in Spanish, and

Luis picked up both bags and headed into the kitchen.

Watching him go, Bonnie said, "Luis is still learning English, but he's been a great help. He knows about a lot of people in the area. He's managed to make connections with a good number of Spanish families in Citrus and the surrounding counties."

Erin said, "We picked up some things at the store too."

Bonnie nodded. "Harold wanted to make sure you were stocked with the basics. Oh, and before I forget, I put together some restaurant suggestions, both for breakfast and lunch as well as dinner. I left a note with some of my favorites on the side of the fridge."

"In that case, *gracias* again."

Darrell felt the slightest prickle on his neck and glanced around. Natalia's words came back to him. *Two visitors.* He hoped two visitors weren't hiding in the walls.

"Could I ask a silly question?" He exchanged a look with Erin and glanced back at their tour guide. "You said this place is one hundred years old?"

"Yeah, it's been in the family most of that time. Why do you ask?"

Darrell swallowed and gazed at Bonnie. "Have you heard any stories about this place being haunted?"

Bonnie and Luis exchanged a few words in Spanish, their hands flying in the air, and both chuckled. When she saw Darrell didn't share their humor, the agent said, "You're serious?"

He gave a quick nod.

"No, I can't say I've ever heard any stories about ghosts roaming around here. Now, if you're looking for some hauntings around the area, you might want to head to Inverness."

Erin broke in, "Thanks, no. I think we'll be busy with other pursuits." She glanced at her husband. "Darrell was simply curious."

"Oh, history and all. I get it," Bonnie said.

After Bonnie had given them keys and final instructions, they stood on the porch as the realtor and her assistant drove away. Watching the SUV and the battered pickup head back the way they came, Erin said, "Well, Doc Simmons has quite the romantic getaway here. I might owe him *two* thank you notes."

"We'll do our best to live up to the romantic part." Darrell leaned in to pull Erin close. "Now, where should we begin our amorous adventures?"

"Easy, tiger." She placed a palm on his chest, giving him a gentle shove. "Bring in the groceries before they spoil in this beautiful Florida sun."

Darrell headed out to the car, hurrying to retrieve the perishables while she went back inside. Opening the car door, he snatched up the two bags off the seat behind the driver and, using his hip, nudged the car door shut. Imagining what romantic adventure they might try first, he started back to the house.

He edged around the car and stepped into the driveway but had to stop. Two kids on small bicycles with training wheels whizzed by, one on either side of him. He turned sideways and raised both bags high. "Hey!" he cried, but neither kid reacted, and they both kept pedaling.

He must've been concentrating on his amorous intentions—he hadn't even seen them. Or heard them. He shot a glance and only got a quick look before they were past, a boy and a girl, maybe five or six. He crossed the distance to the door and, when he turned and looked back where the kids had ridden, he didn't see them anymore. He didn't hear the clatter of their wheels on the pavement either.

He stopped, frozen, and stared. Rotating, he did a slow three sixty, holding a bag in each hand, and scanned the landscape, thinking he'd gotten turned around somehow. He didn't see anyone moving in the little enclave of houses. He heard the echo of a car, and three doors up the street he saw a shiny white SUV backing out of the driveway, the driver the lone occupant. The two kids were nowhere around.

Could they have gone into one of the neighbors'?

A prickle scratched at his neck and ran down his back. He turned again and checked for the two kids, as Natalia's warning echoed in his mind—*two visitors.*

Oh, shit. He'd been here before.

He had the *gift.* He'd been seeing spectral *visitors* since he was thirteen. When he got a visitation from the ghost of his uncle. That visit had cost one kid his life and crippled his brother. And left him with a nasty case of OCD. Then, when the next ghost materialized and demanded Darrell's help, justice came at the price of four more deaths, and Darrell was nearly another one.

He pulled the front door open and halted. Should he tell Erin about the vanishing kids? Absolutely not. He refused to go there.

Shaking his head, he continued through the front door when he caught sight of Erin and saw what she was wearing. Or rather, what she wasn't.

He forgot to put the milk and eggs in the fridge. And completely forgot about the two kids.

Chapter 3

Do manatees sleep in heavenly peace?

"What a view to wake up to," Erin said, staring out at the blue green of the water. She flashed a tired smile across at Darrell, a little sleep still in her eyes.

Darrell said, "Kinda makes me think of the Eastern Shore."

"Yeah, except back there it's twenty degrees right now. We'd freeze to death like this."

He glanced down. All he had on was a pair of boxers, his long bare legs stretching out on the chaise lounge. "Yeah, but you'd look good doing it."

And she did look good.

Erin lay on the navy chaise, wearing one of the long sleeved, button-down Oxford shirts he'd packed in case he took her some place nice. She rolled the sleeves up, and her hands cupped a mug, the steam wafting past a few freckles on her petite face. Her long, red hair, still beautifully disheveled from slumber, hung down, glancing the collar of the shirt.

His Oxford looked better on her.

He lay against the back of the matching chaise lounge and took in the view. They both relaxed under the fine mesh screen on the patio outside the master bedroom.

When Bonnie had showed them the house, she

explained the screens were vital protection from pesky mosquitoes in the summer. During other seasons, they kept out the "no-see-ums," which she said were vicious, tiny, black sand flies that invaded dawn and dusk. Darrell had a momentary vision of a swarm of the tiny black insects attacking his flesh and shuddered. Even though the insects only invaded in the spring and fall, he was grateful to be viewing the scene through the fine mesh.

Beyond lay a long expanse of sparkling blue-green water, its surface slowly rippling. Off to the left sat an island or peninsula—he couldn't tell which—its surface covered in tall, old-growth trees and knotted thick with vegetation. To the right and beyond, all he could see was water. According to the agent, they were looking at Dixie Bay, which emptied into Crystal Bay, which eventually dumped into the Gulf of Mexico. Here at Simmons' place, there was little enough shore, merely a few rocks and small boulders stuffed into a small clump of sand that extended about six feet inland. Dixie Bay lay only a few yards from where they lounged. It looked calm, and peaceful, and soothing. Much like the Chesapeake Bay on a mild summer day, though he recognized a different aroma. The shore here didn't possess the brackish scent he'd grown so accustomed to back on the Eastern Shore. Here the water smelled fresher, cleaner.

For a while, they both sipped their coffee in companionable silence, broken only by the errant calls of birds and the quiet chirp of insects. Contented, they watched the small waves lap against the shore.

Yesterday had been exhausting. After all the traveling and by the time they'd unpacked the car and stored everything in its proper place in the vacation home, they were both drained, their adrenalin spent. However, they did manage to find enough energy to engage in a few pleasurable pursuits. They settled in to their new, albeit temporary, home and stayed in, even splitting the delicious pasta Luis had delivered.

Glancing over at his new wife, Darrell mused, it was a night well spent. They'd slept well. When he awoke this morning to the warbling of some native birds and watched Erin asleep beside him, her chest rising and falling easily, he'd felt so comfortable, so natural. The thought that flitted through his mind was they were supposed to be like this, together forever. From what Erin had shared during their quiet lovemaking last night, he knew she felt the same way.

The last thing he wanted to do was shatter their easy, domestic tranquility with any mention of Natalia's prophecy or the strange appearance of two kids. Or their disappearance. Which he could've imagined anyway.

Erin set down her mug and picked up the stack of brochures she'd discovered in a kitchen drawer. "There are so many things I want to do. Not sure what to do first. Definitely want to swim with the manatees. And we *have* to check out the Gulf Beach at Fort Island." She waved another colorful brochure at Darrell. "Did you know they have six different trails for us to run? It says they run through different forest habitats, through salt marshes, and even along the Gulf of Mexico."

Darrell eyed Erin relaxing on the chaise and lay back, stretching out his legs on his own lounger. "I vote we don't do that today."

"Poor boy. Did I tire you out last night?" She

grinned.

In the end, they settled on a trip to the Three Sisters Springs for the day to get an up-close look at some manatees, which neither had ever seen in person. After they showered in the two-person shower—which took a little longer because it was a two-person shower—and dressed, they drove back into town, purchased their tickets, and rode the trolley, adorned with a life-sized painting of the mammal, from downtown to the park.

Like true tourists, they took their time walking along the wooden boardwalk, holding hands, talking with the docents, and reading the signs. Stands of trees overhung the wooden trail, casting the walk mostly in shade and keeping it cool, the space smelling fresh and moist. Darrell and Erin were surprised to see the springs were quite shallow, only four feet deep in most spots according to one sign, the water a sparkling blue. At the three overlooks built into the boardwalk, they stopped to study the placid creatures, some six to ten feet long with torpedo-like bodies and flattened tails, resting or floating gracefully. Unless a manatee disturbed the silt, briefly sending a murky film through the water, Darrell could see into the springs as clearly as looking into a swimming pool. As he stared across the water, he counted over fifty of the grayish-brown shapes along the bottom of the clear pool.

As they watched, he noticed the manatees spent nearly all their time submerged, only coming up periodically for air before sliding back under the water. Darrell turned to Erin. "I wonder how long they can hold their breath."

A nearby docent must've heard the question because she sauntered over to them. The woman, in her sixties, with white hair brushed back and a friendly face tanned and wrinkled by the sun, smiled. "We get that question all the time. They're mammals, you know, like you and me, so they have to breathe air. But they can hold their breath for a considerable time. If they're awake, almost three minutes. Up to twenty, if they're sleeping."

"What brings them here? To Crystal River?" Erin asked.

"It's the temperature," answered the docent. "The water is a constant seventy-two degrees year-round, thanks to the springs. When the water in the gulf gets too cool, they head here. They usually hang around from December to sometime in early March. And we're thrilled to have them."

Darrell watched as one rose to the surface, the gray snout briefly out of the water, and, after a few seconds, it disappeared below. Without taking his eyes off the curious creatures, he asked, "Are they endangered?"

The woman nodded. "Very much so. In fact, if Jacques Cousteau hadn't come here to study these wonderful creatures in '72, I doubt any of them would be around today. He even filmed a TV special here, and that made the world take notice. Though they were only designated as endangered a few years ago."

Erin reached into her purse and pulled out the small camera. "Would you take a picture?"

The older woman nodded, and Darrell and Erin moved so the docent could capture them under the tree canopy with the boardwalk winding behind them. As they maneuvered into place, he shot a glance at his wife. Today she'd chosen a white cropped top with an open collar. The piece ended in a fancy tie, which hung right below her breast and showed off her flat midriff. The blouse was matched with hip-hugger jeans shorts. He realized she'd make his polo and dress shorts look...well, staid. That was fine with him. Smiling back at them, the volunteer snapped the shot.

Darrell thanked her and started to ask another question when a sharp prickle ran across his neck. A rattle of wooden boards of the walkway behind him made him turn. Glancing toward the noise, he saw two children ride past on small bicycles with training wheels, a young boy and girl, both brown haired. The hard rubber of the wheels slammed onto the separate planks, the clatter diminishing as they rode around the bend.

Hoping against hope, he turned to ask the docent if she knew the kids—maybe they were regular visitors— but when he turned back, he saw no one else had taken note of the noise—or the kids. Mesmerized by the quiet manatees, Erin, the docent, and another older couple were still watching the water. They either hadn't heard or hadn't noticed the racket made by the bikes.

He jerked his gaze back down the boardwalk where the kids had ridden. About fifty feet around a curve, the wide walkway dead ended. Without saying a word, he left Erin and strode down the wooden slats, figuring he'd run into the kids coming back. But when he got to where the boardwalk ended, he saw no one. No other visitors. Definitely no young ones on bikes.

What the hell. He stared, unbelieving. The same two kids he'd seen yesterday? The tingling sensation returned to his neck, this time accompanied by a sense of dread and ugliness. Natalia's tense words, whispered in that booth back in Wilshire, echoed in his head. *"You vill have two visitors.*"

He didn't want this happening, not now, not here. Shaking his head, he strolled back to where Erin still stood, hands on the rail, concentrating on the manatees. When he came up next to her, she must've seen something in his face. "What?" she asked.

He struggled, trying to decide how to answer, watching concern bloom across his wife's features. He couldn't tell her now. Not with the docent beside them and the other couple only a few feet away.

And then, a sick certainty struck him. If he pursued this, if he tried to help the ghosts again, it wouldn't simply spoil their honeymoon. He could bring the consequences not merely on him, but on Erin. His *wife.*

He placed his hand over hers. "It's nothing. I thought I saw a large alligator, but when I checked it out, it was only another manatee."

"Oh, there are plenty of alligators in the springs as well. People think of alligators as dangerous, and they can be, to people. But they never bother the manatees. The manatees' hide is so thick…"

The docent rambled on, but Darrell didn't hear, fixated on one word. Dangerous. Straight out of Natalia's prophecy, the word battered around inside his skull. *"I see a malevolence, great danger lurking nearby."*

Chapter 4

Trading snowsuits for swimsuits

Erin couldn't wait any longer to hit the beach. The next day, after they slept in again, they were up, fed, and off before ten. They found everything they could want in the garage—beach chairs, colorful beach umbrellas, and enough beach towels to outfit an army—and headed off in search of sand and surf.

However, the trip to the shore took longer than Darrell anticipated. First, he drove back to US 19 and almost to town before turning onto FL 44. Instead of the beach being close, the two-lane road wound through miles of forested and swampy land. If he hadn't passed a state park sign for the beach, Darrell would've been certain he'd taken the wrong route.

As he drove, he said, "According to what I read, this beach we're headed to sits right next to some ancient Native American mounds, a really interesting set of different kinds of mounds. Some of the works date back to 500 B.C. They believe these natives—some tribe called Depford—built a settlement here and lived for two thousand years. They abandoned this site a little before European settlers arrived. They don't know why."

He glanced across as they passed more and more acres of trees and choked growth. Erin smiled back and said, "That's pretty interesting, but you know what I'm really interested in today?" She raised her pretty eyebrows.

He smiled back. "I can guess."

"You got it. A little swim and surf in December!" she squealed.

He nodded and kept driving, following the highway almost to the end of a peninsula of land. When they finally arrived, the beach appeared smaller than he expected. Bonnie Bradford had bragged about "the gorgeous white sand beach," explaining it was the only gulf beach in the county, as most of the county's shoreline was tangled in swamps, marshlands, and forests. When he pulled the car into one of the open spots in the small gravel parking lot, Darrell surveyed the shore, which curved in the shape of an elongated C and ran about the length of two football fields. He was surprised to see the beach itself was only about one hundred fifty feet wide, front to back. The sandy stretch was bracketed on both ends by huge copses of trees, bushes, and tangled overgrowth with a few solitary palm trees towering above the other flora.

At least they wouldn't have to walk far. The sand began only a few feet from the edge of the parking lot. Unloading the equipment from the back seat, Darrell slipped one arm through the beach chairs and used the other to lug the colorful umbrella. Beside him, Erin carried a small cooler with some culinary essentials with one arm, and the other clutched their vibrant beach towels.

Struggling with his large load, Darrell let Erin lead, and she headed for an open spot about halfway between the parked car and the water, slightly on the left. As they dodged beach towels and chairs deposited on the sand, they stepped past a small shelter with a raised concrete slab, already claimed this early in the day, picnic baskets and coolers perched atop a wooden table. As they crossed the space, he noticed the beach—unlike others he'd seen—had very little incline, the sand sloping only slightly to the water's edge.

As soon as their cargo was unloaded and set up, Erin stripped off her cover-up, twirled once in her yellow bikini, and plopped into a chair. Shielding her eyes from the bright sun, she said, "Hard to believe we're lounging on a beach a few days before Christmas. Not like any Christmas I can remember."

He leaned over and kissed her, whispering, "One we'll never forget." Pulling his tee over his head, he sat next to her, scanning the shoreline.

A few bathers had ventured into the gulf, wading halfway out into the slow, lapping waves, with the water only up to their thighs. He saw, perhaps three hundred feet out, a long line of rock breakers keeping the wave action more controlled and calm. Glancing left and right, he scanned the beach and saw several other couples lying on matching towels.

Darrell and Erin cranked their chairs back and reclined, holding hands, watching a perfect azure sky with tiny wisps of white clouds skittering across. A small flock of seagulls flew overhead and landed in the shallow surf fifty feet away, their squawks echoing through the air.

"This is perfect. You know that?" Erin turned toward him.

Darrell used one hand to shield their faces from the sun almost directly overhead and kissed her again.

"Only perfect because we're here together."

A father who'd been playing in the surf with two toddlers brought them back and deposited them on a towel nearby. Hearing a commotion, Darrell looked their way. One of the kids, a girl from her pigtails, was tossing sand at her brother, who was grabbing handfuls and pitching them at her. The father growled a few harsh words, and they froze.

Darrell turned back toward Erin. "Do you think I'll be a good father?"

She turned toward him, their foreheads almost touching now. "I know we both said we want kids, uh...but I thought we'd wait a little bit. I mean we've only been married a few days."

"Very funny." He pointed behind him to the small family where both kids were now crying. "I was only watching that dad and wondering how I'll do."

"You'll be a great dad." She grinned. "I mean, when our kids screw up, you'll probably make them run laps."

He chuckled. As they sat there together, quiet again, soaking up a little solar Vitamin D and feeling the nice breeze off the water, the day could not have been better, the sun high in the sky, the temperature climbing through the eighties. Fingers interlocked, they luxuriated in the experience. Soon they were joined by a constant parade of couples, families, and even solitary beach wanderers. Darrell didn't fail to notice many of the guys passing—even those with a partner—stole a furtive glance at Erin in her bikini. Once again, he realized how lucky he was that Erin, this stunning, witty, intelligent red head, had married *him*.

After an hour of relaxing and sunbathing, he asked,

"How about I take a photo of my gorgeous wife?"

She got out of the chair and stood, smiling, with her back to the water, and Darrell snapped two shots. "I think I'm going to do a little run on the beach and then head into the waves. Care to join me?"

"Like to soak up a few more rays. Maybe peruse a couple pages of my beach read." She held up a copy of a romance novel she'd brought along. "Why don't you do a mile or so and circle back? Then I'll be happy to race you. On the sand and into the water."

"Well, if you think you can handle the *Perils of Pauline* by yourself, I'll see you in a few."

She settled back and showed him the novel. "It's Josephine, and I think I'll manage."

Depositing his sandals next to the cooler, he jogged down the shore at a brisk pace, his gaze alternating between the rolling blue of the gulf waves and the matching blue of the sky. As he ran, he inhaled the rich saline tang of the air. Looking at the incredible scene, he had to remind himself it was late December. Probably freezing back home.

As he ran, he passed a few beach walkers coming the other way, singles and couples. Two teen girls, arms linked, grinned at him and giggled when he passed, reminding him of a pair of students in his classes. Farther on, he had to weave around two small families building masterpieces in the sand, and he gave them both a thumbs-up. Another jogger, heading the opposite way, high-fived Darrell as he passed. Darrell pushed on, feeling the moist sand give under his feet and his calves straining in the effort.

He thought back to a time before his adventure last summer in Cape May when the grating sand on his soles had freaked him out. Now, because of his experience on the beach there—and thanks to Erin's patient love and support—he could feel the grains of sand against his bare feet and not cringe. Now, the warm, fine white sand felt soothing against his skin, and he pushed hard against the giving surface and experienced the burn in his legs. Maybe, just maybe, he *could* control his OCD.

Instead of it controlling him.

It had been with him so long, more than ten years now, and at times he could feel its tendrils encircling his head and squeezing. But not today.

He ran harder, finishing the loop and circling back to Erin. She was so engrossed in her reading he managed to sneak up behind her. He leaned and in and grabbed another long kiss.

She kissed him back, smiling. "Now that's better than a little fictional romance." She got up and stretched her long legs.

"You ready for some waves?" he asked.

"If you're up to it, let's do a mile or so on the sand first."

"You're on." Darrell gave a gentlemanly wave of his hand.

"I'll race you." Erin took off like a shot, and Darrell hurried after her. Since the beach was small, they covered the same ground Darrell had a few minutes earlier, passing the family sandcastle builders, another jogger, and the same strolling couples. As usual, she was quick, and he had to hustle to keep up, using some fancy footwork to sidestep sunbathers as they ran. When they got to the north end of the beach where Darrell had turned to double back, Erin headed for a little spit of land that strutted out into the water. He looked beyond and saw what she was headed for. Accelerating, he passed her.

Ahead, at the far end of the beach, a pair of young kids, he'd guess about six, sat in the sand as the waves rolled over their legs. Their small hands busied with a primitive sandcastle. One had long, brown hair tied into pigtails, and the other had a full head of brown hair, unkempt and in need of a trim. He came up to them and stopped, Erin a few seconds behind.

The kids wore street clothes, not swimsuits, but he didn't think much about it. Then he noticed something about the young boy. His right leg was stuck out at a grotesque angle, as if it had been broken and never set. Both kids giggled at the gurgling water that rolled up around their bare feet and pooled in the makeshift moat they'd dug around their sand creation. The castle was crude, a nearly round construction with seashells sticking up like turrets. The two kids glanced up, caramel eyes wide and pleading with half smiles of white teeth. In unison, they said, "*Ayudaños?*"

"Huh?" Darrell said.

"Cute castle, huh?" Erin stared at the sand and looked up at Darrell. "I wonder who made it?" Her eyes roamed around the area. "Out here on this spit of land it isn't going to last very long."

"Those kids—" he started, pointing to the pair. When he looked down, the sandcastle sat alone, the gulf water flowing around the construction and into the crude moat.

His glance darted out to the waves, thinking they'd abandoned their work and ran into the water, even in their street clothes, though he wondered how the boy

31

could have run. No girl or boy.

Oh, God! The same two kids? *"You vill have two visitors."*

"What'd you say?" Erin asked, her gaze meeting his.

The ghosts. Erin hadn't seen them! Shit, he couldn't tell her. Not now. Not here.

"Nothing," he managed around the lump in his throat and glanced back down at the sand.

There at his feet, the crude sand construction they'd been working on, complete with the three blue seashells sticking out of the top, sat alone on the sand. He reached down and grabbed one of the small seashells as the prickle on his neck returned and sizzled. Then he sensed something else, something ominous. No, not ominous, malevolent. More of Natalia's warning came back to him.

I see a malevolence, a great danger lurking nearby.

A big wave rushed in, rolling over their ankles and leveling the mound of sand, leaving the beach empty. As if nothing had ever been there.

"¡*Ayúdaños*!"

Chapter 5

Santa knows when—

Their day at the beach had been perfect—not counting the two visitors.

After their jog together, they'd played in the surf for hours, even as the tide built and the waves got stronger, Erin giggling and frolicking like she hadn't a care in the world. Resting on the sand, Darrell tried to lean over to steal a kiss only to have his beach chair collapse beneath him. Erin couldn't stop laughing. After he gathered up the chair and his dignity, they nibbled on a few snacks from the cooler. She even had fun feeding him plump white grapes, her long, graceful fingers placing each into his mouth. When they'd both had their fill, they charged back into the water, their legs kicking up white froth in the waves.

Watching her enjoying the day, so carefree and relaxed, Darrell couldn't bring himself to dump the news of any ghosts on her. Even though he would've welcomed her help in sorting out what the appearances meant, he didn't want to do anything to shatter their relaxing day at the beach. The whole day, he tried to put the two mysterious kids out of his mind. He was *not* going to let any ghosts ruin their honeymoon.

They stayed so long at Fort Gulf Island, soaking up the novelty of the waves and the warm breezes off the water, that, as the sun dipped into the gulf beyond, its dying rays igniting the blue waters to a bright orange, they sat mesmerized in the two striped beach chairs and had trouble leaving.

Back at the house from the beach, exhaustion struck them more or less at the same time. Darrell could see it in Erin's yawning, and he could feel it in his legs. Fortunately, he'd insisted on liberal use of sunblock, and that had kept them from burning but did nothing to fight the fatigue. It was all they could do to raid their stash in the fridge and collapse in the four-poster bed. Erin had claimed she was even too tired to make love, and for once Darrell was grateful.

He found a night of slumber did much to revive, but when they awoke, still drowsy and bleary eyed, his stomach started growling. Erin rolled over and giggled. "Yeah, well you're not the only one starving. Didn't know lying on the beach all day could give a girl such an appetite."

She shoved him, pushing him part way out of bed, and hustled into the bathroom before he could recover. A few minutes later, they were dressed, riding in the car and heading for some food.

He chose a breakfast joint Bonnie had suggested, a place called Grannie's Restaurant, and her recommendation did not disappoint. As they entered the small diner, a tiny bell tingling, the breakfast aromas wafted over them—the bold smell of strong coffee, the sweet scent of maple syrup, and the enticing smell of sausage sizzling—and Darrell's stomach growled again. Thankfully, it didn't take long to get them seated.

He dove into a tall stack of hotcakes, dripping with butter and syrup, while Erin attacked her veggie omelet with equal enthusiasm. He found the strips of bacon served alongside perfect, crisp, and flavorful, and the hash browns were some of the best he'd ever tasted.

As he ate, his hunger subsiding, he glanced around. The place had a comfortable, down-home quality that all but cried, "Welcome, y'all." From the smiling face of Grandma on the tall exterior sign to the warm, southern drawl of their waitress, to the simple Formica-topped tables, each bearing a small table tent in the shape of a Christmas tree imprinted with the words, "Eat, Drink, and Be Merry." Erin pointed out the black and white photos of classic celebrities hung on white painted walls—Lucille Ball, Elvis Presley, Marilyn Monroe, and several whose faces Darrell recognized but couldn't name. The eatery had the feel of a hometown favorite, right down to the dancing Santa figure at the checkout counter. And it was packed, buzzing with patrons and conversations. They were lucky to get the last table in the small side room.

Famished from their exercise the day before and the light meal before bed, they both wolfed down the delicious food in near silence. Darrell smiled when he stared across the small table and watched Erin eat with as much gusto as he felt. For today, she'd selected a shimmering dress of pale yellow, sleeveless with thin spaghetti straps showing off slightly tanned shoulders and arms. And when she moved, the thin fabric clung to her considerable curves, which Darrell certainly appreciated.

"Not bad for a breakfast," he said, bringing his attention back to the food. His plate empty of all but a few crumbs and two small lingering pools of syrup, he pushed the dish forward and sat back, savoring his second cup of coffee.

Erin slid her empty plate a few inches forward, mimicking Darrell's motion. "Not bad? I haven't seen you leave your plate that empty, even at Ben's." She gestured with her mug at his place. "There wouldn't even be anything left for our favorite pug."

The server came by, refilled their mugs, and cleared both places. She said, "Well, ya said this was your first trip to Grannie's. What'd ya think?"

Darrell pointed to the dishes she held. "We're both members of the clean plate club, as my mom used to say." He saluted with his mug. "It was great, but we're definitely full."

"That's the way we like our customers," said the waitress. "I'll be back in a few with your check."

After she left, Darrell turned back to Erin, "And what would my lovely bride like to do today?"

"Let's do a little shopping. It's December 23rd. The stores will have lots of Christmas sales. Besides, it'll put us in the Christmas mood."

Stomachs full, they set out in search of, in her words, some Christmas treasures. After he found a city parking lot, they got out and strolled among the shops on Citrus Avenue. One store window held a bright holiday display of snowmen dancing, and Darrell and Erin stood, admiring the painted handiwork. Somewhere above them, a Christmas song oozed out of hidden speakers, a choir singing "Joy to the World." While they stood there holding hands, Erin's green eyes crinkled as she sang quietly, "Joy to the world, the Lord is come." When the song ended, they ambled to another shop window, this one with a painting of a group of elves building wooden trucks and sleds. They continued on and ended up in front of what turned out to be their favorite, a store window painted with a large image of Santa and his sleigh pulled by a team of manatees. They lingered there awhile, enjoying the whimsy like a couple of kids.

On the lawn beside one store stood a giant Christmas tree, at least twenty feet tall. Erin wanted to see it up close, so they hurried across the busy street and stood in front of the huge tree, on which oversized red and gold round ornaments glistened in the bright sun. Standing in front, they both inhaled the pine scent redolent in the air and listened as the speaker played a choral version of "O Christmas Tree."

Darrell wasn't much of a shopper, but he saw how Erin's eyes lit up when she discovered a new store, so he played along. Of course, he had no choice but to mingle with other tourists and last-minute shoppers, the avenue busy with them, adults and kids. Through it all, he fought to control his OCD.

Twice, among the crowds, he thought he spotted the same two kids—a boy and a girl, both five or six, two small heads of brown hair. He couldn't help himself. He hustled over to where they stood, but each time he found he was mistaken. Embarrassed, he apologized to the parents and hurried back.

Erin must've caught the reaction on his face. She said, "Is everything okay?"

That simple question made him doubt himself. Should he tell her? Maybe give her a clue without dumping everything on her. He shook his head. "I'm fine. Everything's great." He gave her a warm smile. No ghosts were going to ruin their honeymoon. And maybe, if he refused to get involved, Natalia's "danger" wouldn't even show up.

Erin ducked into another store, this one with a large sign overhead with the words "Heritage House" printed in tall letters. While Darrell waited on the porch outside, a costumed Santa across the way caught his eye. He'd seen these guys often enough, both in Michigan when he was growing up and on the Eastern Shore. With their ringing bell and large red kettle, they were a fixture every holiday season. Some even wore a full Santa suit and beard.

But, as Darrell studied this volunteer, though trying not to stare, he saw this one appeared different. *He* had gone all out. Complete with perfect white beard, rosy cheeks, and large belly, he looked like the real thing. Wouldn't that outfit be pretty hot in the Florida sun? And when the man spoke with a deep jovial voice, the image was complete.

"Ho-ho-ho! Merry Christmas!" he called and rang the bell.

Darrell walked over, pulled out his wallet, and threw in a five-dollar bill. As he watched the money drop into the bucket, the Santa looked up and said, "Ho-ho-ho, thanks."

"You're welcome." Darrell couldn't help but notice the red cheeks and wide smile. All the guy needed was a pipe to complete the Clement Moore creation.

The Santa held his gaze, and Darrell nodded. As he started to walk away, the red-suited man called, "Also, remember Christmas is for children…especially the two who need your help."

Chapter 6

A new wrapped present

Did Darrell hear what he thought he did?

He moved away, taking three steps backward, distancing himself from the Santa. Darrell stared at the man in the costume, who went on ringing the bell, all the while calling, "Ho-ho-ho! Christmas is for children. Let's do all we can to help them." The man didn't even seem to pay Darrell any more attention.

"Thank you, Merry Christmas!" the Santa bellowed to another passerby who dropped some coins into the bucket.

Oh, Darrell *was* getting paranoid. The more he considered it, the more ridiculous it all sounded. A Santa talking about two kids. The same two kids?

The memory of the look in the kids' eyes pulled at him again. Maybe he *ought* to say something to Erin? Maybe she could make some sense of it. He shot another glance at the Santa, who kept ringing his sleigh bell, greeting shoppers coming from and going to the Heritage House.

"*You vill have two visitors.*" Natalia's words echoed in his mind again. He didn't want them there and tried to shake his head to dislodge them. Okay, Natalia had been spot-on with his two other spectral visitors. With the ghost at Wilshire High and the haunted bride in Cape May, her words had proven true, prophetic even. But that didn't mean the medium *had* to be right this time. Damn, he and Erin were on their honeymoon!

"Look what I found in there!" Erin squealed.

He jumped. She appeared next to him while he was focused on the Salvation Army Santa. He glanced at her face, beaming with excitement. Her hand dangled a four-inch-long replica of a manatee, long gray body, flat tail, and funny snout, with "Christmas 1999" etched across the middle in red. She bounced up and down, making the purchase bob with her action.

"A Christmas ornament." Her green eyes sparkled with excitement. "Perfect. It'll be our first ornament for our own Christmas tree."

"We don't have a Christmas tree yet," Darrell said.

She patted his arm. "I know, but we will next year, and now we have our first ornament. The perfect reminder of our honeymoon." She leaned over and kissed him.

Staring into her bright, happy irises, he asked himself, could he tell her anything that would darken those eyes? Anything that would spoil this moment?

Before he had time to consider his answer, she said, "Oh, and I talked with the shop owner. Said we were looking for a small painting, and she told me to check out the gallery a couple doors down."

It took them only a few minutes to get there, and they stopped in front of a small shop with a large picture window, peering at several framed canvases through the glass. A fancy sign next to the largest one proclaimed, GIANT CHRISTMAS SALE. Beside it stood a small Christmas tree with exquisite, hand-painted ornaments and flashing twinkle lights.

"Maybe we can find something here for our new apartment. And it's probably on sale." She smiled up at Darrell.

When they entered, the explosion of color in the small room struck him. Paintings and drawings of all sizes hung on the walls and sat on easels around the room, a little of everything. Tall, skinny canvasses with splashes of some modern art creations. More traditional landscapes of gorgeous water scenes captured in what looked like oils. Even some smaller portraits, a few done in charcoal and others in what looked like colored pencil. They wandered around the small shop, examining canvases up close. Two paintings next to each other on the wall hung crooked, both tilted slightly to the left. He shot a quick glance around—Erin was admiring another work across the room—and he reached out and straightened both. He took a step back and assessed his work, satisfied.

There was another Christmas tree, a little larger than its cousin in the window, adorned with white twinkle lights and dozens of hand decorated ornaments, each with a tiny price tag. Intrigued, Darrell approached the tree and checked out the cost on one of the tags. Yikes. He let it go and checked out the rest of the room.

Then he felt it, or thought he did. The slightest prickle on his neck. It was there…and then it was gone. He scanned the display, his glance sliding from one painting to another, then back to the tree, but saw nothing. He reached behind, rubbing his neck, and the sense disappeared…if it were there at all. He shook his head. It was nothing. He was *not* going to let that happen.

Erin approached one of the landscapes, this one on a small stand about three feet off the ground. The painting captured a sleek sailboat on a crystal-blue sea with the sun setting on the horizon, its rays a sparkling gold slice on the water. She moved closer to the foot-wide painting, turning her head side to side, examining the work. "I think my dad would love this. What do you think?"

Darrell came up next to her, studying the work. "Yeah, this sailboat even has a gold stripe like his." He reached and almost, but not quite, touched the painting. He felt the prickle stir, then decided it was nothing. He pulled his hand back.

"I'm afraid to ask," he said. "How much do they want for it?" He reached down and flipped the dangling price tag. A little high, but not staggering. Still, he wasn't sure he could manage it. Then he corrected himself. He wasn't sure *they* could manage it.

He liked the sound of that. They.

"I see you like the sailboat piece," said a deep voice behind them, and both Erin and Darrell started. An older man with short white hair, grizzled, tanned features, and a small wispy beard crossed his arms and smiled. They hadn't heard him. He must've come from a back room. The man asked, "Do you sail?"

Erin said, "Guilty. My father owns a sailboat, a lot like the one in the picture." She pointed to the painting. "Runs a sailing charter on the Chesapeake, up in Maryland. We're on the water every chance we get. In good weather, of course." She chuckled.

The man turned toward Darrell. "And you?"

Darrell shook his head. "Strictly an apprentice. But I have a great teacher." He took Erin's hand. "But we're here simply to enjoy ourselves…and your charming town. You see, we're on our honeymoon. Erin and Darrell Henshaw." He extended his hand, and the man shook it.

"I'm Ted Shoemaker. Welcome to Crystal River. And congratulations." He stepped between them and picked the painting off the easel. "Glad to see you like this one." He paused a beat. "'Cause it's mine. After I retired, I tried my hand and found I liked it. Now I paint whenever I'm not on the water."

Erin's gaze roamed around the fifty or so pieces on display. "All these yours?"

The owner chuckled. "Heavens, no. Only a few." He gestured around the gallery. "This place is a retirement hobby of mine. Most of the pieces in here are from young artists, either starting out or part time. It's hard for a new artist to get their work displayed. I give them an opportunity to get noticed."

Ted held up the sailboat painting. "How about I give you a special Christmas discount on this? For some honeymooners." He closed one eye. "How about I cut this price in half?"

Erin grabbed Darrell's hand and squeezed. He glanced at her and then at Shoemaker. "I think that means yes."

Darrell and Erin browsed the other paintings and drawings, and she found one she thought would be perfect for their apartment. The two-foot-wide canvas was a painting of a scene in Three Sisters' Springs, capturing the deep green canopy of trees, with the snaking boardwalk beneath and the clear outline of a manatee in the crystal blue water. When Shoemaker made another special offer for that one as well, they were sold.

Ted said, "Let me go back and wrap these up."

The owner disappeared behind a curtain they hadn't noticed when they came in.

Darrell and Erin continued browsing, and he stopped in front of a painting, a close-up portrait of a face of an older man done in wide strokes. He was still studying the work when Ted reappeared, holding the two canvases wrapped in brown paper.

Darrell handed him a credit card, and the owner slid the plastic through the little device. With his other hand, Ted pointed to the painting Darrell stood in front of. "That work is by a new artist named Jared Emerson. He's different and paints with his hands instead of a brush. Sometimes the results are interesting, others not so much. That one is not bad, though."

Darrell was no art critic, but something drew him to the painting. He wasn't sure what it was.

Thanking the man, he took the wrapped packages from him. As he held the paintings in one hand and the door with the other, he felt something on his neck. At first it felt like the familiar prickle, but when they stepped outside into the fading light, the sensation disappeared so quickly he wasn't sure it was ever there in the first place. He probably simply slept wrong last night. After all, he was in a different bed. He'd have Erin massage it when they got back.

Chapter 7

Ayúdaños

"Two Piña Coladas." Erin grinned and held up two fingers for the waitress. "It's December, and look at us. Drinking summer adult beverages and dining outside, enjoying the breeze off the water. Back home, we'd be bundled up in heavy coats."

Taking another of Bonnie's recommendations, Darrell had driven to Cracker's Bar and Grill, a short distance from their shopping excursions, and timed their arrival for four forty-five. When he asked if they could eat outside, the hostess first gave him a questioning glance. But, after a brief hesitation and some gentle persuasion, she led them to a table on the large wooden deck under a broad, blue canvas umbrella. Darrell hoped his charm convinced the young woman to give them the last seats on the crowded deck, but decided it was more likely his ten-dollar tip *and* the fact that Erin had whispered they were on their honeymoon.

Along the top edge of the bar, a set of large black speakers played Bing Crosby's version of "I'm Dreaming of a White Christmas." Darrell glanced to his right, seeing patrons lined up on tall stools at the outside bar, drinking and singing along with the holiday classic. Badly. For a moment, he took in the crowd in their shorts, tank tops, and polo shirts and smiled. If he'd really wanted a white Christmas, he would've taken Erin to some rustic inn in Michigan, maybe even in the Upper Peninsula. They'd definitely have snow. Or they could've stayed on the Eastern Shore. He and Erin had chosen to come here precisely because they didn't want to be shivering through a white Christmas. At least, not for their honeymoon.

Four other tables, crowded with couples and families celebrating the holiday, covered the rest of the deck space. Darrell and Erin settled into their seats, and in front of them lay the reason he had chosen the place. The real estate agent's description had been right on the money.

Not twenty feet from where they sat, rippling waves lapped the shore of this bay, almost completely surrounded on the right and left by snaking shorelines. Just beyond the deck, two dozen berths for sloops and motorboats were attached to a dock, half the spaces filled with boats rocking on the gentle waves. Large personal homes lined the shore on the right, standing two stories tall with massive screened in porches and individual piers extending into the harbor. Down the center of the scene, directly across from them, the sun was setting beyond Kings Bay, igniting the blue waters to a glowing orange.

Watching the harbor open up in front of them with the undulating shore populated with green trees again reminded Darrell of the Eastern Shore. The houses with docks on the water, the slips with boats in them, the restaurants with magnificent views of it all made him think of St. Michaels. But even that quaint harbor didn't have the perfect sunset view like here in Crystal River. He noticed again the odor here was different, a fresher scent. He remembered reading in a brochure the bay was fresh water, fed every day by the springs.

Sitting there, surrounded by music, laughter, and talking, Darrell enjoyed simply watching Erin, his beautiful wife, who seemed mesmerized by the breathtaking scene. Erin's eyes glittered in the sunset, her gorgeous smile broadening as the sun dipped lower in the sky. Their cocktails arrived, yellow and white in tall, frosted glasses, and they both sipped, drinking up the sweet, fruity concoction and drinking in the incredible sight. She said, "Thanks. This is perfect." They sat together, taking in the view and savoring their drinks, and Erin laid her head on his shoulder.

Her head there, relaxed and comfortable against him, made Darrell question himself again. How could he shatter this contentment? This honeymoon was about them, the start of their life together, not some…intruding ghosts.

They'd spent the entire day shopping, or rather Erin had done the shopping while he held the new acquisitions and ferried her finds to the car. In between the shops and the boutiques, they discovered a photo kiosk, and at Erin's urging, Darrell headed there with their now expended disposable camera for the advertised one-hour developing. It had been a fine day. And he had to admit he really did like the painting they purchased for their new place. Even those domestic words, *their new place*, made him smile.

By the time they finished their meal—both enjoyed a local favorite, grouper, which was thick and flavorful—they were blessedly full, and the sun was only a small slit of red in the western sky. Afterward, sitting close together, they sipped a second drink, mango daiquiris this time, as the last bit of light drained out of the sky. Darrell found the slight buzz from the second drink made him *almost* forget about the two kids with the haunting eyes. Almost. He tried to shove the niggling feeling farther back in his brain.

A busser came over to the table next to them and started clearing dishes. Darrell glanced briefly in that direction and nudged Erin, pointing. "Luis?"

The server jerked, surprised at first, but when he looked, recognition dawned in his eyes, a broad smile breaking across his face, his teeth white. "Mister and Mrs. Henshaw."

Erin said, "Hi, Luis. You work here too?"

"*Si.*" He nodded. "Yes, I work here too. Sometime." After a beat, he added, "You like Crystal River?"

Erin spoke up. "Yes, Luis, we're having a wonderful time. Seen the manatees, been to the beach, and did some shopping. It's a very nice town." Then, as if she thought of something else, she continued, "Oh, and thanks so much for the goodies you picked up for us."

Luis looked at her with a question and she added, "At the house. The groceries and the takeout. The pasta was delicious."

He nodded. "That was all Miss Bonnie. She arrange for the food. I pick up."

As Darrell watched the young man work, clearing dirty plates and half-empty glasses, he again noted Luis' thin frame through the uniform, he guessed more from poor nutrition than from any dieting. Darrell knew young people. He had plenty of different aged kids in his classes and would've pegged Luis to be about nineteen or twenty, though he couldn't be sure, as he'd had precious few Latinos in either Michigan or Wilshire.

The young man moved about the table next to them, quietly collecting dishes and utensils and stacking them on a tray. As Darrell watched the young man working at the next table, he thought this might give him a chance to ask the assistant something that had been bothering him. The speakers blared the trumpet finale of "Angels We Have Heard on High" by Mannheim Steamroller and then went quiet for a bit. Darrell figured this was his chance.

"Luis, can I ask you something?"

"*Sí.*" The young man stopped his actions, glancing over at Darrell.

Darrell stared back. "Can you tell me what *ayúdaños* means?" Catching a look from Erin, he said to her, "I heard some kid say that yesterday at the beach and wondered what it meant? I think it's Spanish but wasn't sure." Then back to Luis, "I thought you'd know."

"*Sí,*" Luis said, nodding hard. "It mean…help?" He nodded his head up and down. "Like…help us."

"Help us," Darrell repeated, frowning, but avoided looking at Erin. "Thanks, Luis."

Help us. Not *what he wanted to hear.*

The server picked up his tray and scurried away. When Darrell turned back, Erin was staring at him, a question in her eyes. A question he was afraid he was going to have to answer, sooner or later.

Chapter 8

Not so silent night

Darrell sat straight up in bed.

He'd been deep asleep and something, some sound had intruded. His first thought—prowler—proved wrong. The sound was...different. At first, he figured he was dreaming. But no. When he shut his eyes and breathed slowly, wide awake, he heard it.

It came again. A low moan, almost like weeping.

Erin? No. She slept quietly beside him, her chest rising up and down beneath his Oxford shirt. A small smile tugged at the corner of her pretty mouth, crinkling the freckles on her chin. No, it definitely wasn't her.

Sitting up in the bed, he waited in the darkness and, after a moment, heard it again. It almost sounded like a cat whining or meowing. Was the sound coming from inside the house or outside? Maybe they'd let a cat in while they were bringing in some of their purchases from the car. He hadn't remembered seeing a cat around, but who knows. After a fun day shopping and a delicious sunset dinner, they'd arrived back at the house laughing. They were certainly distracted.

He climbed out of bed, his movements slow and measured, trying not to wake his wife. He stepped into the hall and padded in the direction of the sound.

Halfway across the back of the family room, he stopped to listen. It came again. Quiet, plaintive, but there. It sounded like it was coming from the kitchen. Well, a cat would likely head for where the food was stashed.

Not wanting to disturb Erin, he left the lights off. The glow of the moon reflecting off the water was enough to keep him from bumping into things. He didn't know this house and, with all Simmons' fancy furniture around, he needed to be careful.

When he pushed open the door to the kitchen, the sounds grew slightly louder. The cries came again—two different cries? Could two cats have snuck in without either he or Erin noticing? He listened. Were those cat sounds?

He was still half groggy. Maybe he was imagining or dreaming. He pinched himself, hard. It hurt. The noise persisted.

He crept farther, inching toward the sound, using his hands to feel his way and not trip over anything. The crying—it was definitely crying—was more distinct, and it sounded like...little kids crying? He knew how crazy that sounded. Yes, in this beautiful house—which was NOT haunted—he clearly heard children crying. His mind grasped for some explanation. He didn't want to go to the other possibility, but beneath the crying—innocent, helpless sobbing—he *sensed* something else, something malevolent. He shook it off.

Maybe it was a recording? But coming from where? He remembered seeing an answering machine next to the phone. A prank, maybe? But that didn't make sense.

He turned toward where the phone hung on the

wall, its long, curling cord snaking almost to the ground. The noise wasn't coming from there. Besides, what would a recording of some kids crying be doing on Dr. Simmons' answering machine? He knew that question sounded even more farfetched. Besides, it didn't sound like any recording.

Edging forward, he ran his hands across the counter, feeling the cold granite on his skin. His fingers happened on something, and a shock zapped up his arm. He yanked his hand back, glancing the object and knocking it to the tile floor. He heard something rip.

One of the paintings. Oh, God. He hoped it was the package, not the painting. Erin would be furious. She was so proud of having found the one with a sailboat and was sure her dad would love it. And she loved the picture they had picked out for their place almost as much.

He wheeled back toward the bedroom and checked but didn't hear anything. No movement. Maybe his clumsiness hadn't awakened her. He needed to see what he'd done, see if there was any real damage. In here there wasn't enough light from the moon. He'd have to chance it. Not remembering where, he searched the walls to find the switches. He flipped one. The fluorescents in the ceiling burst on so bright his eyes squeezed shut at first. Then he opened them and shot a quick glance around the room. Everything else looked normal. One brown wrapped package still sat in the center of the island. Shopping bags were on the counter next to the fridge

He heard the quiet whimpering again. No words, only sniffling and weeping—though that sense of evil was still there. Faint, but there. When he turned toward the sound, he saw a painting face down on the floor, the brown paper covering the back torn down the middle. Darrell reached down to pick it up—the last thing he wanted was for Erin to come in and see their new "treasure" shattered on the floor. Besides, he'd have to see if the fall had damaged the piece. If it were only the paper backing, maybe they could go back to the shop and have the owner redo it. As he bent to retrieve it, an electric jolt shot up his arm. He dropped the painting again and heard a larger tear.

Oh, shit. His fingers hurt so fiercely he shook his hand, forgetting for a second about any sound. Then the tingle on his skin receded, and the noise penetrated his consciousness again along with the sense, some premonition. It was coming from the floor. He peered down at the piece, lying there face down, brown backing in two shredded pieces. The weeping grew louder now. The noises, the cries were coming from…the painting?

He knelt and stooped over the torn package. He flipped it over gently and examined the other side. It was the picture they'd bought for her dad, the painting of the sailboat on the shiny blue water. *It* appeared unharmed. Okay. Good. He took a deep a breath, in and out. He turned the piece back over, holding it in both hands.

Beneath the split, brown paper, the image of two small children peeked out at him, though the torn paper still covered the outside edges of both faces. Darrell pulled back the remaining backing to get a better look and studied the canvas. The portrait was of a young boy and a little girl, but it was different than any he'd seen before. The painted image had been created by the colliding of unusual strokes of color, wide and smooth, too wide for a brush. Yet when the broad strokes came together, they formed this perfect, haunting portrait of two young kids with dark skin, darkened even further by smudges and dirt, looking back with deep, caramel eyes.

It hit him. The same two kids. First on the sidewalk at the Simmons place. Then riding on the boardwalk at the manatee park. And playing in the sand at the beach.

The same two kids.

Then, as he stared, he watched both images…cry? Twin streams of tears ran down the painted canvas. His hand edged forward, touching the painting. His fingers came away wet. What the hell?

"Is everything okay?" Erin asked at his back.

He jumped, knocking the painting and sending it clattering to the floor again.

Chapter 9

I thought we were partners

Darrell watched as Erin's eyes went to the damaged canvas on the floor. Stepping around him, she picked it up, cradling it in her hands. She studied the piece, first checking out the sailboat painting, then letting her fingers probe the ripped brown paper backing. She peeled back the remnants of brown paper and examined the other painting hidden there.

Darrell's feet wouldn't hold him up anymore, and he slid down, his back against the island. He trembled, shaking his head back and forth. Erin slid down next to him, her shoulders against the cabinet and legs stretched out in front. "What is it?" She laid a hand on his arm, but he wouldn't look at her.

He kept shaking his head. "No, not again."

Setting the painting on the tile floor, she scrunched around so she sat opposite, face to face. She grabbed his chin, forcing him to look at her. He was crying and shuddering. She reached across and wiped a tear off his cheek.

"I can't. I won't," he mumbled and wouldn't meet her gaze.

She nudged the chin up a bit more. "Whatever it is, we can face it together."

"It's those kids." He pointed to the painting on the

floor. The next words ran out in a torrent. "I've seen them before. This week. First here on the front driveway, then on the boardwalk at Three Sisters and then at the beach."

When she didn't say anything, he pressed, "The same kids."

Releasing his chin, Erin glanced again at the painting of the two children, her brows creasing. "What are you talking about?"

Finally, Darrell raised his gaze and met hers. He shifted his weight on the hard floor, his back a little straighter.

He was here now. He had little choice. He might as well get the whole thing out.

"Look, something woke me up. I heard a noise. I came in the kitchen because it sounded like whatever I heard was coming from in here. Then I accidentally knocked the painting off the island, and when it hit the floor, it ripped."

Erin picked up the artwork with one hand. She flipped it over and showed the sailboat side to him. "It's fine. We can take it back today and have Ted repair the backing."

Darrell shook his head. "That's not it." He took the picture from Erin and turned it over, even as his hand buzzed. The faces of the two kids stared back at them. "When I came in here, these two"—he pointed to the boy and girl—"were crying. The painting was *crying*." He held up the fingers of one hand. "I felt the tears myself." And he mumbled, "They're ghosts."

"What?" Erin leaned in close. "What do you mean they're ghosts? Who are they?"

"I don't know." He sniffled, rubbing an arm across

his nose. "Each time I saw them this week, they would be there and then they would disappear. You know, like ghosts." He brought the fingers of both hands together and then opened them. "On the driveway, these two rode by me on some old bicycles with rusty training wheels when I was bringing in the groceries the first day we got here. I ducked to move out of their way, and when I turned back, they were gone. I figured maybe they'd disappeared inside a neighbor's house."

"Why didn't you tell me about this then?"

"I should have. I was going to…but I got distracted by a beautiful naked woman. Besides, we'd just started our honeymoon."

"Still?" Erin wore a half grin.

Darrell pressed on, "Then, when we were watching the manatees at Three Sisters, they rode right behind us on the boardwalk on the same bicycles."

"You sure? I don't remember any kids on bicycles on the boardwalk at the springs."

"I know. You, and everybody else, didn't see or hear them because you don't have the *gift*." Darrell voice was laced with derision. "And then I saw them again at the beach, building a sandcastle. Remember that sandcastle we saw on the tip of the beach we passed jogging at Fort Island? They were sitting right there playing in the sand in the same street clothes I'd seen them in the first two times. But you couldn't see them, and when I turned around, they were gone."

"Why didn't you tell me then?"

"I would've. I wanted to…but I didn't want our honeymoon to be about chasing ghosts."

Erin reached across and pulled Darrell into her arms. "It'll be okay. I get it. You see ghosts from time to time."

He gently pushed her back. "No, you don't get it. They're haunting me. You know how this goes. Once they start, they won't let up. They need me to *help them*." He uttered the last two words with distaste. "You know, like Hank in Wilshire and Amy in Cape May."

"Maybe you're jumping the gun. Ghosts know you're a sensitive. They reach out to you. Look how many ghosts reached out to you in Cape May. How do you know these two are trying to rope you into some mystery?"

Darrell paused for a moment, thinking. "You know that word I asked Luis about at dinner last night?"

She nodded. "*Ayúdanos.*"

Darrell looked down at the floor. "Yeah, well it's what both kids at Fort Island Beach asked me. The kids who were building a sandcastle. The two you *didn't* see."

Erin frowned. "Still? I don't see why that's got you all worked up. Maybe it's not that big a deal. Hey, I signed up for the full tour." She held up her ring finger and wiggled the small diamond. "Maybe it won't be so bad." She grinned at him. "At least, we have this beautiful Florida weather to go ghost hunting in."

"There's more," he managed, not knowing how he could tell her the rest. This *would* ruin the honeymoon. But he was here, and he couldn't find any way out of it. Darrell faced his wife's beautiful features, with that encouraging smile, gulped again and plunged ahead. "I was warned to expect two *visitors*."

He watched Erin's features cloud over, her green eyes darken. She said, "Not by Natalia?" She slid a few inches away from him, shaking her head. "You said you weren't going to see her without me." Her cold eyes came up. "You promised."

This was going to be worse than he thought. Studying his wife's face, he tried, "I didn't go to see her. She came to see me."

"At your apartment?"

He shook his head hard. "No. It was all Al's fault."

"Al brought Natalia to see you?" She sounded incredulous.

This wasn't coming out the way he hoped. "No, no. She was at the bachelor party."

Erin scowled. "Sara told me about the party. Said Al came home pretty wasted, babbling crazy stories about an *awesome* night." Her two hands did a little shake in the air. "She told me about your brother and the other teachers being there. Oh, and about Jeb Douglass, your principal. But she didn't say anything about Natalia."

"Maybe Al didn't tell her, but she was there all right."

"And I suppose Natalia uttered another of her ghost prophecies?" Erin pronounced the name with the exaggerated Slavic accent.

"Yeah, she said I would have two visitors. Erin, she *knew* we were going to Crystal River. I didn't tell anybody, but she knew. She told me two visitors were waiting for me in Crystal River, two visitors who needed my help. And I had to be careful because there was danger nearby."

Erin started to move, her eyes narrowed at Darrell. "Why didn't you tell me all this? Before."

"I wanted to ignore it. I didn't want some damn

ghosts to ruin our honeymoon."

In a quiet voice, she asked, "Why didn't you trust me enough to simply tell me?"

"I wanted to. I tried."

For a while, she said nothing, breathing in and out, staring at the floor. Darrell sat watching, silent and hoping. Her gaze came up and met his. "Okay, tell me the rest."

Darrell was confused. "That's all she said about the ghosts."

"That's not what I mean." Her words were hard.

"It was nothing," Darrell tried, but it did no good.

"I know you, Darrell Henshaw. There's more, and that's why you didn't tell me. Now, give." She did a little come hither gesture with one hand and not in a friendly way.

Darrell swallowed the lump in his throat and reached across, taking her hands in his. "Well, toward the end of the party, after I'd been through the gauntlet, Al has a server wheel in this huge cake. Must've been three feet tall. With white icing. He made some big announcement—you know how he can be?—and who do you think pops out of this fake cake?"

"Natalia." Erin spat out the word.

"She climbed out of this cardboard cake with icing clinging all over her body."

"Was she...?"

"Naked. No. She had on this bikini, and Al had her pose next to me looking all sultry." Darrell felt the tension in Erin's hands. He dreaded this, but he pressed on. "He announced he'd paid for a special lap dance and pushed me into the little booth behind some divider. And that's where she gave her prophecy."

Erin yanked her hands free. "Natalia did a friggin' *lap dance* for you?" She pushed back. "A damn lap dance."

Darrell started to plead. "NO! No lap dance. She pretended to, but then did her...prophecy." He raised both hands in surrender. "I—I—I didn't have much choice. Besides I was pretty drunk by then."

Her eyes got harder. "Not making it any better, Coach." She broke away from his hands and stood up.

"No, no, it's not what you think. I didn't want to do it. Al dragged me into the booth. You can ask him. He'll tell you. It was all his idea."

Erin chuckled. "Oh, I'm sure you put up great resistance to little Miss Natalia."

Darrell struggled to get to his feet, his legs not cooperating. He stood and reached across to Erin, who backed up.

"No, not now. *I* need to think about this." She turned and headed back across the house. As she walked away, he saw below the bottom of his Oxford shirt the crisscross lines on her bare legs from the impressions of the tile. A minute later, he heard the French door onto the back patio slide shut, sounding like a slap in the face.

Chapter 10

Finding the right words

Fifteen minutes later, Darrell brought her a steaming mug of tea and set it on the table next to the chaise where she lounged, still wearing only his shirt, the collar buttoned up to her neck. Her face was unreadable.

"I'll get some breakfast ready," he mumbled and returned to the kitchen without waiting for a reply. He busied himself with stirring and frying, all the while struggling to come up with the right words of apology. He created this mess, and he had to make it right. Moving about the room, he set the plates on the table and saw the painting of the sailboat sitting alone in the center of the granite island. Well, maybe the ghosts had something to do with it, but he still had to fix it. Cooking helped him focus and settle his nerves a bit, and within a few minutes, his work on the high-end stove produced one skillet holding sizzling strips of bacon and a second with a batch of fluffy scrambled eggs, the delicious aroma filling the kitchen.

When Erin came in from outside some minutes later, Darrell met her at the kitchen door and refilled her mug. "I apologize—" he started.

"Look—" she began at the same precise moment.

They both stopped and, after a bit, she said, "You

go first."

"Okay," Darrell said. "First, you hungry?"

"You know me. I can always eat."

He said, "Okay. You sit and let me serve you some breakfast while it's hot."

"Smells good. Caught a whiff out on the patio." She pulled out the wooden chair closest to the stove and sat.

Darrell scooped some eggs and selected two strips of bacon—done exactly like she liked them—and placed them on a plate. He set it before her. He stood there, hands on hips, and stared at the ceiling, trying to collect his thoughts. Finally, he met her gaze. "First of all, I apologize. I know I should've simply told you about it at the start." Filling his own plate, he slid into the facing chair. "Anyway, when Natalia dropped this on me right before the wedding, I was hoping this was the one time she'd be wrong. And I didn't want to spoil our honeymoon with a stupid ghost hunt."

Erin stopped between bites, a piece of bacon halfway between the plate and her mouth. "Okay, I get that. When we get home, I'm going to have a few words for Al. Or maybe I'll tell Sara and let her take care of him. God knows, this is not what I had in mind for our honeymoon."

"That's what I mean—"

She cut him off. "But after the ghosts appeared to you, after you actually saw the kids, why didn't you trust me enough to tell me then?"

Darrell didn't know how to answer that. "First, I thought I imagined them. At least, that's what I told myself. But you're right. I should've told you right then." He shrugged. "Well, maybe not that night. I mean it was our first night down here. And you looked so incredible. But I should have told you the next morning." He grinned, but she didn't grin back.

Erin took another small bite of eggs, and Darrell waited, silent. After she swallowed, she asked, "And you saw the ghosts two more times? And you still didn't think you should tell me?"

"I wanted to. God, how I wanted to." Darrell shook his head. "I kept telling myself I didn't want to spoil our fun time down here, and I kept putting it off. Looking for the right time."

"I thought we were partners." She left the rest unsaid as she picked up her mug and drank some tea.

"We were, er, I mean we are," Darrell pleaded. "There is no one in the world I trust as much as you. No one I want for a partner other than you." When she still didn't respond, he went on, "I think I told myself I was trying to protect you."

"Darrell, don't give me that. I can take care of myself."

He could feel tears coming. "I know that, but I can't bear the thought of something happening to you. Of putting you in danger again. Each time I thought of telling you, I remembered that timber rattler someone put in our room in Cape May. I could've lost you."

Erin's eyes were hard. "Don't give me that knight-in-shiny-armor crap. I don't need to be rescued. I need a partner."

"You're right. I'm sorry. That's exactly what I want too."

He reached across for her hands. She hesitated a bit, then set her fork down and let him wrap his large fingers around hers. She stared across at him, her bright green eyes focused on his. In a very soft voice, she said, "Darrell, we're married now. If we're going to have any real relationship, we can't keep secrets from each other. It's not like I didn't know what I was getting myself into. Been around for the last two ghost haunts. I never thought Amy in Cape May would be your last."

Darrell hadn't touched his food. He glanced down and noticed his silverware. The knife and fork were in the wrong position...and not aligned. How had he done that? He moved them into their proper place. He saw Erin watching him and settled down. "I only wanted to give us a great honeymoon. Look, when I saw how much you were enjoying our time down here, I didn't want to ruin everything with some ghosts."

She wiggled the fingers of her left hand, staring at the shiny diamond. "Whatever it is, we're in it together." She went back to eating. "By the way, these are quite good. Remind me to have you do a lot of the cooking."

"Thanks." He started eating again.

Erin finished first and picked up her tea. She took a sip and said, "Okay, now tell me what you can remember of Natalia's warning."

Darrell took two more bites and explained about his latest exchange with the medium—as well as he could recall. "I was pretty sloshed by the time she arrived."

"Tell me what she said about the danger."

"As usual, Natalia was pretty enigmatic. Something like, 'I see great danger lurking. Some malevolence.' Ominous, but not much help."

Erin got up and grabbed the painting from the island. She sat down and turned the framed piece over, exposing the ripped paper and the portrait. She studied the two kids. "Awfully cute, aren't they? Look at those smudged faces. Hispanic?"

"Definitely what I thought. When I saw them on the driveway and the boardwalk, I thought they looked like they were five or six. What do you think?"

She studied the picture. "Probably right." Her gaze went to Darrell. "Hey, is this why you asked me what kind of father you'd be?"

"They got me started. When I saw their ghosts and realized they were killed, I got to thinking. Who could kill a couple of cute kids like that? What kind of parent would let that happen? And when I saw the father on the beach, it hit me."

"Well, let's see what we can do to help these two kids before we start thinking about our own."

"I like the sound of that." He grinned. "Especially the second part."

The tension gone now, she slapped him on the arm. Her eyes wandered back to the hidden painting. "Wonder what *did* happen to them."

Darrell shook his head. "It couldn't be good."

"First, we need to find out *who* these two kids are. And the only thing we have to go on is this painting. Right?"

"Yeah, I think." He shrugged.

"Okay, let's find out what's the story with this other painting. I mean, what's it doing hiding on the back of my dad's gift? Is that part of the mystery?"

"Could be. So far, getting to the bottom of these ghost mysteries is pretty twisted. It's not much to go on, though."

Erin said, "No, but Ted can tell us something about

this painting. Wonder...did he paint both of these?"

Leaning across, Darrell took the piece from her and examined it, turning it to the back, glad the sensation was only faint now. "Um...this doesn't look like Ted's work." He did a slow flip from side to side, displaying both paintings to Erin. "If you look at the sailboat and the sun and then at the painting of the two kids." He handed it to her. "Looks like two different artists to me."

She nodded. "Yeah, I see what you mean. But since Ted painted the sailboat on the other side, he has to know something about the painting of the kids. Got to start somewhere."

"Yeah, but what are we going to say? Hey Ted, we ripped off the back and found this other painting. And I've been seeing the ghosts of these two kids around here, and we wondered if you could tell us who they were and what happened to them?"

"Okay, nothing *that* obvious, but we need to start with Ted."

Darrell agreed. "Right, but we need to be careful. We're newbies here. If Natalia is right about this great danger, we have no idea what we're getting ourselves into. Or who to trust."

"No, but if we're going to help those kids, we'd better get started." She got up and pushed her chair in.

Darrell grabbed up both plates and carried them to the sink. When he came back to her, he asked, "You sure you don't mind taking time from our honeymoon to check this out?"

With both mugs in her hands, Erin leaned forward and kissed him. "Well, when I agreed to marry you, I knew our lives would never be boring. Thanks for not disappointing me." She kissed him again. "Now, scoot. You did the cooking. I got the dishes."

Darrell's gaze went from the dishes to his wife. One part of him wanted to clean the dishes and make sure every piece was put away spotless, orderly. But, looking again at Erin, he fought the impulse. "Yes, ma'am."

Over her shoulder, she called, "Why don't you tidy things up in the bedroom and make the bed? That will satisfy your urge. At least, that urge."

When he made it to the doorway, she asked, "From now on, what will you do?"

He stopped, staring at her. "I'll keep no secrets from you. Not even ghost secrets."

Her hands in the sudsy water, she said, "By the time you make the bed, pick up our clothes, and climb into that shower"—she flashed him a smile—"I might join you."

Chapter 11

A dirty Christmas Eve secret

Driving into town, Darrell feared the gallery would be closed. After all, it was Christmas Eve. He shared his anxiety with Erin, but she was the essence of calm, as usual. "Let's not get ahead of ourselves. We'll see in a few minutes."

When they parked the car and hurried to the door of the Coastal Art Gallery, he saw the lights on inside. Maybe his luck was changing. Holding the door with one arm and a bag with the other, he followed his wife into the cramped space.

Before they were three steps inside, the owner greeted them, a wide smile on his weathered face. "Back for another artistic masterpiece?" His hand stroked his white beard. "I bet I can find something else you might like." He walked over and selected another landscape, this one of a thick swamp overgrown with wild vines and trees, sunlight piercing through in broken shafts.

Erin placed a hand on his arm. "Not this time. We have a question for you...about one of the pieces we bought." Darrell handed her the bag, and she pulled out the sailboat painting. They'd agreed she'd handle the canvas to avoid giving Darrell any more shocks, especially here at the gallery. Flipping over the framed piece, she showed him the portrait of the two kids. "What can you tell us about *this* painting?"

She extended it toward him, but he refused to take it, his initial response abrupt. "I'm sorry. We have a no return policy at this shop." He pushed it back toward Erin.

"We don't want to return—" she started, but Darrell interrupted her.

"Look, Ted, all we want to know is how did this painting get on the back of *your* painting?"

The owner turned away, crossed the store, and stood behind the small counter, as if using it as a barrier between them. "I dunno what you're talking about."

Darrell stepped up to the glass counter. "Are you telling us you didn't know there was another painting on the other side of your work?"

Erin came up beside Darrell and set the framed piece on the counter, the faces of the two kids staring up at them.

Ted picked up and examined the painting, turning it from side to side. "Maybe *you* painted this other side."

Darrell leaned in, using his six-foot plus frame to tower over the shop owner. "Look, Ted, we may be new here to Florida, but we weren't born yesterday."

Erin softened her voice. "We're not trying to make any trouble for you. We love your sailboat painting, and I know my dad will too. And we like the portrait of the kids. We only want to learn what you know about this." Her finger lightly touched the forehead of the boy on the canvas.

For thirty seconds, the owner said nothing. Glancing around as if checking for eavesdroppers, he shifted his weight from one foot to the other, unable to meet their gazes. Ted said, "Wait one second." He slipped from behind the counter and moved to the door, locking it. As he returned to his place, he mumbled, "I was getting ready to close up anyway. It's Christmas Eve, after all."

Glancing at the painting lying on the glass, Darrell felt the eyes of the two kids, sad, pleading eyes, boring into him. He gestured at the portrait. "What about this painting?"

Ted brought up his gaze, an inch at a time. "I never dreamt anyone would rip off the backing and even notice the other work." His voice was low now, like he couldn't get his breath behind it. "How'd you discover it?"

Darrell said, "That was on me. I knocked it off our island onto the floor, and the paper ripped. I'm a little clumsy."

"Make that a lot clumsy," Erin said.

Darrell glanced over at his wife and saw her smiling. He realized she was trying to lighten the mood, to get Ted to chill. Darrell grinned and said, "Anyway, when we saw a part of the other painting, we were curious, so we peeled away the rest of the paper and uncovered it." He waited. He was willing to say more if he had to. He wanted to keep Ted talking and tried to think of something to ask him. To get a reply. "We don't think this"—he pointed to the kids—"is your work."

The older man shook his head. "No. It's the work of a young artist." He looked aside and grimaced. "I have a number of artists who bring their work in here, and I try to sell them. Some do okay, others not so well." He shifted again on his feet. "So, after a time, if their works don't sell, I…I…I *recycle* them."

Ted simply hid the other painting, the painting of the two kids? Did he choose this painting to cover, or was it random? Darrell asked, "You do this often? Use the other side for your work?"

"I wouldn't say often. Sometimes…but only after the piece has been here a while and hasn't moved." The owner looked more and more uncomfortable, and Darrell wondered if he was hiding something.

Then Ted blurted out, "Art supplies can be expensive, you know." He added, as if he only thought of it, "And it helps the environment. Keeps them out of the landfill."

Darrell kept his gaze on Ted, trying to appraise the owner. After a bit, he again indicated the painting staring up at them from the glass. "So, who is the artist?"

"That would be Jared Emerson." As if anxious to move on, Ted hustled from behind the counter to the display of canvases on the back wall of the gallery. He picked up one and brought it back, placing it on the counter next to the piece with the two kids. It was another portrait, this one a close-up of an older Hispanic man's face, complete with drooping chin, wrinkles, and tired eyes. Darrell had noticed it on their first visit.

The owner pointed to the painted work of the old man and then to the faces of the two kids. "See how the strokes are broad and smooth, made with his fingers and palm, not a brush. Since you like the artist, I can make you a great deal on this one. Like I did for the two yesterday."

Erin softened her voice again. "Thanks, Ted. We appreciate the offer. Maybe later this week. You gave us a really nice discount yesterday." She reached out and touched his arm. "What can I say? We're mesmerized by this portrait of these two cute kids. We'd really like to meet this artist. Does he live around here?"

"No, not most of the year, but I think I have a local address for him somewhere. Let me go check my records." Without another word, Ted disappeared through the curtain.

He was obviously nervous or maybe guilty about having his practice of *recycling* other artists' works exposed. Or was there more to Ted's anxiety? For a moment, Darrell even thought the man might bolt, head out the back door and leave. Then he reasoned he wouldn't leave them with all these works. They could easily load up quite a few, unlock the front door, and take off.

As if she knew his thoughts, Erin said, "Easy, boy. Give him some time."

Darrell walked over to the Christmas tree and counted the hand-painted ornaments, studying the arrangement. Eighteen in all, and two of them sat in the wrong positions. He couldn't let that be. After measuring in his head, he moved the speckled gold ornament two branches over and then adjusted a blue and silver creation to one branch lower. Stepping back, he admired his work. That was much better. He touched one ornament and sent it swinging in a gentle arc. Then he did the same with one on the opposite side of the tree.

Erin said, "Darrell, come on."

He turned and caught her look. He shrugged.

She glanced toward the curtain where Ted had disappeared, her eyes widening. "You don't think Ted had anything to do with the kids?"

"What?"

"I mean, he did try to hide the painting of the two kids." When Darrell nodded, she asked, still in hushed voice, "You pick up anything? In here?"

"On our first visit, yeah. But that could've been the painting."

"Now?" Erin pushed.

"This time? No, I don't—"

Before he could finish, Ted came out, a card in hand. "If I remember, he bunks with one other artist type over on Dover Street on the other side of town. Here's the address." He slid the index card toward them, next to the painting.

In one move, Erin slid the two-sided canvas off the counter and back into their bag, then pulled out a small notebook. She scribbled down the information. "Thank you, Ted."

As Darrell and Erin turned to leave, the owner hurried around them, unlocking the door. As they exited, he called after them, "Oh, I almost forgot. Jared's from someplace in South Carolina. He comes down to Crystal River from time to time. He may have already headed home for Christmas." He shut the door.

Darrell watched as one fat hand flipped the sign from OPEN to CLOSED.

Great. Probably another dead end. The ghosts never made it easy.

Chapter 12

Maybe not a dead end, but—

As they retraced their steps back to the car, Erin asked, "So what's your best guess about old Ted? Think he's part of this…mystery?"

Darrell considered the question as they walked. "Well, he was plenty nervous, but like I said, I didn't pick up anything in there…except that." He pointed to the bag holding the painting. "My best guess is that Ted's worried about getting caught. And us letting out his secret. There could be more there, but I doubt it."

"That was my take too," Erin said.

As soon as they were inside the car, she pulled out the map. Darrell recalled what the gallery owner had said and repeated it out loud for both their benefit. "Ted said Jared's place was on a street right off something called Nova Bryan Highway, I think."

Getting ready to turn out of the parking lot, he glanced over, but Erin never took her eyes off the map, her fingers following the street markings. She said, "Found it. At least the highway. West Norvell Bryant Highway, and it's also labeled County Road 486. Head west."

"Huh?" Darrell pulled onto the road and stopped at the light. "Which way is west?"

Erin checked the map again. "Straight. Take this

road. Then where Florida 44 intersects with 486, we turn left onto Broad Street." She glanced back at Darrell. "Looks like about ten miles."

With Christmas traffic clogging the roads, it took more than twenty-five minutes, but they found the address Ted had given them and pulled into the lot. Studying the building in front of them, Darrell asked, "You sure this is right?"

"It's the address he gave us." Erin shrugged. "Unless he simply told us something to get rid of us."

Maybe Ted wasn't interested in helping them find Jared, Darrell pondered. Maybe he didn't want them to learn anything about the kids. He did paint over the kids' portrait. Then again, the owner could just be cheap and didn't like being called out on it. Darrell studied the structure.

The building looked like an abandoned warehouse, darkened with age and neglect, cracks snaking through several concrete blocks. The only window up high was broken, half the pane gone. Unreadable graffiti in bright reds and golds stained one end, and weeds grew up around the perimeter, in places almost five feet tall. Most of the gravel had long ago washed away from the meager parking lot, exposing large blotches of mud and dirt. He didn't even see a door.

Erin grabbed the bag with the painting, and they both got out, the racket of the passing cars so loud they couldn't hear each other talk. Tiptoeing from stone to stone and trying to avoid the patches of dried mud, they worked their way around the building. On the side hidden from the street, they saw a battered pickup parked crookedly next to the warehouse and, beyond it, a door, an obvious path to it worn in the hard-packed earth.

On this side of the building, the clamor from the traffic was not as deafening, though still loud, the noise from a large diesel engine echoing off the concrete. When they got to the door, the distinct odor of marijuana drifted through the metal. Darrell found no doorbell, so he used his fist to pound on the rusting door. He heard a solid echo, but nothing more happened. He turned back toward Erin and then repeated his efforts, this time more urgently, yelling, "Anyone home?"

From inside, a muffled voice coughed, then called, "Who wants to know?"

Darrell thought a second and hollered, "Fans of Jared Emerson. Is he here?"

They waited, and for a long minute, nothing happened. He and Erin exchanged glances, and she nodded her head toward the entry. Darrell had just raised his fist to strike again when the door opened. Framed in the doorway stood a young man with long, unkempt blond hair, grinning, a joint in one hand.

"Jared? Jared Emerson?" Darrell asked.

"I wish." The figure inside made a wide sweep with the hand holding the joint. "Come on in," he called over the noise. "Hard to talk out here."

They both stepped through the doorway, and the steel door thumped shut behind them, extinguishing almost all outside sounds, as if they were shut inside some tomb. His paranoia creeping up along his spine, Darrell shot a glance back at the entry. Then he shook his head, fighting to control his anxiety.

Following their host, he and Erin worked their way through the dim interior, having to step around several large objects on the floor. It took a bit for his eyes to adjust to the darkened space, but after a few seconds, Darrell was able to make out the cluttered interior. Against the far wall sat two single beds, both unkempt and unmade, covers halfway on the floor and pillows askew. Next to the beds was an ancient card table with three folding chairs. Pieces of junk, stray car parts, overturned canvases, and empty cans of paint littered the floor. Darrell fought an impulse to organize the chaotic mess and looked up. At least, with the ceiling more than twenty feet above them, the space felt cavernous, offering some relief from the mayhem on the floor. Erin must've read his face, though, because she laid a hand on his arm. It helped, and he took a long, slow breath.

Their host perched himself on the edge of the second bed and offered them the chairs. They declined. Darrell studied the young man—he would've guessed maybe nineteen or twenty—and noticed the guy looked emaciated, with pale, pockmarked skin and hooded blue-gray eyes. He wore a pair of navy shorts held up by a drawstring and a dirty tee shirt. Though not tall, his arms and legs looked like little more than sticks jutting out from the bed.

Darrell tried, "We were told we might find Jared Emerson here."

"Sometimes you can, but not today." The young man drew hard on the joint, holding it in and then exhaling. "Oh, that's good. He crashes here from time to time." Then, as if he was forgetting something, he added, "I'm Len. Len Tackett. Welcome to my domicile, be it ever so humble." He gestured around the space.

Darrell said, "Darrell and Erin Henshaw."

Erin asked, "You're an artist? Like Jared."

Len said, "Kinda. I'm a sculptor." He nodded to the debris strewn around the floor. His face lit up, red-rimmed eyes going wide. "Would you like to see our studio?"

Without waiting for a response, he took a quick toke and crushed out the joint in an ashtray on the bed. He got up and hurried across the floor, opening a door in the tall concrete wall that divided the building in half.

Darrell hadn't even noticed the door before. Maybe if they humored this Len, they could get more information about Jared. He nodded to Erin, and they both followed. When they stepped through the opening, the brightness of the space on the other side made them squint. After a few moments, their eyes adjusted again, and they looked around. This side of the building held an actual artist studio with a bank of windows up high on the far wall, letting in plenty of natural light.

On the closest side of the room, a haphazard structure of metal pieces looked to be in mid construction with more parts scattered around the assembly. Darrell's hands itched to rearrange the miscellaneous pieces into some kind of order, maybe by size. Or shape?

Interrupting Darrell's musings, Len walked over to the "sculpture" and said, "It's still a work in progress."

Darrell crossed to the other side of the studio where a dozen canvases lined the concrete wall and two sat on easels perched to catch the streaming sunlight. He noticed the one on the right easel was off center a half inch. He edged it over, centering it perfectly on the stand. That was better. Ambling around the space, he examined each piece, some painted with more traditional brushwork and others with the broad strokes similar to the portrait of the two kids. Turning back to Len, he pointed to a portrait of a handsome, slightly dark-skinned man with a halo behind him. "Is that—"

"Yep," the sculptor said. "A painting of Christ. Jared is all about his faith, man."

Erin came up alongside and pulled the portrait out of the bag. Glancing from their piece to those scattered across the floor, they compared the painting of the two kids to the others.

"His stuff is pretty damn good, isn't it? Better than mine." Len sounded both honest and embarrassed. "Jared's been experimenting, going from using brushes to painting with his hands. Never seen anything like it."

Joining them, he pointed to a tall portrait standing up against the wall, about four feet high. It captured the image of a beautiful young woman with flowing brown hair and striking Latin features, including full, red lips and startlingly green eyes with tiny gold specks. "See that piece? He painted that with the palms and fingers of both hands. And he did the whole thing in about twenty minutes. If I hadn't been here and watched him do it, I wouldn't believe it. Paints like he's in a trance. When he's done, he's dripping with sweat."

Erin showed Len the piece they brought, the side with the portrait of the two children.

"That looks like his work all right," Len said.

"Is he around?" Erin asked quietly. "We'd really like to meet him."

"Not sure." Len shrugged. "He was gone when I got up this morning." He rubbed the fingers of his right hand. "That's why I was doing the weed. He doesn't like that, so I figured I'd better get a little in while he was away."

"So he's coming back. Do you have any idea when?" Darrell asked.

The sculptor drifted back over to his work-in-progress. "Not really sure. Last night he said he was going to head over to the truck stop for a shower this morning." He gestured around. "Not the greatest facilities here. All we have is a toilet and running water. Gotta have that for our work."

"Did Jared say anything else? Any idea where we might find him?" Darrell asked, his voice getting tighter. He felt they were close to…something. He had no idea what, but something. He needed something, some breadcrumb.

Standing beside his sculpture, Len snatched up a half-empty bag of chips lying among the debris. He crunched, the sound noisy in the studio. "You know, Jared and I go way back. We both went to Bible school together. And when he split and came to Florida to try this art thing, I came with him." He chomped down on four chips and dug in for more. "But we don't hang out together or anything. He kinda does his thing, and I do mine," he said through a full mouth.

Desperate to get something more helpful from this artist, Darrell wanted to wring his scrawny neck. As with many times before, Erin rescued him from himself.

In a quiet voice, she asked, "Have you decided what you're going to make here?" She came over and stood next to the metal assembly.

"Not sure yet," Len said, swallowing the last of the chips. "Some comment on our throwaway society, but it's not finished yet. What do you think?" He glanced at her, angst in his eyes.

She appeared to appraise the sculpture. "I think, um…it has possibility."

"Really?" Len's weed-induced grin returned to his face.

She moved closer to the sculptor, placing her hand on the arm reaching for the chips. "Anything else you can remember about Jared? It's important to us."

He scrunched one eye closed, as if that would help his brain recall. "Oh, yeah. I remember he talked about maybe going home for Christmas, so he could have headed north already. He simply crashes here from time to time. His family's up in South Carolina."

"So he's not coming back?" Darrell's question sounded desperate, even to him.

Len grinned. "Not sure. I'm not his keeper. Besides, we're kinda loose around here. It's almost Christmas, you know. You're welcome to check back tomorrow if you want. Knowing him, if he didn't head home, he'll probably be working here…after church. I'd suspect he'll want to paint even on Christmas."

Darrell could see a few blackened teeth in Len's mouth, and, staring at the guy, figured this was the best they could get—at least for now. His frustration grew at hitting another wall, but he fought to hide it. He walked over and extended a hand.

Len put down the bag of chips and shook clumsily. "Glad you came. Artists are thrilled when someone appreciates their work. I know I am. Oh, could I interest you in a little piece of sculpture?"

Erin asked, "Do you have any finished works?"

Len glanced around the cavernous space. "Not

yet…but I'm working on a couple."

Erin flashed him her winning smile. "Maybe we'll have to come back when you have some completed creations."

Len grinned. "That'll be great."

She said, "Thanks. If you see Jared, would you let him know we'd love the chance to talk with him?"

"Sure will." Len's grin broadened like a little kid who'd got the lead in the school play.

They headed back into the living area, and now Darrell noticed the earlier smell of pot had masked the pungent odor of human sweat, the living area smelling like an untended locker room. He couldn't wait to get out of there. As they were exiting through the door, Erin called back, "It was nice to meet you. We wish you luck with your art."

When the door closed behind them, Darrell called, "I think it's going to take more than luck." He shook his head, his exasperation spilling out. "Damn. Another dead end. I don't know where we go from here."

Chapter 13

A Christmas carol or two might help

Darrell slammed his fist against the steering wheel. "Well, that was a bust. Any ideas on what we should do now?"

He didn't get it. Before last night and the weeping painting, he would've been thrilled to dump the whole ghost thing and simply have a fun, carefree honeymoon. After all, that's why he put off telling Erin about Natalia's prediction. He wanted it all to go away so he and Erin could simply have a relaxing time in the Florida sun.

But after he'd gazed into the pleading eyes of those two young kids—victims before the age of seven—an obsession gripped his heart. Natalia's prophecy hadn't affected him as much as the haunting look in those eyes. They were *so* young. He felt driven to do *something*, anything. To *aAyúdaños*. Now, his inability to learn anything about them ate at him. Made him feel like a failure.

"First, take a breath," Erin said, placing her hand atop his. His gaze moved there, and he noticed his knuckles were white. "Chill a little for me." With her other hand, she turned his face toward her, leaned across the space, and kissed him, slow and gentle. She kept her lips there and whispered, "We've had obstacles before. Figured a way around them. Together. We'll do the same thing here."

She gave him a small smile, which he couldn't resist. Darrell's tension uncoiled. "Together," he repeated in a quiet voice. "Okay, steady one, what do we do now?"

Erin eased back. "Well, it's Christmas Eve. Time for you to treat your wife to some Christmas spirit...and maybe some Christmas spirits." She grinned. "Besides, I'm hungry. Let's grab something to eat back on Citrus Avenue. I read they were going to have a group there this afternoon, carolers or a choir. Sound like fun?"

"With you, it sounds wonderful." He pointed to the bag between them. "What about helping them?"

"Let's celebrate a little Christmas." She smiled. "Something will come to us."

Thirty minutes later, they were relaxing on a bench near a magnificent, towering Christmas tree, the air pungent with the tempting cinnamon aroma of roasted almonds from a street vendor. He couldn't resist. He purchased a bag, and they shared the warm, delicious nuts.

Between crunching, he said, "My dad used to buy us some of these back at the Ann Arbor Christmas Festival. Craig and I would fight over who'd eat the most."

"Yeah, except there it was probably freezing. Not seventy degrees." She gestured to the air.

Their timing proved perfect as a choir from a local high school started their performance. Two dozen kids stood in a grassy area, their red and green outfits twirling as they sang "Deck the Halls" a cappella and followed with a hilarious variation of "The Twelve Days of Christmas." After a few more favorites, they finished with a silly version of "Rudolph the Red-Nosed Reindeer" to spirited applause from Darrell and Erin and others who'd gathered to listen.

As the students sauntered off in twos and threes, he asked, "How's that for a little Christmas spirit?"

"Not bad. Not bad at all."

After a brief deliberation, he went off to get crab cake sandwiches while she headed to the photo kiosk to pick up their developed pictures. Ten minutes later, they returned to the same bench, which by some miracle was still available. At the café, he'd had the server cut his sandwich in two perfect halves, and now he set them on his lap and placed the dill slice precisely in the middle of the two. Using three fingers, he picked up a half sandwich and meticulously worked his way through it. Erin glanced over at his careful manipulation and chuckled, a spot of golden remoulade sauce on her mouth. Grinning, he reached over and dabbed her lips with a napkin.

Her mouth still partway full, she managed, "Thanks."

Not far away sat the "North Pole Hut," and Erin nodded that way. As they ate, they watched as excited children lined up for a last-minute conference with the big guy while the speakers played an orchestral rendering of "Jolly Old St. Nick."

Darrell couldn't help himself. He studied the anxious faces of the young kids, searching for the eyes he'd memorized from the painting. It was no use, he knew. His kids were victims. *The forgotten ones, insignificant and ignored*, Natalia had said. He couldn't get their eyes out of his head.

Erin waved a hand in front of his face. "You okay? Lost you there for a moment."

Darrell shook his head. "Sorry. I saw these children and thought of—"

Erin cut him off. "I know this is hard for you. You care about kids. A lot." He started to shake his head, but her finger on his lips stopped him. "I watched how you are with your players and your students. Don't think any teacher I had cared so much about their students."

"That's not the point. That's what teachers are supposed to do."

Erin wouldn't let him go on. "And I saw how hard it was on you, working to get justice for Hank back in Wilshire. Especially when you realized all he went through." She pointed to the children lining up to see Santa. "And these two are really young, like those kiddos. Kids get to you…and that's a good thing."

His gaze went back to the children in line, jostling and talking, clutching small pieces of paper with bright eyes anxious. Last-minute lists for Santa.

She finished her sandwich first, curled the pale green paper in a tight ball, and picked up her napkin. "You need to have faith. It's Christmas. Something will come up."

"I wish I could be so sure." He turned his attention to the pickle, taking three equal bites.

When he finished, Darrell folded his paper wrapping into four equal quarters. Taking both discarded wraps, he stuffed them in the colorful bag and deposited them into a nearby trashcan. When he returned, he slid an arm around her shoulders, inhaling the slight herbal scent of her shampoo. He loved the smell. Behind them, the music track switched to a rollicking vocal version of "Go Tell It on the Mountain." He couldn't identify the singer but really enjoyed her rendition as he tapped his toes to the beat.

"I love this, and I love being here with you," Darrell said when the song concluded, a brief pause following. "I don't know how to help these kids. This artist, Jared Emerson, he's probably on the road somewhere between here and South Carolina. What if we can't find him? What do we do? We have no idea who they are, how to locate them, or what really happened to them." He shook his head, eyes wandering over the giant Christmas tree. "I think we're going to need a Christmas miracle."

At that exact moment, the lights on the Christmas tree came on, the pine branches bursting with bright yellows, blues, reds, and greens in the fading daylight. In sync, strings of lights on the shops and cafés followed, blinking on one after the other. A few people erupted in applause, and Darrell and Erin sat mesmerized, watching first the tree and then the street erupt in colorful Christmas lights.

Erin glanced from the Christmas tree to Darrell, smiling again. "Good thing I know a place where they do miracles."

Chapter 14

A Christmas Eve miracle?

"You think we'll find a miracle *here*?" Darrell said as they passed through the entrance to St. Benedict's Catholic Church on the Suncoast Highway.

Grinning, Erin whispered back, "You never know. It's almost Christmas."

Stopping at the end of the narthex, the two of them checked out the church. They'd arrived early—the Christmas Eve service wouldn't start for another fifty minutes—but the church was crowding up, and to find open seats they'd have to make their way toward the front. Like churches everywhere, early arrivals had claimed the rear pews.

Outside, darkness had settled over Crystal River, and dim overhead fixtures and candles in the windows provided the only illumination for the interior, creating a quiet and serene atmosphere. Taking Erin's arm, he led her down the right aisle, his eyes roaming around the interior. What he noticed first was the incredible artwork everywhere—ceiling, windows, altar. He guided her down the length of the church, passing several stained glass windows, though they were too close to make out the depictions in the tall colored glass.

At the front, they crossed at the foot of the

sanctuary and stopped briefly to take in the spectacle. Behind the altar hung a three-story-tall glass panel with a huge cross in the center, glorious colors etched into the image. High overhead, a detailed fresco adorned the domed ceiling over the sanctuary, stylized images of saints, angels, and even stags surrounding a figure Darrell guessed was St. Benedict. The painted images flickered in the shimmering lights from the candles.

And at their feet, like at their wedding last week back in Wilshire, forests of poinsettias blanketed the area around the altar and flowed down the outside rows, the brilliant red blossoms exploding against a sea of dark green.

Beside him Erin whispered, "It's beautiful, isn't it?"

Darrell found it hard to speak, so he simply nodded. He didn't have Erin's confidence they were in a place of miracles, but—if there was one in the offing—this was certainly the right setting for it. She tugged his arm, and they made their way to the left side of the altar area and stopped at the Christmas display. Directly in front of them, a large nativity scene flanked the sanctuary on the left, complete with oversized statues of camels, sheep, kings, and shepherds. A bright, five-pointed star hung over the stable, and tall candles bracketed the arrangement. Even at twenty-six, Darrell was still awed by the scene of the helpless little baby wrapped in swaddling clothes and laid in a filthy manger. He held Erin's hand and got quiet, his breathing slow and easy.

Erin must've read his earlier thoughts because she leaned into him, whispering, "Don't know if there's a miracle in store here, but this is the right place to be to ask for one." She continued, her voice low and her green eyes reflecting the candlelight, "We're here celebrating the birth of a young one who was shuttled into a stable because no one would make room for him, and you're..." She stopped and looked into his eyes. "You're doing everything you can to help two lost young ones."

"Thanks." He didn't know what else to say. He felt tears tug at both eyes, so he rubbed them. He was so lucky to have Erin.

After waiting a few moments, Erin tugged on his arm again and led him to a pew on the left side of the nave only a few rows from the front. At least they got two seats on the end and Darrell, claiming the end spot, didn't have anyone next to him, other than Erin. No rubbing elbows with strangers that carried who-knows-what germs.

The familiar aroma of incense and spruce drifted in the air, mixed with a few scents of women's strong perfumes. The fragrance of perfumes caused him to notice others around him for the first time, some dressed in their Christmas finery, suits and ties for the men, colorful holiday dresses for the women. Glancing down at his own wrinkled khakis and a sweat-stained polo shirt, he felt embarrassed and wished they'd taken time to go to the house and change. Catching sight of a couple two rows up in shorts and tee shirts with a store logo, he relaxed a bit.

The service was beautiful as the voices of the choir mixed with chords from a guitar, flute, and piano to create a fitting song track for the retelling of the story of the first Christmas, but Darrell spent most of the time lost in his own thoughts.

Somewhere in the middle of the service, his gaze drifted to a side window, one of the tall windows they had passed earlier. He saw a magnificent configuration of stained glass depicting Jesus surrounded by a group of young children, a toddler on his lap. The lone candle on the sill ignited the deep reds, blues, and purples embedded in the glass, and Darrell thought the colorful scene must be dazzling when sunlight streamed through. Beneath the image he read an inscription scrawled into the glass. "Let the little children come to me and do not hinder them, for the kingdom of God belongs to such as these."

"Let the little children come to me," Darrell repeated softly and then remembered Natalia's words: *They are the forgotten ones. Insignificant and ignored.*

He faced the nativity scene they'd visited and silently asked, are they forgotten? Have you forgotten them? He looked down, his gaze dropping to his scuffed running shoes. He prayed. It was not easy for him, and he struggled.

God, I haven't talked with you much lately. Or at all. But I'm here, and Erin says this is the place to ask for a miracle. You're the one who gave me this... gift. The word, even in his mind, did not come out easily. *Please, if this* is *my gift, help me use it to find these two little ones. Help me help them. Please.*

Darrell must have been distracted for quite a while, for, though he went through the motions of the ritual, the next thing he remembered the celebrant was calling out from the front, "May the God of hope fill you all with joy and peace as you trust in him."

It was as if the priest knew what Darrell craved and had chosen those words only for him. He could certainly use some hope and joy and peace.

After the choir's rousing treatment of "Joy to the World," Darrell and Erin slipped out of the pews and, along with two hundred other worshippers, made their way for the exit. He noticed people everywhere grinning and wishing each other "Merry Christmas." He and Erin followed suit, exchanging holiday greetings with strangers and slogging their way through the crowd.

When they got to the vestibule, someone cried out, "Merry Christmas, Mister and Mrs. Henshaw!" Luis came over and shook Darrell's hand vigorously, his face beaming.

"Merry Christmas to you, Luis," Erin said, her voice warm.

Grinning broadly, Luis slipped an arm around a young woman beside him, a pretty girl with dark skin, a shy smile, and a flawless face. "This is my girlfriend, Juanita."

The young woman, almost as tall as Luis, had beautiful, long black hair that hung down her back and two dangling earrings made from red and black glass. She sported a bright red dress, sleeveless at the top and black and red ruffles at the hem. The whole thing sparkled in the candlelight.

"So very nice to meet you, Juanita," said Erin. "Your boyfriend really helped us get settled in at our rental house when we got here."

The young woman squeezed Luis' arm and smiled.

Luis had on a gray suit that hung loosely on his frame, and he'd added a white shirt and red tie. His glance went from Juanita to Erin and asked, "Is everything okay? With Simmons' place?"

Darrell said, "It's been great, thanks."

Luis said, "If you need anything, Luis get it for you."

Erin said, "We're fine, but we'll keep that in mind."

From ahead of them closer to the door, someone called Luis' name, and he said, "Gotta go." Waving goodbye, Luis and Juanita disappeared into the throng of people heading out of the church.

Darrell took Erin's hand again, her fingers against his palm feeling warm and reassuring. A tall young man came up beside them. He had a handsome face, long blond hair, and a pensive smile. They exchanged holiday greetings and he said, "Happy Christmas to you."

When they came to the celebrant, a priest named Father Tom, Erin said, "Thanks, Father, we enjoyed the service."

The priest beamed a smile and asked, "You new here?"

She turned and indicated Darrell. "Yeah, Erin and Darrell Henshaw. Down here for our honeymoon."

"Congratulations!" His smile got wider, and he reached a hand across to Darrell.

Darrell shook but felt a bit awkward. Erin was always better at these impromptu situations than he. He wanted to say something, so he managed, "I appreciated your wise words tonight."

Father Tom chuckled and said, "It's one of my favorites and kinda a win-win at Christmas. When you're lost, turn to God. If you let him, He will provide an answer." He winked at them. "Enjoy the rest of your honeymoon." After that, he was on to the next group, exchanging more warm greetings.

Darrell took hold of Erin's arm and steered her to the doors, now wide open to the darkness, lit by a few parking lot lights.

If you let him, God will provide an answer. I hope He hurries. We have less than a week.

He took the door from the person ahead and held it for Erin. When they headed toward their parked car, a voice called, "Darrell and Erin Henshaw?"

Stopping, they turned to face the speaker and found the tall young man with the long blond hair, now standing with both hands in his pockets only a few feet behind them. On instinct, Darrell took a half step in front of Erin, blocking her. "Yes, I'm Darrell, and this is Erin. Can we help you?"

The young man seemed hesitant at first and had trouble meeting Darrell's eyes. He raised his gaze and said in a quiet voice, "Uh...I'm Jared Emerson."

Chapter 15

I knew where they were

For the moment, Darrell was speechless, but not Erin. She stepped up beside him and said, "Mr. Emerson, we're thrilled to finally meet you."

The young man glanced at the ground and said, "It's Jared. Len said you were interested in my work. Might want to buy some paintings?"

The artist was tall, about even with Darrell's six-foot-three-inch height and had strong shoulders and powerful arms. He looked to be about the same age as Len, maybe twenty. His clothes, a pair of jeans and a dark blue tee, looked worn but were clean and pressed. A starving artist? That gave Darrell an idea.

"We were just going to get something to eat. How about we buy you dinner, and you can tell us about your art?"

The artist appeared uncertain, or maybe embarrassed, and for a minute Darrell thought he'd blow them off.

Again Erin came to the rescue. "We're visitors here, and there probably aren't many places open now, on Christmas Eve. Bet you know someplace we can get a burger."

Jared pulled his hands out of his pocket, one hand holding a set of keys, and nodded. "I know a place that does a decent burger. And…I'm pretty sure they're still open."

Twenty minutes later, they were seated in a red plastic booth at Fred's Grille, tucked in on a side street in town, away from the waterfront. It looked to be a pretty standard diner, dominated by a long Formica counter with matching stools across from the door. Six booths flanked the doorway, three on either side. They slid into the first one on the left, Jared on one side with Darrell and Erin opposite, the cloth bag lying on the seat between them.

Typical of many diners, the menu was printed on plastic placards tucked into a holder at the rear of the table. Erin and Jared each grabbed one, but when Darrell saw the smudged and stained plastic, he yanked his hand back. He wasn't about to expose himself to all those germs, and he simply read over Erin's shoulder. He glanced around, a little self-conscious, but no one took any notice of them. The place was quiet, with only a few singles and doubles at the counter and taking up one other booth. And no Christmas music. Without the holiday soundtrack that had been running almost nonstop today, the diner felt eerily quiet and, Darrell realized, that would make conversation easier.

Before they even had a chance to start in, the waitress arrived, depositing three ice waters. Touching the end of a short pencil to her tongue, she scribbled on a small pad while they recited their orders—three cheeseburger platters and Cokes.

As soon as the server disappeared into the kitchen, Darrell said, "Thanks for agreeing to talk with us about your work. But first I have a question. How did you know to find us at St. Benedict's? We only decided to attend at the last minute."

Jared grabbed the glass of water and took a long drink, looking as if his throat were parched or maybe deciding what to say. The artist had a small mouth and a long nose, slightly curved toward the end. As the young man finished his drink and looked up, Darrell noticed his eyes were hazel with streaks of gold in the center. And he wore the one-day-old beard look that was so popular—no doubt part of the artistic mystique.

Jared smiled, obviously in comfortable territory. "No big mystery. I had no idea you'd be there. My faith is very important to me and, well, even though I don't usually go there, St. Benedict is one of the few in town that have Christmas Eve service. And they have a pretty good choir. I'll attend First Baptist tomorrow morning. I was behind you filing out and heard you give your names to Father Tom."

Darrell exchanged a glance with Erin. *Miracle?*

Jared said, "When I stopped by the studio, Len told me you were really interested in a few of my pieces there."

"We first saw some of your paintings at the Crystal Art Gallery." Erin slid her arm through Darrell's and added, "We're here on our honeymoon and went in there to pick up something for our apartment. When we asked about you, Ted told us we might be able to find you at the studio address."

The artist brightened. "Honeymoon. Congratulations. Sorry I missed you at the studio. Did you find what you wanted? For your apartment?" He shifted his posture and looked at Erin. "Or could I interest you in one of the paintings you saw at the studio? Most of them are for sale." He shrugged. "Well, all the pieces except for the tall portrait of the young woman."

Darrell and Erin exchanged glances, then he said, "Maybe." Erin reached down into the bag and pulled out the painting, placing it on the table in front of Jared. Darrell said, "First, we wanted to ask you about this one."

Jared shook his head. "That's not mine."

The sailboat side was face up, and Erin said in a gentle voice, "Turn it over."

The artist stared at her, reached down, and his long fingers gracefully flipped the framed piece over. His eyes got wide, and he looked from Darrell to Erin, then back at the painting. "What the heck." Turning the work back and forth a few times, he examined both sides. "What's the story with this?"

Erin said, "Well, we bought that for my dad." She pointed to the painting. "The sailboat. My dad's a sailor. Owns a sailboat something like the one in the painting."

Darrell took it from there. "When we bought the piece, we didn't see your painting. The frame had a brown paper wrapping on the back, covering your work. When we got the painting home, I knocked it to the floor by accident, and the paper ripped, revealing your artwork."

Erin jumped back in. "And when we peeled the rest of the paper off, we found that incredible portrait of those two kids. We were really intrigued by the piece, so we went back to the gallery today, and Ted told us he had 'recycled' your work." She made air quotes. "Because it had sat so long past the agreed time without selling."

"Well, I'll be...That old geezer." His hazel eyes narrowing, Jared looked like he was about to say more, but the waitress returned with their orders, and he went quiet.

The delicious aroma of burgers and fries filled the air, and once the server set down their plates, they went to work passing the condiments and readying the food. After a few bites, Jared paused to talk again. "I'll have to have a little conversation with ole Ted." The burger in both hands, he indicated the painting with his pinkie. "What do you want to ask me about this one?"

Darrell and Erin exchanged another set of looks, and she said, "We're intrigued by the kids in the painting. Can you tell us who they are? Or where you saw them?"

Jared shook his head and set his burger back on the plate. "No idea. I mean, no idea who they are." He grabbed a fry and stuffed it in his mouth. He snatched a second and used it to indicate the portrait. "But I remember where I saw them, where I painted that."

"Great. Where?" Darrell's response erupted, seeming to startle Jared.

After a few seconds, the artist said, "On a side road in Meridian County, the next county over. Sometimes on the trips from Carolina to here, I cut through Meridian. It can be shorter." He stopped to take another bite of the cheeseburger. He chewed, swallowed, and followed it with a sip. "Anyway, I was driving through the county and I'm passing this big group of farm workers, migrants spread out all over, working this field. Picking strawberries, I think. When I pulled up to this stop sign, I see these parents, mother and father, sitting under this big tree, having lunch. Their kids, these two..." He pointed to the painting with another fry and popped it in his mouth. "These two were playing in this runoff ditch. It had rained earlier, and there was about a foot of water running in this ditch. These two kids were playing in the water and laughing."

Darrell didn't want to interrupt, so continued eating and kept his attention on the artist. He nodded to encourage Jared to continue.

Jared took the hint. "Anyway, I know a little Spanish, so I went over to the family and explained I was an artist. I told them I'd like to paint the children. They said they didn't have very long. They only got twenty minutes for lunch and had to get back to work soon."

Erin interrupted, "The kids? These kids had to get back to work too?"

Jared shrugged. "Pretty much everyone in those migrant families have to work, even the little ones. Anyway, I told them it'd only take a few minutes. When they said okay, I went to work. That piece took me about ten minutes, I think."

Erin repeated, "Ten minutes? Jared, you do remarkable work." She stared at the painting. "You captured them so well, with the dirty faces and torn clothes and even their haunting eyes. In ten minutes? You're quite talented."

Darrell blurted out, "Do you remember their names? The kids or the family?"

Jared scrunched his face. "I'm sure they told me. I mean I introduced myself and think they told me their names." He shook his head. "But I don't remember. That was a while ago."

Darrell asked, "Do you recall when this was?"

The artist rubbed his day-old growth. "Not exactly. It was strawberry season last year, so probably...last February."

From her purse, Erin pulled out a folded map of Florida. She pushed her empty plate aside and unfolded the map to the section with Citrus County and the surrounding counties. "Could you show us on the map about where you saw this family?"

She slid the paper toward the artist.

Jared examined the map, one finger tracing the nearby counties until he found Meridian. "I'm pretty sure it was right around here. It was right next to one of those big signs announcing the property." He indicated a point on the map where two solid lines intersected and slid the whole thing back to Erin, who circled the spot with a pen.

Darrell leaned over next to Erin, both studying the spot she'd marked. He glanced up at Jared, who was watching them both. "Thanks," he said. "At least that's a start."

The waitress returned, and Darrell asked for the check. With a flourish, she pulled the bill from a pocket in her apron and set it on the table. "Pay on your way out." Her thumb indicated the cash register in the center of the counter. Grabbing up the empty plates and balancing them on her arm, she left.

After the server made her retreat, Jared asked, "Okay, you got me curious. Why so many questions about this painting? About these kids?"

Darrell started, "That's a little complicated. When I saw this painting of the kids—"

Erin patted him on the arm, interrupting him.

"Darrell's a history teacher, a really great one. His kids love him. He tells them history isn't some old stories about some dead white guys. It's about real people and what happened to them. He has a way to make history come alive for his students."

Jared shook his head and smiled. "Where were you when I was in school? Our history class *was* only a bunch of boring battles and memorizing dates."

Erin continued, "Anyway, when we came down here for our honeymoon, Darrell got this crazy idea to do a little research about the history of migrant workers in the South." She patted her husband on the arm and raised her eyebrows. "Everywhere we go, he's doing historical research. He says the best research is from primary sources, from the people themselves. Only, he doesn't know any...any migrant workers."

She picked up the framed painting of the two Hispanic kids. "We fell in love with these kids, and Darrell thought maybe we could interview this family and get a start on some real research. Since we now know where you met them, it might give us a place to start."

As she talked, Darrell studied Jared. The artist looked conflicted, like he was trying to decide how much to say. After a bit, he shook his head. "Sorry guys, what I told you won't be much help. I met that family almost a year ago. The migrants move from farm to farm with the crops. I doubt they could be there. It's not strawberry season. They could be anywhere right now."

As Jared slid his long legs out of the booth, he stood up and nodded. "Thanks for the meal, and good luck." He turned and, in three seconds, was out the door.

Disappointment flooding over him, Darrell watched the artist leave and disappear into the darkness…just like their Christmas miracle.

Chapter 16

A Christmas picture is worth…

The next morning Darrell awoke to an empty bed. Groggy, his eyes only half open, he reached his hand across and landed on a clump of lilac sheets. No Erin. Last night his sleep had been tormented with questions about the two kids—and no answers. His subconscious still was stuck in the nightmare, and when he didn't find Erin beside him, he sat up quickly. "Erin?" he called, his voice hoarse. "Erin?" he repeated louder, a little more insistent.

"Easy, big boy." She appeared in the doorway, holding two steaming mugs and dressed in his other Oxford shirt, this one a pale yellow, her long beautiful legs extending beneath. The sight of her there calmed him.

Her wavy, red tresses fell easily onto both shoulders, and he realized she must have risen earlier and brushed her hair. Was she wearing lipstick? She looked tremendous. Releasing a slow breath, he slid his legs off the edge of the huge bed. Smiling, she came over to his side, set both mugs on his nightstand, and stepped in between his legs.

Standing with both hands on his shoulders, she leaned in, kissed him, and whispered, "Happy Christmas, my husband."

His eyes shot open. "Christmas?"

She pulled back. "Don't tell me you forgot today is Christmas?"

"Uh...no, not exactly. I had a rough night...last night," he stumbled. "I kept thinking about the kids. And then when I woke up and didn't find you here—"

She placed one finger on his lips. "No talk of ghosts today. It's Christmas, our first Christmas together." She closed one eye. "Okay, I'll allow one mention of Marley's ghost."

Darrell looked up. "Who?"

"Dickens' *Christmas Carol*, silly." She snatched one of the mugs. "Now, get yourself together and meet me in the family room. Those presents won't unwrap themselves."

A few minutes later, they stood together, mugs in hand, in front of the Christmas tree. Darrell shot a quick look at the dark liquid—Christmas tea with cinnamon and cloves from the aroma—and at the Persian rug and stopped.

"Hang on a minute. I'll be right back." One hand balancing the tea, he headed to the kitchen. Setting the mug on the counter, he rummaged through the drawers until he came up with two coasters, ceramic squares with images of manatees printed on top. He grabbed the coasters with one hand and snatched the white paper bag they'd gotten at the gourmet bakery yesterday. Coasters and sack in one hand, he went to pick up his mug and noticed the packets of the photos they had developed. He thought about grabbing them too to add to their morning celebration, then shook his head. He didn't think he could juggle all of it. They'd have to wait until later.

When he arrived back at the family room, Erin was kneeling, still holding the mug and using her free hand to pull the gifts from under the tree and arrange them on the rug. Darrell laid the coasters on the soft carpet, one on either side of the gifts. Settling into his position, he took a sip and set his mug atop the manatee. "This tea is delicious and perfect for Christmas, but I thought we had better be careful with this beautiful Persian rug."

"Good idea. Hadn't thought of that," Erin said and joined him, sitting directly across with the gifts between them and the tall Christmas tree above, lights ablaze. He extracted a Danish and handed the bag across to her. She did the same, and they sat, enjoying their pastries and sipping the savory brew.

Checking out the gaily colored gifts, Darrell noticed there were a few more than the four they had brought on the plane. "Hey, how'd you get more presents? I thought we agreed—"

"Shhh and open your presents," Erin said.

Darrell recalled the last-minute advice his dad had given him on his wedding night. His father had said, "Son, you'll have a happy marriage if you only remember two words." Darrell decided it was a good time to follow his father's advice. He smiled and said, "Yes, dear."

He pulled the paper off the first gift and took out a blue tee shirt with "CRYSTAL RIVER" across the front and a large picture of a manatee on the back. Then he reached into the box and found a matching tee in Erin's size. He tossed it over, and they both held the shirts up to their chests. "Good choice," he said. Laying the wrapping paper on the beige and red rug, he folded the sheets into four neat quarters, smoothing out the creases with the palm of his hand.

A second package was wrapped with brightly colored paper covered with footballs and candy cane goal posts. He held up the cute pattern, and she grinned back. When he undid the wrapping and opened the box, he found a shiny metal clipboard, the front personalized with his name. When he turned it over, he read aloud the engraved saying, "It's not whether you get knocked down; it's whether you get back up.—Vince Lombardi."

"I love it. It's perfect. Thanks." He kissed her and repeated the same process with the Christmas sports paper, leaving two folded sets. When he finished, he gestured to her. "Your turn."

She made even quicker work of the wrapping paper, ending up with the ripped, colorful paper in haphazard heaps on both sides of her, the boxes in the middle. Out of the first box she pulled a flimsy nightgown and held it up, the lights twinkling through the sheer fabric. "Oh, look. Apparently, I opened your gift," she said, her eyebrows raising. She started to hand it back and stopped. "Expect me to sleep in this?"

"When you put that on, you'll look so sexy I'm not sure either of us will get much sleep."

Erin laughed and took her time opening a second box, withdrawing a long sleeve turtleneck top in a shimmering teal. She held it up in front of her. "I really like the color. You have good taste." She laid the cloth against her chin. "And it's so soft. A little warm for Florida, though?"

"We do have to go home to the cold Chesapeake eventually." He shrugged.

"I guess." She replaced the top and released a

breath. "But this is a super Christmas." She smiled that gorgeous smile. "Christmas in Crystal River has been great for our honeymoon."

He started, "Even with the two—"

Leaning across, she moved a finger to his lips. "No talk of ghosts yet."

"Come here." Darrell opened his arms, and she snuggled into them. For a little while, they lay there together on the plush Persian rug and stared up at the blinking Christmas lights on the tree, content to simply drink in the holiday calm. Two married folks lounging around on Christmas morning. Darrell grinned at the thought. They lapsed into comfortable silence, the only sound the soft Christmas tunes coming from the twenty-four-hour Christmas station. As one song finished, Erin sung quietly along with Mariah Carey, "All I want for Christmas is you."

Darrell said, "And you." He nodded. "Oh, that reminds me." He shoved her gently. "I'll be right back." He got up, walked around the Christmas tree, and pulled something from inside the branches in the back. Returning to where Erin still sat, he leaned down and offered a small box wrapped in a deep green velvet, tied with a red ribbon, and topped with a red and white bow. "I have something else for the woman I love."

A broad smile lit up her face as she accepted the present. In only a few seconds, she undid the ribbon and tore open the wrapping, tossing both aside. She opened the box, and her green eyes sparkled. She squealed, "They're gorgeous." She jumped up and wrapped her arms around Darrell's neck. Standing next to him, she held the diamond stud earrings up to the Christmas lights and watched the facets sparkle. "I. Love. Them.

They're perfect." She held them against her earlobes for Darrell to admire.

"They'll make those pretty ears look even better," he said.

"Here. Hold these. I know we're not going out anywhere today, but that doesn't mean a girl can't add a little bling." She handed him the velvet box and then deftly popped out the silver posts she had in her ears. "Trade you." She gave him the posts and took the box back. With careful fingers, she inserted each diamond stud and then twirled her head for Darrell to admire. "What do you think?"

"Exactly like I thought. They look stunning on those beautiful ears."

She wrapped her arms around him and kissed him, slow and long this time. "Thank…you," she whispered.

"You're quite welcome." He wrapped his arms a little tighter.

After a bit, they each called their parents and shared how much fun they were having in Florida and how the weather was perfect. They made sure to check on the family's holidays back home, snow on the ground in Ann Arbor and cold and blustery on the Chesapeake. Afterward, they even took a few minutes to call Sara and Al to wish them a Merry Christmas. Of course, Al had a Christmas pun for them.

"What did the wise men say after they offered up their gifts of gold and frankincense? Wait, there's myrrh," he hollered through the phone and laughed at his own joke. Darrell rolled his eyes but gave an appreciative hoot—it was Christmas after all—and Erin burst into a fit of giggles.

Later, Erin offered to cook him dinner, one of his

favorites, meatloaf with carrots and potatoes. Sitting at the farmhouse table, he watched her mixing the egg with the ground beef and forming the loaf. He grinned again. A wonderful, domestic scene. *She* was the best Christmas gift he could ever wish for. He recalled the banner with their wedding theme, "When we're together, it'll always be Christmas!" He hoped so.

Still, he couldn't shake his foreboding about the ghosts of the two children—even if he wasn't allowed to mention them. The premonition still hung over him like an ugly, black cloud, threatening to block out the sunshine of their holiday celebration. Without willing it, his thoughts drifted back to last evening. His prayers asking for help finding the two lost children—which surprised even himself. Meeting Jared and learning *something* finally about the kids. Then, the chance of a miracle evaporating.

How was he supposed to find out what happened to them? His gaze drifted out to the view through the rear windows. The sun hung high over the blue-green water, the waves slowly lapping the shore. He stared at the orange ball and, much to his surprise, found himself praying again.

God, what good is my gift *if I can't use it to even find these missing children, much less help them in some way? Please let me know what to do.*

Erin must have seen him staring out at the Kings Bay because she turned and said, "Hey, a penny for your thoughts."

Embarrassed for dwelling on the ghosts after promising not to, he covered. "I was thinking you look just as great at the stove as you do in bed."

She rolled her eyes. "You can't sweet talk me into

doing all the cooking," she said but came over and kissed him. When she raised her greasy hands up, Darrell grabbed them, and they wrestled until she eventually smeared the mess on his shirt, all the while both of them laughing.

After dinner, he insisted Erin relax at the table while he did the cleanup, stacking the dishes and utensils in the dishwasher. Filling up the farmhouse style sink with sudsy water, he noticed again the package of photos sitting on the counter. He tossed them to Erin.

"We don't want to get these wet. Why don't you go through them and let me know if there's anything you want me to see."

"Will do." Erin opened the envelope while he started working the roaster pan. A minute or two later, she said, "Darrell, you've got to see this."

Wiping his hands on a towel, once then twice, he pulled out a chair next to her. He sat down and leaned in close.

Flipping through the photos of one couple after another, she stopped at one and pointed. "This must be from your brother's table." She held it up. "Look at Craig grinning. Who's that with him?"

"That's Sharice." Before she could ask, he added, "I don't know if it's serious. He wouldn't tell me."

"She's pretty and...she came all the way to Maryland for our wedding." She smiled. "Doesn't sound *not* serious."

She edged through the others without comment, her fingers turning over one after another, until she got near the end. She stopped and picked up a picture. "Hey, look. Here's the one we had Bonnie take of us by the gorgeous Christmas tree. We look great, if maybe a little tired." She held it up, admiring the pose.

Darrell inched his face closer to the photo. His eyes got wide, and he glanced from his wife to the picture. Taking it from her, he examined it even more closely. "Tell me..." He was breathless. "Uh, tell me you see them." He handed the picture back to Erin.

She must have seen his stark expression because the mirth left her face. "See who?" Her gaze went from him to the photo and back to Darrell. "What are you talking about?"

He pointed to a corner of the photo. "Look at the French doors. To the right of the Christmas tree. There, in the glass. Two faces looking in. The faces of *two kids*. You *can* see them, right?"

She raised the picture up a few inches from her eyes. "Yeah...I see *something*." She glanced at him and back at the photo. "Yeah, I think I *can* make out two sets of eyes." She moved her head from side to side. "And they do look a little like the faces in the painting."

"You really can see them? It's not just me." Darrell released a breath.

"I see *something*. You really think it's them?"

"Who else can it be? I didn't see any peeping Toms around." He had an idea. "Hey, let me see the other photos. The others we took down here—to finish the roll."

Erin fumbled with the package, flipping through to get to the final two photos. She handed him the one of them at Three Sisters Springs, and Darrell studied it. He held it up for her to see as well. "Look. There on the boardwalk. See the two children riding little bikes behind us?"

Erin peered at the photo and nodded. He grabbed up the remaining picture, the one of her on the beach. There in the background was an image of two young kids, dark hair and wide pleading eyes.

"It's the same two kids." Laying the three photos side by side on the table, he pointed from one to the other and gave his head a small shake. "And *you* can see them! All three! You can actually see them. I don't know what that means, but it's got to mean... something."

Erin said, "I don't know either, but I'm glad. I can actually see something from the other side that you can."

"Yeah, you can." He nodded, smiling. Then his glance flicked from Erin to the images on the table and back to Erin. He raised one finger and whispered, "What if...maybe...maybe it means they're *not* dead? Maybe I'm supposed to find these two little ones...*alive.*"

Chapter 17

A little run can't hurt

Darrell stood at the metal railing panting, his chest heaving in and out. He dripped with sweat, his thighs hurt, and his calves screamed. He glanced over at the sleek body of his wife next to him, also wet with perspiration, but who didn't look nearly as winded. Her figure was stunning in the running clothes, a top striped in bright pink, purple, and blue with shorts in hot pink, the same outfit she wore on their first date, another run back in Wilshire. Then, as today, Erin pretty much kicked his butt.

It wasn't hot, only in the low seventies this morning, but with their exertion the last sixty minutes, they were both slick from head to toe. They'd just finished the Withlacoochee Bay Trail.

She got her voice first. "Now...wasn't *that* worth it?" She pointed out over the water.

He raised his drooping head and stared at an endless expanse of blue. The water stretched to the horizon and met a near perfect azure sky, with streaks of billowy white clouds perfectly placed as if painted by some unknown hand. The sight *was* remarkable.

The picturesque scene made him think of the peculiar artist they'd met Christmas Eve, the one who'd painted the Hispanic children. Without willing it, he pondered again whether what Jared Emerson had told them would actually lead to the kids. Did Jared know more than he shared? Was he tied up somehow with what happened to the dead children? Or maybe the missing children?

Darrell's sense told him Jared was only an innocent participant, but he wasn't sure he could trust that ability. It didn't seem to be of much help finding out about the ghosts this time...or whatever they were. At least, not yet.

Once again, standing there, half hunched over and sweating, the question struck him. *The* question. Why was he the one with this *gift?* He'd never asked for it. He didn't want it. At least...he didn't think he wanted it. Besides, he didn't seem to be able to *use* the gift very well. He had no idea who the kids were or how to find them. Or rather, find out what happened to them. He fought to push aside his anxiety, and he drank in the scene.

Right beyond where they stood, the trail ended at the water's edge, the shoreline dotted with clumps of trees, rocks, and boulders, and the occasional patches of sand. Beyond the jagged and uneven shore lay the Gulf of Mexico.

"Yeah...it's gorgeous." He gasped another ragged breath. "But we had to run five miles to get here."

Erin took her eyes from the water scene and glanced over her shoulder. "Must be a great idea. We're not alone this morning."

Darrell turned to see the dozen or so bikes—road, touring, and recumbent—pulled onto a concrete pad next to a set of restrooms. "Yeah, but most everyone else rode here."

As they had jogged through swamps with trees, moss clinging to the branches, across long, slatted, wooden bridges, and across the paved asphalt strips skirting rivers and bogs, bicycles of all shapes and sizes had whizzed by them. Now, behind the assembled cyclists, two lone runners trotted to the end. At least, Darrell and Erin weren't the only fools running this morning.

He didn't want to be here. Well, that wasn't exactly true. He loved being with Erin, even if that meant torturing his body on an early morning five-mile run. But after their wonderful day yesterday, his slumber was again haunted by his two ghost visitors. Okay, not in the literal sense. He'd fallen asleep next to Erin, contented and exhausted, but his pleasant dreams were interrupted by visions of the two pairs of caramel eyes, staring, pleading for help. More than once, he thrashed about in the bed, only to have Erin wake him and hold him until he fell back asleep.

Once they awoke, she talked him into "a little run." A five-mile little run. But Erin had been right. Pounding the pavement had allowed him to jettison much of his anxiety, leaving it with the drops of his sweat on the black path. His muscles ached, but his head had cleared some.

Erin knew him and must have seen something in his face. "You okay? It's more than the run, isn't it?"

He faced her. "I can't get the vision of the kids' pleading eyes out of my head, you know, like in the three photos."

"Which I could see, remember?"

"How could I forget?" The fact that Erin could see the images of the ghosts was something new. It buoyed him somehow. He was glad to share the gift. Maybe he wasn't simply…crazy. Which was often how he felt in the middle of these ghost adventures. Did the gift make him crazy? Or was he already crazy and simply wanted to blame the ghosts?

He shook his head. "But I've still got no idea what that really means." He met her gaze. "Maybe, just maybe, the kids *aren't* dead, but I don't know. This is new territory for me."

She flashed him one of her wonderful smiles. "I didn't know marrying you would come with such…mystery. I love it."

Her smile helped, but he sensed time slipping away, could almost hear a clock ticking. "We only have a few more days down here, and if we can't find the kids, or at least find out what happened to them, they might be forever 'ignored and forgotten.' I know it's not much of a honeymoon, but I feel like we should drop everything and search for them."

Erin patted his hand. "Today is Sunday, the day after Christmas, and we're not likely to catch anyone at home." She gave her head a small shake. "Besides, if we need to go to an office or see someone at work, no place will be open."

Erin, the practical one, was right, of course. She added, "Not to mention, last week we made reservations to swim with the manatees this afternoon. Which we already paid for."

He knew Erin had really looked forward to swimming with the manatees. It was what she talked about most from the day they first discussed coming to Crystal River. He did not want to disappoint her. He heaved a deep breath and released it. "You're right."

Erin turned back to face the water, and he joined her. She stretched one arm out and pointed to the right. "See that? Almost on the horizon."

Looking in the direction she indicated, Darrell squinted. He saw something. A long, white smudge on the water.

"Looks like a cruise ship," she said, excitement in her voice.

He stared and thought maybe he could make out the windows or balconies across the top. Probably a cruise ship.

She turned toward him. "Would you go on a cruise with me?"

Images of hordes of people crowded into small spaces—dining rooms, elevators, stairs, bars—flooded his brain. Literally, millions of germs everywhere. He'd read those ships carried between fifteen hundred and two thousand passengers. Not counting the crew. He did an inward shudder but tried not to show it.

"I'd love to be with you, but we might have to work on that," he said, nodding toward the smudge.

Erin glanced over, smiling. "All in good time. How much longer you want to wait before we start back?"

"Oh, yeah. We have to run back the way we came," Darrell pretended to complain.

She looked over and saw him grinning. She glanced at the slim gold watch on her wrist. "We've got about three hours until our reservations for the manatee swim."

Darrell did the calculations in his head. "Well, let's hit the facilities, get some more water, and head back. I'm sure the manatees are waiting to meet you."

By the time later that day they finished their swim,

Darrell would be surprised how right he'd been.

Chapter 18

Maybe manatees know something

It turned out their timeline was tight, as they needed all of the three hours. They had to jog back—they were both a little slower on the return trip—drive back to the house, shower, change, and head to the Plantation on Crystal River. They had barely enough time to grab a burger, fries, and Coke at a drive through.

Still, the hustling proved worth it as the manatee experience turned out to be everything they'd hoped for. The excursion began with an hour-long cruise on Kings Bay, where the captain shared a few interesting facts about the area and its history. Erin, ever the sailor, was surprised to learn the bay was only three to six feet deep, which accounted for why they saw so few sailboats. Most sloops carried a keel too deep to navigate the shallow water. Darrell got his sports and history fix when the captain steered the flat bottom boat past a peninsula with the oldest building in Crystal River, a dilapidated and broken-down cabin with a long wooden porch facing the water.

"You'd never know it to look at it now," the sunburned old captain explained, "but that place was a fishing cabin, back when there was nothin' else here. Back in the day, baseball greats like Babe Ruth and Ted

Williams came here to relax on days off during Spring Training."

Darrell finished off the roll of another of the disposable cameras Erin had brought along, clicking shots of the old structure. They also floated past an old, rundown motel called Port Paradise where they learned Elvis Presley had stayed while filming a movie neither Erin nor Darrell had ever heard of.

"That's okay," chuckled the captain. " 'Follow That Dream' wasn't one of his best anyway."

After the relaxing boat ride, everyone went to don wetsuits. Darrell took the one handed him by the assistant, holding it out at arm's length and examining it. Draped on the hanger, it looked like a blue skin of thick foam with a zipper up the side. His gaze went from the wetsuit to the assistant, and for a moment, he didn't move. This...thing was worn by others, he thought, others with who knows what germs.

The guide, a slim, middle-age woman with blonde hair and a wrinkled forehead, came over and noticed Darrell standing there, holding up the line. Taking his inaction for confusion, she explained, "The water from the springs is a constant seventy-two degrees. That's perfect for our swimming mammals but a little cool for humans, especially since the air temps are only in the seventies today."

Still holding the covering at arm's length, Darrell glanced at Erin and saw the pleading in her eyes. He leaned close to the guide and asked in a quiet voice, "Are these sanitized?"

The guide chuckled and said out loud for the group's benefit, "After each use, each wetsuit is dunked in a special sanitizing bath for cleaning. You can be sure they are completely safe." She grinned at him and added, "Of course, inside the shop they'll be happy to sell you a brand new wetsuit. They start at around a hundred and fifty dollars."

Seeing the desperate look on Erin's face, Darrell sucked it up and stepped into the neoprene, the sticking wetness sucking on his skin in places. It took a bit, and he needed her help with the zipper. Finished, they followed the others onto a second boat, Darrell bringing up the rear, trying to ignore the looks from the others.

Once they went over the side of the boat, though, they understood. The cold water was a shock at first, but after a few minutes their internal temperatures adjusted. Still, they were glad for the extra layer.

The body of water was indeed shallow, and they both could easily stand up. But Molly, the guide, directed her guests to float on top of the water, looking and breathing through the snorkel so as not to disturb the manatees resting along the bottom. They all did as Molly directed, letting their natural buoyancy keep them afloat. He and Erin, holding hands, followed the line of tourists and floated into the springs area. The change was dramatic. Unlike the canal where they boarded the boat, the water here was crystal clear, and Darrell stared through the transparent plastic screen, catching slight movements in the silty bottom. The strong musty smell of the springs struck him, causing him to wince. But after a while his nose got accustomed to the scent, and he was able to enjoy the sensation. Once his eyes got used to the mask, he widened his view and saw ten—no, maybe fifteen—of the magnificent animals lying on the bottom, floating nearby, and rising through the four feet of water to breathe through their hippo-like snouts. Up close, the manatees looked almost like the long gray torpedoes Darrell had seen at the naval museum on Lake Erie years before, though broader and with egg-shaped heads ending in their unusual snouts. Their smooth, round, gray bodies ended with a flat tail a little like a whale or seal, and their fins seemed to be almost hidden on the sides.

Floating there in the springs, his face in the water, extinguished almost all sound. The effect was immediate. Serene, quiet, part of another whole world. Studying the manatees, he recalled the docent explaining these creatures were on the brink of extinction only a few decades earlier, yet here they were, satisfied and unperturbed. The giant lumbering beasts seemed to exude a kind of gentle peace. They swam and floated about, coming up for breaths and occasionally eating the tape grass, long, thin, green submerged plants. They seemed perfectly content with their lot. Watching them, Darrell felt himself relax, and he breathed slowly in and out, the sounds of his breaths rattling in the snorkel. Then and there, the haunting premonition lifted, and the sense of uselessness that accompanied it eased. At least for a while.

Floating above and watching the massive, serene beasts, another thought struck him. Maybe he needed to be a little like them, to accept *his* lot in life. Maybe he needed to stop fighting his ability to see ghosts and communicate with those on the other side. Maybe it was time he acknowledged he was a…*sensitive*. Perhaps it was even time to acknowledge his *gift* as a gift.

He glanced over to Erin, who smiled at him as if

she knew his thoughts and made the okay sign with her hand. He wasn't sure it was all okay yet, but her assurance made him feel better.

One mammal swam beneath Darrell, interrupting his musings. First the creature lagged behind, and then, as Darrell hovered, easily slid past, his huge body moving with ease. A few days earlier, he and Erin had watched the same manatees, peering down into the Three Sisters' Springs from the platform, but being here, close to these magnificent creatures, was an entirely new sensation. Up on the boat, the guide had explained this species, a branch of the West Indian Manatee, was large and could grow to twelve feet long and weigh up to one thousand pounds, the females larger than the males. Darrell watched as one swam past him beneath and did the quick calculations in his head. At least eight feet long and maybe two feet wide. Probably a male and seven hundred fifty pounds. Yet the mammal swam with a grace and ease that appeared to be effortless.

Before they went over the side, the guide had repeated her instructions—and the law—not to initiate contact with the manatees.

"One of them may get curious and come up to you, but do not poke or fondle the creature. We're here to simply observe and enjoy."

Which was precisely what Darrell did. As he and Erin floated aimlessly, drifting farther into the center of the springs, a pair of manatees swam beneath them, a mother and calf, he realized. Only a few feet away, both mammals surfaced for some air, and he saw the mother glance at him as the two breathed noisily. Not wanting to disturb the pair, he and Erin hovered in the water, their masks half submerged so they could watch the action above and below the waterline. After a few seconds, the mother and calf slid beneath the water and swam away. Using gentle paddling motions with their hands, Darrell and Erin moved on.

Of course, one of the manatees chose Erin as a cuddle mate. One medium-sized manatee, larger than the calf they'd seen but not nearly as large as others, swam slowly up to Erin and rubbed its snout against the deep blue neoprene on her thigh. His wife froze in the water, her eyes wide with excitement and a huge smile on her lips. As Darrell watched, the animal slid alongside and brushed Erin's shoulder with its flippers, as if making an inspection. Even though this one was a middleweight, it looked so large next to Erin's slim body, Darrell would've been concerned had they not been assured the manatees were merely gentle giants. Erin's wide grin at the encounter, clearly visible behind the mask, also eased his concerns. After a few moments of inspection, the manatee swam away, its rear fin giving Erin a slight nudge as it passed.

Not long after that, the guide gave the signal their time was up, and all the swimmers moved to exit the water. As soon as they were back on the boat, Erin took off her mask and said, "That was incredible! See how that big guy wanted to dance with me?"

Darrell said, "How did you know it was a he?"

She peeled the wetsuit off her torso, revealing the top half of her yellow bikini, and pointed to her chest. She said in a quiet voice, "He was a little fresh." Grinning, she leaned closer. "Don't worry. I told him I was a married woman." She straightened up and looked at him. "Did you enjoy it?"

"Very much. You said it right. It *was* incredible." He peeled the rest of the neoprene suit off his legs and nodded. "It was like being in another tranquil universe. Hard to be stressed watching those magnificent creatures. Exactly what I needed."

"So, you ready for...?"

"Yep," he whispered, so none of the other passengers on the boat could hear. "Ready to do a little ghost hunting."

Chapter 19

Over the river and through the woods

Early the next morning as the fingers of dawn crawled into the bedroom, Darrell lay awake, watching, breathing. He knew where he was headed, or at least sensed it. And after his encounter with the manatees, he felt a little less stressed. This morning he was focused and gripped by a sense of anticipation…and foreboding.

He didn't say anything at first, but he knew from the pattern of her breathing—slow and easy, but not as deep as in slumber—that Erin lay awake too. Without moving, his gaze on the huge ceiling fan making lazy circles, he asked, "You ready for this?"

Without opening her eyes, Erin reached across the covers and took his hand. "I think so."

"I'm so glad you're with me. I love you," he said, his voice still hoarse with the tendrils of sleep.

"I know. Same here." He could hear the smile laced into her words. "I love you too, Coach."

They moved a little faster than normal, even cutting short their time in the shower. Erin grabbed some fruit from the fridge and breakfast bars from the pantry while Darrell poured coffee into some to-go mugs. When they set the food on the seat and the drinks in the cup holders, Erin cried, "Wait!" She ran inside and came out a minute later, carrying a Florida map and a cloth bag. "Might need these."

Still, they were turning onto US 19 less than forty minutes after they rose from bed. Which was where their problems started. The highway was packed with thick traffic hurtling past, both north and south. Impatient, Darrell waited, and when a small opening appeared, he squeezed into the stream of cars. As they neared town, the traffic slowed to a stop-'n'-go pace. At least, it gave him plenty of opportunity to drink some coffee and nibble on the crunchy breakfast bar. Along with about a hundred other cars, they crawled past the sign for the Plantation on Crystal River, and he checked out the marquee. When he glanced over, Erin was studying the sign as well.

She nodded toward the billboard. "I know you were anxious to get started on this yesterday, but thanks for taking me. I really enjoyed swimming with the manatees. And I loved doing it with you. Something we'll be able to tell our kids we did on our honeymoon."

"Kids? Like *our* kids?" He glanced at the sign as they passed the entrance.

"Don't get ahead of yourself, big boy. Someday." She chuckled and pointed ahead. "Up here, we're going to turn right onto FL 44."

The traffic flow improved a bit, and when Darrell saw the sign with the face of the smiling, older woman, he edged over to the outside lane. The cars slowed again, and it took them another ten minutes to cross the next mile, but when Darrell saw the road sign with the numerals 44, he released a breath. Of course, when they got to the intersection, they missed the light. And there was no break in the oncoming traffic for him to turn right on red, so he waited, fingers drumming a staccato on the steering wheel.

He called up the experience in the water yesterday and tried to recapture that sense of calm. He took in a slow, deep breath. Staring out at the crowded traffic, he wondered if all this was part of some test, a test to see if his *gift* would survive. Did he want it to survive? He wanted to find the two children, whatever happened to them, wherever they were. The urge to find them bordered on desperation now. And if that meant his gift—

Erin interrupted his thoughts. "Looks like the light's changing."

Darrell edged into the new stream of traffic, only slightly better than the gridlock on US 19, and had to stop again after moving a mere two hundred feet. He'd battled traffic bottlenecks numerous times before, but today he resented the congestion of cars, trucks, and SUV's, as if they conspired against him, one more force trying to keep him from finding "his kids," as he was starting to think of the two little ones. Or maybe he was merely projecting from Erin's earlier suggestion. They weren't "his," certainly not like his own flesh and blood, or even his high school students and players. But now that he was in this deep, he felt a certain sense of protection and obligation toward the two missing children.

Perhaps his internal grumbling helped, as on the edge of town the traffic jam eased up and their pace improved. They rolled past Broad Street on the left, and he shot a quick glance in that direction. As they passed, he managed a glimpse of the ugly warehouse their search had taken them to, recalling again the unusual artwork by Jared Emerson. And the haunted painting in the bag between them. A mile farther, as if someone had unstopped a drain, the congestion let up, and they sped ahead at a normal pace.

Traffic slowed again as they made their way through Inverness, but only for a mile or so, long enough to recognize the stately old houses lining the road and the classic architecture of the old courthouse—reported to be haunted by the ghosts of dead prisoners. He did not want to go there. He didn't need any more ghost complications and was glad not to pick up any spectral "signals." He had enough trouble sorting out the truth about the ghosts of his two unnamed young ones. Once through the warren of small-town streets, he left Inverness and the courthouse ghosts behind him, and they moved faster again, heading almost straight east.

As he drove, he noticed the landscape shift around him. Many of the roads they had driven in Citrus County had been edged with thick growth and towering palm trees. Around Crystal River, every few miles they crossed a bridge over water—streams, lakes, swamps. But as they headed east, the tall vegetation shrank first, then disappeared altogether, and the land transformed to rolling hills, broken only by the occasional body of water. After they passed under I-75, the hills gave way to flatter ground covered with rows and rows of plants. Farmland.

With the driving easier, Darrell glanced over at his navigator, who looked great, as usual. Her choice today was casual, another sleeveless top, navy dotted with white. Beneath a scoop neckline, four white buttons marched down the center of the blouse, which ended just short of the waistline of her tight jeans. Her nose buried in the map, Erin hadn't noticed his inspection. When she did, she said, "Eyes on the road, buster," though she was smiling. "We have got to head a little northeast. Turn onto 301 up here, and then we'll have to take a few county roads."

He did as directed. He drove on, able to go the speed limit and beyond as they saw few other cars out here. It was amazing. Only thirty minutes earlier, they were mired in bumper-to-bumper traffic, with commuters and travelers battling for the same road space. And out here, with so little traffic, they felt almost alone at times.

Crystal River and Citrus County had this incredible small-town-Florida vibe, with the water and the swampy growth carrying off the Florida "Everglades" theme. The springs, the manatees, and the quaint small towns with period architecture completed the postcard images. Out here, less than an hour away, cutting across the state on county highways, lay a completely different world—acres and acres of farmland, planted with rows of green crops, with few signs of people. It felt vast, impersonal almost, though Darrell realized he was biased because of how much they enjoyed Citrus County. These miles and miles of farmland were critical. They fed America.

But it wasn't merely the change in scenery. As they drove, he felt like he was distancing himself also from the peace and calm he'd experienced yesterday with the manatees. Now, a sense of foreboding replaced it, the sensation intensifying with each mile traveling east. As he watched the fields fill with rows and rows of crops, he realized he was observing the toil of migrant workers, immigrants like his two kids. And he sensed that among these fields of sprouting and greening crops lay buried the secrets about the two children— "abandoned and forgotten." Perhaps not for much longer. He hoped, and then prayed, they were moving closer to that elusive Christmas miracle.

As the miles passed, he read the signs for towns on roads breaking off left and right. Homosassa. Ocala. Leesburg. Okahumpka. Wildwood. From their names alone, he recognized the melding of the Native American with the European and pondered the many interesting stories—and probably conflicts—the names represented. Different, intriguing histories. Right now, though, he was only focused on one history, one story. What happened to the two children? Were they still alive somewhere, abandoned and forgotten and waiting for him to find them? He didn't think so—he saw them as ghosts, after all—but with this *gift,* he simply wasn't sure. Either way, he sensed he was getting closer.

Erin disrupted his deliberation. "Turn here onto Hampton Road." She glanced up from the map. "We're almost there."

Darrell turned where she indicated, then sped up. The road ahead was winding, and he had to brake into curve after curve before speeding up again. Coming out of the third sharp bend, the road straightened, and the land opened in front of them, giving a wide view all the way around. A quarter mile ahead on the left another county road intersected with theirs. He glanced over at Erin, who again checked the map.

"Not this corner. This should be Seminole." One finger pointed to the circle she made on the paper. "Next one, Ontario, *should* be the corner Jared told us about."

When Darrell glanced back up, he saw a car, some convertible, barreling down the road ahead that intersected with theirs. In the bright sun, the body shone, a dazzling silver or bright blue cutting across from the right. He exchanged a glance with Erin, who looked in the same direction.

"She's got a stop sign. We don't," she said, as much to herself as anyone else.

Darrell watched the speeding sports car and didn't see it slowing. He flicked his gaze from the road to the car headed their way. He caught sight of long blonde hair flowing wildly behind the driver. A few quick calculations told him they were going to arrive at the intersection at the same time. Surely, she was going to stop. Surely, she was not going to blow through that stop sign.

Beside him, Erin squirmed in her seat. She shot a glance from him to the speeding car. She screamed, "That idiot's not stopping. Hit the brakes!"

He did. The tires screeched as the brakes engaged. From sixty miles an hour to zero, the rental fishtailed to a stop barely short of the intersection, a half second before the other car blew through. Darrell caught sight of a young woman wearing large sunglasses, golden hair flying as she passed. Smiling, she gave them a short wave.

Darrell struggled to hold in a curse, and they both fought to get their breaths back, heaving in huge sighs.

Erin was able to speak first. "Like I said," she gasped, "life with you is *never* boring."

Darrell barked a short laugh.

Easing off the brake, he straightened the car out

and continued. A mile farther, they hit their own stop sign and stopped, of course. They glanced at the street sign marking the crossroad. Ontario Road. Sitting at the intersection, they scanned the area. There on the left stood the tree, some old growth tree, maybe some kind of oak, where Jared had said he found the parents having lunch. And there, along the side of Hampton Road right in front of them ran the ditch where the artist said he captured the kids playing in the water. There were no other cars on the road, so, for a moment they sat there, staring through the windshield at the scene. Then, hearing the distant rumble of an engine, Darrell rolled the rental forward, turned, and parked beneath the large tree.

They got out and wandered over across the street. Beyond sat a field that seemed to stretch forever, perfect, neat rows of green plants marching off to the horizon. Alongside the field, running into the distance, was a culvert, which no doubt carried water. Jared had said the day he arrived water filled the ditch, and the kids were playing in it in the hot sun. Darrell looked into the ditch and saw a trickle. On impulse, he reached down, and his fingers came away damp.

"Anything? Getting any vibes?" Erin asked.

He straightened. "There's something here, but it's faint." He reached his other hand behind his neck and felt only the slightest twinge. Not much. "It's very…faint." As he spoke, the sensation on his skin seem to slither away altogether. Of course, it couldn't be that easy. With the ghosts, it was *never* that easy.

Erin stepped next to him, staring down into the culvert. "Any ideas? What do we do now?"

Darrell let his gaze roam over the area, taking in

the road, the huge field, the endless rows of plants. Off to his right, he noticed a large sign edging the field. He read it out loud. "The Harrington Plantation. We grow only the BEST produce. Office: 304 Cool Springs Rd. Hancock." A phone number was listed at the bottom, and pulling his cellphone from his pocket, he flipped it open. No signal. Of course.

He turned to Erin. "You think you can find that place on the map?"

"If it's on the map, I'll find it."

"Okay then. Let's go there and ask at the Harrington Plantation if they know our kids."

Chapter 20

Not exactly Grandma's house

Only Erin couldn't find Cool Springs Road anywhere on the map.

She'd folded the large, unruly sheet so she could study Meridian County, moving her face close to the tiny printing. "I don't see it listed here. Do you think it could be a new road? Maybe added since they printed the map?" She glanced up at Darrell, who sat ready to put the car in gear.

"I don't think so." He backed the car onto Hampton Road and pointed to the right. "That sign doesn't look new. You can see the weathering."

"Well, how do we decide which way to head?"

Darrell put the car in drive and eased forward. "Put the map aside for now and keep an eye on the fields." He jerked a thumb to the right. "I'm guessing there are more of these Harrington Plantation signs. If we drive around the property marked by the signs, we'll probably find the big house."

He drove slowly at first, and Erin stared out her side window. Accelerating, he followed Hampton Road for miles, the perfectly planted rows running alongside them. Only one vehicle passed them on the other side of the road, a new Ford F-150 pickup. All this time, Erin watched but didn't see another sign for the farm.

Darrell shook his head. "I don't know."

"Don't know what?" Erin asked.

"Okay, we're out here. What exactly do we ask someone…assuming we find someone to ask?" He kept his eyes on the road, not looking at her.

"We ask them if they know the two kids?"

His frustration growing, Darrell glanced over at her. "What if they ask what the kids' names are? What if they ask why we want to know?"

Erin shrugged. "We'll think of something."

Darrell let his gaze drift from the curving road to the hundreds, no thousands, of planted rows on the right. "This place must be huge."

"Unless this isn't all part of the Harringtons' farm." Erin shot a glance at Darrell before resuming her scanning of the countryside. "I haven't seen another sign for the plantation since the corner at Ontario."

They rolled on, searching, uncertain they were on the right track. Twice, as he drove, a powerful chemical smell of fertilizer worked its way inside the car, making him glad they were traveling with the windows up this morning. Five miles into their search—Darrell had the presence of mind to check the odometer when they left the corner—they came to a stop sign, and he rolled to a slow stop. Another four-way stop. Erin peered over and read the crossroad sign. "Six Steppes Road." Scrambling to pull the map back up, she scanned the folded section. "Here," she called.

"And that's what we're looking for." Darrell pointed out her window.

At the corner, as if marking a property line, another sign for Harrington Plantation stood facing them. Staring ahead, Darrell noticed the landscape had changed again. Across Six Steppes Road, the countryside had gone wild with massive clusters of trees and tall grasses, which he figured marked swampy terrain.

He said, "I think this is the end of their property. Let's head right here and see if that gets us where we want to go."

He turned the corner, and Erin went back to studying the map, bringing it closer to her eyes. "A little way down here on Six Steppes there's a cut off. A small road, I think. It's not named, but maybe it's Cool Springs."

He followed the new, narrower road, paralleling bright green rows on the right with the swamps on the left, and less than a mile down came to a turn off. He slowed so they both could read the sign, this one with "Cool Springs Road" in some fancy script. Turning onto the smooth asphalt, he didn't know how far he drove—he'd forgotten to check the odometer numbers when he turned—but he figured it must've been more than two miles. He pulled to a stop.

In front of them, a tall post held a much larger replica of the sign they'd first seen on Hampton, this time with the title "Harrington Plantation" in the same elaborate font. Here, the cultivated rows ended, replaced by a huge, near-perfect green lawn surrounded by an actual white picket fence. In the center sat a large house, looking more like a nineteenth century mansion than a farmhouse. The driveway circled around the lawn, and, as Darrell drove, he and Erin peered out, studying the large, rambling house. The two-story structure was wrapped in siding, in a color Darrell thought of as Florida flamingo pink—he'd seen plenty of it down here—though Erin called it light rose. The entire house was topped by a red-shingled roof, itself accented with a single, tall red turret and two chimneys. A long porch edged with a decorative white railing wrapped around the front and left of the structure. As he pulled the car around, he saw a three-car garage tucked off to the left. A shiny blue convertible sat in front of the first garage door, a new Porsche Boxster, if he wasn't mistaken.

After he stopped, he and Erin got out and she whispered, "Doesn't that look like the same car that almost ran into us?"

"Yeah. Not likely to be two of those around here."

They stopped at the foot of the sidewalk leading up to the house and stared ahead. The walkway to the front door was composed of red bricks the same color as the roof, the stones fitted tightly together. Sets of tall, decorative bushes bordered both sides of the walkway. Bent together and trimmed with mechanical precision, they created a storybook-arch feel for the entire length of the walk. As they made their way across the bricks, Darrell noticed strands of tiny Christmas lights entwined around the arching branches.

Climbing the four steps, he glanced down across the porch. He counted six old-style, wooden rocking chairs, all painted white. A stuffed life-size Santa and a matching Mrs. Claus perched in the first two. Stepping forward, Erin rang the doorbell, setting off a melodic version of "Joy to the World." Twenty seconds later, the door opened to reveal an attractive, middle-aged woman with a full head of blonde hair and wearing a stylish, thin Christmas sweater and what looked like riding pants.

"Can I help you?" she asked in a polite tone.

Erin said, "Good afternoon. We apologize for disturbing you, but we were hoping to speak to someone about a family who worked on your farm."

The woman said, "Well, we can't have you standing out there. It wouldn't be in the Christmas spirit. Come on in." She gestured them inside.

Eyebrows raised, Darrell shot a glance across at Erin, who led the way as they stepped through the wide doorway.

Erin waved a hand around. "You certainly have a beautiful place here."

The woman beamed. "Thank you kindly. We like it here."

Darrell caught the southern lilt of the long i's in her speech.

"You'll wanna speak with my husband...about the family. Sterling." She called the last word down the hallway. "This way. I think I left him in the great room."

One wall of the hallway they passed through held a line of paintings, four expensively framed works of art hung one after the other, each with its own small spotlight. The other side of the hall was crowded with a collection of Santas of all types and sizes on a bench and across the floor, standing, sitting, even sleeping—traditional ones, whimsical bearded figures, Santa nutcrackers, St. Nick figures. Counting as they followed, making their way along the foyer, he got to thirty-three.

Erin said, "Quite the place here. And I love the Santa collection. It's truly beautiful."

"Well, thank ya for that," the hostess replied, her

southern accent prominent. "I do love them and always hate to see them go." She sighed. "But next week Maria will have to pack them away. For the season." She nodded at the display with a sad smile. "I'm Savannah Harrington."

Erin said, "We're the Henshaws. Darrell and Erin."

Mrs. Harrington said, "Welcome to our home."

Darrell tried to study their hostess—blonde hair dark at the roots, a pleasant smile now that crinkled around her mouth, and alert, olive eyes. He struggled to *sense* something but wasn't getting much.

As they made their way, he glanced at Erin and noticed her gaze swing from the Santas to the paintings on the opposite wall. At the fourth framed piece, she pulled up short, and he turned to look. Savannah, now a few steps ahead and mumbling something, stopped and retraced her steps to where he and Erin stood.

Erin turned to him. "Isn't that...?"

Scrutinizing the work, Darrell realized why Erin had paused. The painting was done in deep earth tones—golds, browns, tans. It captured the face of a beautiful young Hispanic woman, her skin a shimmering brown and her hair almost golden. And the image was painted in broad strokes, like those made with a finger or palm, not a brush.

He leaned closer to catch the signature. "I think so."

"Isn't she beautiful?" Savannah said, pointing to the work. "I found it in this quaint little gallery in Crystal River, and I simply *had* to have it. Sterling bought it for me as a Christmas present. The owner said it's by some new, young artist. I forget his name."

"Jared Emerson," Darrell and Erin answered

together.

"I see you've heard of him." Their hostess looked pleased with herself.

"Savannah, is someone here?" a voice called from down the hall.

"Yes, dear, we're coming," she called and led the rest of the way.

Before he moved, Darrell's gaze jumped from the painting to the Santas again.

A Christmas miracle?

The Harringtons had a piece by the same artist who painted the portrait of his two kids. Was that a coincidence...or was there some other connection? Maybe there *was* more Jared hadn't told them...though Savannah didn't even seem to know the artist's name. When they approached the painting, Darrell felt no tug, no prickle, but still. Mulling it over, shaking his head, he hurried to catch up with the two women.

The end of the extensive hallway opened into a great room. *Great* room, Darrell thought. The room had to be thirty feet across with a vast cathedral ceiling overhead, making the space appear even larger. One wall held the traditional fireplace complete with a hearth of red bricks from the same batch as the ones on the sidewalk outside. Beside the fireplace towered a Christmas tree that made the one in Doc Simmons' place look puny. Sixteen feet tall at least, with hundreds of twinkling lights. The room held the strong, pleasant aroma of pine.

Atop the hearth sat a long wooden mantel displaying a series of framed colored pictures. With little time for inspection, Darrell's quick glance took in photos of George Bush and Bill Clinton, each with that president posing next to a short man, who stood erect and grinning.

"Sterling, this is Mr. and Mrs. Henshaw."

The man, the same one as in the photos, set down the newspaper he was reading and rose from a recliner. Darrell stepped forward. "Darrell and Erin," he said, nodding toward his wife.

"Sterling Harrington, but I guess you already know that," he said with a deep bass voice, a warm smile on his weathered face. "What brings you to our little corner of the world?"

Darrell didn't catch any hint of Southern inflection in his words, unlike his wife. The man stood maybe five six, with brown hair trying to decide if it wanted to go gray or disappear altogether. Beyond and above the short man, a movement caught Darrell's attention, and his glance went there. Around all four walls of the massive room hung a foot-wide shelving, about eight feet off the floor with a miniature train track attached. On the track chugged the Lionel Christmas Express, complete with a shiny black engine puffing smoke and two open cars, one carrying six tiny evergreen trees and a second stacked with colorful, miniature, wrapped presents.

"You like the train?" Harrington asked, seeing Darrell looking over his shoulder and glancing that way himself. "Savannah's idea, but my handiwork." He motioned to his wife, who beamed.

Savannah said, "You designed it all, but Luis did the real work." She caught her husband's scowl and announced, "The Lord says to give credit where credit is due."

Darrell's eyes went from husband to wife, and he

said, "We had a similar one around our Christmas tree when I was a kid." Then he chuckled. "A lot shorter track, though."

Sterling Harrington flashed a small smile, though it never made it to his eyes. Darrell studied the man before him. Harrington had broad shoulders and stood erect in a manner as if he were trying to make himself taller. Darrell thought, military. Back in Wilshire, Darrell had a colleague, Frank Tolbert, who was retired military and now taught PE. Frank carried himself with the same bearing, strong, straight, and confident. Rumor around the school was his PE classes looked remarkably like basic training. Harrington extended a hand and Darrell shook, though his knuckles hurt in the exchange.

Beyond the bearing, Darrell detected something else. A slight twinge ran from his neck down his back.

While he was trying to decipher its meaning, Harrington asked, "You wouldn't be shopping for some property down here? We heard from a realtor a couple was coming by to talk about buying some acreage from us."

Darrell shook his head, allowing his fingers to rub the sensitive area as the sensation ebbed. "No, we're only down here on a little vacation."

Erin squeezed Darrell's arm. "Actually, we're from Maryland. On our honeymoon down here."

Savannah said, "Well, congratulations!" She eyed them over. "Aren't you quite the couple?" she said, again the accent on the "*i*."

Mr. Harrington's brow furrowed. "You're from Maryland and you're honeymooning in Meridian County? I mean, we love it here, but I can't see it as a honeymoon destination."

Erin chuckled. "Actually, we're staying in Crystal River. Only came over here for the day."

"Then what brings two beautiful young lovers to the Harrington Plantation?" Sterling asked.

His tone was polite enough, and Darrell didn't detect anything beneath it. Still, he remembered the sensation and figured he should be careful how he answered.

Mrs. Harrington interjected, "They want to ask about some of our farm workers, dear. I told them they needed to talk with you." She clapped her hands together. "Where are my manners? We were getting ready to have a little lunch. Won't you join us?"

Darrell said, "Thanks, but if we could only have a few minutes of your time, we'll be out of your way."

Savannah stepped close to Erin and patted her arm in a matronly manner. "Nonsense. We have plenty. I'll ask the cook to put out two more plates. It would hardly be in the Christmas spirit to send ya out hungry." She released Erin's arm and disappeared through a doorway.

Darrell wasn't sure if they'd received an invitation or a directive. Then he felt the twinge on his neck again.

Chapter 21

A little something to chew on

"I wouldn't argue if I were you. A force of nature, that one," explained Sterling Harrington, shaking his head.

Darrell moved his hand to the back of his neck, rubbing the skin. The prickle slid away. He checked out Harrington and shot a glance at Erin. She gave a brief nod.

"I'm back, Daddy," called a petite young woman who came in the way the Mrs. had exited. She bounced into the room but pulled up short at the sight of the guests. Darrell observed the long, flowing blonde hair and large sunglasses above a tight pink top and even tighter black shorts.

He and Erin exchanged a glance.

Harrington must have caught their look because he turned to the young woman. "Darrell and Erin, may I introduce our daughter Steph? Though from the look on your faces, I suspect you may have already met her. Let me guess. On the road?" His gaze flicked from his guests to his daughter.

Steph started to retreat back the way she came.

"Not so fast, young lady." Then to Darrell. "What'd she do this time?"

Not wanting to create a scene, Darrell struggled

with what to say. The last thing he wanted to do was antagonize Harrington—they needed some information—but couldn't figure out how to sugarcoat it. He glanced at Erin and shrugged. "She blew through a stop sign and came close to clipping us."

The father turned toward his daughter and extended one hand, palm up. "Keys."

"Dadd—eee?" Steph pleaded.

"Keys. And we'll talk about this later."

The young woman dumped the keys into the outstretched hand, glared at Darrell, and sulked down the hall, all eyes following her progress.

Erin said, "We didn't mean to get her into trouble."

"Not your concern," Harrington announced. "Her mother spoils her." He sighed, his strong shoulders dropping. "And truth be told, so do I. Let's head over to lunch. I believe we're eating in the sunroom. We can talk there."

Without waiting, he headed into the hallway where his wife and daughter had retreated. They walked past a large formal dining room, stepping around a table set with china, crystal, and silverware for twelve. The center of the table was festooned with a huge arrangement of pine boughs dotted with red and gold glass ornaments.

Harrington stopped. "New Year's Eve we host a little get together for the other owners. It's an important holiday tradition for my wife." He gave his head a shake. "They're simply getting a little head start on the set up." Their host led the way through the room.

As they rounded the table, Darrell surveyed the dozen place settings, amazed to find every one laid with precision, each plate, glass, and piece of silverware in the precise, exact place. He couldn't help but admire the perfect symmetry until he felt Erin's nudge on his arm. He followed her through a door to the right.

They stepped into a brightly lit room with floor-to-ceiling windows on three sides. Through the glass panes at the rear, a large, kidney-shaped swimming pool shimmered in the sunlight surrounded by white striped chaise lounges. In the center of the sunlit room sat a glass-topped table surrounded by four wicker chairs. Wearing a bright smile, Savannah already sat at the foot, and Sterling took the chair at the head. Darrell and Erin grabbed the other two, one opposite the other.

Once they were all seated, Savannah bowed her head, and they all followed her lead. In a flat tone, she recited, "Lord, we thank you for this food and all the gifts you have given us. Please bless our crops and keep us in your good graces always."

"Amen," Sterling said, Erin and Darrell echoing in hushed voices.

Down the center lay a table runner embossed with a bright poinsettia pattern, vibrant red flowers amid a cluster of dark green leaves. At each place sat a clear glass plate with a sandwich of toasted wheat bread—cut into two perfect triangles, Darrell noted—and a long dill slice. And beside the light green of the pickle wedge lay a red-and-white striped candy cane.

Still, Darrell noticed something was off about his place setting. The silverware looked right, fork on the left and spoon and knife on the right, each piece with proper spacing. Then he saw it. The glass wasn't set in the right position, an inch too close to center. He glanced at the others, trying not to look obvious. Erin was complimenting Savannah on the beautiful table, and they all seemed preoccupied, so he took a drink and replaced the glass in precisely the right place. Satisfied, he released a breath and took a small bite of the sandwich, which turned out to be delicious chicken salad.

Darrell couldn't figure out how to start, how to ask the question he wanted to ask, so he began with the obvious. Setting his half sandwich down, he said, "This is delicious. You must be a magician. How'd you do this so fast?"

Savannah chuckled. "Oh, that was Juanita. I couldn't manage without her. She always prepares extra...in case someone drops in." She touched a hand to her mouth. "Oh, and she probably thought Steph would be joining us, but she's pulling one of her teenage pouts." She glanced across the table at her husband.

Harrington mumbled, "I'll tell you about it later."

Darrell decided he'd better change the subject. "We drove around some of your property. It looks like quite the spread. How many acres do you farm here?"

Mr. Harrington took a long swallow. "A little over ten thousand. Mostly in strawberries and blueberries, though we still have a small citrus patch, oranges mostly."

"A good bit of land," Darrell said. "It must be a lot of work."

"It is, but we have a lot of help." Harrington grabbed the pickle slice and held it in midair. "Now, Savannah said you wanted to ask about some of our farm workers."

"Yes..." Darrell stared down at the plate, seeing the trail of tan crumbs from the toast. "Well, um…we're trying to locate one of the migrant families that worked for you."

Harrington took a loud bite of the crisp dill pickle. "Son, I don't know how much help I can be." He chewed and went on. "I have hundreds of workers who help with the fields. I couldn't begin to know every wet—"

"Sterling!" Savannah scolded from across the table.

"Okay, every…farmhand who works for me. Hell, I don't even learn their names. I simply sign the checks," Harrington finished, eying his wife.

Erin chimed in, "We have a picture. Could you tell us if, uh…if they look familiar?" She looked toward their hostess.

Savannah smiled. "Of course, we'll have a look. Won't we, Sterling?"

He nodded, still crunching on the dill slice.

Reaching into her bag, Erin pulled out the portrait and slid it across the glass.

Savannah looked down at the artwork. "Look, Sterling, it's a painting. Quite different. Of two Hispanic children." His eyes went from the portrait to Erin. "This style looks a little like the one you were admiring in the foyer." Turning her head, she stared at the painting. "Is this by the same artist?"

Erin nodded. "Yes, Jared Emerson. That's why we recognized his work in the hall."

Savannah pointed to the framed work. "Look, Sterling. They bought a painting by the same guy. Small world." She beamed. "Maybe he will be somebody famous."

Her husband harrumphed. "We'll see."

Turning back to Darrell, Savannah pointed again to

the portrait. "Cute kids. You said the family worked for us?"

"Yes. At least, we know they did last season," Darrell said. "Jared told us he painted this down the road last February when the family was on a lunch break."

Savannah shook her head slowly. "Like I said, cute kids, but I don't recognize 'em. How 'bout you, Sterling?" She held the framed canvas out. Erin took it and passed it to the head of the table.

Sterling Harrington accepted the painting and turned it from one side to the other. He held the sailboat painting toward his wife, and she smiled. "I didn't even notice that painting. Good lord. There's a painting on both sides?" Her eyebrows raised, she glanced at Erin, who nodded. Then she turned back to her husband. "But I think they mean the other side, dear."

"Too bad. I like the sailboat painting." He turned it over and examined it, giving one definitive shake of his head. "Nope, can't say I recognize them." He shrugged. "Of course, I don't interact with the workers enough to have time to tell them apart. I certainly don't have time to notice their children." He handed the painting back to Erin, who stowed it in the canvas sack again.

A few moments of awkward silence followed while all four returned to their food. While Darrell finished the last of his sandwich, he caught a quick glance exchanged between Mr. and Mrs. Harrington. As he studied their faces, the prickle returned to his neck, and his left hand went there. Did they know more and weren't saying anything? Or was he imagining motives where none existed? As he took in the couple and the beautiful view outside, the sensation subsided slowly, so slowly he wasn't sure it was ever there.

"I wonder if Tom might be able to help 'em," Savannah said, sharing another look with her husband. "Whadda ya think?"

Harrington set his glass down. "Maybe. He'd know better than us."

"Tom?" Erin asked.

"Tom Stickley," answered Harrington. "He's our farm supervisor. He supervises the migrants who work our fields. He might have some idea. His place is about a mile or so farther down on Six Steppes. Long gravel driveway. You can't miss it."

Darrell and Erin finished their meal and thanked their hosts for their hospitality. He grabbed the candy cane and stuck it in his pocket. Erin did the same and said, "Thanks for the holiday candy…and the whole lunch. We're truly grateful for the warm welcome."

Savannah slid her chair out. "You're quite welcome. Come back anytime. I'll walk you out."

Erin gave a short wave. "Don't trouble yourself. We can find our way out." With the bag on her shoulder, she slid an arm through Darrell's. "You've been very kind, and lunch was delicious."

Savannah relaxed back into her wicker chair. "Well then, I want to say congratulations again…and Happy New Year." She smiled broadly at them.

They both echoed, "Happy New Year to you too." Darrell extended a hand to Harrington. "Thank you, sir."

Harrington took the offered hand, and Darrell felt the prickle tug at his neck again. As he released the handshake, Harrington said, "Enjoy the rest of your honeymoon and…I hope you find those two kids you're looking for."

On their way out, as they neared the wide foyer, they heard a high female voice. "You just came here to ask about a couple of migrant kids?" Steph slouched at the corner of the hallway. "Why do you care about a couple of spics, anyway?"

Erin stopped. "We didn't mean to get you into trouble. We simply wanted to know if—"

"Steph?" Savannah called from the other end of the house.

The teen did a classic eye roll and mumbled, "Whatever." Then she screamed down the hallway, "COMING!" Without giving Darrell and Erin another glance, she sulked away.

Darrell held the door open with one hand and his other rubbed his neck, still feeling the burn. He didn't see how they were closer to any Christmas miracle.

Chapter 22

The road leads here

Back in the car, they followed the long, circular asphalt driveway around the house and past the multi-car garage, checking out the Porsche convertible. Definitely the same one that almost T-boned them…and could've killed them. A sudden chill ran through Darrell. He glanced over to Erin, whose gaze was also fixed on the shiny, blue Boxster. Sucking on the peppermint, he accelerated the car out the driveway and turned back onto Cool Springs Road. He followed it to the end and turned right onto Six Steppes.

Checking his odometer, he alternated his glance from the road to his dials. Harrington had said the turnoff was about a mile ahead, so Darrell drove easily, watching the tenths slide by and sucking on the candy. When he got to seven tenths, he slowed, giving them ample time to spot the gravel driveway. All he saw was more uninterrupted rows of bright green plants, and he glanced to Erin for confirmation. She gave a shrug.

He kept going, though more slowly now. Eight tenths. Nine tenths. A mile. A mile and a tenth. Now he was only doing about ten miles an hour. A mile, three tenths. A mile and a half.

"Didn't he say a mile down this road?" Darrell asked, alternating his gaze from the odometer to the side of the road.

"That's what I heard," Erin said. She shot a glance at him. "Maybe a different road. Cool Springs, maybe."

"Nope. When we drove back onto Cool Springs, I checked the road out, and it only ran another hundred yards and dead-ended at some outbuilding." He looked over to his wife. "You think he could've sent us on some wild goose chase?" Bringing his eyes back to the numbers, he watched a mile-seven roll past.

She said, "Doesn't make sense. They know we'd simply show up back at the house again."

Darrell started to respond and stopped. As the two-mile mark on his dash rolled into place, he saw something. Straight ahead, two hundred yards maybe, a gravel driveway interrupted the procession of planted rows. He made the turn and accelerated, the bumpy stones punishing the cheap suspension of the rental. They followed the gravel driveway about another half mile, shooting up a rooster tail of dust and small pebbles until the path circled around a yard and a small structure. He stopped the car across from the house.

Darrell scanned the area, noting the contrast between these surroundings and the home they'd just left. The gravel driveway encircled a small yard, if it could be called that. Tufts of grass struggled to break through the rocky soil and, in most places, were losing the battle. Off to the right, two scrawny chickens pecked the ground. In the center of the yard sat a run-down, one-story structure, its siding badly in need of a fresh coat of white paint and its cheap metal roof scarred with brown streaks of rust. A small, cracked concrete slab served as a poor excuse for a porch beneath a weathered wooden door. Beyond the house where the gravel drive circled around, two vehicles were parked, a shiny, new black pickup truck complete with gun rack, maybe a Ford F-150, and a dented, dark green, ten-year-old sedan, Darrell would've guessed a Monte Carlo.

They got out and started across the lawn. When they'd taken two steps, a large black and gray dog shot around the far side of the house and ran snarling at them. On instinct, Darrell stepped in front of Erin, and they both halted. He assessed the canine. It looked to be some kind of German Shepherd/Airedale Terrier mix, and as it closed on them, it bared an angry set of teeth. Right before the dog reached them, it was jerked to a stop, its neck yanked by a taut rope.

"Easy, boy," called a deep voice from inside the house. "Heel."

Darrell looked up to see the front door open and a short, squat man step out onto the concrete slab. The dog obeyed, first turning its snout from the man to Darrell and Erin, then it relaxed and trotted back to the side of the house.

"Harley won't bother ya now. Ain't too fond of strangers, though," the man said.

Darrell and Erin continued across the lawn with a little more care, eying where they stepped. Piles of dog excrement lay everywhere, some of it fresh, its ripe stink almost overpowering. In the air, he caught the whiff of another acrid odor, thinking first it came from the manure, then he remembered it was the same smell they noticed driving along the fields. The sharp stench of fertilizer. The sights and smells got to him, and he fought back the dry heaves. He felt his condition rising up, threatening to pull him under, and shot a desperate glance at Erin.

She took one step forward, rescuing Darrell, and gave a small wave. "Good afternoon, Mr. Stickley," she said, her voice with strained pleasantry.

Trying to hold it together, Darrell stared ahead and didn't look over at her, but he knew she was smiling. It might be a forced smile, but she was smiling.

She went on, "We're Erin and Darrell Henshaw and—"

"I know who ya are. Mr. Harrington called and told me you was comin'," the guy growled.

The sun had started its descent and hung barely above the roof, and as Darrell and Erin approached, they had to look up and shield their eyes to make out the figure. A stout fireplug of a man, he slouched on the stoop, hands inside deep pockets of ripped blue overalls, the top of his chest bare, bristles of black hairs sticking out. He chewed on the stub of a cigar, which bobbed when he spoke. Because of the bright sun behind him, Darrell had trouble reading his face, but when he did, he caught a stern gaze scrutinizing them.

This wasn't going to be easy. Erin had given him some time to recover, and it had helped. He'd got himself centered again, focusing on why they were here, rather than the horrid surroundings. He decided to switch to another tactic. "Yeah, Mr. Harrington told us you're the man. He said he depends on you to get everything done around here."

The pudgy little man's shoulders came up an inch, his head of dark, disheveled hair turning a little sideways. Stickley said, "He did?"

"That's what he told us. Didn't he, Erin?"

Erin caught on and added, "Said you supervise all

the work around here. Said nothing would get done around this place if it wasn't for you. He said if anyone knows what goes on around here, it was Tom Stickley."

At her flattery, the supervisor relaxed his bare shoulders and allowed the smallest of smiles around the cigar stub, though it never reached his eyes. He stepped down from the stoop and offered his hand to Darrell. At first, Darrell stared at the fleshy hand, stained with God knows what. Then, remembering the two little kids, he extended his own hand and shook, the supervisor's skin like rough sandpaper and his grip like iron. Darrell grimaced inside but was careful not to show it.

Once Stickley let go, he shook his head. "Yeah, well, he told me what you was askin' him, and I don't think I'm goin' to be much help. He said you was askin' 'bout some migrant family. Said you got some kind of pixure."

Erin pulled out the painting, turning so her body blocked the glare of the midday sun. Stickley's one pudgy hand took it from her, and he looked it over, eyebrows scrunched together.

Darrell moved behind the man so his larger shadow fell over the piece. "It's a painting of two kids whose family worked the farm here. A local artist was driving by, saw these kids, and painted this. He painted it with only his hands. No brushes. Something else, isn't it?" Darrell spoke, rambling on so the guy would take his time and look. Not simply dismiss the whole thing.

"Who are these two kids?" Stickley turned and looked straight at Erin.

This was what Darrell was worried about. They didn't have any names. How were they supposed to ask about the kids if they don't even know their names? He started, "Well, we think—"

"Can I see the pixure?" asked a timid female voice from behind them.

Chapter 23

They all look the same

Darrell turned and glanced back to see a tiny woman, not even five feet tall, who had stepped out onto the porch. He hadn't even heard the door open. As skinny as her husband was portly, she looked so thin Darrell could see her ribs through the fabric of an old tee shirt. Stickley shot a withering look at the woman, who shrank back and dropped her gaze to the crack in the concrete slab.

After hesitating as if he was trying to decide, Stickley thrust the painting at her. The small woman took it. Once it was in her hands, she clutched the framed canvas as if it were a valuable heirloom. Her gaze focused on the portrait, and Darrell caught something in her eyes. Recognition? Anxiety? Fear?

"Tom...?" the woman started, the single syllable barely an entreaty.

"Helen, hush!" the man barked and turned back to Darrell. "Name don't matter none. Likely wouldn't mean nothin' to me anyway. These people ain't around long enough for us to learn many names. Ya know, they're not very dependable. Here one year, gone the next. If I only had a dollar, ev'ry time I had to chase down a worker and find he's in the slammer. Or drunk. Or picked up by immigration."

Darrell glanced back at the small woman. "Maybe Helen might have some idea—"

"She don't," Stickley barked, shooting a glare at his wife. "Hell, hard 'nough tellin' the adults apart. Don't have time to pay attention to any damn kids."

Erin asked, "You sure you have no idea. Helen?"

The woman formed a small "o" with her mouth, and Darrell felt certain she was about to say something. Stickley stepped up on the slab and snatched the painting from his wife's hands. The woman cringed.

Staring at Erin, the supervisor said, "Look, we'd like to help ya, miss, but do ya know how many migrants wander through here each year? Hundreds. God, you know them beaners all look alike. I swear they do. Most time, I never give no never mind to their rug rats. Sorry."

Darrell came back around in front of the man. "Is there anything you can tell us? Anyone else who might be able to help?"

Stickley shoved the painting back at Darrell, and without thinking he took it. An electric shock ran up his arm, and he almost threw the painting to Erin, rubbing his exposed skin. The jolt so intense he missed what the small woman was saying.

"—could check with Mrs. Hudson. She might have some idea, but it's a long shot. She's got to deal with thousands."

Even though he'd let go of the painting, the sensation in his arm wouldn't let up. Now the familiar prickle ran along his neck and spread down his back. He sensed they were close to something and surveyed his surroundings. A small metal outbuilding, the white almost orange from the rust, sat at the far end of the dusty yard beyond the gravel circle. A huge tractor with one of those high cabs, the bright green body shining in the sunlight looking like it just rolled off the showroom floor, sat perched in front of the building. Next to the tractor was another long piece of farm equipment, maybe twenty feet across with tines that stretched down into the ground. Beyond that was a long, cylindrical tank with a hose and spout in the middle and an ag corporate logo. Which, he guessed, held the chemical fertilizer. Beyond that stood an even larger metal building.

None of it meant anything to him, but the sensation wouldn't abate. He searched between the buildings and a little farther back saw what looked to be a long pile of dirt about eight feet tall and ten feet wide with the irregular growth of grasses and weeds sprouting out of the brown soil. When his glance returned to Stickley, the man was staring at him.

The supervisor asked, "Ya all right?"

Inwardly Darrell did a shudder but couldn't shake the feeling. He managed, "Yeah. Fine."

Erin rescued him, asking, "Who is Mrs. Hudson?"

The supervisor shot another look at his wife and turned his attention to Erin. "Mrs. Hudson is the public school lady. She tries to get them migrant kids in school. Would ya believe it, a lot of those parents make their kids work, 'stead of goin' to school? Anyway, she knows most of 'em."

Glancing at Darrell out of the corner of her eye, Erin flashed a warm smile at the supervisor. "Thanks, Mr. Stickley. We'll check her out. Where can we find Mrs. Hudson?"

Stickley said, "She travels a lot. Been here

checkin' on kids a bunch a times. But she has an office in Dixon."

"Dixon?" Erin asked.

"Yep. Dixon's the county seat. It's where all those wetbacks go to get them guverment checks. She got an office in the school district building there."

The sensation, the buzzing hadn't gone away, but Darrell dragged his attention to Stickley. "Dixon. Think if we head there now we might catch her?"

The man looked down at his watch, a beat-up Timex sitting alone on a hairy arm. "Doubt it. It'll take ya a while, and by the time you get there, office's probably closed. Ya know, they keep them guverment hours. You need to check back tomorrow." He shook his head. "Still, it's the week after Christmas, don't even know if anybody be in the school office."

Erin gave the short man an even wider smile. "Mr. Stickley, we really appreciate your help. I can see why Mr. Harrington puts such store in you."

The man grinned back in return, showing yellowed teeth around the cigar butt. "Tom. Name's Tom."

Erin said, "Tom, thanks for your time. And you too, Mrs. Stickley."

The thin woman offered a weak smile. "It's Helen."

Erin continued, "Thank you, Helen. If either of you have any other idea on how we might find these two little kids, we'd appreciate hearing it."

Stickley shook his head and said, "Sorry, nope."

In a frail voice, Helen said, "Well, if ya wanted, you might could check at the Settlement."

Tom Stickley whirled on his wife, and she recoiled.

"The settlement?" Erin asked.

Keeping her eyes on her husband's hands, Helen offered, "Yep, that's the housing complex where lotta migrants live. Over in Crooked Creek."

"Thanks. We'll check out there too," Erin said.

Stickley said, "Hey, do either of ya speak Spanish? *Español?*"

Darrell and Erin shook their heads.

He snickered. "Well, if ya head over to Crooked Creek, ya better have somebody who does. Ya know most of them spics never bother to learn our language." He turned back, stepped up on the stoop, and opened the door, all the while muttering. "Yeah, come here and work. Take our paychecks and that guverment money, but can't even learn decent English. Git inside, Helen."

His short bulk disappeared through the opening, the door slam sounding like a gunshot in the warm afternoon air.

Chapter 24

Suffer the little children

After Mr. and Mrs. Stickley disappeared inside the dilapidated house, Darrell and Erin started back across the yard. As they made their way through the yard, Darrell divided his attention between navigating around the disgusting dog poop and rubbing his arm and neck, trying to get the sensation to abate. Erin studied him, concern on her face.

"You look almost white. Is it bad?" He nodded, and she continued, "So there's something here?"

Stopping, Darrell looked at her and then scanned the area. "There's something, but I can't tell what."

"What about Helen Stickley? You get anything from her?"

Darrell shook his head. "I don't think so, but I'm not sure."

Erin glanced at the closed front door. "Don't know. I got the feeling she wanted to tell us something."

Not wanting to attract any more attention, they climbed back into the car. His flesh still stinging, Darrell felt like he should press on, do something. But, after Erin checked the distances and confirmed they wouldn't get to Dixon until close to four thirty, he realized it was a no go. From his years as a teacher and coach, he knew school office hours during break were pretty limited, and no one would likely be there at four thirty on the Monday after Christmas. Disappointed, he turned the key, the engine throttling.

He said, "We could head over to Crooked Creek. We'd have better luck catching the migrant families at home."

Erin shook her head. "If Stickley's right, we need to have somebody with us who can speak Spanish. We'll be outsiders and don't know the language. I doubt anyone would share anything with us."

Seeing no other options, Darrell put the car in gear, and they headed back to Crystal River. He felt like he'd hit another wall. They didn't know much more after another whole day gone. They still didn't even have the kids' names, for God's sake. And the clock was ticking. Some Christmas miracle.

They are vaiting for you. He heard it again.

"At least we have something," Erin insisted. "We have a few more leads. This Mrs. Hudson. Somebody we can talk to."

So Darrell drove as fast as he dared, and he let Erin console him. Or try to. By the time they pulled into the parking lot of Charlie's Fish House back in Crystal River, the sun hung low over Kings Bay. Since they were too late to get any of the seats on the terrace, they settled for an inside table near the rear, where they could at least watch the water ignite with the glow from the setting sun. Inside, they took in the nautical décor, with huge, mounted fish and nets strung along the ceiling, all festooned with twinkle lights.

Common menus were stuck in the condiment display on the table and, his stomach growling, Darrell reached for one. As he pulled one from the stand, he noticed some food stains on it and dropped it. He cringed and glanced at Erin, who got the message and grabbed up the menu scanning the options. His gaze returned to the display, and something else in the arrangement of the tray caught his eye. Square white napkins were stacked on each side of the display with the menus and condiments in the center. He stared for a few seconds and then realized what bothered him. The stacks of the paper napkins were uneven, with the right side holding almost twice as much as the left. Being careful not to touch the remaining smudged plastic cards, he moved napkins from the right to the left, a few at a time. When he put the last one in place, both piles even now, he looked up, satisfied, and noticed the waitress staring at him.

Erin started rattling off their orders, and the server moved her glance and jotted down on her pad. Erin ordered beers and shrimp scampi with jasmine rice. She added a side salad for both and sent the server on her way.

After he left their booth, Erin didn't even mention his behavior. Instead she said, "You catch the attitude we got today? From the owner and the supervisor."

"You mean the 'wetback' and 'beaner' comments from Tom?" Darrell whispered, checking to make sure they weren't overheard. "And I think Sterling would've used a word or two, if Savannah hadn't stopped him. I think for these people that's the norm. Most of the time, the migrants are simply laborers, numbers on a spreadsheet."

"Still, Stickley was so casual about it. Didn't even try to hide it from us. Like that's the way it is, take it or leave it."

"Maybe in their world it is." He shook his head. "I didn't like it any more than you did, but I'm afraid it's pretty standard down here. But that doesn't mean anything. Not about our kids."

"But your arm went crazy at the Stickleys'," Erin said.

"Yeah, but it might've been because I grabbed the picture. Up until then, we'd been careful and made sure only you handled Jared's painting. But I was concentrating on trying to get something from Stickley and completely forgot. When I took the piece from him, I got a major jolt that wouldn't let up."

"So you don't think it had something to do with that place?"

"I don't know. I can't tell. I checked around, but nothing came to me."

Erin looked pensive. "Maybe it's female intuition, but I think Helen Stickley knows more." She stared at Darrell. "Think she might tell us too, if we could get her away from her husband."

Darrell took a pull of the bottle, the beer cold and sharp going down. "You'd think with my past 'experiences' with the ghosts it would get easier, but here we are again. Trying to solve a mystery when we can't even figure out who the victims are."

The waiter returned with their salads, and they stopped talking. They ate then in comfortable silence, enjoying the music, which Darrell noticed was no longer Christmas songs. Instead, the speakers oozed with smooth jazz, though the tunes did little to calm his spirit. He found himself driven to help these kids but realized they'd gotten nowhere. Natalia's words haunted him. *Darrell Henshaw, you must care.* He cared. A lot of good it did. What good was his gift anyway?

He and Erin had plane reservations for Saturday, the first—and real life and work to get back to in Wilshire—which left only four days down here. If they didn't find something by then, he'd be forced to give it up and admit his failure. He needed to face it. They couldn't help kids whose names they didn't even know. Maybe they would learn something tomorrow...with either Mrs. Hudson or at the Settlement, though that was a longshot. He thought over what Stickley had said about the language barrier. He hoped they'd find someone at the Settlement with passable English, at least. He didn't know what other chance they had.

The server returned with their entrée, and he ordered another beer. Erin declined. The second beer felt even better going down, but it didn't wash away his anxiety. Every time he set the bottle down on the glass table, it left a smudged ring of moisture. He couldn't help himself. Each time he felt compelled to use a napkin to wipe up the wet ring, returning the clear glass to its pristine condition. Then, after another draw, he set it down again, and the whole process would start over. Erin eyed him but said nothing.

As they enjoyed the rice and shrimp, he caught her smiling at him between bites. He knew she was trying to cheer him up, to buoy his spirits. But this weight felt so heavy he wasn't sure even she could help him.

When the busser came by to clear the plates on a nearby table, Darrell didn't notice, lost in his own thoughts. The server's quick word to another diner, "*Gracias,*" grabbed his attention, and Darrell's head jerked up.

"Luis?"

The young man stopped collecting the dirty dishes for a second and grinned, beautiful white teeth showing on the almond-colored face. "*Sí*. Mr. and Mrs. Henshaw. Hello." He seemed surprised but pleased to see them.

Erin asked, "You work here? Thought you worked at Crackers?"

Returning to his task at the nearby table, Luis nodded. "*Sí*. Need...*dinero*. Money. Work where I can. Need money to treat Juanita right." He smiled.

Erin's face brightened. "We're glad we got to get to meet her at church on Christmas Eve. She's a beautiful young woman." She looked from Darrell to the busser. "Hey, Luis, you working tomorrow?"

Balancing the final glasses atop the tray he was carrying, he said, "Ms. Bradford not working much. She say no one buying house over holidays."

"We could use your help. Could you work for us? Tomorrow?" she asked.

Luis shrugged. "*Sí*. I guess. What I do?"

Darrell said, "We need somebody to translate. We're going to see some migrant families at Crooked Creek. In Meridian County."

"*Lo conozco*, Crooked Creek. The Settle-ment?"

"Yeah. We've been told they speak very little English." After a bit, Darrell remembered, "And we'll pay you...whatever Bonnie pays you."

"Twenty-five dollar," Luis said proudly.

"Deal," Darrell said, extending his hand.

The server set down the tray and shook. "What time you want me?"

"Let's say..." Darrell glanced at Erin. "Eight

thirty?"

Erin nodded, and Luis followed. "*Sí*, at the Simmons place."

"Good," Darrell said.

The young Hispanic man flashed his wide smile again. "*Gracias*. Tomorrow." He nodded twice and snatched up the dishes. In five seconds, he disappeared with them into the kitchen.

Erin reached her hand across the table. "Maybe he'll be able to help us."

Darrell looked at his wife. "I hope so. Smart thinking, by the way." His gaze moved to the kitchen door. "I think we're going to need the help."

Chapter 25

What mess were they getting into?

Unable to sleep, Darrell was up, pacing the same imaginary line, back and forth, in the large bedroom. Even in the semi-dark, his feet maintained the same precise pattern, each step onto the identical footprints in the soft carpet. His head down, he'd made the nth sweep when Erin stepped into his path, intercepting him and making him stop.

"The weeping portrait wake you again?"

"What?" He looked up and met her gaze in the darkened room. "Oh...no. I simply couldn't sleep. I went on the computer and checked out Sterling Harrington."

"What'd you learn?" Her eyes looked alert, even in the dim light.

"Harrington is one important dude." He shook his head. "I did a search on 'Ask Jeeves' and got all these hits. Rotarian Man of the Year for 1998. President of the Florida Growers Association for the past four years. On the board of some of the really big names in ag, like that fertilizer company we saw. And that was only the first page."

Erin tilted her head slightly to the side, a few long red tresses drooping in front of her eyes. She brushed them aside. "Well, that pretty much fits with the guy we met…and his place."

"Yeah, but I'm not excited about taking on another guy with money. That didn't go so well in Cape May. We need to be really careful which hornet nests we stir up."

Erin took his hand. "Yesterday, we both caught his inuendo about the immigrants, but I really can't see him having much to do with the individual farm workers, much less their kids. I've got to believe he simply pays the bills, like he said, and lets others do any dirty work."

"You're right, but I know the answers about the kids are there. In Meridian County. They have to be. Somebody has to know what happened, if we can find them. And if they'll even talk to us."

"Well, we'll have a better chance with Luis along." She reached for his other hand. "But, hey, it's only a little past six. He isn't going to be here for two more hours."

"I should've made the time earlier. So we could get started. So we'd get there—"

Erin stopped him. "Nonsense. We went over this last night. If we leave here around eight thirty, we should get to the school office a little before ten. You figured we had a good chance to catch Mrs. Hudson, even on reduced hours for the holiday break. That should give us plenty of time to get to the Settlement and back." She wrapped her arms around him. "Now, come back to bed for a while."

Darrell allowed her to lead him back onto the wide, comfortable mattress, and they lay in each other's arms, foreheads touching. For a while, neither spoke, both breathing in sync together. Through the open French doors, the song of the morning's first birds floated into the room along with the chirp of insects. A soft breeze blew the slight freshwater scent from the bay into their space. Darrell could feel his heart rate settle back into normal range.

Without moving, he said, "Have I ever told you how lucky I am to have met you, Mrs. Henshaw?"

He could hear the smile in her words. "Once or twice."

For a long time, they lay there, not sleeping, simply hovering in the comfort of each other's presence, bodies close together in the same space. Instead of feeling cramped with his OCD kicking in, Darrell felt relaxed and secure here next to Erin. And after a few moments, they both fell back asleep, Erin first and he shortly after.

More than an hour later, morning sunlight flooded the room, rousing him. Groggy but less anxious, Darrell awoke and nudged Erin. After showering, dressing, and a little breakfast—both too nervous to eat much—they were standing in the driveway when Luis pulled up in his battered and rusting pickup at eight twenty. And they were out of town heading west a few minutes later.

Out on Novell Bryant Highway, Darrell turned and glanced at their passenger, who'd taken the seat behind Erin. This morning he wore a white tee shirt with a few words in Spanish across the front and a clean but worn pair of jeans. Luis grinned back. The young man reminded Darrell of a few of his favorite students back at Wilshire High. Not the coloring. He'd not had many Latinos in his classes, maybe a few in Michigan. And Luis had a few years on his kids. But the teens he had in mind came to school with bright eyes, open smiles, and willing postures, eager for whatever academic challenge came their way. In his instant appraisal of Luis, Darrell read the same enthusiasm in the young man's features.

He said, "We're glad to have you with us. We're headed to Dixon first this morning. We're hoping to catch a Mrs. Hudson. She works for the school system, and we were told she might be able to help us."

He glanced in the rearview mirror to see Luis wearing a wide smile. "I know Mrs. Hudson. She…good lady. Help kids in school."

Erin turned in her seat. "Luis, did you live in Meridian County? Go to school there?"

"*Sí*." He nodded. "My family…*trabajado en los campos*. Worked the fields. Many years. *Recogimos fruta*…we pick fruit. I move to Crystal River after I graduate."

Erin asked, "Do you remember if your family ever worked for the Harrington Plantation?"

Luis didn't answer at first and then said, "*No*, but I know of Harrington. *Granja grande*…big place, no?"

Erin said, "Yes, really big. Told us they employ hundreds of migrant workers."

"Mrs. Henshaw, can I ask question?" the young man said, and Darrell caught the hesitancy in the words.

Erin said, "Of course, Luis. Just a sec." She held up the printed MapQuest page. "Take I-75 north for a few miles." Then back to Luis. "What would you like to ask?"

"Why you want to talk to Mrs. Hudson? What you want to know?"

That was the killer question. Last night he and Erin had tossed around some ideas and came up with a possible explanation—which didn't include ghosts—though Darrell wasn't sure they'd be able to sell it.

"Take Florida 40 here west," Erin said and launched into the sales pitch. "Well, you know Darrell is into history."

"Ms. Bonnie told me. History teacher, no?"

"Yes, Darrell loves history, especially local history. Well, while we're down here, he thought he'd explore a little local history. Anyway, we bought this painting." She pulled the frame out of the canvas bag and handed it over the seat back.

Luis studied the picture and handed it back. "How you say…cute kids."

As Darrell exited the interstate and turned onto the state highway, he peered into the rearview mirror, checking.

Erin continued, "*Sí*. Yes. Well, to make a long story short, we fell in love with these two kids, and Darrell decided he wanted to find them and learn about their family history. We chased down the local artist, and he told us they were from Meridian County, probably worked for Harrington. Now we're trying to locate them. Maybe learn about them and their family's history. We're even hoping we can give them this painting."

Listening, Darrell was dividing his focus between the highway ahead and the rearview mirror. He turned to catch Luis' expression and saw him nodding.

After a short pause, Luis said, "I think it…nice."

Darrell went back to switching his gaze between the mirror and road. Erin watched him and said, "What? What is it?"

He shook his head. "Nothing. For a while I thought

someone was following us. I saw a car fall in behind us when we exited 75, but I don't see them now. They must've turned off. I'm a little paranoid, I guess."

Erin and Luis both turned in their seats to look out the rear window. As they stared, Darrell checked the rearview one more time. Nothing. He drove on, cautious, paranoid maybe, remembering his favorite line about that. "Just because you're paranoid doesn't mean they're not out to get you." He tried to chuckle, but, shooting another glance at the rearview mirror, couldn't quite pull it off.

Why was he doing this, really? Last night in bed he realized before this week he knew practically nothing about the migrants, the immigrants. Okay, unlike Harrington and Stickley, he knew they did *not* all look alike but not much else. Oh, he remembered reading in one of his college classes about Cesar Chavez and the grape boycott and strike by the farmworkers. About the terrible working conditions. Sometime in the sixties, he thought, thirty years ago, and that was in California. Surely things had improved since then here in Florida.

Like everyone else, he bought the fruits and vegetables grown in Florida and elsewhere in the south and west, glad to be able to get the fresh produce. But before this week, he'd never given much thought to the migrant workers who labored in the fields to harvest the fruits and vegetables. He had no idea what the lives of migrant families were really like.

Thinking about meeting Mrs. Hudson, his teacher instincts kicked in. He considered how hard it would be to try to teach kids who had to change schools every few weeks as their families moved from farm to farm. If he'd had more time, he'd love to chat with Mrs.

Hudson about how she helped these students. About what she did to make sure they weren't forgotten or left behind. Then he realized that might be one way to connect with the woman—if he needed it.

But there wouldn't be much time for any academic discussion. This morning he had other more pressing questions for her. He only hoped she had a few answers.

Chapter 26

Maybe the educator had some answers

Twenty minutes later, they were stopped at a light, facing a sign proclaiming "Dixon, a friendly little Florida town," the whole thing bordered in drooping pine garland. Erin used the MapQuest directions to guide them through the town streets to the Meridian County School Office. There, after they got out and went in through the front door, Darrell employed his facility with educational bureaucracy to negotiate and get them to the office they wanted.

They stood in front of a closed door bearing a large evergreen wreath complete with tiny gold and red glass ornaments nestled in the artificial pine needles. Beside the door was a gold plate with the lettering, "Gloria Hudson, District Liaison for Itinerant Children." Darrell knocked.

A high-pitched voice from inside called, "Com'on in."

He opened the door, allowing Erin and Luis to enter first, and followed, closing it behind them. When they stepped into the office, they found very little room to stand and no place to sit. The office was good sized, but almost every space—floor, chairs, shelves—was filled with boxes and colorful plastic bins of all different shapes and sizes. Most of the boxes contained scores of books, their spines indicating some were in English and others in Spanish. Some tubs contained book bags and jackets. Others had collections of crayons and pencils. His eyes going wide, Darrell's gaze flicked around the untidy room, his claustrophobia closing in on him. He sucked in a deep breath.

Erin must have noted his anxiety because she jumped in. "Good morning, Mrs. Hudson. My name is Erin Henshaw, and this is my husband, Darrell." She turned, and Darrell stepped up next to her, maneuvering around two stuffed boxes. Then she indicated Luis. "And this is Luis Hernandez."

The woman pushed away from her desk, a green metal military standard, its surface covered with a scattering of pencils and pens in apparent disarray. They looked like a tossing of pixie sticks Darrell remembered from when he was a kid. He focused on the mess of writing utensils and fought against the impulse to straighten them, put them in some kind of order. He took another slow breath and turned his attention to Mrs. Hudson.

She was a short, stout woman and wore a wide smile under a wrinkled brow and a head of gray hair, cut tomboy style. She was white, but her skin, like a number of Floridians he'd met, had turned darker from so much time in the sun. Her eyes were some of the deepest blue he'd ever seen, and when she stared at you, the azure eyes held real kindness and understanding. Darrell could easily see how the smile and kind eyes would win over parents and kids and decided she was probably quite good at her job. If she could get a recommendation from the Stickleys...

She rose, and he saw she wore stylish jeans and a

tee with the image of a sun alongside the words "Florida—the Sunshine State." She worked her way around another box on the floor, stepping closer to Luis. With both hands, she gripped his shoulders and gave him an appraising look. "Luis Hernadez, is that really you? You've grown into quite the man."

Looking like a little kid, the young man wore a sheepish grin and startled rattling off words and phrases in rapid-fire Spanish, his hands making quick gestures. Partway through, Gloria Hudson interrupted in a kind voice, "Let's do English, Luis. You need the practice."

"Right, Mrs. Hudson. I living in Crystal River now. I am assistant for real estate person. Today I help Mr. and Mrs. Henshaw." He flashed a proud smile.

"Very good, sir." Mrs. Hudson turned toward Darrell and Erin. "I've known Luis since he was a teen, fifteen, when he first came to this country. Right, Luis?"

"*Sì*," the young man said and quickly added, "Yes."

Mrs. Hudson looked to Darrell and Erin. "It's great to see one of my charges do well, but I suspect you didn't come here to show off a star pupil. You can see I'm right in the middle of my project." She gestured to the mess that surrounded them, then looked up, meeting Darrell's gaze. "Is there something I can do to help you two?"

He answered, "We're looking for a migrant family who worked for the Harringtons last year, and we were told you might be able to help us."

"Why me?" the school liaison asked.

Erin said, "Well, we're really looking for two Hispanic kids, and we were told you know pretty much all the migrant families and their children. We've got a picture of the two we're looking for." She reached into the bag and extracted the painting, passing it over.

Gloria Hudson took it, looking quizzically at the painting of the sailboat.

"Not that one. The other side." Watching her, Erin took and turned the canvas over, showing the kids' portrait. Gloria Hudson looked up with a question in her eyes and Erin added, "It's a long story."

The older woman shrugged and studied the portrait of the two children, holding it in both hands, the deep blue eyes concentrating on the picture. "What an interesting work of art. I don't think I've seen anything like it."

"We found that painting at an art gallery in Crystal River," Erin continued. "We were so taken with the image of the two kids we tracked down the artist. He said he painted it while the kids were playing in a ditch at the Harrington Plantation. We visited with the Harringtons yesterday and when they didn't remember who the kids were, their supervisor suggested we check with you."

The woman's eyebrows went up at his reference to the landowners, and Darrell noticed a certain hardening of the blue eyes. Gloria Hudson said, "Did they now?" She took another close look at the picture. "I don't recognize these two. From this painting, it looks like they might've been too young for school. Some of the migrant families don't put them into school until they are six or sometimes even seven." She shook her head slowly. "And some of the owners force the kids to work. Sometimes, I have to fight to get them into school at all." She glanced up at Erin. "Do you have any names for them?"

Erin shook her head. "We don't have their names yet. We're hoping you might have an idea."

The woman examined the work again, turning it so the light from the one window in the room struck the painted strokes. "If they weren't in school, I might not have met them yet. But they look a little like the Sanchez family. I don't think Enrico and Isabella have any children that young, but these two could be cousins." She turned toward Luis. "Do you remember the Sanchezes? They have three kids. The oldest would be about five years behind you, maybe fifteen?"

Luis closed one eye and tilted his head. "I think so. The oldest. His name Carlos?"

"Yeah, I think that's right." Hudson looked back at Erin and Darrell and pointed to the canvas. "When was this painted?"

Darrell said, "Almost a year ago."

Hudson handed back the painting to Erin. "Okay, why is this so important? Why are you really trying to find these two?" she asked, her tone halfway between curious and suspicious.

After Darrell and Erin exchanged a brief look, he let her take the lead. Erin repeated the story she'd given in the car, but when she finished, Gloria Hudson did not look all that convinced.

Luis said, "I think it very nice they go to all this trouble to find kids." He pointed to the painting. "I glad to help."

"Uh-hum." Gloria Hudson navigated her away through the clutter on the floor back to her chair. She saw Darrell watching her and said, "Sorry about the mess. These are all books and supplies I've collected in our Christmas drive, and after the New Year, I'll be delivering them to kids who need them."

Glancing around the crowded room, Darrell said, "Well, you've certainly put together quite the collection here." Understanding why the disorder was there helped him to dial back his OCD. "Do you know where we might be able to find the Sanchez family? The ones you said might be cousins."

Hudson leaned back in her chair. "Might is the operative word. But if Enrico and Isabella are in town, you might find them at the Settlement. You know where that is?"

Erin piped up, "Crooked Creek. We were heading there next. And we asked Luis to come along to translate."

"I'm sure Luis will be a fine translator. Good luck then." Gloria Hudson shook her head. "I hope you find them. A lot can happen in a year. Especially to these folks."

Chapter 27

No reason for holiday spirit here

After they thanked Gloria Hudson for her help, they worked their way back through the maze of office corridors and out to the car. Sitting in the front seat, Erin checked the second page of directions they'd run off, from Dixon to Crooked Creek.

"According to these"—she held up the paper—"it's going to take an hour to drive to the Settlement." She turned. "Luis, any place to eat between here and there?"

"No. No restaurant from here to Crooked Creek."

"Well, I guess we're eating here," Darrell said. "An army travels on its stomach."

"Army?" Luis asked.

"It's a saying from history—they think from Napoleon Bonaparte. It means you function better when you're not hungry."

"*Quien*...who *es* Napoleon?" Luis asked.

"A famous French general." Darrell chuckled. "Never mind for now. Since you're our assistant today, you choose where to eat."

Luis selected a taco place he knew, and they all enjoyed the authentic Mexican fare. When they were full, they climbed into the rental and headed back onto the highway. The route took them east on FL 40 and then south on a series of back country roads. As they neared their destination, the roads got worse, going from paved surfaces to potholed, ancient asphalt badly in need of repair to gravel roads. Several times Darrell had to slow the rental down to a crawl to prevent them from being tossed around like ragdolls inside the car. Crooked Creek turned out to be little more than a fork in the road, and they needed Luis' help to even find the pitted driveway that led to the Settlement. There was no sign or marker for the "complex," if it could be called that. When they pulled up, they all got out, and Darrell stared at the Settlement.

He hadn't expected much but was appalled by what he saw. The Settlement was little more than a series of small barracks, badly maintained with a broken-down fence running around what might have served as a yard. Some buildings had weathered wood siding, long since turned gray, and other shacks were covered with mere tarpaper. On the front of each dwelling, clothes hung on hooks attached to the boards, stained shirts and jeans drooping in the slight breeze. At the end of the first set of barracks, a clothesline was strung across the space, yellowed underwear and socks dangling over the muddy earth. Each dwelling had one door and a small window, the whole place no larger than five hundred square feet. Darrell tried to imagine a family of four or five living in one and shook his head.

He caught a small splash of color in the drab gray and brown scene, the window of the second apartment. Dark green with a little red. Studying it, he could barely make out a hand drawn and colored Christmas tree. His gaze went up the row of shacks and realized it was the only Christmas decoration, the only evidence of the holiday.

Little *Feliz Navidad* here.

The wind shifted and blew past them the acrid odor of rotting garbage from somewhere on the other side of the Settlement. Darrell used his arm to cover his nose and then, afraid of offending, he brought it back down. If these people had to deal with that smell all the time, he'd have to tough it out.

Behind the buildings, a group of three kids kicked a soccer ball in and out of the rut that ran along the row of structures. In front of the first shack, an older Hispanic woman sat in a broken-down, upholstered living room chair, one that looked like it had been rescued from a dump.

Darrell had trouble taking in what he saw, and his eyes searched Erin's. She shook her head slightly and frowned. Both looked to Luis, who shrugged and let out a long breath.

Darrell stepped up to the older woman and said, "We're looking for the Sanchezes. Enrico and Isabella. Do you know if they're here?"

The woman shook her head. "*No Inglés.*"

Darrell turned back to Luis and raised his eyebrows. The young man hesitated at first and then stepped up next to Darrell. Luis went through a quick expression or two in quiet Spanish, his hands punctuating the words and a reserved smile on his face.

The woman never moved from the ancient chair, but hollered, "José!"

One of the kids stopped kicking and ran over to her. The woman had a quick exchange in Spanish with the boy, who took off running.

Luis explained, "This is Mrs. Corzo. She asked José to get someone who may know something."

"Thanks, Luis," Darrell said quietly. The young man nodded twice.

When the messenger boy emerged from a house near the end, he was followed by a group of five little children, Darrell would've guessed ages three to six. As he studied the little ones, trying to see if any looked like "his kids," he noticed they all wore few clothes, and those they had on were tattered and ripped. Behind the group of kids strode a middle-aged man with strong shoulders and a full head of black hair, hobbling one foot after the other. As he came closer, Darrell noticed the man had a scar down the side of his face and a badly broken nose over a large moustache. Like Luis, he wore a white tee shirt—no saying though—and a worn pair of jeans. Darrell pondered if this was the person in charge.

"Hello, I'm Miguel Romero. I help you?" the man said.

"Do you speak English?" Darrell asked, anxious.

"Yes, some," Romero said.

"We're looking for two kids who would be six or seven. Their family worked the Harrington Plantation last year." The man looked confused, and he turned to Luis. "Maybe you could try to explain in Spanish."

Luis jumped in, less hesitant now, talking half in Spanish and half in broken English. When he finished, the man looked less confused but still suspicious.

Romero asked, "Which kids? Names?"

Erin stepped up and handed him the painting. "We have a picture of them, and we think their names might be Sanchez, but we're not sure."

Romero took the painting and examined it, shaking his head. "Sanchez not here. Enrico take family to see *abuela.*" He looked from the visitors to the painting. "Why you ask about kids?"

Darrell and Erin exchanged glances, and she got the silent message. Stepping up alongside of Luis, she placed a hand on his arm and nodded. Together, they told the story, tag teaming between English and Spanish when necessary. As they spoke, Darrell watched the man's face and didn't think Romero was buying the pitch. If anything, his features seem to cloud over.

Darrell slid his gaze around the barren surroundings, trying to decide what to do. Several other adults, mostly older, bent individuals, had come out of the shacks, now standing on their stoops, observing the exchange. Each adult face, male and female, bore expressions of concern and suspicion, inching Darrell's anxiety up a notch. He tried to smile and nod, hoping to convey, without the language, some semblance of friendliness. He couldn't detect if his response had any impact, and he took a step closer to Erin.

As Erin, Luis, and Romero talked, Darrell kept focused on the group of people gathered around, scanning each individual face, and realized how different they looked. Different from him, yes, but also different from each other. They all looked like they came from Central America—Mexico and other countries—but that was where the similarities stopped. As he examined one face after another, he noticed their skin tones covered quite a range, from a deep brown like Luis to a light sienna to an almost beige. Most of their hair that wasn't gray was dark, variations of brown and black, but their eyes ran the gamut from green to gray to blue. Stickley's comment, "They all look the same to me," came back to him, and Darrell laughed to himself at how ludicrous it sounded.

Studying the children huddled around, who had as much variety in appearance as the adults, he wondered how were they going to find out what happened to the two kids?

By the time Erin and Luis finished their fractured tale, Romero was shaking his head, scowling. He thrust the painting back. "Can't help you. Don't know them."

Darrell couldn't tell from his tone if Romero really didn't know anything or if he simply didn't trust them enough to tell them anything. Darrell's eyes searched out the rest of the adults, looking for an ally. He said, "Is there anyone else here we could ask? Someone who may know something? It's important."

"No." Romero shook his head again, definite.

Studying the stern features of the older Latino man, Darrell pondered another question. Was Romero simply suspicious of the gringos, or was there something else? Did he know something about the two missing kids or maybe…he was involved somehow? Perhaps what he read on the man's face wasn't suspicion but guilt.

Before he had time to weigh any possibility, another older woman, one of those who had come out to watch, stepped carefully off her stoop and hobbled over to Darrell and Erin. As she crossed the fifty feet, she used a knobby stick as a cane, her movements slow, stiff, and awkward. She looked to be quite old, with a face of tanned, mottled skin, hair a snow white. She wore an old house dress, its floral pattern long since faded, which swished around her stick legs as she stumbled slightly across the uneven ground toward them. Once in front of the visitors, she seemed to straighten her posture and stared at Darrell. One hand balancing the makeshift cane, she thrust out a second wrinkled hand with crooked, arthritic fingers. "See painting?" Up close, Darrell noticed her eyes were a soft blue.

Erin handled her the framed canvas, and the old woman's gaze focused on the faces of the two kids.

Erin asked, "Do you know them?" When the woman didn't answer, Erin blurted out, "We think something maybe happened to them."

At Erin's last words, the old woman's face jerked up, her eyes becoming hard like blue ice, and then she returned her attention to the portrait. Romero stepped in and hunched next to the old woman. He exchanged a few quiet words in Spanish with her, and she barked back two syllables. Darrell didn't understand the words, but he knew she told him to back off. Romero looked indignant at first, then he shook his head and eased his shoulders back.

The woman looked from the picture to Luis and began an explanation in Spanish. All Darrell could catch was two names, Daniel and Mia, and later two other names, which she said so quickly he didn't understand. When she finished, Darrell turned to Luis.

Luis took a breath. "This is Mrs. Morales. She think these two"—he pointed to the painting—"might be Sanchez kids. Daniel and Mia. Not Enrico's kids. His brother's, Juan's kids." He looked from Mrs. Morales to Darrell. "She ask how you know something happened to them?"

Darrell knew he couldn't go there and wished Erin hadn't blurted that out, but he was stuck with it. He certainly couldn't tell them he'd seen their ghosts. He fumbled for some explanation and managed, "That's complicated. Uh…tell her we don't know. We're not sure."

At first, Luis' features clouded, and he scrunched his eyebrows together. He met Darrell's gaze, then turned slowly and gave the translation, pointing back once. Darrell watched, holding his breath. At the end, the old woman's bony shoulders shook, and she started to speak, but before she got a few syllables out, Romero edged forward again and barked a few words, pointing angrily at Darrell. Undeterred, Mrs. Morales gave a curt, almost unintelligible reply. Romero huffed and stomped away, his gimpy leg hobbling, all the while muttering under his breath. After he took a few steps away, the older woman turned back to Luis and uttered a few more sentences in Spanish, more subdued this time.

Luis bowed his head and nodded solemnly. He turned back to Darrell. "Mrs. Morales say last year the kids' parents came into camp, screaming something about 'accident and hurt my babies.' The father, Juan Sanchez, got into fight."

"What fight? And with whom?" Darrell asked. Then, before Luis had time to translate, Darrell pushed. "Wait. Ask her if she remembers when this happened?"

Luis translated, and they watched as the old woman's gray eyebrows scrunched together. For a while, she was silent and then her face came up and she spoke in rapid-fire Spanish, one gnarled hand gesturing in the air. When she finished, Luis said, "Mrs. Morales say it right after holiday last February. She say she remember 'cause they never get off, but news talk about it."

"Presidents' Day?" Darrell asked.

"*Sí*, right after Presidents' Day last year."

"Ask her where the parents are. If we can talk to them." Before Darrell finished his thought, Luis began translating. When he stopped, the woman shook her head once, the white curls making a quick flip, and said something more in Spanish and spit on the ground, her blue eyes hard.

"She say they not here. Juan got arrested for fighting, and he and wife Lucia deported." Luis wore a grim expression.

Erin asked quietly, "What about the kids? What happened to the kids? Were they deported too?"

Luis translated the questions, and again the old woman shook her head, the azure eyes turning soft again. She mumbled a few words in Spanish and closed her eyes. A silence hung in the air and, impatient, Darrell asked, "What'd she say?"

Luis took a deep breath. "She say she no know. She never saw children again."

Chapter 28

It came out of nowhere

Darrell felt like he'd been punched in the gut.

After thanking everyone and shaking hands, he nodded at the adults and grinned to the children, fighting to hide his disappointment. When the three of them climbed back into the car, he started down the rutted gravel path. He couldn't hold it in any longer. He slammed his fist on the steering wheel three times, making the car shimmy a little.

"I was so sure we'd get some answers there." He nodded his head back toward the Settlement as they turned onto Crooked Creek. "I thought everything led to there."

The warm afternoon had heated up the inside of the car, even with the windows cracked. Darrell glanced over at Erin and saw outside her window the huge dust cloud their car was raising in the filthy gravel. Great. All he needed was to have the car filled with sand and grime. He buzzed the windows all the way up, flipped on the AC, and set it to max.

"Mr. Henshaw, you not happy with what I learn for you?" Luis asked, his voice seeking confirmation, just like Thad in third period American history did. Darrell was frustrated but didn't want to take it out on Luis.

Before he had a chance to say anything, Erin

turned and looked back, twisting the seatbelt. "No, it's not you. *You* did a great job. I don't know what we would've done if we hadn't had your help."

Darrell added, "You did great. It's not you. I was simply hoping to learn more."

Erin said, "Well, we know more than when we came here. We have names to go with...with, uh, the kids in the painting." She cut a quick glance to the back seat.

Darrell said, "Yeah, but we still don't know what happened to them."

Erin countered, "Mrs. Morales said something about an accident. Maybe they were, um, hurt in some accident?"

Darrell shook his head. "I don't know. An accident doesn't make much sense." He shot a look at Erin to convey the rest, about the ghosts' request.

Erin paused and then raised her voice, as if she just thought of something. "Do you think Steph could've hit the kids...with the way she drives that Boxster?"

"Maybe...who knows?" Darrell said.

"Who Steph? What boxer?" Luis asked from the back seat, and both Darrell and Erin turned to look back.

She answered, "Steph is the daughter of the plantation owner." She shook her head and went on, "Yesterday, when we were on our way over here to ask about the kids, she almost sideswiped us at a stop sign. With her car. It's a fancy sports car called a Boxster." When Luis nodded, she turned back to Darrell. "Maybe we could check with body shops, you know, like we did in Cape May."

Darrell shook his head again. "Maybe later. What

I'd like to know is who Juan, the kids' dad, got into a fight with, but I've no idea who else can we even ask? It'll be damn near impossible to talk with parents who've been deported."

He shot a brief glance into the back seat. "Luis, when I watched that guy, Romero, I had the feeling he knew more than he told us. I got a bad vibe from him. Did you pick up anything?"

"I no think so." Luis leaned forward, his head over the top of the front seatback. "Mr. Romero and others not know you. Know you are good people." His gaze went from Darrell to Erin. "That is hard life. Taught them not to trust gringos. Most gringos they know only…how you say, take…?"

Erin offered, "Take advantage?"

"*Sí.* Yes. Take advantage of them."

Erin nodded. "I get it. If we lived that life, we'd probably not trust many people, especially outsiders."

Keeping his eyes on the road, Darrell pressed, "Luis, do you think there is any chance Romero could've been involved, uh, somehow with whatever happened to the kids? He was definitely holding back. Did you pick up anything from his Spanish?"

Luis paused this time before answering then shook his head. "It's possible, but I no think so. Mr. Romero hurt in the field. He no walk right. That's why he not working the fields today. I see many like him. Angry at world and at gringos. He might know more than he say, but I no know about him and these kids."

Erin added, "I think I understand." She turned toward Darrell. "You know, looking at those kids, those families, I felt so bad for them. I saw those children and wished we brought some candy or something. Makes you think about all we have." She shook her head. "The one little kid, the one with the reddish gold hair, did you see him?"

"Yeah, I think. Maybe, three years old?" Darrell said.

Erin nodded. "Notice his nose and mouth? I couldn't be sure, but I think he has impetigo. Easy to treat with antibiotics, which I'd guess they have little access to."

Luis said, "Mother no afford doctor."

"Which way here?" Darrell asked, stopped at an intersection, head swiveling both ways. "Can you check the directions for the route back to Crystal River?"

Erin shuffled through the papers and came to the one she wanted. "We go back the way we came. Turn right here and take it back to Florida 404."

Turning the rental onto the street, Darrell focused his attention on navigating the country road. A long ribbon of asphalt snaked ahead of him, two black lanes curling through bends and twists bordered on both sides with groups of dense woods. As he drove, he alternated his gaze between the road ahead and the rearview mirror.

Erin asked, "See something?"

"Not sure," Darrell said. "When we turned onto this road, a gray pickup pulled onto the road a little ways behind us." He glanced at the mirror again. "It's still there."

Erin twisted in her seat again so she could see out the back window.

Darrell said, "Wait till we come out of this bend. Now, watch. See, there he is."

Erin kept her eyes focused out the rear window.

"Yeah, well, it's not like there are lots of places to turn off."

"Mr. Henshaw, Mrs. Henshaw, can I ask something?"

Erin leaned into the middle of the seat. "Sure. What would you like to know?"

"My English is not that good yet. I work on it, but English difficult."

"You're doing fine," Erin said, a smile in her voice.

Luis shook his head. "Thank you, but not my question. Because my problems with English, some people think I stupid."

"We don't think that, Luis. Do we, Darrell?"

Darrell took his gaze from the road and mirror for a second. "Definitely not." His eyes flicked back to the road.

"I not know how to say this." Luis lowered his gaze and gave a slight shake of his head. "I think…think you know something about these kids. More than what you say."

Still hovering in the middle of the seat, Erin glanced over at Darrell.

Darrell caught the look on her face and started, "Like I said back there, it's complicated. We—"

Erin's side window exploded. The fractured glass shot slivers across the front seat. The sound of an explosion followed a beat behind. Erin screamed. Something stung Darrell's right arm. He reached to grab it. He saw a cut open on his skin and then looked across the seat. Damn. Erin's arm was bleeding, bad.

He couldn't breathe. "Erin?" he got out. He stared at her for a second and then jerked his gaze back to the road and straightened the car.

Something hit the rear window. Luis yelped. The glass shattered, and a second later, another crack followed. Luis fell forward. Was he hit? Darrell's gaze jumped from the road to Erin to the back seat. Luis had fallen to the floor. Darrell couldn't see him.

"Luis?" Erin called.

No answer.

Dragging his eyes from the road, Darrell shot another glance at Erin. Her entire arm was now turning red, the edge of her short sleeve wicking up the scarlet. The fingers of her left hand gripped tightly around her right arm, the knuckles turning white. The blood still seeped through.

Shit. "Erin, are you—" he cried.

"I'll be all right, I think," she managed between gritted teeth. "What about Luis?"

Dragging his eyes from Erin for a second, he turned in his seat to try to look into the back. He screamed, "Luis!"

Darrell wrenched farther around to look, and his leg bumped the steering wheel. He heard an ugly thump. Too late, he jerked back around to see the car careen over the berm. In three seconds, it slammed into a tree. He heard another explosion and was slammed back against the seat.

Everything went dark.

Chapter 29

Just because you're paranoid—

When Darrell dragged his eyes open, all he could see was a fuzzy whiteness. Where was he? He blinked, forcing his gaze to focus. And his chest hurt. He shook his head, trying to clear it and stared again. The airbag.

Erin! Frantic, he shoved the canvas away and looked to his right. "Erin?" he screamed. No response.

In a flash, the memories exploded in his head. The side window shattering. The glass shards raining down on Erin. Her bleeding!

"Erin!" he tried again, his voice hoarse now.

Beside him, he heard movement and a groan. Erin. He shoved the stiff material back toward the steering column, sending a wave of white dust floating in the air. He'd read the powder had something to do with airbags going off, but right now he didn't care. He caught a whiff of some foul smell. Fighting to unleash his tangled seatbelt, he slid over to get to her.

"Erin? Erin, can you hear me?"

He watched her turn her face toward him in slow motion like the action hurt and saw her cheek was covered with blood. *Oh, God, no.* He bashed in her partially deflated airbag toward the dash to make a little room. Darrell cradled her face in his hands, and one hand came away wet and red.

"Are you…is your face…?" he choked out.

She shook her head slowly. "Just my arm." She raised her right arm, and he could see the long cut right beneath her shoulder, still gushing blood. Her voice grew weaker. "Losing too much, I think. Need to stop the bleeding." She adjusted her left hand on the wound and clamped down hard, her knuckles white again even as her fingers were stained with scarlet.

His first aid kit, Darrell thought, and leaned over the seat to retrieve it. As soon as he turned, he remembered this was not his car. It was a damn rental. His movement had him peer over the seat back onto the floor. Oh, Jesus, Luis. He had another flash of a memory, the rear window exploding and Luis crying out. He had fallen into the footwell, turned so Darrell couldn't see his face, only his shoulder. And it was bleeding. Badly.

Erin managed, her voice getting weaker, "Is Luis all right?"

Feeling a humid breeze on his face, Darrell looked up and saw the shattered back window. His gaze jerked from Erin to Luis, both bleeding.

Erin said, barely a whisper, "Go see about Luis. I'll be okay. I'll…"

Darrell could see her fading. Probably shock from loss of blood. It wasn't squirting, so it didn't look like any of the shards had cut an artery, but what did he know? God, how he wished he had paid more attention at those mandatory first aid trainings the nurse gave at school. He remembered some things.

He pushed against his car door and, yes! it opened. It must not have warped in the collision. He ran around to Erin's door, yanking off his shirt. Ripping it into pieces, he made several large strips. Holding the cloths in one hand, he yanked on the door with the other. It fell open. Balancing himself in the ditch, he gently eased Erin's body around, placing her back against the seat. The fingers of her left hand still wrapped around the long gash. Blood was seeping between her fingers. Darrell noticed her grip was no longer tight—no white knuckles.

"Okay, you can let go," he said. "I'm going to wrap this around it to stop the bleeding."

She released her grip, and the scarlet flow immediately quickened. Darrell wrapped the cloth around the upper arm once, twice, and even a third time, and then pulled it tight, gently tying the two ends.

"Ow-w," Erin got out.

"I know, but it's got to be tight to stop the blood."

She nodded feebly.

In several seconds, the wound went from a flow to a trickle and then stopped. Darrell saw another gash closer to her wrist, not as bad, but still bleeding. He repeated the same process with the second cut, and after a few seconds had stopped that flow as well. His hands now slick with blood, he wiped them on his pants, leaving scarlet handprints. He examined the rest of her arm and shoulder.

"Are there any more cuts?"

Erin whispered, "No...don't think so." She leaned forward like she was nodding off. She got out, "Luis?"

Darrell eased her back against the beige material of the seat, which was now stained with streaks of red. He struggled up the slight incline and pulled on the rear door. He had to tug a few times before it gave way, and when it did, he fell backward and lost his footing, ending on his butt. He scrambled to stand, looked in, and saw Luis huddled on the floor.

"Luis? Luis, are you all right?"

What a stupid question. Darrell stared at the guy's right shoulder, the red spreading down the fabric of the tee shirt. It didn't look like it was bleeding as much as Erin's had, but he couldn't see much of the man's body down in the footwell. Placing both hands under Luis' armpits, he tried to pull him out of the well and onto the seat so he could take a better look. See if there was anything else. Luis' body was so limp, Darrell struggled to get him up, like pulling a life-sized rag doll. Halfway to the seat, Luis uttered a sharp cry, and Darrell slowed. As easily as he could, he lowered Luis back against the seat like he'd done with Erin

Darrell needed to get Luis' shirt off so he could take a look at the wound—and make sure there wasn't more damage—but he knew it would hurt like hell. Darrell wished he had scissors to cut the cloth. It'd be a whole lot less painful. He made a mental note to add a pair of scissors to his first aid kit when he got home.

"I've got to get this shirt off you," Darrell said to the slumping figure. "It's going to hurt like a bitch, but I need to see how bad you're hurt."

As gently as he could, he pulled the shirt over Luis' head, the young man grimacing the whole time. The effort and anguish paid off. Studying the thin torso, Darrell noted the only injury he could see was the shoulder wound about an inch from his neck. It was bleeding, the red flowing down his bare front now. It didn't look like a cut, like Erin's. It looked like some kind of gash.

Since there was little left of his own shirt, Darrell

tore Luis' shirt into strips. He used one dry strip to try to clean the cut as well as he could and threw the crimson-soaked rag behind him to the ground. Layering two strips of cloth across the wound, he pressed down. He said, "The way this thing is, I can't tie it off. You need to press down hard to stop the bleeding."

When Luis didn't immediately respond, Darrell called a little louder, "Luis, can you hear me?" He watched as the young man's dark face came up and something seemed to register. He took Luis' left hand and held it atop the wound. "Now press down and hold it. I need to get us some help."

Darrell backed out of the car. He reached into his pants pocket and pulled out his cellphone. He flipped it open and stared at the small screen. "Come on!" he urged as he watched the cell go through its cycle. "I hope they have 911 down here. Come on, come on," he repeated, his voice rising with impatience. "Of course, no service. Damn."

He slammed the phone closed and stuffed it back into his pants pocket. He looked at Luis and Erin, both now slumped against the seatbacks. He'd have to do this himself.

He backed away and closed the rear door, then did the same for Erin's door. He struggled down the incline and examined the tree he'd struck. When they hit, he hadn't noticed any steam escaping from the radiator, so he hoped the car wasn't crippled. The front fender was bashed in pretty badly, the grill broken in half. The engine was still running at least. The bushes and brambles around the tree were so thick he couldn't get through them. So, holding onto the body of the car, he dragged himself up the hill and around the back of the car.

They'd been shot at?

As he made his way to his front door, he kept his head on a swivel, checking again for something, anything. There were copses of trees and bushes lining the rural road on both sides, plenty of places to hide. A primitive part of his brain told him his precautions were futile. If someone crouching in one of these thickets had a rifle and was a decent shot, he'd have no trouble hitting Darrell. He tried hard not to think about that. Still, he jumped through the opening and yanked the door shut.

He released a huge exhale. He punched the deflated airbag most of the way back into the center of the steering wheel. At least he could get his arms around the steering wheel and turn. It would have to do. The keys? Where'd he leave the keys? Automatically, Darrell patted his pants pockets and then glanced at the ignition. The keys were still there, the spare dangling from where his leg brushed it. He reached to turn on the ignition and realized again the car was still running. He put the car in reverse and gave it a little gas. The wheels spun, the car rocked once and stopped. Darrell let off the gas.

He shot a glance over at Erin, who had managed to sit up, her back against the seat, her color going paler. Darrell turned and looked at Luis. He lay against the back seat now, eyes closed, but left hand on the strips, which were now turning red. Darrell couldn't be sure how bad either of them was. He needed to get them to a hospital. Now.

He turned his attention back to the rental. He'd have to rock it to get it off the berm and onto the asphalt. Applying slight pressure on the accelerator, he eased the car backward a few inches at a time, his other foot on the brake to keep them from rolling farther into the ditch. It seemed to take a maddeningly long time, but after several tries, he got the car back onto the road, the front tires spinning as they slipped out of the berm, gravel, sand, and soil flying out in front of the car. He straightened the rental back into the west lane and, from the bounce of the chassis, he could tell the suspension was messed up. He prayed the car would still get them to Dixon, or at least to some help.

As he put the gear into drive, the yelp of a siren behind him made him jerk. A cop? He can help. In the rearview mirror, he saw a cruiser pull up behind him, siren wailing. The flashing strobe whipped through the broken rear window a second later. Darrell shoved the car in park, opened the door, and jumped out.

Chapter 30

Time is blood

Darrell didn't have time for this. He tried to muster up the energy to run, but all he could manage was to trot toward the cop car, his feet making heavy thumps beneath the *ee-ow* whine of the cruiser. When he'd covered half the distance, an officer threw open his door and jumped out with gun raised.

"Halt!" the cop commanded.

Darrell stopped in his tracks. "You don't understand," Darrell blurted out, pointing back toward his car.

"Don't. Move," the cop yelled, and Darrell could see the barrel of the handgun quiver. "Raise your hands. Over your head. Now." The arm with the gun stretched out straighter.

Darrell did as he was told, lifting both hands slowly over his head, blinking in the sun. As he lowered his gaze to escape the glare, he glanced down and saw the blood splattered across his chest. It blotched both hands and streaked scarlet down his arms. He felt sweat running from his underarms. At least, he hoped it was sweat.

He tried again. "Please, you don't understand." Keeping both hands up, he turned his head back toward the rental idling on the asphalt, exhaust floating from

208

the tailpipe. "Two people are hurt, bleeding."

The officer didn't move, though the gun wavered a bit. He nodded toward the car. "You've been in an accident. That how they got hurt?"

Darrell shook his head. "Yeah...no...yeah, I hit a tree...but that was after. Erin and Luis, they're both bleeding. I'm not sure how bad, but I need to get them to the hospital."

The officer—Darrell could see now he was young, several years younger than himself—chinned toward the idling car. "They get hurt in the accident?"

"No, that was after." Darrell heard the desperation in his own voice. Couldn't the officer hear it? He lowered one hand and pointed back at the shattered rear window. "Look, we're wasting time. I think they were cut from the flying glass when the windows exploded."

The cop looked confused. "Not in the accident? How did the windows explode?"

Darrell used the one hand to point to the trees lining the road. "When someone shot at us! Look, I'll answer all the questions after. I need to get them taken care of."

The cop looked from Darrell to the car. He said, "Let me see your license."

Reaching a bloodstained hand into his back pocket, Darrell eased out his wallet. He noticed the gun's aim never left his center mass. He pulled out the plastic card and saw the red smudges left by his fingerprints. Without moving, he offered the card.

The cop sidled over and, using his free hand, snatched the license. Darrell watched as the cop's green eyes went down, scanned the license, and shot back up at him. The pistol stayed aimed at his chest. Darrell didn't move.

"Darrell Henshaw. You're from Maryland," the officer said in a flat tone. "What are you doing in Meridian County?"

"We're on our honeymoon. That's my wife in the front seat. She's hurt. Please. We need to get her to the hospital. And Luis too."

The cop slipped the license into a shirt pocket and barked, "Stay right there. I'm going to check myself."

He edged around Darrell, keeping his distance, and approached the running car. Gun still drawn, he walked first to the driver's side, opened the door, reached in with his other hand, and turned the key. The rental gave up one chug and quit. As Darrell watched, the young cop stood there and stared inside, looking across at Erin and into the back at Luis. He moved around the other side, opened each door, and used his free hand to check first Luis and then Erin.

Holding his breath, Darrell peered as the figure in the sand-colored uniform stretched inside the back seat and then the front. Thirty feet away, Darrell stared and prayed. When neither head moved at the cop's inspection, Darrell felt the pit in his stomach harden. Oh, God.

The officer holstered his weapon and ran to where Darrell stood. He practically threw Darrell's license back at him. Darrell caught it and stuffed it back in his wallet.

"Follow me," the cop hollered as he passed, and Darrell hustled right behind him. The officer stopped at the driver's door of the cruiser. He slid into the seat and took the radio mic off its stand. He talked, but Darrell couldn't hear what he said. Desperate, Darrell only wanted to get going, to get Erin and Luis to the hospital.

When he came out, the cop was shaking his head. "I just checked with dispatch. We're too far out. It'll take the ambulance at least twenty-five minutes to get out here and then another twenty to get them to Dixon Memorial. If we hustle with this, we can have them to the hospital before the ambulance can get here."

The cop hurried to the rear of the cruiser and popped the trunk. He grabbed a first aid kit and handed it to Darrell. He turned and sprinted back to the rental, Darrell on his heels.

As they ran, the officer said, "You did a decent job with both of them, but before we move them, I want to get a proper compression dressing and some antibiotic on those wounds. Then I'll give you an escort all the way to the hospital."

They arrived at the rear passenger door, and the cop yanked it open. "I think this guy...what's his name?"

"Luis," Darrell supplied.

"Yeah, well it looks like Luis needs the most help, so I'll take him. Give me that." Darrell passed the kit to him.

The cop's small hands rifled through the contents of the kit, pushing items to the side. While he worked, Darrell read the nameplate above the badge on the tan uniform. "Atwater." Darrell studied the kid's face. That's the thought which jumped into his head—a kid. The deputy didn't look any older than twenty, his young face with a few pimples still to prove it.

A few seconds later, the cop came out with several bandages and two small tubes. He thrust two bandages and a tube into Darrell's hands and kept the same for himself.

He nodded toward the front seat. "Looks like you did pretty good for the woman, so you take care of her. I'll take care of Luis here."

For a while both men worked in silence. Darrell tried to be gentle so as not to hurt Erin any more than necessary. In the middle of his efforts, she turned her head toward him, opened her eyes, and gave him a weak smile. He smiled back, though he felt his stomach clench. Head close to Erin, he caught the sickening sweet odor of blood, the stench almost overpowering, and wondered how he hadn't noticed it before.

He inspected his earlier work and was relieved to see little blood seeping through the torn pieces of cloth. Not wanting to disturb the strips already in place, he covered each cut with one of the sterile gauze bandages Atwater handed him.

Atwater finished first and said, "That should hold them till we get to the hospital." He looked over the seat as Darrell was applying the second dressing. "Tell me again how this happened." He nodded toward what was left of the rear window and picked up a large sliver of glass. He held it in his hand and turned it, examining it.

Darrell didn't answer until he'd finished attending to Erin. When he did, he straightened up and stood next to the still open door, one hand clutching the scarlet-soaked strips of cloth. He balled them up in his hand. The cop matched his posture next to the open rear door, still holding the sliver of glass.

Darrell pointed to the glass shard and said in a low voice, "I think someone in your fine county just tried to kill us."

Chapter 31

No place for the holidays

Siren wailing, Atwater swung the cruiser around the rental and sped down Mineola Road so fast, Darrell barely had time to turn over the ignition and hit the gas. Since the cop knew the roads, he was able to hit the bends fast, and Darrell had all he could handle to keep up. Of course, Darrell kept glancing over to check on Erin, fighting his rising panic. Not to mention young Luis. Even with the wind whipping in from the shattered windows, the odor of spilled blood still hung in the air, its smell reminding him of Erin fading. Of what he got them into.

He shot another look at his wife, whose head lolled lazily. Was her color paler? He didn't think so, but he couldn't be sure. And because he was driving so fast, he couldn't even chance turning in his seat to look at Luis. Twice, as they approached four-way stops, the cop would slow, checking both ways, then speed through the intersection without stopping, siren yelping. Darrell did all he could to match Atwater's movements so as not to lose the cop car.

The siren and strobe worked. They made it back to Dixon in twenty-one minutes, a little more than half the time it took Darrell to make the reverse trip earlier. As they pulled up to the ER entrance, damaged rental immediately behind the cruiser, two sets of medical workers ran out the doors, pushing gurneys toward his car. Atwater must have radioed ahead. Darrell jumped out of the driver's seat. He ran around the car as the first pair was lifting Erin onto a gurney. Her eyes were closed.

"It looks like she's lost a lot of blood," the first medic said. "What's her blood type?"

Darrell stammered, "Uh...um...yeah." He tried desperately to think. Oh, God. Right, they had joked about it when they got tested for the marriage license. She was the same type as he. "Yeah, she's type O positive," he blurted out. Then he added, "Oh, and she's a nurse."

The EMT said, "Okay, good to know. One of ours." Then to his partner, "Get two pints of O positive ready soon as we roll her in." He made a quick turn back to Darrell. "Thanks. We'll take care of her. You do what you have to do." The two men ran through the sliding doors, propelling the gurney with Erin. His new wife. Oh, God.

He turned to check on Luis, but he was gone. Darrell looked toward the hospital again. He saw the other pair of medics with another gurney already inside the ER, Deputy Atwater striding alongside. He had no idea what Luis' blood type was. Hopefully, the young man was conscious enough to tell them.

Darrell stared back at the rental, both doors wide open. Did he need to move the car? Did he need to check in, give them Erin's information? On the floor inside the open car door, he saw her purse. He snatched it up and held it to his bare chest. He only wanted to be with her, to hold her hand. To tell her how sorry he was. His gaze went from the glass doors of the hospital to the car.

He froze. What the hell had he gotten them into? And poor Luis. He had nothing to do with all this. He'd only come along to help. The weight of it all bore down on him, paralyzing Darrell. What did he think he was doing here? He and Erin were supposed to be on a carefree honeymoon. Now she was inside the hospital, bleeding. He had no idea how bad it was. How much blood had she lost? There were large smears across her seat. And what if the glass had slashed a ligament or tendon? What if she had permanent damage? Oh God, exactly like what had happened to his brother Craig fifteen years ago, all because of *that* ghost, the first damn one.

What was the matter with him? What the hell was he doing chasing some phantoms down here in Florida?

Deputy Atwater broke Darrell's recrimination. "Don't worry about the car. I'll go ahead and move it for you. The keys in it?" Darrell nodded dumbly. "The head nurse was asking for you. They need your help getting Erin registered. You know, paperwork. We can talk after."

He must've seen the look of shock and fear on Darrell's face because he said, "Don't worry. They're good here. They'll take good care of her."

Darrell nodded, feeling like some automaton, and stumbled in through the sliding glass doors.

"Mr. Henshaw?" a cheery nurse called, and he looked up.

"Erin? My wife?" he croaked.

"She's in very good hands. They have her in bay three, and Dr. Shelton is with her right now. It looks like you did quite the job staunching the bleeding." The nurse stopped and stared at him, examining his bloody chest and arms. "Are you okay?" Her hand probed the scarlet smears on his chest.

Darrell looked down at her hand, barely registering her words. He nodded. "Not mine. Erin's blood. And Luis'."

"Okay. You can go see your wife in a minute. Let's get her registered and let the doctor do his thing."

Darrell let her lead him through the hallway to the registration desk, and he slumped into a stiff chair.

"Name?" an officious voice snapped.

Darrell raised his gaze to meet the stern face of a woman in a blue hospital smock, black hair in a tight, old-fashioned bun. The nameplate on the counter read, "Gloria Ferguson, Registration." She scowled at him, eyes slanted together and lips almost a straight line.

"Henshaw. Darrell Henshaw," he managed, his voice raspy.

The woman's eyes—the color of dark chocolate—narrowed. "No. The patient's name?"

"Oh, Erin…Erin Henshaw," he said, feeling the lump in his throat.

"Identification?"

Darrell reached into his back pocket and pulled out his wallet. He slid out the license, seeing again the dried bloody fingerprints. Reaching across, he extended the card, and, in the motion, his arm glanced the miniature Christmas tree on the counter. He hadn't even noticed it. The short artificial tree stood atop the white Formica counter, blinking with tiny twinkle lights. When his arm brushed it, the small glass balls hanging on one side of the tree swung back and forth. The tree, with its bright lights and gaily colored ornaments, seemed like an insult right now. It didn't feel anything like Christmas. Couldn't be Christmastime. Not like this.

"Watch it!" snapped Ferguson, and she reached a hand out to steady the little tree. The sides of her mouth had wrinkles curving down as if she wore a permanent frown. She picked up the license by the edges, stared at it, then shoved it back at him. "Not yours. The patient's ID."

Erin's ID. It would be in her purse. With her. He started to stand up, then realized the handbag hung from his shoulder. Sitting back down in the stiff chair, he set the purse on his lap and flipped it open. He'd never looked inside Erin's purse before, and it felt like some kind of personal intrusion. Pulling items out slowly, he set them on his legs, picturing features of his wife with each article. Her hairbrush with strands of tangled red hair still in the tines. The deep red lipstick she liked. Her favorite gum she chewed hard when she was nervous. A tampon in a pink wrapper. A ticket stub from the Chesapeake Bay Maritime Museum. He saw the date and felt a lump in his throat. This past summer. The day he asked her to marry him. Now she was here in this hospital, bleeding and…He shot a glance down the corridor.

"Sir?" the woman asked, her tone barely civil, hard eyes unyielding.

He turned back to the purse. Finally, at the bottom of the handbag he found her flower-patterned wallet. He fumbled with the closure, got it open, and located her license. Saw the photo of her with that incredible smile. Tears leaked out of his eyes, and he felt them drip onto his bare chest. He handed the card over, feeling like he was giving her away.

Ferguson grabbed the license and scanned it. "You said her name was Erin Henshaw." She pointed to the laminated card. "This says Erin Caveny."

Darrell felt his throat tighten again. "We were just married. We're on our honeymoon."

Her head came up, and for the first time her brown eyes softened. "I'm sorry." Her hands started in on her keyboard, making tiny clicking sounds. "Would this address be correct?" She held up Erin's license.

Darrell shook his head. "No, you'll want my address." He handed her back his license.

"Insurance card?" she asked next.

And on it went. Darrell felt like it took forever before he was finally able to step away. Groggy, he made his way through the tight corridors, back to the ER.

Erin? Where did the nurse say they'd taken her? The nice one? He thought, trying to remember back. It was foggy, then it came to him. Bay three. She said bay three. His eyes scanned the black numerals outside each space and found number three. But no one was there. It was…empty.

Chapter 32

Another ID required

His gaze jerked around. Where was Erin? His mind raced through possibilities, each one more catastrophic than the last. She lay bleeding on some operating table. She'd lost too much blood. They had to rush her to ICU.

He had to find someone. Ask somebody. He hustled back to the nurses' station. No one was there, the entire area empty. Frantic, he glanced around, but the whole ER seemed deserted. He stood alone in the space, looking, staring. Panic swelled inside his chest.

No Erin. Instead, what he saw were other Christmas decorations he hadn't noticed before. A wooden plaque on one nurse's station with "Have a Cool Yule" printed across it beside a snowman with sunglasses. More miniature lights around one computer station. In the corner of the waiting room stood another decorated Christmas tree, larger, maybe five feet tall, with brightly wrapped presents crowded around the stand, each with a perfect, shiny bow.

His eyes taking it all in, he grew desperate, then angry. It all felt like an abomination. He realized the workers, the nurses and orderlies, were merely trying to inject some holiday spirit into their workplace—which must see a lot of tragedy. But, with Erin and Luis lying on some gurney or hospital bed bleeding, or worse, the whole Christmas shtick felt obscene right now. Where the hell was *his* Christmas miracle?

One nurse came through a pair of double doors and went to the nurses' station, sitting at a computer.

"Can you help me?' he squeaked.

The nurse, this one younger with a cap of brown hair and soft, olive eyes, looked up from the monitor even as her fingers worked the keys. "I'll try." Her voice oozed sympathy.

"I-I-I came in with my wife." He jerked over to the bays. "She was bleeding from some cuts. They took her to bay three...I think. They made me go to registration, and now when I got back, she's not there. Is she...okay? Do you know where she is?"

The young nurse smiled. "Don't worry." She leaned over and scanned a chart next to the computer, a finger running over a list of names. "That would be Erin Henshaw? She your wife?"

Darrell gave two quick nods. "Where'd they take her? Can I see her?"

"Not to worry, Mr. Henshaw. They simply took her to radiology. They want to take a few pictures to make sure there were no structural damages from the glass. They should be back here in a few minutes. If you'll have a seat, someone will get you as soon as they bring her back."

Darrell nodded again. "Thanks." He released a big breath and walked over to the chairs but couldn't sit down. He paced across the length the room, eyes searching each corner. He was alone, no one else waiting for dire news. He stared down at the floor and saw the regular pattern. Without thinking, his compulsion seized him, and his feet followed the pattern, stepping on each gray tile, back and forth, back and forth, each repetition a little faster. Visions of another small hospital up north in Cape May, not that much different than this one, rushed back. Him pacing, waiting for word on other casualties of another ghost hunt.

His *gift*. Just when he was getting close to accepting this...this...this ability, someone gets hurt. No, not someone. Erin. No, no, no. This *couldn't* be happening. If something happened to her, he'd never forgive himself. The hell with his damn *gift*. She was more important to him than any gift.

He could be so stupid. Why did he get sucked in? Look where his *gift* had gotten him. With *Erin* in the hospital this time. Oh, God.

And Luis. He'd been so consumed with his concern about Erin he hadn't given much thought to their young translator. He needed to see how he was doing. Darrell's gaze jerked around the space again. It was eerily quiet. Most of the bays sat open, the curtains pulled back, except the last one. Bay six. The drape was pulled all the way closed. Glancing around, he approached the area with a black numeral six above it. He didn't want to disturb someone else, so he whispered, "Luis?"

At first, no sound came from the bay, then Darrell heard some movement, someone shifting on the bed. He said a little louder, "Luis?"

A hoarse voice from behind the curtain said, "*Sí*. Mr. Henshaw?"

Darrell dragged the drape back and stepped into the space. Luis lay on the hospital bed, naked to the waist, both arms at his side. Darrell stared at the young man's thin, blood-streaked chest and right shoulder. The wound looked like it had the same bandage Atwater had applied in the car.

"Luis, are you okay? Did they check you over? What'd they say?" Darrell's hand went to the dressing and fingered it gingerly. The blood had saturated the gauze, turning the white a dark scarlet.

"I don' know, Mr. Henshaw." He leaned his head forward and then eased back as if the action pained him. "They rolled me in here and asked my name. I told them and gave them wallet." He took a breath. "Then, another man, no doctor I think. He had suit and tie. He say they no treat me. I need to go another hospital."

"Why?" Were Luis' wounds too serious and they needed a trauma center to treat them? Why didn't they take him to the other hospital by ambulance? Why was he lying here alone? "Why did they say they couldn't treat you here?"

Luis stared down at his bare chest and wouldn't meet Darrell's gaze. "Man say I could be illegal. He say they no treat illegals here."

Chapter 33

He will have to bleed elsewhere

"You want to explain why you're not caring for Luis Alvarez," Darrell demanded of the surly registration woman.

"Who?" Gloria Ferguson's head jerked up, on guard.

Anger had replaced Darrell's anxiety and guilt. White hot fury as he grasped what was going on. He said through gritted teeth, "Luis. Alvarez. In bay six. He came in with my wife and me. He was injured in the same attack. He's still lying there. No one has even examined him."

"Attack?" The woman's chocolate eyes widened, the curtness replaced by concern. "What did you say his name was?" She hit a few keys.

"Luis. Alvarez," Darrell spit out. "Do you need me to spell it for you?"

"Uh…Uh…No." Her fingers hovering over the keys, she looked up from her screen. She tried to force a smile but couldn't bring it off. "Um, uh…let me get someone who can answer your question." She got up and disappeared through a door behind her.

Impatient and his fuse burning, Darrell stared, his fingers drumming on the counter. Minutes passed, and no one appeared. He was tempted to reach over and yank out the cord connecting the dinky little Christmas tree. He glared at the door the woman had disappeared through, but it remained motionless. Maybe he should head back to see one of the ER nurses, who at least had been nice. See if they had any answers or could get help for Luis.

Right then, the door behind the counter opened, and the surly woman returned, followed by an older man in a black suit, white shirt, and blue tie. The man stopped on the other side of the counter. "Mr. Henshaw, I'm Thomas Anderson, hospital administrator here. I understand you have questions about the status of someone you brought to the hospital." His tone was officious, his words clipped. He was short, with a small round face with jowls that had gone to fat, his nearly bald head reflecting the bright fluorescent lights above. His diminutive size and pretentious manner made Darrell think, Napoleon complex. The man glanced down at a yellow Post-it. "A Mr. Luis Alvarez?"

"Yes. I brought him here along with my wife, Erin Henshaw."

Anderson interrupted, offering a tight, ostentatious smile. "Yes, your wife is in very good hands and doing well they tell me."

That made Darrell pause. "Thank you. I appreciate hearing that." He nodded. "Mr. Alvarez came in with us. As I was explaining, he was wounded in the same attack as my wife."

"Attack?" Anderson asked. "I was told it was an accident."

Darrell felt his anger rising again. "It was no damn accident. Someone shot out the windows of our car. And a bullet struck Luis."

"A bullet wound? No one told me it was a bullet wound." The administrator shot a look at Ferguson, who shrugged. He looked down, shaking his head. "Well, that doesn't change anything. We'll need to have him transferred to Ocala General."

"Change what?" Darrell barked.

The administrator tried to meet Darrell's glare but couldn't maintain eye contact and instead glanced down at the small yellow paper in his hand. When he did, Darrell stared at the spreading bald spot amidst the thinning salt-and-pepper hair. "Well...it appears...um, well, we had questions about Mr. Alvarez's, um, identification...uh, we believe...Luis Alvarez may be an illegal."

Darrell's stare didn't waiver, but he held his tongue.

"We tried to talk with him but couldn't tell. Mr. Alvarez doesn't speak very good English. And he didn't have an insurance card."

Looking up, Anderson scrunched his features together, and Darrell read the coldness in the steel-gray eyes.

"In the past few years, this hospital has been overrun by...um, Hispanics...by migrants with health problems...you see, they come here and don't have insurance. We're not a public hospital. They were bankrupting the entire organization. And on top of that, immigration officials were coming in here, looking at papers. Well, we didn't want to get in the middle of all those problems." He dropped his head and shifted from one foot to another. "A few months ago, the board voted not to offer service to any migrants without clean papers and insurance."

Darrell glanced around and noticed everything in the hospital seemed to be new—computer stations, chairs, gurneys. Fresh paint on every wall. Newly printed signs. No wear on the vinyl flooring. New vinyl flooring.

He gritted his teeth again. "I thought this was a *hospital*. You know, a place where people come when they need help. I didn't know this was the kind of place where whether you would get care depended on the color of your *skin*."

"Now see here, no one said anything about race—" Anderson tried, but Darrell cut him off.

"Don't give me that crap." He reached across the counter and grabbed the man by the necktie. And yanked. Darrell moved in so his face stopped mere inches from Anderson, their noses almost touching. "For your information, Luis Alvarez is *not* an illegal. He's the professional assistant of a realtor in Crystal River." Without letting go, he turned to the receptionist. "That would be Bonnie Bradford, of the Citrus County Realty Company, Crystal River. You can look her up." Without letting go of the tie, he turned his attention back to the administrator, whose gray eyes now shone with fear. "I'm a historical researcher, and I was doing some research in the area. I asked Luis to accompany us as a professional translator. By the way, his English is fine."

He released the man. Anderson stumbled back, regaining his footing, and tried to adjust his tie and maybe his dignity. Darrell continued, steel in his voice, "None of that should matter. Luis and Erin and I were shot at by someone in your fine county, and he needs your help."

"But Alvarez has no insurance," Anderson squeaked, his early bluster evaporated.

Darrell barked a sharp laugh. "Don't worry. I'll cover your damn bills. Just get him looked at and taken care of."

"Do we have a problem here?" Deputy Atwater appeared at Darrell's shoulder.

Ferguson must've sent someone a message alerting security, and Atwater happened to be close by. Darrell took a quick glance at the deputy and returned his glare back to the hospital administrator. "Do we?" he asked, his tone still tight. "Have a problem?"

The small administrator looked from the woman to the officer and finally met Darrell's glare. "No, sir. We'll make sure Mr. Alvarez gets taken care of. Right away." He turned to the cop. "Thanks, Deputy Atwater."

Darrell shook his head. "Okay. Thanks." He looked again at Anderson. "I think I'll go check on my wife. Whom you said the staff took such good care of. Thanks again for that."

He walked away, heading back to the ER area. Darrell knew he was mad, at himself as well as the hospital. Maybe he went a little overboard, but it felt good to let out his anxiety on someone else. He'd beat himself up later. Hearing quiet footsteps, he realized the deputy had taken up alongside him.

Atwater said, "I know you're worried, but you don't need to take it—"

Darrell stopped and interrupted the cop. "Did you know they were doing that? Denying service to Hispanics?" He looked into the deputy's eyes. "Of course, you did. It's your county." Darrell shook his head again.

Atwater tried, "Look, these are good people. Well, most of them."

Darrell said, "They ignored Luis. With a *gunshot* wound. If it had been more serious, he could have bled out, right there in their damn ER."

"It wasn't that serious. And we did a good job stopping the bleeding." The deputy shrugged. "They would probably have taken care of him...if it had been serious."

Darrell stared at him. "You think so?"

"They will now." Atwater grinned. "I think you might have made Anderson pee in his pants." He lowered his voice. "He can be a real prick...but I didn't say that."

Darrell relaxed, and they resumed their trip back to the ER. When they arrived, he noticed bay six was empty and hoped they'd moved Luis to get him taken care of. In bay three, Erin sat up, drinking orange juice through a straw, and smiled at him. Oh, God. Seeing that smile felt good.

He hurried over, leaned in, and kissed her, wrapping one arm around her unhurt side. When he straightened, she displayed her right arm, wrapped in gauze in two places. "My first stitches. A battle wound."

The nurse beside her addressed Darrell, "She's doing much better. The x-rays were negative, thank heaven. And no damage to ligaments or tendons. A small miracle with where the cuts were." She went over to the IV bag, checking the dial. "But she lost a lot of blood. They may want to keep her overnight."

"I feel fine," Erin protested.

Darrell examined his wife—whom he could've lost. Her color was better, though still a little pale. "Erin?"

"Okay, I feel much better. I don't need to stay in the hospital. I'm a nurse, and I'd know if I needed to be kept overnight."

"Mrs. Henshaw," the nurse said, "you know as well as I, medical people are the worst patients."

The deputy had stayed a few feet behind but now stepped forward and took off his cap. Hat in hand, he said, "Mrs. Henshaw, you are looking better than when I saw you last."

"Thank you," Erin said.

"But I'd like to offer a compromise." Atwater pointed to Darrell. "We're going to need Mr. Henshaw to come to the sheriff's office to fill out a report about what happened. And he's going to have to get some new wheels. You can't drive that rental back to Crystal River. All that's going to take a while." He turned to the nurse. "Nurse Higgins, how about you keep Mrs. Henshaw under observation until Mr. Henshaw can return, and then you medical people can fight it out?"

Nurse Higgins—who Darrell now realized was the nurse he'd met earlier at the nurses' station—broke into a broad grin. "An excellent suggestion, Deputy Atwater."

Darrell saw a little twinkle in her olive eyes, and when he checked Atwater, saw a similar glimmer in his blue eyes. They must *know* each other.

Erin gave a little pout. "I guess I can live with that."

Darrell added, "Well, we're not leaving here until I'm sure Luis is squared away anyway."

Erin's eyes got wide. "Is Luis okay?"

Nurse Higgins patted Erin on the arm. "He's going to be fine. Thanks to your husband's insistence, they're taking good care of him. He's in radiology now to make sure the wound isn't worse than it looks. He's a lucky man."

Not as lucky as if he hadn't come with them.

When he met the nurse's gaze, Darrell realized he had another ally. Maybe they were good people and didn't like turning away needy migrants any more than he did.

Darrell leaned in and kissed his wife again. "Okay, I'm off with this guy." He pointed to the deputy. "If I'm not back in an hour or so, send out the search teams." He grinned at her and hoped she knew he was kidding. Well, mostly kidding.

Chapter 34

Good will toward which men

"Before we head inside, I'd like to take a look at your car with you," Deputy Atwater said. "I did an examination of the vehicle before we had it moved over here, and I want to show you what I found and see what you think."

It had taken them less than ten minutes to make the trip from the hospital to the county sheriff's office. Alone with his remorse and anger, Darrell hadn't spoken in the car, and Atwater had only broken the silence to make a call on the radio letting the dispatcher know he was heading in. After they pulled the cruiser into the parking lot and got out, Darrell automatically headed for the steps, but the deputy had stopped him with his words. Darrell shrugged and reversed his path, following the cop to a lot in the back.

When they arrived at the impound lot and Darrell caught sight of the rental, its front end bashed in and side and rear windows shattered, he let out a small gasp. He'd been so consumed with trying to get Erin and Luis to the hospital he hadn't taken in the extent of the damage.

"Looks to me," Atwater said, "your vehicle was struck by two stray rounds." He walked up to the rear of the rental. "One through the back window here." The cop pointed to a spot barely right of center of the window, or at least where the window had been. He was careful not to get too close to the pieces of broken glass that still clung to the frame. Walking around the driver's side, he opened the rear door. "And the bullet lodged here." His pointer lit up a small hole near the bottom of the bucket seat. He stopped and looked at Darrell. "You guys were lucky. A few inches farther right or higher the bullet would've hit you. Or given your friend a lot worse than a graze."

Darrell felt his face get hot. Oh, God. How close they came.

"I extracted the bullet and sent it to the lab. Look to me like a .30-30 Winchester, but it was pretty messed up. Don't think there's enough left to do any matching." All professional, Atwater continued, "The second bullet struck this window." He indicated Erin's side window, now almost completely gone. "Shattered the glass that cut your wife and punched a hole in the windshield." He aimed the pointer through the window, and a red dot struck a small opening in the windshield. "Of course, that bullet is long gone." Sticking the pointer back in his pocket, he turned to look at Darrell. "Does that fit what you remember?"

Darrell said, "Mostly. It happened so fast. Only the first bullet shattered Erin's window and the second struck the rear. Both within a few seconds."

They stood there observing the damage, Darrell's guilt growing with the sight. The deputy said, "My best guess would be a hunting accident."

"A hunting accident?" Darrell heard the incredulity in his voice and struggled to contain it. "You really think this was all a *hunting* accident. What exactly is in season in December down here?"

Atwater shifted on his feet. "Well, nothing is in season right now. But some of the locals don't pay much attention to hunting season. They, uh…hunt pretty much whenever they want. And they are not all great shots." He pointed to the damaged car with two windows exploded. "Looks like two stray bullets got your car."

"Stray bullets?" Darrell shook his head. "I don't think so."

"Okay, what do you think it was?"

"Like I told you before. Somebody tried to kill us."

Deputy Atwater looked Darrell up and down. "Now why would someone try to kill you? You have major enemies here in Meridian County?"

Darrell realized he was stuck. He sure as hell couldn't tell the cop the real reason they were down here asking questions. He figured he'd employ the story he'd used at the Settlement, but before he had a chance the deputy threw another question at him.

"You told me you were down here on your honeymoon?"

"That's right."

Atwater gave a little chuckle. "Well, we like Meridian County well enough, but I don't see it as much of a couple's destination. What kind of honeymoon activities have you guys been doing in the county?"

Darrell glanced down at the black asphalt at his feet. "You might find it a little strange."

"Try me."

Glancing inside the car, he saw the bag with the painting on the floor. He grabbed it up, opened it, and showed it to Atwater. "I'm an amateur historian. Well, actually, I'm a high school history teacher, but I'm big into local history. I find it fascinating. Anyway, since we were down here, I decided I wanted to learn a little history about some migrant families who work your fields. We don't have any in Maryland where we're from, so I figured I wouldn't get another chance."

He checked Atwater to see if the cop was buying his story, but the deputy's face remained impassive.

"So we were taking a little time to interview some of the local workers. Over at the Settlement. A family named Sanchez. The family of these two kids." He pointed to the picture and hoped the details might help sell the story. "And I'm lucky to be married to a woman who allows me to pursue my hobby. At least, every once in a while."

When Atwater still didn't respond, Darrell said, "Now let me ask you a question."

"Sure, but let's head back inside so you can file the report and get out of here."

Before they reached the first step to enter through the rear door, Darrell put a hand on the deputy's arm, halting him. "Do you know any reason a local would take potshots at us simply because we were interviewing a few migrants?"

"People down here don't take to outsiders snooping into their business." Atwater shrugged. "But to actually shoot at you. That seems pretty extreme. I guess I could ask around."

Turning, he led Darrell in through the door, and Darrell had to duck under a small banner across the doorway proclaiming, "Peace on Earth. Good will toward men," with a picture of an angel next to the words. Exhausted, Darrell realized he could use a little peace and good will.

They headed down a corridor to a small room with a single table and two chairs. Darrell perched on a seat, and once down, realized how exhausted he was. Making sure his arms didn't touch the surface, he stared at the table, marked with scratches and black stains. He tried not to think of the accumulated germs the tabletop held. He slid back, careful not to lay his hands on the surface and keeping any contact with the table to a minimum.

In three minutes, Atwater returned with a blank Meridian County Incident Report, a cup of strong coffee, and a long sleeve tee with the words, "Property of Sheriff's Department" printed across the front. Darrell stood up and immediately slid on the shirt. It felt great to have something on, especially since it covered the ugly scarlet stains of dried blood on his chest. He'd seen how the staff at the hospital had looked at him, but no one offered a shirt. And Darrell didn't have a spare in the car.

The coffee felt good going down, and he hoped it would sustain him. He had a while to go. Glad to have something between his flesh and the ugly tabletop, Darrell went to work. It took him about twenty minutes to write up his report. Wanting to make sure he got it right, he read it over twice to be certain he didn't leave anything out.

When Atwater wandered back in to check on him, Darrell handed him the paper. The deputy took the other chair and read Darrell's handwritten account, nodding a few times as he made his way through it. When he finished, he handed it back.

"All you have to do is sign it, and you're done here."

Darrell took it and scribbled his signature, barely legible. When he extended it back, he said, "I never thanked you for the help with Luis and Erin. And for getting us to the hospital so quickly."

"Protect and serve." Atwater grinned. "Glad I was there at the right time."

"Of course, you really scared me with the drawn gun routine. *I* almost peed in my pants."

The cop chuckled. "Sorry about that. When we're on patrol alone, we're trained to take every precaution."

"I get it. But, after being shot at twice and staring at the gray barrel of your pistol, I thought I was going to pass out."

"You did okay." Atwater stood. "You want me to drop you at the car rental place? We only have one in town."

Darrell didn't move. "Thank you, yes. But first I have a request. Well, really two."

"Shoot." The deputy leaned on the table, his nightstick clinking against the edge.

"Remember the migrant family I mentioned earlier, the Sanchezes?"

"Yeah, what about them?"

"Well, when we interviewed them, I learned two of the kids went missing almost a year ago. Maybe last February. Daniel and Mia Sanchez, I think five or six years old. Could you see if anyone ever filed a missing persons report?"

Atwater nodded. "I can check. You said two requests?"

"Yeah, about the same time, I gather their father

Juan Sanchez got into some trouble with the law. This happened February, maybe around the fifteenth or twentieth. Could I have a look at the arrest report?"

When Atwater didn't answer, Darrell continued, "I'd like to see if they told me the truth. And I assume reports like that are public records down here, like they are in Maryland."

The deputy paused and said, "Okay, wait here. I'll go have a look and see if I can find the record." He pulled out a small notebook. "You said those names were Mia and Daniel Sanchez and Juan Sanchez and this happened February 1999?"

"That's what they said."

Atwater left, leaving the door open this time, and Darrell could hear his heavy boots echoing down the hallway. He wasn't sure the deputy had bought his whole story. Still, he was helping. Darrell knew that, if Florida regulations matched Maryland, the sheriff's office had up to seven days to grant any records request, so it would've been easy to put Darrell off.

He looked behind him, noticing the one-way mirror for the first time. Studying the glass, he saw an oily stain partway up the surface toward the center. Probably the grease from the back of someone's head. The blotch mocked him. His compulsion struck him again, and the nearly unbearable need urged him to wipe the mirror clean. But the only thing he had was the shirt, and he wasn't taking it off to clean the glass. He struggled to tamp down the impulse. Forcing his gaze to roam around the room, he saw the black camera in the far corner, a red eye blinking at him. He stared back.

Atwater returned, single folder in hand. "Nothing on the two missing kids, but here's what I found on the father."

As Darrell took the file, he read across the top, "Juan Sanchez. February 18, 1999. A & B. Disposition: Immigration/Deported." He glanced up at the deputy. "That was fast. Was this your arrest?"

Atwater shook his head and pointed to a line on the folder. "Before my time. That'd be Robertson."

"Is he here? Could I talk with him? If I have any questions?"

The cop shook his head again. "No longer here. Took a better slot in Tampa. Higher rank, more pay." He grinned. "I got his spot."

Atwater started to go and stopped. "Holler when you're finished, and we'll head over to the car rental. Oh, and you can read, but the report stays here. You'll have to file a formal request for any copies."

Darrell nodded at the officer. Nothing on the missing kids. That was no help. What the hell happened to them?

He turned back to the report. Opening the folder, he pulled out the single sheet of paper and started reading. Not easy. He was used to reading teenagers' hurried scribbles, but this cop's handwriting was as bad as any Darrell had seen in his classroom. Still, he pressed on and got the gist.

The accused, one Juan Sanchez, had struck and bloodied the victim, one Tom Stickley. There was a note the officer detected the strong smell of alcohol on Stickley's breath but none on Sanchez. Stickley's speech was somewhat slurred, but he had mumbled something about an accident.

The accused was very agitated and kept pointing at the victim and had to be restrained several times.

Robertson wrote he had trouble understanding the accused as Sanchez spoke Spanish with only a little broken English, and there was no one available to translate. The cop recorded only a few words of Sanchez's testimony without comment. Among the man's cramped scribbling, Darrell could make out *niño, niña,* and *el daño.*

Darrell stopped reading. He'd heard the same words uttered in rapid-fire dialect at the Settlement. Luis had translated them for him.

"Hurt my little boy and girl."

Chapter 35

No place like home for the holidays

By the time Darrell picked up a new rental and returned to the hospital, he found Erin sitting up, legs dangling off the side of the bed, talking and laughing with a small gaggle of nurses and orderlies, all female.

When she saw him approaching, Erin smiled at him. "And here is my handsome prince! Come to whisk me away in a jeweled carriage."

Darrell leaned in between two of the group and gave her a hug, careful not to bump the injured arm. Checking her over, he noted her color looked much better, only a little pale, and the good humor didn't seem forced.

He turned to the nurse he'd spoken with earlier. "Nurse Higgins, what's the prognosis? Didn't you say the doctor wanted to keep her overnight for observation?"

The nurse laid a hand on Erin's leg. "Dr. Shelton did, but Nurse Caveny, er, I meant Nurse Henshaw, convinced the doc she'd be able to convalesce at home. Well, at the great vacation home you're staying at. Sounds like you guys have been having fun in Crystal River. She's been telling us all about your adventures."

Darrell hoped not *all* about their adventures.

He caught a gleam in his wife's eyes, which had

some of their sparkle back.

All false innocence, Erin said, "I explained we only have three more days on our honeymoon. Don't want to spend one of them in the hospital." She stretched her good arm behind her across the mattress. "These beds work fine for hospital patients but aren't so great for other important life…experiences."

The nurses and orderlies giggled. Nurse Higgins continued, "But she has to swear to take it easy."

Erin raised her right arm carefully, wincing a little, and gave the three-finger Scout salute. Higgins turned toward Darrell, arching her eyebrows. "And you need to be gentle with her."

"Yes, ma'am."

While they got a wheelchair for Erin, he went to check on Luis. Like his wife, the young man sat up on the bed in the same bay Darrell had left him in, but his wound had obviously been tended to, and his right arm hung in a sling. Someone, probably one of the nurses, had given him a smock top. Or maybe someone didn't want to look at his mocha skin.

Nurse Higgins followed a step behind Darrell. "Same thing goes for this young man." She eased to the side of the bed, looked inside the blue top, and did another check of the dressing. "Looks okay. Luis is very lucky the bullet only grazed his shoulder. The doc would rather he spend the night here, but Luis said he wants to head back home with you. Your wife has agreed to check on him and change the bandage as needed. I'll have a wheelchair brought up for him. Luis and Erin have already signed the discharge papers, so they're all yours."

Administrator Anderson was no doubt thrilled to be

rid of the "migrant," but Darrell let it go.

Darrell drove the rental up to the sliding glass doors, and a pair of wheelchairs rolled across the space to meet him. He helped Erin ease into the front and fussed with the belt. By the time he got to the second wheelchair, Luis had already leveled himself into the rear seat and buckled himself in, head back against the headrest.

As he pulled away, Erin was fingering the dash with her left hand. "Not exactly a jeweled carriage, but it looks like you moved us up. What is this?"

"The rental guy called it a Toyota Rav4."

"An SUV? Thought you weren't much of an SUV man."

Darrell said, "I didn't have much choice. It was either this or a GMC Yukon."

"A Yukon Cornelius?" Erin giggled, and he figured she was still feeling the effects of the painkiller.

Back on the highway, he turned the radio on but kept the volume low. Relieved he found a station not broadcasting Christmas songs, he smiled when he heard Shania Twain sing "That Don't Impress Me Much." He knew Erin loved the song and hoped it might take her mind off everything. At least, for a few minutes. He glanced over and saw her head swaying and her lips mouthing the lyrics.

Turning to check out the back seat, he saw Luis still had his head against the seat back, eyes closed, the blue smock collapsing around his slender frame. Sleeping, Darrell hoped. He checked the road and shot another glance at Erin. Keeping his voice low, he said, "After I filled out the incident report, I asked if they had anything reported on our two kids, Mia and Daniel

Sanchez."

"Did they?"

He shook his head but kept his eyes on the road. "Nothing. No missing person's report or reports of their death. I did get a look at the arrest report for Juan Sanchez though."

"And?" Erin's voice was low but impatient.

Darrell turned to check on Luis. No change. Eyes still closed. He whispered, "February 18, he was arrested for assault and battery on Tom Stickley, who it looks like was drunk at the time."

"That matches what they told us at the Settlement."

"Yeah. The report said Stickley kept mumbling something about an accident."

"An accident?" Erin asked. "What kind of accident?"

"Don't know. That's all they had in the arrest report."

"What was Juan's story? Cops must have taken a statement from him at least."

Darrell shot another glance at his back seat passenger. He couldn't tell if Luis was sleeping...or quietly listening. He whispered, "That's the thing. Apparently, Juan didn't speak much English and the officer, a deputy named Robertson, didn't speak any Spanish. The cop only included a few words from Juan in his report." He looked across at Erin and then brought his eyes back to the road, "*Niño, niña* and *el daño.*"

"Didn't we hear the same words from Mrs. Morales back at the Settlement? And Luis translated them for us. Do you remember what they meant?"

From the back seat, Luis answered, "Hurt my son

and daughter."

Darrell turned toward the back seat. "Sorry. We weren't trying to leave you out. I was only trying to give you time to rest."

Without opening his eyes, Luis said, "I rest enough at home."

For a while, neither Darrell nor Erin spoke, though he exchanged a quick glance with her. A few miles rolled on, the silence broken only by another song from the radio, "I Want It That Way" by the Backstreet Boys.

When the song finished and the DJ started talking, Erin reached the volume knob with her left hand and turned it down. She asked, no longer in a whisper, "The file have the disposition of the case?"

Darrell nodded. "It stated he was deported. Exactly like Mrs. Morales said."

Luis added, "And that's why Latinos no trust gringos. Especially migrant workers."

Another silence followed, more profound this time, as the radio was little more than a whisper. Luis broke it. "Mr. and Mrs. Henshaw, I like you both."

Erin spoke up, her words running together, "And we like you, Luis. And we're so grateful for your help. And we're so sorry about what happened and about you getting hurt."

"I know, Missus." He held up his sling. "I have real story to tell when I get home. But not what I mean. Remember when I say I not know English that well, but still smart?"

Erin said, "Yeah. We can tell you're quite smart."

Luis waited a beat and asked, "Then why do you not tell me real reason you ask about kids in picture?"

Darrell cleared his throat. "I don't know what you

mean."

Luis leaned forward as far as his seatbelt would allow. "Mr. Henshaw, I can tell from you and the missus that finding about these children more than history, uh…how do you say, *por curiosidad?"*

Erin offered, "Curiosity?"

The young Latino said quickly, "*Sí*, more than curiosity about history. If you want my help, why lie to me?"

Chapter 36

Easier to believe in Santa

Darrell knew he was caught, and his mind reeled. Trying not to be obvious, his gaze slid over to Erin, who gave a small, one-shoulder shrug. Worst part of all, Luis was right. He and Erin had used his limited lack of English and hoped they could give him the cover story and he'd buy it. And they almost got him *and* Erin killed. That reality froze Darrell.

But how could they tell him the truth? Even after so many encounters with the spirit world, when Darrell verbalized it, said it out loud to anyone other than Erin—and maybe Al and Sara—the whole thing sounded preposterous. And now, the ghosts of little children? Luis would probably think Darrell was merely feeding him a new line.

For his part, Luis said nothing more, and his patient silence only made Darrell more anxious. When he turned to check, he saw Luis still lay back, head against the headrest but eyes open. Waiting.

Erin made the decision for him. "Well, Luis—"

Darrell stopped her with a hand on her good arm. "We used that story because the truth is so strange, no one would believe it anyway."

Without moving his head, Luis said, "I hear plenty strange stories. Try me."

So, as he drove on, Darrell told him. The road they traveled was impossibly dark, no streetlights, no lighted highway signs, and very few headlights passing them. The encroaching darkness seemed to envelop them, as if creating the perfect sinister setting for the strange story. He adjusted the rearview mirror so he could watch Luis' reactions and plowed on, explaining he sometimes *saw* people from the other side, ghosts, and they often wanted him to help in some way. He'd been visited by the ghosts of these two children and, until a few days ago, had no idea who they were. Stumbling a few times, Darrell finally got out that the kids' ghosts were asking for his help.

There he came to a halt. To him, it felt like a screeching halt, and for a while the young man in the back seat didn't say a word. Finally, Luis asked, "This ghost visit, this happen before, you say?"

Erin answered, "Yeah, Darrell helped two other ghosts. Last year in Wilshire, where we live. Then last summer in Cape May, the ghost of a murdered bride."

"I know it's pretty unbelievable." Darrell glanced in the rearview mirror to watch for any reaction.

Luis shook his head. "No. *Extraño*, yes, but unbelievable, no. My *abuela,* she sees spirits too. She say dead talk to her."

"Really?" Darrell said. "I'd like to meet your *abuela*."

"Be hard. She live in Mexico."

For a while no one spoke in the car, the music playing low now, some song by Britney Spears the only intrusion in the silence. Darrell exchanged another look with Erin, his eyes wide.

After a while, Luis said, "What these ghosts,

Daniel and Mia, want you to do?"

"Help them. That's it, all they said. *Ayúdaños.*"

Luis stirred in the back seat, leaning forward again. "*Ayúdaños.* That's why you asked. At Charlie's."

Darrell nodded.

Luis said, "Help them…how?"

Darrell turned to meet his passenger's gaze and then brought his attention back to the darkened road. "We're not sure. Find out what really happened to them…and expose the truth?"

"Something about an accident, you think?" Luis asked.

Darrell said, "Yeah. We think. We're not sure."

Erin spoke up. "Sorry for dragging you into this. And for getting you hurt."

Luis leaned forward and waved off her comment with his good arm. "Still no understand something. Why you care about two Latino children you not know? Why waste honeymoon on them?"

Darrell didn't know how to answer that, wasn't sure *he* knew the answer.

Erin turned in her seat to meet Luis' gaze for the first time. As she moved, she let out a low gasp, drawing Darrell's stare. She took a breath, released it, and started in. "Darrell's a teacher and a coach. I mean, like the best teacher. He cares about kids. Last summer he almost got himself killed because he wouldn't give up looking for a runaway teen who was a sister to a kid in a football camp he was coaching."

"Real *fútbol.* Like soccer?" Luis asked. "Or American football?"

"Doesn't matter. Darrell only knew this kid for two weeks, had only met him a few days before. But he saw this teenager was hurting, and Darrell did everything he could to help. So when these two called out to him, two little kids, he couldn't turn his back on them."

Luis asked, "And *you* okay with this?"

Erin smiled for the first time since they left the hospital. "It's part of what I love about him." She threw a glance at Darrell, who caught it out of the corner of his eye. "Not my ideal way to spend a honeymoon, I admit, but we have a lifetime together, and these kids only have our help for a few days. Besides, I know when we have kids of our own, he'll protect them just as ferociously as he fights for these ghosts."

Luis settled back against the seat again. "Okay. I happy to help." Darrell could hear his smile through his words. "Not know when I agree that trip be so exciting."

Erin chuckled. "Take it from me. Life with Darrell is *never* boring."

Once back at Crystal River, using Luis' knowledge of the back roads, Darrell got off the highway and cut through to deliver Luis to his place on a side street, a road lined with small ranch houses. When he pulled up in front of the one-story house with lights burning in the windows, Darrell counted six cars parked in the driveway and on the street. He asked, "A lot of drivers in the house?"

"I live with two other families. Only way I can pay." Luis started to slide out of the seat and stopped. "I left my truck at Simmons' house. Tomorrow, Fredo will bring me by to pick it up. Okay?"

Erin said, "Sure, and don't worry about it. Darrell and I can get it to you tomorrow. Depends on how you feel." She glanced at Darrell who gave a quick nod.

"And thank you again. We meant what we said. Couldn't have done it without you today."

Darrell handed three ten-dollar bills over the seat back.

"*Gracias*, Mr. and Mrs. Henshaw." He turned and loped toward the door.

Darrell pulled the car back onto the street and threaded his way back to US 19 and to their long and winding road home. When he pulled into the circular Simmons driveway and stopped behind the rusty pickup, he saw the hundreds of twinkling lights which edged the frame of the house and were nestled in the trees and bushes in the front yard. He'd seen the brilliance of the display a few nights earlier when they returned after dark and remembered the lights were on some kind of timer. Thinking of his journey through town, he realized most of the displays of lights on other houses had been darkened, and many Christmas displays had even been taken down. Not like up north where people kept the Christmas lights burning at least until New Year's Eve and sometimes beyond. He was not home, but he was with Erin.

Tonight, though, rather than finding the colorful Christmas display welcoming and comforting, the bright lights rattled him. With two dead kids and an attempt on their lives, it didn't seem like any holiday. As he came through the front door a few steps behind Erin, he flipped the switch turning the front of the house to utter darkness.

He almost got Erin—and poor Luis—killed today. He stared at the darkness outside. The blackness was a far better fit for his mood.

Chapter 37

Anything in the paper?

The previous day's events had exhausted Darrell, and though Erin had put on a brave face, he knew she was wiped. They both barely made it through the fancy front door of the Simmons' place before shedding their clothes and crashing in bed.

From the sunlight streaming through the French doors, he could tell he'd slept in more than he planned. When he awoke fully, his head still swimming from yesterday's attack, he tried to shake the sense of dread that had seized him in the hospital. He slipped silently from bed and threw on some clothes. He wanted to give Erin some down time today to simply rest and recuperate. And he'd love to simply lie in bed beside her, but his anxiety wouldn't let him. And he had things he wanted to do.

As he stood there watching Erin sleeping, he was torn. On the one hand, he wanted to swear off the ghosts, swear off his *gift*, and use the few remaining days of the honeymoon to enjoy their time together and show Erin how much he loved her. God, he could have lost her. He shuddered as Atwater's words came back, "If either of those bullets had been a few inches off, they could have killed any of you."

Was anything worth that risk?

On the other side of his brain, Natalia's warning echoed. *"The kids are lost and forgotten."*

He didn't even have to see the painting. The kids' gazes were burned into his brain—desperate brown eyes, silently pleading for help.

"No one cares. You must care, Darrell Henshaw."

If he *was* going to find out what happened to them, much less do anything about it, he knew he'd have to get on it. Darrell felt the time slipping away, could almost hear the seconds clicking down. He and Erin had to fly back to Maryland in only three days, and if he didn't come up with some way to help the kids, it would be too late. If there really was a way. One that didn't get them killed.

He moved soundlessly around the bed, but by the time he tiptoed to the bathroom, he heard her sleepy voice. "Leaving me already? I almost take a bullet for you yesterday, and you're going to desert me?"

When he glanced over, he noticed Erin hadn't even opened her eyes yet, but still knew. He wasn't going to be able to get away with anything. "I was simply trying to be a considerate husband and not wake my sleeping beauty of a wife. Besides, I promised I'd make sure you'd take it easy."

She rolled over so she now faced the bathroom doorway where Darrell stood frozen, one leg in a pair of slacks. As she turned, the Oxford shirt shifted, revealing a lovely V of her chest, and her green eyes focused on him. "A little flattery is nice but won't get you off answering my question. Where're you going?"

Jamming the other leg into the pants, he pulled them up and zipped. He took a step and sat on the side of the bed next to Erin's still prone body. "I was going to leave you a note. I'm heading into town to spend a few hours at the library going through newspaper archives to see if I can find anything about Juan's arrest...or Stickley's accident...or anything about our missing kids."

He figured he could at least do the research without committing one way or the other. He'd see if he turned up anything...and then decide what he'd do.

"Not without me, you don't." She sat up in bed, and her movement made her wince, though she tried to hide it.

Darrell jumped on it. "See, your arm still hurts. It's going to hurt for a while, Higgins said. You're supposed to rest." He leaned in and kissed her. "You know I'd love to have you with me, but I promised."

She shoved him back with her good arm to make room. Sliding her legs over the edge of the bed, she stood up quickly, as if testing herself. She raised both arms in triumph. "See. No fainting. I'll be fine."

"Erin—"

She cut him off. "Look, I am going to take it easy. I'm not running a marathon. The way I look at it, I can sit around here for most of the day, or I can sit on a chair at the library. Not much diff."

He shook his head and she finished, holding up her left arm, "And I promise I'll only use my good arm."

Darrell realized it was futile and caved.

Sixty minutes later, together they climbed the three stone steps and entered the Coastal Region Library of Crystal River. Though the exterior sported a kind of art deco look, the inside looked remarkably like most of the other libraries where he'd spent so much time. Front desk for circulation and information sat off to the right, and as they entered, he nodded to the woman behind the desk, who smiled back at them. Stacks of books lined both sides of the space with volumes running twenty feet deep in each direction. Standing in the entrance getting their bearings, he inhaled the comforting aromas of paper and mildew. He was in familiar territory. At the rear of the building, he saw the local research room, separated by a tall glass wall and beyond it a half dozen wooden carrels, all empty at the moment. They headed that way.

On the way, he passed a display of local and area newspapers and stopped. The headline in the local paper, *The Citrus County Courier,* caught his eye. LOCAL BANK BRACES FOR POSSIBLE Y2K DISASTER. Shooting a glance at Erin, he stopped and pulled the paper from the rack. He scanned the article and after a bit read part of it to Erin in a stage whisper. "Officials at Florida Federal Bank in Crystal River say they are prepared for any mishap that might be caused by the changing of the millennium. 'We have every confidence in our computer systems but are prepared to take all systems offline if the need arises,' explained bank president, Frederick Talbot."

Meeting Erin's raised eyebrows, Darrell shook his head. "And we think we have problems. At least we're not dealing with the meltdown of the internet."

Once inside the research room, he worked to get the workstations ready. Before they started, he wiped down both carrels and the readers, including the knobs and the twelve-inch screens—all to the bemusement of the library personnel. Darrell didn't care.

Once the helpful librarian—a homely, middle-aged woman with warm, friendly eyes and brunette hair pulled back in a ponytail—got the spools of microfilm on the reader and threaded through the machine, both Erin and Darrell took it from there. He decided they'd focus on February 1999, since they'd gained that much from yesterday's excursion—though it was hardly worth the injuries to Erin and Luis. At Erin's suggestion, they split up duties, her tackling the *Meridian Bugle*, that county's weekly, and him the *Ocala Register*, the closest paper with any sizable circulation.

Before he climbed into his chair, he checked on Erin. She'd slipped on another sleeveless top, this one white, which wrapped her torso. The top hung loose by a pair of spaghetti straps, chosen no doubt so as not to brush against the bandages on her arm. As he watched her work, he was amazed at her dexterity with one hand—and not her dominant hand—moving between one handle and the next, the images of the newspaper pages flying in and out of focus. Satisfied, he slipped into his carrel and went to work on his microfilm reader.

This research should have been a little easier. After all, they had an actual date, and he figured they'd only have to review the papers from a little over a month. Last summer they had to search through archives of five years of newspapers, and in Wilshire before that, the time span for research had been even greater.

Three hours later, though, they'd come up with nothing. At least, nothing about the Sanchez family or the Harrington Plantation.

They had cranked through every issue twice, three times for Erin since she had far fewer to check, and examined each page—front page, regional sections, local gossip, even opinion. In desperation, they extended their search into early March, thinking maybe some of the reports might not have gotten posted until later. Their search turned up nothing to confirm what they were trying to find.

The *Meridian Bugle* had a weekly sheriff's report, mostly speeding tickets and the occasional DUI. Strangely, Erin found no mention of the arrest and deportation of Juan Sanchez in Dixon. She showed Darrell that particular weekly, dated February 25, which listed only one "drunk and disorderly"—Silas Warner, his second offense—and a sheriff's auction of an eight-hundred-acre farm.

The *Ocala Register* proved more fruitful, only not with the information they were looking for. In addition to various crime reports—breaking and entering, property theft, and domestic disturbances—Darrell found several reports of injuries from farm accidents from areas around Ocala, but nothing mentioning the Harrington Plantation. One farmworker had lost an arm to a cultivator, and another had a leg crushed by a tractor tire. The month's issues carried two reports of missing children, but each article was about a white boy and girl who had gone missing from Ocala or Dixon.

In fact, as Darrell and Erin reviewed all the sections from both papers, comparing notes and sharing ideas, he noticed there was barely a mention of migrant workers. It was almost as if the hundreds of immigrants who worked the fields were an afterthought, at least to the readers of the papers. In fact, the only reference to the immigrants came from an editorial about an article from a national magazine on the conditions of the migrant workers. An article that was hardly complimentary, he gathered from the scant mention in the *Ocala Register*. He was so intrigued he followed the lead to the actual article in a back issue of *The Atlantic*.

By the time the librarian found the issue with the piece entitled "In the Strawberry Fields," Darrell was exhausted, eyes bleary from hours of reading the small print on the computer screen. He almost didn't bother. The article probably wouldn't get them any closer to solving what happened to the two kids, and when he checked her over, Erin looked like she needed a nap. But once he started reading, he got hooked, knee-deep in the harrowing world of immigrant laborers.

Darrell was surprised to learn the strawberry crop—the one that dominated the Harrington fields—was one of the riskiest but also the most profitable of the row crops. But it is also one of the most devastating to the workers who had to spend hours upon hours bent over, walking the rows, and picking the berries. Disability was common among the migrants—their work was some of the most dangerous in the nation—and even more prominent among the workers who pick strawberries. Like the Sanchez family. As he read on, he kept sharing passages in a loud whisper to Erin, who no longer looked tired.

What he read was an exposé of some of the conditions of these workers, conditions even worse than what he witnessed at the Settlement. Living in dilapidated trailers or tiny, shabby bungalows with no electricity or running water. Working in the fields for long, twelve-hour days with no portable toilets and no faucets to even clean their hands. Workers having to drink from the same cup as sixty of their fellow laborers. Children working in the fields alongside the adults.

He learned there were almost an estimated one million migrant farm workers in the U.S., who averaged less than $5,000 a year. And unlike the stereotypes, the vast majority of migrants rather than take government handouts keep moving from town to town, from crop to crop. From Florida to the Carolinas to Georgia to West Virginia, never able to spend more than a few weeks in any one place.

Maybe things for the migrants hadn't improved much in the last thirty years.

"Less than $5,000 a year. *This* had been the life of the Sanchez family, of Daniel and Mia," Darrell whispered to Erin with a shiver.

"Hard to believe." Erin gave a slow shake of her head. "You got enough?"

Catching the fading look on her face, he nodded and undid their two rolls of microfilm, returning them along with the issue to the accommodating librarian with his thanks. They left, and Darrell helped Erin back into the car, taking care with her injured arm. Still, he saw her cringe again.

"You didn't use your right arm in there, did you?"

Erin shook her head. "No, I was careful, but it's hurting a little more. Need to go home and rest in our beautiful bed. Let's pick something up and head back."

"Your wish is my command." He gave a quick bow, making Erin grin, and that eased his tension some. A half hour later he pulled into their circular driveway, jumping out and grabbing the carryout from the back seat. Before he got to her door, Erin had it open with her left arm and was sliding out. She tried to smile, but Darrell could see the ache in her eyes.

He ran ahead to hold the front door open for her and almost stumbled over a delivery on the stoop. A large floral arrangement wrapped in clear cellophane sat on the concrete, a small envelope sticking out of the top. Turning the key, he pushed the large door in, holding it open for Erin to pass through. He grabbed the bouquet and carried the food and flowers into the kitchen, setting both on the island.

After hours squinting at the microfilm screens, they were both starved, but Darrell found himself more immediately fascinated by the arrangement. When he glanced over, Erin's gaze was on the flowers, not their sandwiches. Even through the plastic, the bouquet exploded with color—bright red roses, vibrant yellow sunflowers, and orange day lilies, bright greens with red holly berries interspersed among the flowers, and even a sprig of mistletoe in the center. Her eyes came up, expectant.

"Any guesses?" he said, smiling. "Maybe Doc Simmons?"

Erin shook her head. "Not likely. Not this late in our stay. Don't know." She pulled at the small envelope with the logo of a local florist, breaking it free and tearing the cellophane in the process, the rip echoing in the room. The delightful scent of the flowers filled the room, adding to the delectable smell of the grilled sandwiches they'd bought.

She held up the card, reading the message silently, her green eyes going wide.

"What is it?" Darrell asked, anxiety rising in his voice. He felt no prickle, no premonition, but still. His paranoia kicked in. Erin handed the small card to him. Scanning it over once, he read the message out loud.

"A Special Holiday Bouquet for the Honeymooning Couple

We've heard about your dreadful accident yesterday on Mineola Road. So glad to learn you're both okay. Perhaps, as one loving couple to another, we could give you some sage marital advice. Take care of each other and use what time you have to enjoy your honeymoon. You'll never get this time back. Maybe let Floridians take care of their own problems—Savannah and Sterling Harrington"

Chapter 38

Okay, now what?

"I'm not sure we can take that chance." Darrell set the mug down on the farmhouse table, his gaze watching the steam rising from the ceramic edge. "Atwater said if the second bullet had been a little higher, you could've been killed."

When he remembered the deputy pointing out the bullet hole bored into the frame of the bucket seat—the perforation small, black, and deadly—he shivered at the thought.

Erin took a sip of her coffee and set the mug down using only her good arm. Watching that sent another tremble through him. She said, "Hey, I'm not keen on getting in anyone's line of fire, but do you think we should quit now that we've come this far? I mean, what about Daniel and Mia? Their parents were deported, the rest of the immigrants don't seem to know what happened. Not that they have time to care. You read what their lives are like."

Darrell tried, "I feel terrible about the migrants, but those kids are still dead. Nothing we do can undo that. Whatever happens, they'll still be dead."

Even as he heard his own words, he recognized the hollowness of his argument. It was *because* Daniel and Mia were dead they reached out to him. Because of his gift, they believed *he*—and not anyone else—could do something about what happened to them. Whatever that was.

Erin echoed his thoughts, almost as if she could read his mind. "What about your gift? You told me you were trying to come to terms with it. Trying to recognize it as a *gift*. Daniel and Mia reached out to you because of your gift."

"I know I said that, and I meant it. But that was before someone tried to kill us, kill you. I know it's Christmastime and everything, and I feel horrible about those two little kids." He let his voice drop. "Besides, you read the *friendly* advice from the Harringtons."

Erin stared at him. "Doesn't that seem fishy to you?" She glanced over at the oversized arrangement on the island. "These wealthy landowners, who couldn't help us with the two migrant kids, send these beautiful flowers and politely told us to mind our own business. Doesn't that bother you a little?"

"Of course, it bothers me," Darrell replied a little too quickly and then saw the flash in Erin's eyes. "I just don't want to take a chance. I can't put *you* in danger." He glanced at the bandage on her arm. "Any more danger. The cop said I could've been burying you." He fought to hold back tears.

Erin started, "We can be careful—" Then she must've seen the look in his eyes because she stopped. She took another sip and stared across the scarred wooden table. "So we're simply going to abandon those kids."

"I don't know. I just don't know."

Erin turned her head until they were face to face. "Darrell, why do you think you've been given this gift?"

"What?"

"Why do you think you have the gift of seeing, um…those on the other side?"

Darrell shook his head. "I don't know. I guess it's like you said before. Some people have artistic talent, others can swish a basketball from half court. I have…this."

Now Erin shook her head. "I think it has to be more than that. Surely you can't be the only one. I mean, we found out in Cape May Cassie has a similar ability. There has to be more. There are probably a number of sensitives down here in this area, this town even."

"Um, yeah, I guess. So?"

"Well, I'm asking you why you think these kids reached out to you? Why did Hank and Amy reach out to you?"

Darrell looked across at his wife, clearly puzzled. "Because I *could* see them when others couldn't? I don't get it."

Erin appeared definite. "I think it's more than that. These kids, or Amy or Hank, could have reached out to others who have the same gift, but they chose you."

"Great. Lucky me." Darrell gave her a sad smile.

"I'm serious. I think these lost kids reached out to you, like Amy and Hank did, because they somehow know you care. You're willing to go the extra mile when a lot of people wouldn't bother."

Darrell shook his head again. "I don't know. I think you're stretching it."

Erin reached her hand across and touched Darrell's chin, her soft fingertips tracing his stubble. "If you think about it, you'll know I'm right. It's the same quality that makes you such a great teacher...and one I love about you. You think about others first. Maybe the ghosts knew getting some help would be quite a challenge. So they reached out to you because they sensed you'd go the extra mile for them. Just like you do for your students." She closed the distance and kissed him softly.

After they broke, he said, "I appreciate you for saying that...and even if it's true, that doesn't mean I want to take any chances with your life."

They'd had several versions of this exchange since they returned yesterday from the library to find the flowers from the Harringtons. With the not-so-subtle warning.

Since then, the conversation or discussion or argument had started and stopped a number of times, each exchange without any final resolution. In between, they tried several distractions. For dinner, Darrell had gone out, picked up Chinese, and they ate cross-legged at the foot of the shining Christmas tree, trying to savor the impromptu holiday picnic.

Later, they took turns flipping through the brochures, exploring possible fun options for the next two days before they returned home to Maryland. Darrell suggested a tour of the Yulee Sugar Mill Ruins in Homasassa. Erin wanted to head over to Inverness to ride an airboat into the Everglades. But their hearts weren't into it, and sooner or later they found themselves returning to the dilemma of Daniel and Mia.

They even tried the TV for a little diversion. *Will and Grace* provided some comic relief, but when *Chicago Hope* came on, they couldn't concentrate on the story. They had enough drama in their life right now.

The only real respite they found from the tension was when they agreed to call it a night. Even then, when Erin undressed revealing the two white bandages covering the stitches on her arm, Darrell pondered again how he'd almost lost her and had to fight back tears. She must've known what he was thinking because she kissed him, softly at first, then fiercely. Conflicted, he was worried about hurting the arm, but she was enthusiastic. Using her lips and one good arm, she urged him, brought him to the edge, and made him banish any other thoughts. All he could think of was completing her, becoming her other half. So, in the large four poster bed with the quiet slush of the waves outside, they made ardent, deep love, finally surrendering together to an exhausted slumber.

When the gray mist of early morning crept into the bedroom, they both awoke without speaking and ambled into the kitchen. The breeze off the water was gentle, the wind ruffling the sheer curtains at the kitchen windows. And here they were back at the same discussion.

Darrell broke the silence. "We don't even know what really happened to them."

"The older woman at the Settlement…" Erin started.

"Mrs. Morales?"

"Yeah, Mrs. Morales said something about an accident."

Darrell shook his head. "I've been thinking about that. I don't think it was a normal accident, like a hit-and-run."

"You don't think Steph could've hit them with her car? Why not?"

"Well, if that happened, why did the dad, Juan, get into a fight with Stickley?"

Erin didn't say anything for a moment, then offered, "Maybe he wanted to get to Harrington. Sterling, I mean. Maybe Juan found out the teen hit the two kids and went after her father, and Stickley tried to stop him?"

"I don't think so." Darrell shook his head. "But there's something about Harrington. And he'd definitely have the clout to get the two parents deported." He paused and then said, "It wouldn't surprise me if Romero was involved somehow. He was definitely holding back. Maybe he was working some farm equipment and hurt Daniel and Mia somehow. And then went to Stickley..." He dropped off.

Now Erin was shaking her head. "I picked up the vibe from Romero, but remember Luis told us he was injured and can't work in the fields."

For a few minutes, neither spoke. Then Darrell said, "Mrs. Morales did say something about an accident, but that doesn't make much sense. I mean, ag accidents aren't that uncommon. Remember the article said farm workers have one of the highest rates of job injuries of any profession."

"But these were kids, not really farm workers," Erin said.

"Still. My guess is for these families, the migrant farm workers, injuries on the job are not uncommon. I mean, I can't see Harrington and Stickley putting in the most up-to-date safety provisions, can you? And even kids might get hurt sometimes. It's sad, tragic even, but there has to be more to the story."

"More?"

"Yeah, if it was only an *accident*, why go to the trouble of deporting the parents? What's the big deal?" When Erin started to shake her head, he continued, "If it was merely an accident, what unfinished business do Daniel and Mia want my help with?"

Erin leaned back in her chair. "Unfinished business?"

Darrell nodded hard. "Yeah, like Hank and Amy. Both of those ghosts needed my help to conclude their unfinished business."

"You mean, bring their murderers to justice?"

"Yeah, that was *their* unfinished business. There has to be something like that for Daniel and Mia." His finger stabbed at the painting lying on the table but didn't touch it. "But with an accident, I don't know what that is. It doesn't sound like anyone murdered them…I mean like with Hank or Amy."

"That makes sense," Erin said.

"Besides, I haven't a clue where we would go next. There's nothing in the police file that could help us. You and I couldn't find anything in the newspapers. No mention of any hit-and-run or any farm accidents that could have involved the kids." He stared across the table at his wife. "Do you have any idea on what to do or who to talk to if—and that's a big *if*—we would pursue this?"

Erin hesitated and then shook her head. "I don't know, but it doesn't feel right to abandon those kids."

"I know." Darrell let out a big sigh. "Maybe the universe is trying to tell us—"

The house phone rang, its bleating loud in the

contained space of the kitchen.

Both Darrell and Erin's gaze went to the white phone hanging on the wall next to the fridge, its curling cord dangling almost to the floor.

"Who would be calling?" Erin asked.

Ring.

"Who did you give this number to?" Darrell asked in reply.

"No one. We called our parents on your cell, right? Bonnie, maybe?"

Ring.

Darrell's paranoia started to kick in. "The Harringtons knew where to deliver the flowers. Wouldn't be that hard to get the number." He looked from the large floral bouquet to the ringing phone and made a decision. He hustled over. "Hello?" he called into the receiver.

"Mr. Henshaw? This is Luis. I hope I not calling too early."

Darrell shook his head for Erin's benefit. "Oh hi, Luis," he said aloud. "No, we're both up. Is everything okay? How's the shoulder?"

Getting up from the table, she came over to join Darrell. He held the phone sideways so she could hear the voice coming out of the receiver. "Good morning, Luis," she said, her voice bright.

"Halo, Mrs. Henshaw," the young Latino replied, the smile coming across the line. "I okay. Shoulder hurts some, but not bad."

Darrell said, "Saw you came and got the truck yesterday. Can we help with something?"

Luis said, "Do you have time to meet? If you have plans—"

Erin answered first. "We'd be glad to see you. It'll give me a chance to check out your dressing. Need our help with something?"

"No," Luis blurted, excitement obvious in the single word. "Oh, I mean fine with the bandage. But I no need your help. *I* help you."

Darrell asked, "What do you mean, help us?"

"I think I may have information about your...ghosts." He uttered the final word in a whisper.

Chapter 39

Maybe he *knows something*

Luis' call moved them off the dime.

Darrell hadn't changed his mind, but he wanted to hear what Luis had to say. He was still conflicted, the weight of abandoning those two kids eating at him.

They both got dressed quickly, and he drove into town and pulled into a packed parking lot at Grannie's Restaurant. The line of hungry patrons snaked out the door, but when Darrell and Erin stepped up, they heard, "Mr. and Mrs. Henshaw!"

The young Latino led them through the line and to a red-topped booth. He wore sneakers without socks, a pair of worn jeans, and a plain white tee shirt. And a white sling for the arm of the injured shoulder. Face beaming, Luis slid into one side, good hand balancing on the table and skinny legs scuttling into the space beneath. Darrell and Erin eased in opposite, gazes roaming around the diner. The Christmas tree table tents had been swapped for blue and gold ones picturing an exploding bottle of champagne bearing the words HAPPY 2000! The dancing Santa figurine next to the cash register had been replaced with a diapered baby doll complete with black top hat bearing the words HAPPY NEW YEAR in large white letters.

"The shoulder doesn't hurt too bad?" Erin asked,

her left hand pointing to Luis' right arm wrapped in a sling.

The young man shook his head, grinning. "I big hero at home. Not too bad." He used his left to lift the injured limb. "I keep it like this, like you say."

Erin reached across the narrow table and fingered the bulge under the tee Luis wore. "Looks okay. I'll check it outside when we're done eating. I brought a fresh bandage if you need it."

The waitress came, and they all ordered, Darrell making it clear he'd pay. When the server left, scribbling quickly on a small order pad, Erin spoke quietly. "We're really sorry about what happened. About your shoulder." She pointed to the sling. "We had no idea we'd put you in danger."

Darrell reached into his wallet and pulled out some bills. "Here's another twenty-five dollars." He slid the money across the red Formica.

Luis looked up, confusion in his brown eyes. "But you already pay me. Thirty dollars Tuesday, more than we agree." He stared at the bills sitting on the table. "And you pay for hospital."

Erin reached across again and set a gentle hand on the arm in the sling. "We got you involved in all this and got you injured. Besides, we figured you could use the money."

Darrell added, "Sometimes this ghost thing—" He looked around to see if anyone was listening and didn't catch any eavesdroppers. His gaze returned to the table, and he noticed his placemat was crooked. He straightened it, taking time to align the bottom of the paper along the edge of the tabletop. When he brought his eyes back up, he saw the other two watching him, and he stopped. "This ghost thing can become dangerous. We certainly didn't want you to get hurt." He shook his head. "That's all we've been discussing." He wondered if he should share Harrington's warning and decided not to. "That's why we've decided to let it go."

Erin's head jerked toward him. "We did?" she asked, her voice incredulous. "When did *we* decide this?"

Darrell met her hard gaze. "Right now. Sitting here, looking at your injuries, both of you." He pointed to the two bandaged arms.

Luis shook his head hard. "Mr. Henshaw, you can't—"

He stopped midsentence, interrupted by the server bearing a very full aluminum tray. The waitress set the plates down, getting each one correct from memory, Darrell's french toast and bacon, Erin's scrambled eggs, and Luis' fried chicken and waffles. No one spoke as she worked, the savory aroma floating up from the dishes. She refilled coffees, checked to make sure everything was okay, and backed away.

Before she left, Luis was already digging into his dish, slathering the waffle with pungent maple syrup, then taking a large bite of the fried chicken. Darrell watched their companion eating, the juice from the large breast dripping down the side of his mouth and figured the young man couldn't afford a breakfast like this very often. He joined him. Darrell cut his soft, buttery french toast into pieces, each slice becoming six nearly flawless rectangles, perfect for dipping in the circular pool of syrup he created on the edge of his plate. Bite after bite, he ate slowly, trying to give Luis time to satisfy his hunger. Once or twice, his eyes met Erin's, and he saw her questioning glance, but she didn't say any more.

Like their first visit to the restaurant, everything was delicious, and after only a few minutes, all three were shoving nearly empty plates to the center of the booth table. Besides small pools of amber liquid, the only things remaining on the plates were the skeletons of the chicken pieces and a stray green sprig of parsley. The server must've been watching because she appeared at the table and cleared the dishes with efficiency and a broad smile.

When she left, Luis grinned across the booth. "Thank you, Mr. Henshaw. You take good care of me."

Looking at the sling lying on the tabletop, Darrell swallowed a lump in his throat. "I'm not so sure about that." He pointed with his coffee cup. "Like I was saying, I think we need to give this ghost thing a rest. At least for a while." He could feel Erin's gaze boring a hole in him.

"I no think so." Luis used his good arm to hold up a tentative hand. "Think you need to hear something first." Darrell could see the excitement in the young man's face, his eyes wide and a small smile tugging at the corners of his mouth.

Darrell did a quick visual sweep of the diner and leaned in. Erin did the same.

"Last night a friend call. At home. He heard about *accident*." He lifted his sling slightly and rested it again on the table. "He live at Settlement and heard we ask questions. About Sanchez kids."

Darrell and Erin exchanged another glance, and she asked in a soft voice, "What's your friend's name?"

Without hesitation, Luis said, "José. José Guzman. José and me go to school together. Anyway, he say he heard we were asking questions about Daniel and Mia." His gaze went from Erin to Darrell. "He said he know something about the kids, about what happened to them."

Darrell frowned. "Why didn't he come see you when we were there at the Settlement?"

Luis shook his head hard, side to side. "He wasn't there. He only got back last night. He say he know more about kids."

Both Darrell and Erin waited, then finally Darrell blurted out, "What'd he tell you?"

"No." The young Latino shook his head again. "He say he only tell me in person. Not over the phone. He thinks someone listening."

Now Darrell shook his head. "We can't get you more involved. We can't take the chance. It could be dangerous."

Erin spoke again, her voice the essence of calm. "We're very grateful for your help, but we don't want to take a chance something else might happen to you. Something worse than a flesh wound." She pointed to his shoulder. "Could you call your friend and ask him to meet with us? Darrell and I will go back to the Settlement and see him." She glanced over at Darrell, who nodded.

"He won't." Luis frowned and shook his head again. "He no trust gringos. He said he only tell me. Besides he won't talk at Settlement. He say too many eyes and ears there."

"Where does he want to meet?" Darrell asked.

"At special place him and me know. A place we

used to go when we were in high school. In next county, Iberia."

Darrell looked from Luis to Erin, who pursed her lips. He asked, "How far is it? How long will it take to get to this place?"

"About an hour, I think."

Erin asked quietly, "You already told your friend you'd meet him, didn't you?"

Luis' face broke out into a broad smile. "*Sí.*"

"When?" Darrell asked.

Luis stared above the counter and found the clock. "In about an hour."

Chapter 40

Suffer the little children still?

A few minutes later, Darrell paid the bill, and they hustled out to the parking lot. Luis tried to insist he'd go alone, but Darrell and Erin wouldn't have it. They maintained they'd all go together in Darrell's new rental.

Even though time was tight, Erin demanded to check Luis' wound first. She had the young Latino sit in the back seat of the SUV, and she examined his shoulder, pulling back the short sleeve on the tee and undoing the dressing. Satisfied, she applied some salve and covered the area with a fresh bandage. Standing next to her, Darrell looked down at their companion and saw the imprint of his ribs under the skin. Luis looked incredibly thin.

"At least we can be sure there's no infection," she declared when she was finished.

Darrell and Erin got in, and he drove out of the parking lot into the traffic on US 19. By the time he was stopped at the first light, Erin had the map out and with Luis' help had found the place where this José said he'd be waiting. Using the map, she guided Darrell onto FL 44 and then to the interstate north to get to Iberia County.

His entire body tense, Darrell checked the rearview

mirror every few miles. He told himself it wouldn't do any good. Two days ago, someone shot at them with a rifle from who knows how far away. Still, his eyes kept darting to the mirror and back to the road. He didn't see anything, but that didn't make him relax.

Erin must've have sensed his apprehension—or maybe she felt it as well—because she turned to talk with Luis. To break the tension probably. "Tell us about this guy you're meeting. Your friend José."

Luis shrugged. "I no say we friends. Not exactly. We used to be. We went to high school together. He same age, but we not the same. He wanted to stay in fields. He in charge of small crew. He responsible for numbers."

"Numbers?" Erin asked. "Numbers of what?"

"He must make sure crew picks number of crops…blueberry, strawberry, even oranges. Responsible to the supervisor, to Stickley." Luis shifted on the seat, leaning forward to put his good arm on the back of the bucket seat. "He stay, and I go, so we different."

Darrell's gaze went from the rearview to check on Luis, then back to the road ahead. "But he heard you were asking about the Sanchez kids and called to tell you something? Why'd he do that? If he's not your friend?"

Luis said, "José said he care about kids." He paused, then added, "Maybe he trust me 'cause his family and mine come from same town in Mexico. And he wants money. Twenty dollars."

Erin said, "We'll take care of that."

Using the map, Erin got them to the correct exit and turned it over to Luis to navigate from there. Once off the main artery, he had Darrell turn onto some winding back roads, the asphalt snaking through towering trees and across bridges over meandering creeks. Luis now leaned fully forward, stretching the seatbelt to the max and scanning the oncoming geography through the windshield. Twice, just before Darrell passed a turnoff or intersection, Luis recognized a sign or landmark and hollered to take a left or right, apologizing afterward.

"I haven't been here for long time," Luis said by way of explanation.

"Why do you think José chose this place to meet?" Erin asked.

"This was place he and I found when we were kids. Sometimes we come here to escape...and fish." He grinned. "And drink. We ride here on our bikes."

As Darrell tried to picture where they traveled, he realized even though they had maneuvered through some slow hairpin turns and even onto a few unnamed back roads, they weren't all that far from the Settlement. They simply came around the back way. He'd guess maybe fifteen minutes by car from the Settlement, if you knew the route, twice that by bike. And the boys may have known some back paths to cut through the woods.

As they traveled farther on the back roads, the timbers that bordered both sides of the asphalt, mostly towering palms, pine, and other evergreens, grew thicker. The babbling of a waterway beyond the woodlands became louder. Coming out of another S bend, he slowly drove up a rise and came to the mouth of a large covered bridge.

"Stop," Luis hollered. "This it."

Darrell hit the brakes and pulled the car onto the gravel shoulder, the stones crunching under the tires. Luis had the door open before Darrell got the car in park.

Throwing open the front door, Darrell hurried after. "Wait. I'll go with you."

Luis turned and raised his good hand, the sling swinging round in the motion. "No. José say he only talk to me. No gringos."

"Okay, then, here's the money." Darrell pulled two tens out of his wallet and thrust them at the young Latino.

Luis took the money, turned back, and trudged up the rise toward the bridge. Darrell watched as he approached the ancient wooden structure, his gaze checking all around. "José?" Luis called in a strained whisper. "José?"

"You see anyone?" Erin called.

Standing outside his open car door, Darrell watched Luis head toward the bridge, his blue jeans and white shirt a dramatic contrast against the background of the trees and high weeds bordering the wooden structure. He turned and whispered, "No one so far," and then returned to his surveillance of the bridge. In those few seconds, Luis disappeared. Darrell's glance darted up and down the deserted road. No one and no Luis.

Darrell scurried up the hill, following Luis' path and passed the overgrown trees and the wall of large rocks and boulders that had been assembled at the end of the bridge. He stepped in front of the wooden bridge and, standing at the tall mouth, scanned the length. Nothing. No Luis. The wooden structure ran for two hundred feet, its weathered crossbeams creating large x's along both sides. A red-shingled roof shone in the late morning sun that broke through an opening in the thick foliage. Darrell took a step onto the bridge roadway, huge, hewn timbers running crossways. He stopped.

He stepped back out, ready to call to Erin to have her join the search, when he heard something. Beneath the wooden structure, two hushed voices spoke in rapid Spanish, the sounds barely carrying above the gurgle of the water rushing somewhere close by. Darrell retreated out of the covered bridge and signaled to Erin to stay put. She got the message and sat back on the seat, her legs out the open door.

Darrell stood and listened. He didn't understand the words spoken but could tell much by the cadence and tone. José—he could make out two distinct voices—was agitated and angry even. He heard Luis give what must've been entreaties to settle his companion down. They may have worked because José sounded less distressed, though still tense. Darrell would recognize that tone in any language.

It was killing him to stand there and do nothing. Darrell was used to being the one doing something. Making things happen, even when that hadn't always turned out well. And he knew Erin would not be happy to simply sit and wait.

He leaned in, listening more intently, trying to decide if he needed to scuttle around the rocks and join the two Latinos beneath the bridge. He tried to detect any danger, but Luis' voice remained cool and relaxed—and he still had no idea of the actual meaning of the words spoken. In fact, Luis was doing most of the talking with José giving the occasional response, usually only a few words uttered in quick Spanish.

Luis had made it clear José would *not* talk to any gringos and said he had good reason not to trust white guys. Still, his desire to protect their new Latino friend, to not let anything more happen to Luis almost overpowered Darrell's caution. Three minutes passed, the Spanish exchanges continued, sometimes in slightly raised voices, usually hushed. Darrell could almost picture the two young men gesturing wildly and whispering in loud voices. He checked his watch. Five minutes. He listened and again didn't hear anything. That raised the hairs on his neck.

Glancing back at the car, his gaze met Erin's, and her eyes implored him. Even without her saying a word, he knew she was worried for Luis as well—and wanted Darrell to do something. He strained and continued listening, leaning toward the tumbled boulders. He checked his watch again. Eight minutes. He looked back to the car and saw Erin raise both hands in the air. He made a decision.

He stepped over to the boulders and put one foot on them when he heard the sound of someone coming up the creek bank. Darrell hurried and took a step or two back toward the car, waiting to see who emerged. He watched a brown hand come up over the highest boulder followed by the white sling being set atop the rock. Then Luis' brown face, bright with exertion, shone above the stack of rocks, and he stepped onto the pile and came over to Darrell.

"Everything all right?" Darrell asked as they walked over to the rental. Erin stood to join them.

"I fine," Luis said, glancing around. Darrell and

Erin followed his lead and did the same. "Let's get out of here." He pointed toward the car.

Darrell got the message and hustled everyone back into the car. Starting up the engine, he executed a one-eighty and had the car heading back the way they came before anyone said a word.

"Sounded like a heated exchange down there," Darrell said.

"José not happy you came with me. He no trust any gringos. He wanted to know why gringos care what happen to two Mexican kids?"

"What'd you'd tell him?" Darrell asked, turning in his seat to glance at the young man.

"This is our turn. Left here," Luis said. "I tried same story you told me about history research." He shook his head. "José didn't believe it. Finally, I ask him to tell me what he knew and, after arguing, he did. Then I pay him money."

Seeing a wide spot in the road ahead, Darrell pulled the SUV over so he could concentrate on what Luis had to say. The thick copse of trees on both sides of the road shrouded them, cutting off the sunlight again. No other cars passed them going either way. It looked safe enough.

Putting the car in park, he glanced into the back seat and asked, "Why all the cloak and dagger?"

"Cloak and digger?" Luis asked.

Erin said, "He means the secrecy. Why didn't we simply meet him at the Settlement?"

Luis looked around the car, scanning the windows on all sides. "José say Harrington threaten. Anyone talking about the Sanchez kids deported."

"Jeez," Erin said, letting it set. She glanced at

Darrell. "Maybe that explains how Romero acted. Why he was holding back." She turned back to Luis. "Okay. What did he tell you? About the kids?"

Luis faced her. "He say what Mrs. Morales say, only he say more. José say Daniel and Mia playing in ditch and got hurt bad in accident when equipment Stickley driving run over their legs."

"Oh my gosh," Erin gasped.

Luis continued, "José say Daniel and Mia's father working in the fields with him when they all found out. He say Juan grab someone's truck and drive to where accident happen on Ontario Road."

Darrell looked across at Erin, and she nodded. It was the same road where Jared had painted the kids. Maybe even the same afternoon.

"Anyway, José say kids not there, but he heard Juan went after Tom Stickley and started beating on him. It took three men to pull him off. Stickley called sheriff, and they come and arrest Juan. A few days later, he got deported along with his wife Maria."

Darrell's voice was so tight it sounded strangled. "Then what happened? What happened to Daniel and Mia? Did they go to the hospital?"

Luis' eyes searched Darrell and Erin, both turned in the seat to face him. "José say something strange. *Los niños todavía están en Stickleys.*"

Darrell snapped, "What does that mean?"

Luis swallowed. "He say Daniel and Mia never left plantation. He say they still at Stickley's."

Chapter 41

To be or not to be...dead

For a while no one spoke, the area around them so quiet Darrell could hear the gurgle of the creek deep inside the woods.

Erin repeated softly, "They never left the plantation? They're still at Stickley's? What does that mean?" She jerked her glance from Luis to Darrell. "They're alive someplace? At Stickley's?"

Darrell shook his head. It didn't make any sense. He still didn't get how the whole sensitive thing worked...with the ghosts. He wasn't sure he'd ever figure it all out. But before, he only got visits from those who were...well, dead. His uncle. Hank. Amy and the others at Cape May.

His mind raced to recall what Natalia had said, her exact words. *You vill receive two visitors from the other side.*

Visitors from *the other side*. Didn't that mean they were, had to be...dead? Wasn't that why the kids could contact him?

Luis broke his concentration. "Sorry, I no know what it mean. That is all José tell me. He just say, *Los niños nunca abandonaron la plantación."*

"What?" Erin asked.

"Oh, sorry," Luis said. "He say, kids never left the

285

plantation. That all he say. When I tried to get him to, to…explain more, he say he could not. Said he say too much already."

Erin said quietly, her voice almost wistful, "Could the kids be alive all this time? Somewhere at Stickley's place?" She turned in her seat and faced Darrell. "Maybe we're supposed to find them…alive." The last word came out in a whisper.

Darrell could read the excitement in his wife's eyes and didn't want to crush it, but he thought—no, in his bones, he knew—it was a false hope. He didn't want to get her hopes up only to be devastated later by the cruel reality. He had seen the two kids, Daniel and Mia, and each time they or their images disappeared. First at the Simmons place, then at Three Sisters, then at Fort Gulf Island Beach. Not to mention the damn painting *that came alive*. Those were all consistent with what he'd experienced before. The apparitions with Hank. And Amy and the others at Cape May. And they were all *definitely* dead.

Then he remembered the pictures. The three snapshots that each captured an image of the two young Hispanic kids, large, wide eyes beseeching the camera. He realized something was different about the snapshots. First, the impression of the kids captured on the film didn't disappear or dissolve the way the other images of ghosts had. Like the image of Hank on the videotape. *And* Erin could see the two kids as clearly as he. He and Erin had gotten the photos out and checked several times, last night even, and she could clearly see the two brown-haired kids huddled together in each of the pictures. Did that mean something? Hell, he had no idea.

"Let's not get our hopes up." He stared at his wife, seeing the spark of anticipation in her eyes. "How could they be alive all this time and no one see them or hear them?"

"Well." Erin looked down, and then her gaze came up. "Weren't there several buildings on Stickley's place? Maybe they have them stashed in one of those. Uh, maybe holding them prisoner or something?" Her words got more desperate as she went on.

Darrell reached across the seat and took Erin's good left hand in his right. "Why would they do such a thing? Keep them there and not tell anyone? They'd have to keep them fed and everything. Do you really see Tom Stickley as the paternal type?"

"No. I don't know." Erin shook her head and looked up at Darrell again. "Maybe Helen and Tom Stickley wanted kids and couldn't have them...so they had the parents deported and kept Daniel and Mia."

Darrell paused a bit before continuing. Erin wasn't going to like it. "I'd love to think the kids could still be alive too. But—"

"But what?" Erin asked, her eyebrows arching.

Darrell glanced away and then met her gaze. "Natalia said I'd have 'two visitors from the other side.' "

"Damn Natalia!" Erin blurted out. "Maybe that crazy medium is simply wrong this time."

"Medium?" Luis asked.

Darrell glanced at the young man in the back seat. "Yeah, before we came down here, this medium told me I'd have two visitors—her word for ghosts—when we were here." He nodded. "She helped make some sense of some ghost appearances before."

He took a slow breath and met his wife's stern stare. "I'd like to think Natalia could be wrong in this case. Hell, I didn't want her to be right about *any* ghosts on our honeymoon." He shook his head. "Besides, I simply can't picture Tom Stickley wanting to raise, um…" He tried to decide if he should utter Stickley's slur but couldn't figure out how else to say it. "See him raising two 'wetback' kids…like he called them. Can you?" Then to Luis, "Sorry, man."

"Okay. I know you only repeat what that man say," Luis said.

Erin hesitated, then shook her head. "I've got to admit it's pretty hard to imagine." She turned to the back. "You're sure José said they never left the plantation?"

Luis said, "I sure he say that. *Los niños nunca abandonaron la plantación.* I not sure what he mean."

Erin tried again. "Yeah, but if they're somewhere on Stickley's property, that might explain why they don't want anyone asking questions about the kids."

"Maybe," Darrell conceded.

Erin rushed on. "I mean if they simply died in an accident, it wouldn't be that big a deal. Isn't that what you said? A tragedy, but an accident. From what you read, farm accidents are common, right?" She didn't give Darrell time to respond. "But if the Stickleys held them, kept them prisoner or something, wouldn't that explain the secrecy and the threats?"

Darrell said, "I can't think of any reason he would do that. But you're right. There has to be more than merely some farm accident, but I'm not sure what it is."

"But it *could* be the two kids are alive and waiting for us to rescue them," Erin pleaded.

Darrell was torn between wanting what his wife wanted and what he feared—the kids were just as dead as Hank or Amy had been. If José was right and Daniel and Mia never left the plantation, then their bodies were probably buried somewhere there. He dreaded his job was *not* to find and rescue two young Hispanic kids, but to discover their corpses, uncover what really happened to them, and make those responsible pay.

Still, he didn't want to extinguish the smallest bit of hope Erin clung to. At least, not yet.

Luis spoke up. "From what José say, it is not good for Daniel and Mia, no matter what." He looked from Erin to Darrell. "Some things worse than dying."

For a few minutes, no one spoke in the car, the silence oppressive and worrisome. The sun broke through the clouds and sent a ray through the green canopy, illuminating Erin's side of the car. Darrell wondered if it were a sign. He glanced over at her, red hair glowing in the sunlight. "Well, José accomplished one thing for us. If there's any chance to help Mia and Daniel, we can't abandon them now."

"Good." Erin nodded twice. "I agree."

"So what we going to do?" Luis asked from the back seat.

"One way or the other, the answers are at the Stickleys'. I'm almost sure." Darrell put the car in drive again and pulled back onto the asphalt, looking both ways. Still no traffic coming in either direction. "But before I go back there, I need to be prepared."

Chapter 42

Girding for battle

Darrell's first instinct was to get Luis home and out of trouble. Not to mention his urge to keep Erin from any harm. Keeping her safe meant taking her back to the Simmons place in Crystal River. He couldn't *see* trouble coming, but he sensed it was there barreling toward them. He didn't feel the prickle on his neck. Not yet. But he knew things were going to get dicey.

When he went there, neither would even consider it.

"My place is with you," Erin declared.

Luis said, "I not afraid. And I want to find what happen to kids."

It would consume almost three hours to take them both back, drop them off, and return. With the hours slipping away and only two days till they had to board their flight back to Maryland, Darrell knew he didn't have time to spare. So instead they all headed into Dixon to grab a bite to eat, pick up a few things, and plan. While his cellphone had a signal there, he called Deputy Atwater. He didn't get the officer and left a message, saying they'd gotten a lead on what happened to the two Hispanic kids, and they were headed back to Stickley's at the Harrington Plantation to check it out. With what Atwater had told him about the bullets,

Darrell hoped the deputy would read between the lines. He prayed he wouldn't need the cop, but seeing the fresh bandages on both Erin and Luis, he decided he had better have some backup.

On the trip from Dixon back to the farm, he watched as the sky began to darken, the clouds thickening in various shades of silver and gray, the change quite noticeable. Every day they'd spent in Florida the past two weeks had been bright, with the sun strong against a vast azure sky. A few times, a couple of cirrus clouds had skittered across the heavens and then disappeared. There had even been two early morning showers, which were over almost before they started. But this sky looked different. Though the clouds hadn't blotted out the sun yet, they were filling the sky and casting immense shadows on the land below. Darrell hoped the change in the weather was not a grave omen.

When he arrived at the corner of Cool Springs and Six Steppes again, he stared down the gravel road. Though he couldn't see it yet, he knew the supervisor's place lay around the bend on the dusty road. He stopped the car and glanced both ways but saw no traffic coming in either direction on Cool Springs.

Darrell pointed to the pitted and bumpy track ahead. "No matter where we park out here, anyone coming up Six Steppes will see our car."

"If you ride in slow like, they might not hear us." Erin said. "We could park the car behind one of the outbuildings near the house. It'd be out of sight."

"As good a plan as any." Darrell rolled the SUV onto the gravel road and proceeded slowly, trying to kick up as little dust tail as possible.

"What about this?" Luis held up the bag from the diner.

"We'll need that in a minute," Darrell said.

When he drove up to the house, he saw no movement. Keeping his pace measured, he edged around the small, scraggy yard and turned right onto the hard-packed earth. Grateful for the all-wheel drive, he steered the SUV slowly around a large metal shed, the stiff suspension bouncing on the uneven ground. When he was sure the car was out of sight from the driveway and the house, he stopped.

He put the car in park but decided to leave the keys in the ignition. If they had to get out in a hurry, it might save a few seconds. Turning in his seat, he said, "Now hand me the doggy bag from the diner."

Using his good hand, Luis lifted the sack over the seat back, and Darrell took it. Back at the diner where they grabbed lunch, Darrell had noticed the heading on the menu, "We make all our burgers by hand." That gave him an inspiration. He asked for four half-pound burgers to go—raw. When the server looked at him funny, he simply held up his own burger and said, "Like these so much, I'm going to grill up a few at home tonight."

He extracted the package enclosed in butcher paper and unwrapped it. Using one hand, he formed the four loose burgers into one round, red mass.

He pointed to the white plastic bag with the "Dixon Drugs" logo at Erin's feet. "Now I need the sleeping pills we bought."

"Let me do that. We don't want to kill the poor thing, only knock him out." Taking out a black box marked "Sleep-Eaze," she tore open the cellophane and pulled out the bottle. She read the label and then scrunched closed one eye. She dumped out a few of the green capsules and stuffed them one at a time into the meat. "That ought to do it...without really hurting the dog."

She handed Darrell back the large ball of ground beef, and he wrapped it in the paper again then stuffed it back into the bag. From the Dixon Drug bag, he took out a container of wipes, pulling out two for himself and handing one to Erin. He took his time cleaning his hands, working to remove even the tiniest remnants of beef from his fingernails. This time it was more than OCD. They couldn't have the dog distracted with the smell of beef on their hands. Satisfied his fingers were free of the ground beef, he extracted two more wipes and repeated the entire process again, double cleaning his fingers, then stuffing the used sheets back into the drug store sack. Erin, using only the one sheet, finished well before Darrell but waited patiently for him to complete his ritual.

Luis had observed the whole thing from the back seat. "I curious when you ask server for extra burgers." He looked from Darrell to Erin. "Stickley has guard dog?"

Erin said, "A particularly mean one." She pointed to the bag containing the meat. "But hopefully that ought to take care of him."

"Let's do this." Darrell got out, holding the paper bag from the diner. Once out of the car, he took his cell phone out of his pocket and flipped it open. No signal, again. He tossed the useless phone on the front seat and headed out. He led them around the back of the metal structure, which, from the size of it, must have been a barn of some kind. As they walked around it, he realized it was larger than he first thought, running almost two hundred feet long and about half that in width. Coming to an entry door, he opened it and stepped inside. It was almost completely dark. By the time his eyes adjusted, Luis and Erin stood beside him. He could make out the darkened silhouettes of large, hulking machinery, but he felt nothing, no sensations.

"Daniel? Mia?" Erin got out in a hoarse whisper and drew no response.

They all retreated out of the barn and came around the front and stopped. From here, they had a clear view of the house. There were no cars parked behind, where they'd seen them on their last visit.

When they sketched out the plan together, huddled in the back booth at the diner, all three talking in hushed voices, Darrell explained he believed the key to the whole thing was the accident. If he could find some specifics about the accident, some record for the insurance, or something that would tie to the kids, they *might* have something to go on. And he was pretty sure any records were at the supervisor's home. If Helen Stickley were home, Erin thought she *might* be able to get through to her. But they didn't want to run into Tom Stickley, who Darrell hoped would be working with the migrants in the fields. He stared across at the empty driveway. Maybe they were in luck.

As they came around the shelter of the building and emerged into the open space, the smells hit him again, carried on a breeze that had picked up. The distinctive odor of fertilizer and the pungent stench of excrement filled the air as dust clouds of dirt were blown at them. Using his arm to shield his eyes, Darrell scanned the straggly yard but didn't see the mongrel. Two scrawny chickens walked among the dirt and grass, occasionally pecking the ground, their feathers ruffled by the wind. He stepped across the gravel path toward the house, Erin and Luis close behind, when the sensation struck again. The prickle on his neck erupted so strongly Darrell stopped in his tracks and glanced around, searching for…something?

His gaze landed on another metal building off to their right, this one about half the size of the one they parked the car behind. He turned to Luis. "Could you go check out that building? See if anyone is in there?" He didn't have to say, "See if the kids were in the outbuilding."

Luis took off across the space, his one arm in the sling at his side. As Darrell and Erin watched, he opened the door using his left arm, stepped inside, and a minute later, came out shaking his head.

Darrell kept scanning, watching for the dog…and anything else. Still no sign of Harley, the huge German Shepherd mix. The sensation didn't let up. He held his breath and tried not to inhale the strong odors. Beyond the second outbuilding lay the mound he'd seen before, dirt piled about ten feet high and running about the length of a football field. As he examined the pile, he realized his earlier assumption about it being some sort of experimental crop patch had to be wrong. One section of the mound, mostly on the end of the pile closer to the house, looked fresher, as if the soil had been added more recently. There was little growth in this front section, only small tufts of wild grasses and weeds sprouting. Could this be some kind of soil hauled in and used where they needed it? The portion farther away, the last twenty feet or so, looked older, the weeds and sporadic growth taller, popping through the surface.

When Luis joined them, Darrell led the three off the gravel path onto the dusty yard that surrounded the dilapidated house. As soon as they set foot onto the yard, the dog shot from around the other side of the house, where he was dozing probably. The chickens took flight briefly to get out of the dog's path. The animal came straight at Darrell, snarling and snapping. Seeing how close they'd gotten to the house, he realized they were no longer outside the length of the rope attached to the mutt's collar.

"Get back. Hurry!" he yelled and took several rushed steps away, almost back to the gravel drive. Like before, the rope pulled taut, and the guard dog was jerked to an abrupt stop only a few feet away from them. The beast's jaws opened and closed, white teeth sharp and menacing and saliva dripping onto the ground. Darrell tried to talk, forcing some fake calm in his shaky voice. "Hey, Harley. I brought something for you." He held it up and let it sway away from his body.

The hound sniffed at the bag in Darrell's hand and snarled again, an ugly, vicious sound.

"Mr. Henshaw?" Luis said, his voice shaky.

"It's okay, Luis. He can't get to us," Darrell said, trying to convey some semblance of composure.

Luis pointed to the frayed rope the dog tugged on, pulling and pawing, trying to get to the intruders. "It don't look like it hold him for long."

"I got this," Darrell said, sounding more confident than he felt. He waved the bag again and saw the dog's nose come up. "Yeah, you smell it, don't you?"

The dog barked, a sharp, angry growl. Darrell

knew if anyone were home, they would've heard. Making sure the dog was watching, he threw the bag in a long arc, and it landed on the other side of the yard. The mongrel took off in a shot and covered the ground in less than two seconds. In another few seconds, he tore the bag and paper with his teeth and began gulping at the meat.

No one moved. Darrell's gaze went from the dog, snout down, devouring the beef, to the front door of the dwelling. He thought any minute the door would open and someone, Tom or Helen, would step onto the porch, gun in hand. But the door remained closed. No one came out. He glanced back at the dog who looked like he had almost finished wolfing down the meat. While he ate, Harley's black eyes came up and looked toward where they stood, as if checking to be sure they hadn't intruded on his domain. None of them moved. When the dog finished, he used his front paws to hold down the now shredded paper so he could lick the last of the hamburger off it.

The three of them stood there, watching, and Erin exchanged a worried glance with Darrell.

Luis uttered, "Mr. Henshaw!" He pointed to the dog, who had risen and started across the yard again toward them, a little slower this time.

Darrell managed, "The bottle said the pills were the fastest working on the market." He stared at the approaching dog and gulped. The dog took a few more steps and seemed to be studying them. And still looked hungry.

The animal kept coming slowly, black eyes focused on the three intruders, until the rope yanked him to a stop again. Jerking his snout back and forth, he looked back along the cord and then at the three of them. Darrell took another step backward, closer to the outbuilding, and had Erin and Luis do the same. He was ready to bolt inside the shed if they needed to, along with Erin and Luis.

Harley uttered a low, guttural growl.

His eyes fixed on the dog, Luis whispered, "What we do now, Mr. Henshaw?"

Chapter 43

Hardly what they expected

Darrell stared at the mongrel, searching for any signs the drugs were working. Seeing Erin shift next to him, he shot an anxious glance her way. He had no idea what he'd do if the pills didn't incapacitate the dog. They needed to get inside the house. The animal stood on all fours and glared at them, black eyes blazing and posture rigid, all four legs primed to spring. Studying the mutt, Darrell had the eerie feeling the dog knew what he'd done.

"You sure you gave him enough?" Darrell said out of the side of his mouth without taking his eyes off the guard dog.

She said, with a lump in her throat, "I think so. I guessed his weight and put in about twice what it recommended. Should be plenty to knock him out but not enough to do any real damage."

The hound backed up a step or two and paced back and forth, tugging on the frayed rope. His stride was more deliberate than hurried, back and forth, back and forth, always keeping the three intruders in his sight. Then, as Darrell watched, the dog's pace slowed a bit, a change so subtle Darrell wasn't certain he detected any at first. Harley stopped, eyes still on Darrell, and lowered his back legs. In a few seconds, his front legs trembled a bit and collapsed, the animal crumpling onto the ground.

For a few seconds, no one moved. Then Darrell took three tentative steps forward and stood over the dog. Beneath him, Harley lay in a slumbering heap, eyes closed, chest moving rhythmically in and out. Erin and Luis came to join him, both studying the animal sprawled in the dirt.

Darrell turned. "It's okay. Let's go, but watch where you step. There's a lot of dog crap on the ground."

The three proceeded across the small yard toward the front door, keeping their gaze on the ground to gauge where to step next. Darrell tried to rein in his compulsion, staying focused on why they were there. When they got to the small slab porch, Darrell stepped up and tried the handle. It turned and opened. He reasoned the Stickleys had few visitors and they figured Harley would handle any unwanted guests. Turning to Luis, he said, "Could you pick up the remnants of the bag from the diner? No reason to advertise we were here if we don't have to."

Luis said, "I can do that."

Darrell continued, "How about you wait out here and warn us if anyone is coming? Or if Harley starts to wake up."

The young Hispanic gave a little salute. "Got it, Mr. Henshaw."

"Maybe we can simply go with Darrell, hey?"

"Sure, Mr. Henshaw, er, Darrell." Luis threaded his way back across the yard.

Darrell hollered at the worn wooden door, "Mrs. Stickley? Helen? It's Darrell and Erin Henshaw. We met earlier this week."

No response from inside.

Darrell nodded to his wife, pushed the front door open, and stepped inside, Erin right behind. They both stopped in the front room and took in the small house. As he scanned the interior, he was stunned by what he saw. Outside, the yard looked unkempt, with rusted tools scattered about, dog excrement dumped everywhere, and no real lawn or no sign of any garden. The siding and front door both needed attention, long past the time for repainting. But as he stared at the inside of the small house, it was as if he'd been dropped into a different world. The entire place was pristine.

No dishes were piled in the kitchen sink off to one side. Atop the small counter, a toaster and a coffee maker sat alone, their chrome exteriors sparkling clean. The kitchen appliances he could see weren't modern, but the stove top was spotless, and the clean white front of the fridge held a picture of the nativity, Mary and Joseph with Jesus resting in a manger surrounded by farm animals. Next to a back door, he spotted a rifle leaning against a corner.

The front room, the room they were in, had a comfortable sofa and a recliner, both covered in tan upholstery. The furniture appeared old, but each piece looked clean and well cared for. On each end of the couch sat a Christmas teddy bear, one with a green tee shirt and a second with a red one. Between the sofa and chair sat a wooden end table, its lower shelf holding a stack of used paperbacks of Christmas mysteries. Next to the sofa was a curio cabinet with figurines behind glass doors.

For a moment, Darrell felt like he'd entered an

OCD sanctuary. He took two slow breaths then shook his head and remembered why they were there. He said, "I'm going to check the bedrooms. I'd guess that's where they'd keep any records. You have a look around out here and let me know if you find anything."

"Will do," Erin said.

He headed down a small hallway. He opened the first door he came to on his left, which revealed a small bedroom stuffed with a queen-sized bed and two dressers and little room for anything else. Like the front room, the bedroom was well kept, bed made and three brown throw pillows arranged atop a colorful bedspread. Closing the door, he headed down the hallway. Sensing something—though not a prickle—he hurried, worrying they were running out of time.

He tried a door on the right, half expecting it to be locked, but the handle turned easily in his hand. When he swung it open, he found an office with a small wood desk and beside it a three-drawer, metal file cabinet. Unlike the rest of the house, this room was a mess. Papers strewn across the desk, half-full coffee mug to the side, a curdled tan liquid floating on top. A small bookcase sat against the wall with the volumes stacked on wooden shelves. Some books were stuffed in backward, uneven pages sticking out. Other hardcovers lay on their side, their titles reading sideways. Darrell stepped over to the bookcase, feeling the instinctive need to rearrange the books, spines out, in neat rows. Not what he was here for. He moved to the file cabinet.

None of the drawers were marked, but he found each folder inside was labeled in hand-written capitals. Unable to recognize any filing system, it took him a while to locate what he wanted. In the rear of the second drawer, he came upon a file marked INSURANCE. He flipped through the pages, mostly annual cost statements for insuring the farm equipment. The very last entry in the file was a stapled group of papers with the title INCIDENT REPORT in bold red letters across the top. He pulled it out and laid it on the desk. Scanning the bureaucratic language on the three pages, he found what he'd come to see. The date for the accident was listed as February 18, 1999, and the equipment damaged was something called a Blueberry Harvester number three. His fingers scrolling down the printed lines, Darrell read the description of the incident. "On February 18, an employee of Harrington Plantation was operating the Blueberry Harvester number three on a plot of land bordering Ontario Road. The operator did not see a downed tree trunk left in the ditch and ran part of the machine over the obstacle, damaging the tines of the harvester. As instructed by the Farmers Eco Insurance Company rep, the equipment was sent in for repair, which cost $3402.37."

That was it. He kept reading. At the bottom of the third page, he found the big red letters CLAIM DENIED FOR NON-PAYMENT. The insurance company had refused to pay...because they let the policy lapse. Had they known all this when...?

Even though he felt time closing in, could hear the clock ticking in his head, Darrell read the rest of the pages, thick with insurance jargon, but learned nothing else helpful. He whispered, "A downed tree trunk. An obstacle?" He shook his head. No mention of children hurt. Maybe he'd been wrong about this. Still, the date lined up. Even the location was near where Jared had said he'd painted Daniel and Mia. And Juan's fight with

Tom? Clearly, Stickley had been the employee operating the machine. He got that much from the sheriff's report.

Darrell had learned when it came to the ghosts there were no coincidences. Maybe what was important was what *wasn't* in the report.

He needed to show Erin and see what she thought. Looking around the office, he didn't see a copy machine, so he grabbed the report and closed the file drawer.

"Darrell, you need to see this," Erin called from the front room.

Insurance report in hand, he joined her, standing in front of the curio cabinet. She had the doors open and was examining the half dozen figurines inside. As she was about to say something, he heard a howl from outside that sounded like a coyote. He glanced at Erin, who'd obviously heard it too.

She asked, "Is that a—"

"A coyote," he finished. "Yeah, I think so. I didn't know they had coyotes in Florida." Both stared at the open window and watched as the curtain fluttered in the breeze. He turned his attention back to her. "What'd you want me to see?"

"Oh, yeah." Erin pointed to the curio cabinet. "See these figurines. Notice anything about them?"

Darrell studied the figures, each one cleaned and shining under the light in the cabinet. He noticed a tag which read "Hummel" and another with "Precious Moments." He said, "Nice. Thinking of starting a collection?"

She frowned at him. "No, silly. Look at the kind of figurines."

"I still don't see it. What?"

"They're all kids." Erin pointed to a pair closest to the edge. "Each set of figurines is a pair of little kids, a boy and a girl."

"So?" Darrell didn't understand. He simply wanted to show her the insurance report.

Erin placed one fist on her hip. "Did you see any evidence of any children around the house?"

Darrell's eyes came up. "No."

Erin started, "Well—"

"What are ya two doing in my house?" an angry Helen Stickley yelled as she came through a back door, dropping two grocery bags on the red Formica table. She reached for the rifle leaning against the corner.

Chapter 44

Things are not what they seem

Darrell watched as Helen Stickley raised the rifle and aimed it at them. The gray-black barrel looked long and deadly. The ugly gun looked to be almost longer than the woman was tall, but she had little trouble handling it. She used one hand to brush at the slim yellow housedress that wanted to bunch around her thin legs and then returned it to the rifle stock.

Erin's eyes met his, and he nodded. "We apologize, Mrs. Stickley," Erin said. "We came to see you and your husband, and when we got here, we noticed something was wrong with Harley, your dog?"

"He ain't my dog," Helen said, jerking the rifle left and right. "That ugly mutt is Tom's. Harley gives me the creeps."

"Well, anyway, when we saw something might be wrong with the dog, we came to the house to tell you or Mr. Stickley. We knocked and called out, but we didn't get any answer. So we tried the handle and came in. We just got here and were admiring your home. We're sorry for intruding."

Erin shot a side glance at Darrell, who snuck the report under his shirt in the back. He watched as Erin feigned nonchalance even as a bead of sweat trickled beneath her hairline. She let her hand float around the room. "You have a truly beautiful home here."

Helen Stickley peered at Erin with a curious look. After a beat, she said, "Thanks." She seemed to relax some, the muscles in her narrow shoulders easing, but didn't lower the rifle.

Erin kept on. She pointed at the open door to the curio cabinet. "I was mesmerized by your amazing collection. How long have you been collecting these?"

Helen glanced at the gun in her hand and then she seemed to think about it and make a decision. She took a step back and returned the rifle to the corner, the faded housedress swirling in the motion. She came to join Darrell and Erin in front of the cabinet. "Not that long. Almost a year now." She picked up the pair near the front of the top shelf and held them in her small hands. "I found these two in Orlando when Tom and me went there last summer."

"They're beautiful," Erin said. "I noticed they are all of little kids." She left the sentence hang in the air, more question than statement.

Helen let out a long sigh. "Yeah. All I can have."

"Darrell and I haven't been married that long, but the question of kids has already come up." Erin nodded at Darrell. "I apologize we never asked before. Do you and Tom have any children?"

Helen shook her head. "No, though we tried. We can't." She stared at the figurines in her hands. "Them as close as I get." Gingerly, she placed both porcelain figures back on the top shelf, shut the glass doors, and brushed imaginary specks of dirt off the top of the curio cabinet. She took another deep breath. "Why'd you come back? If you want to talk to Tom, he'll be back sometime later. I never know exactly when."

Darrell spoke up. "We had a few more questions about the migrant kids, the ones we came to ask about before." He studied Helen Stickley's features, trying to read her, but wasn't sure. "Thanks for your suggestion about talking with the school lady, Mrs. Hudson. She was very helpful. The children's names are Daniel and Mia Sanchez, by the way."

"I...know," Helen managed before starting to sob, her tiny shoulders shuddering. She stumbled over and collapsed onto the couch, clutching one of the stuffed bears to her chest, the one with the shiny red tee. Erin moved and sat beside her. Helen went on, "Those poor children. I think about 'em all the time." Her eyes, dull olive and bloodshot, stared at Erin and Darrell. "I know this sounds silly, but from time to time I swear I still hear 'em singing and playing outside."

Right then, as if she summoned them, the sound of two children's voices—voices singing a song in Spanish—came floating through the air, almost as if they were right outside the open front window. Darrell thought he could make out the words *Feliz Navidad*." Helen's eyes got huge, and she stared from Erin to Darrell.

"Tell me ya hear them," she said. "Tell me I'm not goin' crazy, like Tom says." She stopped again, staring at the curtained window, perhaps to see if the children's singing would continue. It did, the voices coming and going as if carried by the breath of the wind.

Erin, a question on her face, glanced at Darrell, who nodded. He heard the voices clearly, singing the familiar Spanish Christmas carol. "I hear them too, Helen. I'm guessing we're hearing Daniel and Mia Sanchez. Is that right?"

Helen nodded, large tears running down her cheeks, both arms hugging the stuffed animal.

"Have you seen them too?" Darrell asked.

Helen nodded again. "Sometimes." More tears streamed down her face.

"How long have you been getting these visions?" he asked quietly.

"Is that what they are?" Helen barked a short laugh. "Ever since…" Her voice trailed off.

Erin reached over and placed a hand on Helen Stickley's arm. She asked, her voice almost a whisper, "What happened to the two kids, Helen?"

The older woman shook her head. "It was an accident. He didn't mean it. He said those kids were playin' where they weren't supposed ta."

She stopped, quiet for a few seconds. Darrell noticed the kids' singing had quieted too. Instead, he heard the clear baying of a coyote again. He exchanged another glance with Erin, who shrugged. He decided they needed to spur Helen on, to get the rest of the story.

"Your husband had been drinking that day, right?"

Helen's gaze came up. "How do ya know that?"

"I read the sheriff's report about his fight with Juan Sanchez, the kids' dad." Darrell added quietly, "There was something about him being under the influence."

"This job is really hard," Helen got out. "You have no idear how hard it is on my husband. Sometimes he drinks a little. He needs to."

When she halted again, Darrell prompted her. "And the kids were hurt when the Blueberry Harvester ran over them?"

Helen's eyes got hard. "How'd you know about the

equipment?" She shook her head. "I guess it don't matter none. Yeah, the kids were hurt bad, and Tom came and told me. He was really upset and wanted to take them to the hospital right then, but first he had to call Mr. Harrington. Them are the rules. Anything happens out in the fields, he has to call Mr. Harrington and report."

"What happened to the children?" Erin asked again, tears in her words.

"Don't say another word, woman!" Tom Stickley yelled.

Chapter 45

But they were kids

Darrell jumped at the voice and turned. Stickley's broad form filled the back door. He pounded across the kitchen toward them, rifle aimed at Darrell's chest, finger poised on the trigger. Darrell stared at the ugly black barrel, which never moved.

"You are some dumb shit, Henshaw," growled Tom Stickley. "We tried to warn ya off, but I guess you're jus' too stupid to take the hint."

"The shots at the car?" Darrell asked, suddenly angry. "You could've hurt us... badly. Deputy Atwater said a few inches either way and you could have killed us."

Standing at the edge of the kitchen, Stickley let out a short bark. He wore another set of blue denim overalls, his chest between the straps bare again, wiry black hairs snaking out. But what Darrell noticed was the gun, an even larger rifle than the one Helen had pointed at them a few minutes ago.

Stickley said, "Hell, if I wanted to kill ya, I would've. Looks like now ya give me no choice." He gestured toward the front door with the rifle. "Let's go outside. I'm not having your brains splattered all over my wife's pretty things in here." He turned and glanced at Erin. "You too, Mrs. Henshaw."

Her eyes wide and pleading, Erin looked at Helen next to her on the couch. The older woman seemed to get the message. Mrs. Stickley said, "Jus' wait a sec', Tom."

Darrell watched as Stickley's eyes moved from him to Helen on the sofa. For a moment, he contemplated going for the gun. Just as quickly, he realized the big man had turned his aim along with his gaze and now had the gun pointed straight at Erin. Darrell decided to bide his time.

Then another thought struck him. Where was Luis? How had Helen and Tom gotten to the house without him warning them? Right then, Darrell heard the baying of the coyote again. Closer this time. Then it hit him. Man, was he stupid. Luis had been trying to signal them with the coyote call right before Helen arrived. Once again before Stickley came through the door. Now, the young Latino was outside, close, waiting.

From her spot on the couch, Erin said, "We're not trying to make trouble for you. We're simply trying to find out what happened to those two kids."

Stickley grunted, "A little late for that." He shook his head, and the rifle barrel bounced once. "What's the big deal about them damn kids? Here's what I want to know—why do a couple of Yankees like you care about two snot-nosed, wetback kids? I don't get it." His stance relaxed a bit, but he still held the gun aimed at Erin.

Erin said, "Helen must think the children are important. She was just telling us about her having visions of them."

Helen pleaded, "Maybe their comin' here's a sign. Ya know how I have them dreams. And, and I told you

I could hear them kids and even see 'em a few times when I was awake." She pointed to Darrell. "He sees them and hears them too. A few minutes ago, we just heard them kids singing some Spanish Christmas song." Her thin finger jabbed at Darrell and back at herself. "Both of us."

Tom Stickley's face got red. "That's crazy talk, woman. They're jus' fillin' your head with crazy talk."

Even though his heart was pounding in his chest, Darrell tried to feign calm. "Tom, Helen's not crazy. I know it's a lot to take in, but your wife Helen is a *sensitive* like me. She can see and hear ghosts. The ghosts of those two kids. It's a gift few people have."

"Some *gift!*" Stickley crowed.

Darrell plowed on, "You asked why we care about these two kids, who we don't even know. Okay, I'll tell you." He looked to Erin for confirmation, and she gave a small nod. They didn't have anything to lose. "Erin and I, we only came to Florida for our honeymoon. Two beautiful weeks in the Florida sun. But when we got here, the ghosts of those two kids appeared to me and asked me to help them." He glanced over at Stickley to see if he was buying it, but the scowl on his face didn't change. Darrell hurried on. "The kids kept showing up, more than once, and wouldn't let me alone."

Helen offered, "Tom, all that makes sense to me. I told you I was being haunted by them two little Spics."

"Shut up, woman. All this talk about ghosts is just hooey. I told you before there ain't no such thing as ghosts."

Darrell thought maybe he saw an opening and went for it. "Tom, it's not hooey." He glanced at Helen.

"And your wife's not crazy." He put both hands up, palms out. "It may sound crazy, but ghosts do exist, and some people see and hear them more than others. It's like anything else, basketball or shooting." He pointed at the gun. "I know, I know how crazy it sounds. I've been a sensitive for years and tried to fight it. For some reason, the ghosts come to me looking for help. I've been able to help…help them find peace. It really is a gift—one I only recently came to appreciate." Darrell pointed to Erin and himself. "Whatever you do to us, the ghosts won't go away. They'll keep haunting until—"

Stickley cut him off. "I've heard enough. I'm done talkin' here." He moved the barrel toward Darrell again. "Now, I ain't going to say it again. Let's go. Outside." He glanced back at the couch. "You too, Missus."

Erin's eyes grew even larger, and her gaze jerked from Helen Stickley to Darrell. She reached an arm out to the older woman, who glanced at her husband and then stared down at the rug. Erin's features tight, she rose and took slow steps over to Darrell, who put an arm around her. Helen rose to follow.

Stickley barked, "You don't need to come out, Helen. You don't need to see this."

"Tom?" Helen implored.

Stickley said, "I got 'em. You know what to do." His head twitched to the kitchen and turned back to Darrell. "Out the door. Move."

Darrell met Erin's gaze, his eyes doing a quick jerk to the door and outside. He hoped she caught his meaning. Using his arm, he guided her in front of him, heading through the doorway first. He needed to keep himself between the rifle and Erin. They filed out the door and onto the small stoop, first Erin, then Darrell, followed by Stickley. Each step out the door, onto the small porch, and down the cracked step, Stickley jabbed the rifle barrel hard into Darrell's back. Once outside, the breeze hit him again, though it had picked up while they'd been inside. The wind carried the nauseating odors of the yard, and Darrell put his hand over his nose.

He glanced around, blinking in the wind, but tried not to let Stickley see. His brain raced, searching for some way out. Where was Luis? His gaze swept the yard and the area around, but he didn't see him. The little guy had to be here somewhere. Darrell tried to guess what Luis might have in mind and what *he* could do. He'd heard the last coyote call clearly, so Luis had to be close, not that far outside the window. He must've heard most of what Stickley had said. The young man had courage and determination. No way he'd take off. He'd try something.

Darrell let his gaze roam around, searching. The two hens still roamed the grass and dirt space, occasionally stopping to peck the ground. The German Shepherd mix lay on the edge of the yard where they left him, obviously still sleeping. No sign of Luis.

Stickley must've seen Darrell's glance in the dog's direction. He asked, "How ya get past my dog?" His eyes stared out at the animal. "D'ya do something to Harley?"

Erin tried her line again. "Like I told your wife, we only came by to ask a few questions and found your dog like that. We'd just told her about Harley when you came in screaming at us. You can ask her."

While Erin was talking, Darrell kept his gaze

roaming the yard, searching for Luis. Not seeing him, he looked for something, anything they could use to defend themselves with. All he could see—and smell—was dog crap. Could he use that? Could he bring himself to pick that up and…

When Erin finished, the older man glared at her, his oval face frowning. "I don't believe ya." He laughed, showing the yellowed teeth again. "I was just goin' to say if ya did anything to old Harley, I'd kill ya. Then I realized I can't kill ya twice."

Darrell looked to Erin and figured they had nothing to lose…and he had to buy them some time. Where was Luis? What was he planning? As he turned to the angry supervisor, his eyes kept searching. What he had to say would make Stickley even more pissed off, but he had to chance it. "Okay, you got us, Tom." He raised both hands in the air. "Your dog scares the shit out of us, so we gave him something to help him sleep." He saw the rage burn in the man's gray eyes and hurried on. "Erin's a nurse, and she made sure we didn't hurt Harley."

Stickley's eyes moved toward the dog slumbering on the other end of the yard, and Darrell hoped he'd head over to check. But the man only deepened his scowl. "If he ain't okay, I swear I'll come back and shoot you twice. Now git moving." He pointed the rifle toward the rear of the property, in the direction of the smaller outbuilding and large mound Darrell noticed coming in. "Might as well put you where I stashed the others. Head that way. Let's get this over with."

Erin led, and they started across the hard-packed ground, all three staring down, stepping around piles of dog turds. When they emerged past the corner of the house, the wind pressed and stung their faces, stronger now. Darrell caught a blurred motion and turned.

Luis ran out from between the parked car and the pickup. His reedy arms struggled to hold a small boulder overhead. He screamed, "A-a-a-r-g-h!"

Chapter 46

It wasn't his fault

Stickley whirled and tried to bring the rifle in the direction of the scream, but not in time. Luis was on him and slammed the huge rock onto the side of Stickley's head. With his momentum, Luis landed on top of the fat man with an "Umph." The supervisor crumpled to the ground, his large belly straining the denim. Darrell pounced and ripped the gun out of Stickley's hands as soon as he hit the ground. A line of blood trickled down the side of the man's head, and his gray eyes fluttered and closed.

Holding the rifle and leaning over both men, Darrell said, "You can get off him now."

He stepped back, keeping the gun aimed at the prone figure and making room for Luis. The young Latino struggled to his feet, grunting, a red stain blooming on the right sleeve. The sling hung limp on his side.

Darrell shifted the rifle in his hands, getting comfortable. He was no expert with firearms, but he'd gone hunting a few times in the Upper Peninsula with his dad and brother. He knew enough and settled the rifle in his arms, barrel aimed at Stickley, finger on the trigger. He checked to make sure the safety was off.

The front door of the house banged open, and

Helen Stickley scrambled down onto the porch, yellow dress billowing in the wind. She ran across the front of the house. Darrell turned, expecting her to have the other rifle, but she hurried over, her hands empty.

"Oh, no, Tom," she cried. Collapsing next to her husband, she cradled his head in her small hands. She glared up, fire in her eyes. "You hurt him. Bad, maybe." Her fingers dabbed at the scarlet smear of blood on his temple.

Darrell pulled a white handkerchief from his back pocket and gave it to Erin but stayed where he was. He kept the rifle aimed at both Stickleys now.

Kneeling down beside Helen, Erin handed her the folded cloth. "Here. Hold this against the cut. I'll check him over." Uncertain, Helen glared at Erin, who said, "It's okay. I'm a nurse."

With a huff, the older woman accepted the handkerchief with a trembling hand and pressed it against the wound. Erin leaned over the now unconscious form, checked his vitals, examined the wound, and nodded. She said, "He'll be okay, probably unconscious for a while. Going to have a doozy of a headache when he wakes up, though. And it wouldn't hurt to have him checked for a concussion. We'll get him to the hospital after."

Luis said, "I not know what else to do." Standing just off to one side, he looked from the prone form to Darrell. "When I came back from car, after I pick up papers, I see woman coming and didn't want to call out, so I do coyote. I hide on side of house and see man pull up in truck. I do coyote again." With his right hand, he pointed at the unconscious Stickley, and Darrell again noticed the sling hanging loose around his neck and the wound bleeding. "Then, after he go in, I wait near window and hear him say he kill you. I had to do something."

Darrell said, "You did great. Probably saved our lives."

"Great?" Helen stared at Darrell. "Looked what he did to my husband."

Darrell watched as the end of her yellow sleeve turned bright red where Helen leaned against her husband's wound. Darrell shook his head. He was at the end of his rope. Some honeymoon. "Your husband said he was going to *kill* us. All because we were asking about two poor kids."

"You don't understand," Helen Stickley mumbled. "He got no choice."

Darrell let the gun barrel drop to the ground but held onto it. "What do you mean he had no choice."

The older woman didn't answer and instead said, "Tom, Tom?"

"Helen?" Erin said, still kneeling on the ground, her face only a foot from the other woman. "Tom said he was going to put us where he stashed the others. What was he talking about?" When Helen didn't answer, Erin reached over and turned the other woman's face toward her. "Are the kids still alive?" she asked in an anguished voice.

Helen began to cry again, huge, heaving sobs. In between, she tried to answer but couldn't get any words to come out.

Leaning on the rifle, Darrell crouched down so he was at her level. "Tom killed both kids in the accident, didn't he?"

Helen shook her head hard, back and forth, tears

dripping off her face onto the dirt. "No. He hurt both the kids pretty bad in the accident, but he didn't kill them. Hell, he carried 'em in his arms back into the house. We was going to take 'em to the hospital in Dixon." She stopped suddenly. Her eyes got a faraway look. "I thought maybe…" Her voice drifted off.

"They didn't make it to the hospital, did they?" Erin asked softly.

The woman shook her head again, this time slowly. Erin whispered, "What happened?"

Helen sniffed a few times. "Tom was going to, he was. But first, he had to call Harrington. Them's the rules. Anything happens in the field, we have to call Harrington." She halted again, as if the next was too hard to get out.

Darrell handed the rifle to Luis and crouched down close to the two women. "What did Mr. Harrington tell him?"

Helen looked up at Darrell. As she talked, more tears ran down her face and into her mouth, but she never bothered to wipe them away. "He told Tom he couldn't take the kids to the hospital. Harrington said he let the policy lapse, and they had no insurance on the plantation. He said when their parents found out, they'd sue us. Said the whole place would go bankrupt." She dropped her gaze to her husband again. "He said them damn wetbacks would, would take everything. Said me and Tom be out on the street. After seventeen years of working for that man."

Darrell said, "That's why they made up the thing about the fight with Juan Sanchez and had the parents deported. Awful hard to sue in Mexico, huh?"

Helen glared up at him. "Oh, there was a fight all

right. Nothing made up about that. Juan found out his kids had been hurt and came after Tom. Gave him six stitches." She reached over and fingered a tiny scar under her husband's jaw.

Erin spoke up, still quiet. "So you just let the kids…die. They were hurt bad in the accident. I'd guess broken legs and significant internal injuries."

Helen said, "Don't know about no internal injuries but both had badly broken legs. They was real bad off."

"So you just let the kids die?" Erin repeated her question, a little louder this time.

Helen's weeping started up again, big sobs, and she shook her head. "Harrington said it wasn't humane to have the kids suffer like that."

Everyone got quiet. A horrified look in her eyes, Erin glanced at Darrell. She pushed, "What happened to the kids?"

Helen was crying loudly now, sniffling and sobbing so much she had to force the words out between sobs. "He…he…broke…their little necks."

Chapter 47

Perhaps some old-fashioned justice

Erin rose slowly and she, Darrell, and Luis exchanged stares, too stunned to speak. It felt like the air had been sucked out from around them. Even the wind seemed to die down for the moment. Finally, Darrell found his voice. "What did you say he did?" He glared at the unconscious man on the ground.

Helen must've seen the horror on her visitors' faces. She tried, "You gotta understand. We didn't want to hurt them kids. They was only kids. I pleaded with Tom. I told him we could keep them, raise 'em as our own, after, um...they got better." Her gaze jerked from one to the other. "But my Tom, he said them kids weren't going to get better. He knows Spics better than anyone. He works with 'em every day. He made me see them kids ain't like us. He said they don't feel things the way we do."

Hearing her words, Luis handed Darrell the rifle. He stomped over and picked up the large rock from where he chucked it. He came over next to Darrell. Both arms straining, he raised the rock chest level. Luis said through gritted teeth, "Maybe I bring this down on him a few more times. See if he *feel* things the way we do."

Helen gaped up in terror and leaned over her

husband, trying to shield him.

He continued, "When I finish, I hit her. Maybe a few good hits in the head." At this, Helen cowered, backing away.

Darrell reached out a hand, laying it on Luis' hurt arm. "I get it. They deserve it after what they did to those two children." He nodded to the red-soaked sleeve. "Put it down. Don't make that shoulder any worse."

For a few seconds Luis stood there, the huge rock held in two hands, arms straining. He exchanged an angry glare with Darrell, eyes narrowed. Finally, he nodded, tossing the rock away from the group again.

A prickle returned to Darrell's neck, the impression deep and expanding. He urged to rub the area, but he knew he didn't dare, and he kept both hands on the rifle. Then, without warning, another sensation struck him, this more uncomfortable and foreboding. He had the uncanny feeling—no, the certainty—that someone was watching them. The ghosts? No, this felt like, like…something else. He sensed this was far from over.

Natalia's warning came back to him. *"But you must be careful. I see great danger lurking nearby. There are those who do not vant them found."*

He chanced taking his eyes off the Stickleys and shot a hurried glance around, ending in the direction of the gravel drive. He couldn't see any rooster tail of dust. The sky had darkened, the clouds edging from silver to dark gray. The wind whipped across the open space, hurtling grasses and soil into the air, but he saw no telltale plume on the gravel drive. Anyone coming would have to come that way, wouldn't they? He'd get plenty of warning. Darrell shifted his gaze back to the supervisor and his wife.

Erin asked, "Helen, Tom said he was going to take us where he stashed the others. What others? Was he talking about Daniel and Mia?"

Helen didn't respond but kept her head lowered next to her husband.

Erin pressed, "Where was he taking us?"

Helen lifted her head and nodded in the direction of the smaller metal building and the dirt mound but still didn't say anything.

Erin asked, "Is that where he put the kids after…?"

The older woman stabbed a thin finger at the pile of dirt. "We, Tom had no choice. Mr. Harrington came over to make sure everything was taken care of."

Darrell turned to look where she pointed. When he did, Helen sprang from the ground and grabbed for the barrel of the gun. He caught her movement out of the corner of his eye. He turned just in time. He brought his foot up and kicked her, sending her tumbling backward atop her husband. Rage burned through him. Slowly, he brought the rifle up and sighted the barrel at the pair sprawled on the ground.

"No, please!" Helen squealed.

Darrell curled his finger around the trigger.

Erin came over and placed a hand on his arm. She whispered, "Darrell, don't."

He didn't flinch but tightened his finger on the trigger, feeling the cool curve of the metal. Without moving his aim, he spat out, "They killed Daniel and Mia, two little children. They broke their necks, for God's sake. And they dumped their bodies. Like trash." His gaze flitted over to Erin and then back to the gun sight. "I'm supposed to see the kids get justice. Maybe *this* is justice."

For a moment, no one spoke, the air thick with tension and rage. Darrell didn't look at Luis or Erin but knew they were both staring at him. Helen Stickley's eyes were on him too. Huge, terrified eyes. The prickle returned, another jolt of electricity starting at his neck and running down his back. Was that a signal? Was *this* what he was supposed to do?

The other times, with Hank in Wilshire and Amy at Cape May, Darrell had been certain he was doing the right thing. Both of those deaths had called out for justice and had driven him to keep going no matter what.

But these kids' deaths, executions really, struck him differently. There was something hideous, inhuman about such casual extinction of beautiful young lives. Daniel and Mia were little children, five and six years old! Anyone who could snuff out the lives of some so young and innocent were...monsters. And what were you supposed to do with monsters?

A jagged bolt of electricity split the darkened sky. Two seconds later, the explosion of thunder broke. Darrell jerked in the direction of the boom and then back, staring at his prisoners.

Erin whispered, "Darrell, I love you, and I understand your anger. You have every right to be furious. What they did was gruesome, unforgivable even. But you know this isn't right. This isn't *you*." When she got the last words out, he could hear the trembling in her voice.

He shot her another quick glance and caught her pleading eyes. "If we turn them in, you know what will happen. They'll simply deny everything and get off."

Helen said quickly, "No, I promise we won't. I'll tell the sheriff everything. I promise. The whole story. Please...don't kill us."

Darrell shook his head slightly. "She'd say anything right now to save her scrawny neck. She'll simply change her tune later. It'll be our word against hers. Two *Yankees* and a...an immigrant! You saw how these people are. You saw how they treated Luis at the hospital. You heard how Stickley described the *wetbacks*. Hell, Harrington probably has some high-priced lawyer on retainer...to deal with all these 'nasty wetbacks.' The lawyer will get them off, and they'll never see any justice."

The dust at Darrell's feet exploded, pebbles shooting in all directions. A half second later, the report of the bullet echoed off the metal buildings. Darrell's eyes shot in the direction of the sound. From behind the nearer outbuilding, a voice hollered, "Drop the rifle, or the next one will make the head of your pretty new wife explode."

Chapter 48

You can join the damn kids

Stunned, Darrell hesitated a fraction of a second. Two more shots struck the ground inches from his feet. He jumped. The deep bass voice yelled, "I'm not kidding. You wanna watch your wife die, keep holdin' on to that rifle."

"Okay, okay," Darrell called back and set the rifle on the ground at his feet, but not out of reach. He could grab it up in a few seconds if given the chance. He raised his hands above his head.

The voice must've known what Darrell was thinking and yelled, "Now kick it over toward Tom and Helen."

Using his right foot, Darrell did as directed, sending the gun about half the distance. As soon as his foot met the metal, the prickle returned to his neck. He wanted to slide his hand there but kept both raised. The prickle went from a buzz to a sizzle, the sensation running like electricity from the base of his head down his spine. Again, he scanned the area, looking for something—or someone. It was a sign, a warning, but he had no idea what he was supposed to do.

The voice called, "Helen, go and get the rifle."

Helen hesitated at first, glancing at her injured husband.

The voice barked, "Move it, woman. I don't have all day here."

Helen jerked her head toward the smaller building and then, after a few seconds, she let her husband's head down gently. She rose, anxious eyes darting from the structure to Darrell. She scurried over, picked up the rifle, and hurried back. Standing next to her unconscious husband, she aimed the gun at Darrell. Jerking the barrel at Erin, she motioned her to join Darrell, then did the same to Luis.

"Well done, Helen," the voice called. "Is Tom okay?"

The older woman said, "I think so. This one"—she jerked the barrel toward Erin again—"she said she's a nurse and she said it wudn't serious. Maybe a concussion."

"Well, that's good. No permanent damage then," the man called.

Darrell recognized the voice. He'd heard it before and glanced at Erin. She nodded.

A small man stepped out from the corner of the small metal outbuilding and strode toward the group. As he neared, Darrell studied the short figure with the thinning brown hair. Harrington. He remembered Stickley telling his wife she knew what to do. She must've called the boss when Tom walked them outside.

Staring at the owner, a strange thought struck him. The pale-yellow polo shirt, pressed khakis, and fancy loafers seemed at odds with the large rifle the guy was holding, aimed at Darrell's chest. Once again, Darrell moved so that Erin and Luis were behind him, or at least he was between them and the gun sight. As he did, he wondered why Harrington hadn't already shot all three of them. No witnesses...except Helen, and Darrell didn't think she'd talk.

The short man approached, a broad smirk on his face. "Well, I guess I'm not too late to the party."

"I'm so glad to see you, Mr. Harrington," Helen gushed. "You got here just in time. I think they were going to kill us, me and Tom, and I wuddn't tellin' 'em anything—"

"I heard everything, Helen," Harrington snapped as he closed the last few feet. He shot an ugly glance at the older woman, whose face went pale, but she didn't utter another word. He glared at Darrell. "I know these two, the *honeymooners*." His gun jerked at Darrell and Erin. "But who's the wetback?"

"I dunno, Mr. Harrington," Helen answered quickly. "I never seen him before. When Tom marched them out of the house, this guy came rushing out and bashed Tom on the head—"

Luis stepped from behind Darrell. "My name is Luis Alvarez. I help Mr. and Mrs. Henshaw."

Darrell said, "Luis was kind enough to offer to help us find out what happened to the two poor Latino kids, Daniel and Mia Sanchez."

Harrington shook his head. "The two poor Latino kids." His tone mocked Darrell's words. "No great mystery there. Just an unfortunate accident. Wrong place, wrong time."

Darrell was still reeling from what Helen had revealed about the kids' deaths. "Except you had Tom execute them?"

Harrington shook his head again. "You just don't understand. Tom simply put them out of their misery.

Out of their pain."

Darrell needed to keep Harrington talking so he could maybe think of something to do. "Helen said she wanted to take them to the hospital, to save them." He glanced at the woman to see if she'd try to deny it, but she didn't.

The owner shrugged. "Helen's a nice woman. She's got a good heart, but she's soft. She had no idea what the medical bills for those two would've cost. I checked on the way over here that day. Over a hundred thousand dollars! Each! And that would only have been the beginning."

"Well, you couldn't have that now, could you?" Darrell asked, his own tone mocking.

"Hell, no!" thundered Harrington, his eyes wide. "Might as well give their parents our whole Goddamn checkbook. They would've taken everything."

"Well, I guess your friends in immigration took care of that problem for you, didn't they? Kinda hard to sue from Mexico."

"Shut up!" Harrington brought the rifle up, barrel pointed at Darrell's head. For a moment, Darrell thought it was over. Harrington was going to pull the trigger. A bead of sweat rolled down the side of Darrell's face.

Instead, Harrington jerked his rifle at Luis. "These...these people are like vultures. Whatever you give them, no matter how much you do for them, it's not enough. I give 'em a place to live and a chance to earn a decent wage, and all they do is complain. They ought to be grateful, but they ain't. They got no rights in this country. They're illegals. We let them work here and pay them more than they can make back home.

Still, it's not enough. It's never enough."

Lightning split the grayness, and the sky rumbled again. For a moment, everyone's gaze jerked west toward the oncoming front. The wind that blew across the space smelled heavy with rain. Darrell was certain in a few minutes getting wet was going to be the least of their problems.

Erin said in a quiet voice, "You saw two kids suffering and you simply had them killed?"

"It was for the best," Harrington said, his voice getting hoarse. "It was the humane thing to do. It's what you do when something is suffering."

Erin asked, "Did you just call two little children 'something'?"

"Damn Northerners," Harrington spat out and brought the gun back on Darrell and Erin. "You got no idea how things are run around here. Those kids live, and their parents take us to court. We could've lost EVERYTHING. Half the families in the county depend on our farm for work…and hundreds of…of migrants would've been out of work then too."

Erin said quietly, "They were merely little kids who never did you any harm."

"Well, missy, you're so anxious to see what happened to those two. How about I show you?" Harrington jerked the rifle in the direction of the smaller outbuilding. "You, whatever your name is, go in there and get two shovels." As he watched the young man start toward the metal shed, he added, "And don't try anything or I'll put a bullet in both your friends."

When Luis disappeared inside, Harrington turned toward Helen. "Tom still out?"

The older woman nodded, and the owner

continued, "Well, then I want you to come over here and help me cover them. I don't trust these guys."

Helen took another look at her husband, still unconscious on the ground, and joined the group, raising up the second rifle. In less than a minute, Luis returned with two rusting shovels. Darrell's glance went from Luis dragging the two shovels to Harrington and Helen with the rifles, and he got it. Harrington was going to make them dig their own graves…before he killed them.

The wind swirled around them, raising the dust into the air. On instinct, everyone raised their arms to shield their eyes from the swirling debris. Darrell thought it might give them an opening and pondered taking action but realized that both Harrington and Helen were too far away.

The owner yelled over the wind, "Don't even think about it," and he pointed to Darrell. "Give him one." To the whole group, he said, "Let's head over to that mound." He nodded toward the large pile of dirt.

Staying a few steps behind, Harrington and Helen marched Darrell, Erin, and Luis down the length of the mound, dirt and grasses blowing around them. The trek took some time. When they were back at the house, Darrell hadn't realized how long the mound was. A shovel in his hand, Darrell swung it a little as they walked, feeling its heft and dragging it through the dirt. Could he use the shovel somehow to…? He had to find some way out of this mess. He chanced a look back and saw Helen and Harrington still a few steps behind. As they walked alongside the dirt pile, Darrell glanced across and up, noticing the soil was fresher, darker golden, almost brown in the nearer section. Then as they got farther down the mound, he saw the ground looked more settled, undisturbed. Starting at about three-fourths of the way down, the grasses and weeds were taller, and the soil had dried to an almost pale yellow.

Harrington stopped and gestured to the top of the mound. "That ought to be about right. Climb up there and start digging."

Chapter 49

Daniel and Mia

Darrell wanted to run at Harrington, shovel in
hand, and bring the heavy tool down on his head. That
would be suicide. And would do nothing to free Erin
and Luis.

Harrington interrupted Darrell's thoughts. The
owner barked, "Helen, you stand here and start shooting
if they do anything." He turned to the three captives.
"Up there." With his rifle, he pointed to the rise of the
mound.

Dragging the shovels, Darrell and Luis climbed up
the incline. Erin stood off to the side. A pace or two
behind, Harrington followed them up the ten-foot rise.
Then he backed down on the other side, the side nearer
the outbuilding, all the while keeping the rifle aimed at
Darrell and Luis.

Darrell stared from his position atop the hill,
surveying the fields, the gravel road, the buildings, even
the little farmhouse. Then he brought his gaze back to
Harrington and Helen holding the guns at them at cross
angles. They were trapped, and there was no one
coming. Maybe his message hadn't gotten through to
Deputy Atwater…or maybe Atwater didn't want a
confrontation with one of the most powerful growers in
the county. He and Erin and Luis were on their own.

His stomach clenched.

Darrell stuck the shovel into the dirt. He started slowly, breaking the hardened crust and fighting the tall weeds and grasses. When the rusted metal tip struck the earth for the third time, a host of sounds erupted, a cacophony of indistinct voices dancing around them. Trying not to be obvious, he peered around, searching for where the voices were coming from. He looked at Luis to see if he heard, but the young Latino seemed only intent on digging, one shovelful at a time, and grimacing, the effort obviously painful to his injured shoulder. Still, as Darrell listened, the voices rose and fell, as if borne by the wind, and he could now make out moaning, a string of Spanish words and…some children singing? The sensation on his neck streaked down his back. Afraid to take his hands off the shovel, he arched, but it did little to ease the buzzing.

His head swiveled as he lowered the shovel for another bite of the soft earth, but he still couldn't see anyone else. Neither Erin nor Harrington seemed to notice the voices, but in his peripheral vision he saw Helen looking around as if *she* heard something. And, of course, he sensed something, but that was little help.

Harrington yelled, "Let's go. I don't want to get caught in this damn storm." He jerked the rifle barrel in the general direction of the marching clouds, which had turned an ominous gray black.

Darrell had to admit Harrington had planned this part well. If he or Luis tried to get to Harrington with a shovel, Helen could simply open fire, hitting Erin first then shooting the two of them. If they went for Helen, the owner would simply do the same thing. The three of them stood atop the dirt, sitting ducks. No place to hide.

Nowhere to run.

He dug, his shovel stabbing into the brown earth. A few drops of rain, large and full, plopped onto his shoulder, back, and head. Glancing up, he saw that the clouds had turned dark all around, the sky an ominous ceiling of black above them. Not a good sign. But even as he dug, Darrell's gaze kept roaming, trying to search for the source of the voices. He thought maybe the voices…or something would give him an opening. At one point, he thought they were coming from behind him. A minute later, they seemed to be on his left…or front. The wind was playing nasty tricks with the sounds, and the voices rose and fell with the gusts.

He stole another quick look at Helen. She still guarded her side, rifle on them, but her eyes kept darting from side to side, always bringing her vision back on them. Darrell realized he wasn't imagining it. The older woman heard the voices, too. And she was getting anxious.

Darrell strained his eyes to search for something, anything around them that might help. His mind raced for any option out of their predicament. Like a fool, he'd gotten them into this. Well, no, the ghosts had gotten them into this, but Darrell felt no rage at these ghosts. They were just children, crying for help. Still, he and Erin and Luis were going to end up dead all the same.

His eyes returned to the earth, and as he stuck the metal shovel into the soft soil, he realized again they were digging their own graves. Literally. He fought his rising panic and tried to think of something. Concentrating on the voices, he jammed the shovel into the ground again. He could make out men moaning and some rapid-fire exchange, but it was all in Spanish and meant nothing to him. Then, erupting through some angry and anguished words, he distinctly heard two children's voices singing. He caught the song he'd heard back at the house, *Feliz Navidad.* He shot another quick glance back and saw that Helen was still looking around, her gaze darting from side to side. She heard them too. Could he do something with that?

Darrell's eyes met Harrington's, but he only jabbed the rifle barrel at him. The owner took a few hurried steps up the side of the mound and looked at Helen. He shouted, "Helen, what are you doing?"

The woman reacted, jerking her gun up toward the captives. "Nothing. I've got them," she yelled over the rising wind, her voice high and tight.

"You better," Harrington called and backed down to his position, rifle at the ready.

Darrell looked from Erin to Luis, both of whom behaved oblivious to the voices. Erin's face bore only fear, tears drifting from tortured green eyes. Luis showed only pain. The young man's eyes were huge as he tossed another shovelful of soil over the side and grunted, the effort wearing on him. Scarlet streaks now mixing with the fresh dirt stains, blood seeped from Luis' bandaged shoulder and ran down his white tee shirt.

Helen and Harrington stayed rooted their spots, only shifting their feet from time to time. Helen's eyes kept searching, though their movement was more subtle now. They both kept their rifles aimed up the incline while twisting their heads from time to time to keep the dirt out of their eyes. The wind gusts whipped past them, grabbing some of the loose soil from their shovelfuls and flinging it in the air. Darrell watched Harrington raise a hand to keep the errant dirt from hitting him.

Maybe he could use *that*? Maybe he could toss soil at the owner and Luis could throw the dirt toward Helen and grab her gun. Someone would probably get shot— God, he hoped it wouldn't be Erin—but at least one or two of them might survive. As he plotted, the prickle became a sizzle again on his neck and back, the feeling intense. He leaned on the shovel handle and tried to reach around to scratch. Was that a signal for him to act? Darrell knew it wasn't much of a plan, but it was better than nothing. They had to do something. He leaned over to whisper to Luis.

The dirt at their feet exploded, and the air cracked with the sound. Both Darrell and Luis jumped backward, almost falling down.

Harrington yelled, "Just shut up and keep digging. I don't want to be out here all day."

Darrell gave up that idea, at least for now.

He and Luis straightened and hurried back to their positions, worried where the next bullet might land. They dug, scooping up chunks of earth and sending them down the side of the mound. Across from each other, they worked methodically, shoveling out dirt and tossing it, widening the hole, opening their graves, oblivious to the fat drops that continued to splat on them. Once they'd broken the surface and cleared the growth and got past the roots, Darrell found the soil loose with only a few small rocks and pebbles, almost like topsoil. The digging was not difficult, but before long they were both soaked, sweat dripping from their arms and foreheads, mixing now with the raindrops.

With almost every shovelful, Luis would glance over, a question in his eyes. The labor was taking its toll on his thin frame and his wound. His eyes begged for an answer. Each time, Darrell would meet the young man's gaze, shaking his head, out of solutions.

Erin came forward, placing a hand on the young Latino's back. She pointed to the bleeding shoulder. "Why don't you let me switch? I can take over for a while."

Harrington laughed, the sound carrying in the thick air. "Isn't that cute? The missus wants to help." He gestured with the rifle. "You let the wetback do the grunt work. It's what they're good for."

At first, Erin didn't move, looking at Darrell. He shrugged. She stepped back, and both guys continued digging.

A few minutes later, Luis' shovel cracked into something. Peering into the gap, Darrell put a hand out to stop him and reached down to clear the rock. Leaning over the hole, he froze, and his breath caught. Luis set his shovel down and knelt on the ground, peering into the opening. Darrell met Luis' wide eyes for a second, and both stared down at a tiny, partially uncovered white skull. Whisps of curling brown hair still clung to the skull. A mouth with tiny teeth grinned at them.

Even though he should've known what they'd find, Darrell couldn't help himself. He felt the vomit coming up, rushing from his stomach, and he turned away. A second later, Luis stumbled away from the hole and did the same, his brown eyes wide with horror.

Harrington climbed up the mound, smirking at the two of them crouched over, retching. "I saw far worse than that in combat, you wusses." He peered into the hole. "You were so damn determined to find these two. Well, meet little Daniel and—"

Harrington stopped midsentence. *He* had heard something. The owner turned, jerking his head around to look back the way he came. Then Darrell heard it again, the same sounds louder now. The cacophony of Spanish voices argued, growing stronger, and then slowly the singing came through, kids singing the same Spanish Christmas song. "*Feliz Navidad. Próspero año y Felicidad.*"

And now Darrell could tell it was coming from the end of the mound.

Chapter 50

Bullets don't always work

"What the hell?" roared Harrington, glancing from his prisoners back toward the end of the mound. The wind carried the angry bickering in Spanish and the painful moaning past them. Then, louder than the other sounds, the sing-song cadence of two children's voices echoed on the back of the next gust.

"*Feliz Navidad.*

Feliz Navidad.

Feliz Navidad. Próspero año y Felicidad."

Jerking his head back and forth, Harrington hollered over the rising wind and rain, "Helen, keep them covered, and I'll check this out. Whatever it is, I'll take care of it." He marched toward the sounds, ignoring Darrell and Luis. And Erin.

Hunched over and stomach aching, Darrell tried to make sense of the sounds—the angry bickering in Spanish, the moaning and the singing—and thought he knew what it meant. His extra *sense* was clamoring, the electric prickle zapping painfully from his neck down his back. More ghosts were making their presence known. His premonition screamed at him, warning these spirits weren't friendly like the kids. These spectral signals conveyed true malevolence.

Wiping the last of the vomit off his mouth, he

pushed himself up and checked Helen's reaction, figuring—if she really was a sensitive—she'd be picking up much of the same psychic messages. As Darrell watched, the woman's eyes went wide, and her face paled. She couldn't help herself. She was drawn to the sounds. Head jerking around, she headed the same direction Harrington had gone, leaving Darrell, Luis, and Erin alone.

Darrell turned back and saw Luis dragging himself up, Erin helping him to his feet again. To be sure, Darrell watched Helen and Harrington at the far end of the mound and made sure both were preoccupied, neither glancing back. Realizing they needed to do something and quickly, he hustled over to where Luis and Erin stood together. Keeping his voice low, he said, "I'm going to go for Harrington and try to wrestle the gun away. You two take care of Helen. Knock the rifle down. Get that—"

The crack of a bullet exploded in the air. All three cringed and turned. Darrell expected to feel the pain in his back or see the look of horror on Erin or Luis' face—but the bullet hadn't been meant for them.

"No, it's not possible. You're *dead*!" Harrington's scream tumbled back to them with the wind.

Darrell turned and watched, but all he could see were the backs of Harrington and Helen, side by side, both facing away from them. As he crossed the distance, the owner raised the rifle and fired, three more explosions ripping the air.

Helen shook her head and cried, "I can't take this anymore." She sighted the barrel, firing twice in the same direction. Darrell saw the rifle butt kick in her arms, but he couldn't tell what they were shooting at.

Though he had a pretty good idea.

He hustled down the length of the mound, Luis and Erin a step behind. A rumble of thunder bounced around the darkening clouds, not loud but threatening more to come. Covered by the roll of the thunder, they didn't need to be quiet, but all three moved in a crouching position, trying to be stealthy. It didn't matter. Harrington and Helen were both fixated on what was in front of them and didn't even turn around.

Harrington yelled, "No, it can't be."

He and Helen raised their rifles again and started firing, the bullets striking the ground and sending dirt and pebbles into the air.

Darrell gestured Erin and Luis toward Helen, and he crept up behind the owner. When he edged closer and had the right angle, Darrell got a glimpse of what they had been shooting at. The two young kids, Daniel and Mia, appeared at the edge of the dirt pile digging in the soil, much as he'd seen them at the beach. Daniel's right leg was bent back in that ugly manner he'd first noticed on the sand. They sat there in their street clothes, dirty jeans and soiled tee shirts, and looked back, those brown eyes large and pleading. Their images were less substantial than his vision at the beach, their figures shimmering in the wind as if they were fading in and out of focus. They sat, singing bravely as the bullets passed through them and spit into the earth behind them.

"Feliz Navidad. Próspero año y Felicidad."

Beyond the image of the children, three other figures shimmered in the wind and rain. Darrell could make out three adult Hispanic males, the first two tall with angry eyes and muscular arms, both arguing, though their words were whisked away in another gust. The last was an image of a third Latino man, but scrawny, hunched over and bleeding. A large slash cut across the left side of his face, and blood streamed out toward the ground, dark scarlet. Though when Darrell checked he noted the drops never reached the earth, no bright red splotch in the soil.

Darrell had no idea who these phantoms were, but they looked to be more migrants, mocha coloring, dark hair, mottled skin from days in the sun. Unlike the kids, though, the spectral signals they gave off were evil, wicked. No doubt, they were the malevolence he'd sensed a few times hanging around the children's aura. He couldn't guess what they wanted—though he sensed it held evil intent—but he was glad *they* hadn't tried to reach out to him. Maybe his *gift* was okay after all. It had only channeled a connection to the two children, the innocents.

Glancing at the kids again—no, the kids' ghosts— Darrell had a bit of déjà vu. He flashed on the scene back in Wilshire, that night with Hank on the widow's walk. Then Amy on a deserted street outside of Cape May. Like Hank and Amy, the ghosts of Daniel and Mia had come to *his* rescue. And he needed to do something, to seize this chance. He gestured to Luis and Erin, and then he ran, half trudging, half stumbling down the side of the mound toward Harrington.

A jagged streak of lightning ripped out of the dark clouds and struck the ground at the far corner of the small shed less than a hundred feet away. A millisecond later, the sky exploded with a huge boom. Everyone froze and cringed, arms shielding their eyes against the sudden, impossible brightness. As Harrington turned toward the strike, he must have caught sight of Darrell in his peripheral vision because the owner swerved sharply, bringing the rifle around. But Darrell ran up on him and stepped in close. He grabbed the rifle barrel with both hands. It was hot, burning his fingers, and he almost let go. But Darrell knew if he did, he'd die. So he ignored the pain and ripped at the weapon.

The clouds opened up and sent down a torrent of rain now, quickly drenching them and making the barrel slick. Still, Darrell tightened his grip and would not let go. The wind picked up the rain and threw it at their faces, the drops feeling cold and hard. Darrell's instinct was to wipe the moisture out of his eyes so he could see better but couldn't chance it. As he struggled with the wet metal, he and Harrington twisted, turning, and he caught sight of the others. Luis knocked Helen to the ground, and Erin wrestled the gun away. At least, they'd gotten it done. Now he had to step up.

Harrington snarled at him, "Who do you think you are, you pissant?"

The rain came harder then, the downpour dropping rivers of water on them now and turning the tan dirt at their feet to a brown swamp of sloppy mud. Darrell felt his feet slipping. With a quick move, he chanced to slide his hands down the rifle, one after the other, grasping the stock. Using a firmer hold on the gun, he shoved hard, knocking Harrington back onto the wet and slippery earth. Darrell came down hard on top of him. As they went down, Harrington kept pulling the trigger, spewing bullets one after another in a deadly arc. *Crack. Crack. Crack. Crack.* Darrell fought to keep the aim away from Luis and Erin. He prayed he'd been successful but had no time to check.

Entangled together, they rolled on the ground, the oily mud lathering their arms, clothes, and even their hair. The mud and slop creeped Darrell out, and he felt his OCD emerging. He fought to keep his compulsion under control. He needed to stay alive.

Darrell slipped in the mud, having to throw out one hand to brace himself. Harrington used the opportunity to try to wrestle the gun away, but Darrell kept the grip of his one hand like iron. He was *not* going to give up that hold. He was surprised how strong the older man was. It was almost as if Harrington, like Darrell, was fighting for his life.

The rain kept coming, only increasing in intensity, and the thunder echoed again, this time farther away. The water poured as if some huge faucet had been unleashed, drenching their clothes, their hair, their skin, running into their eyes and mouths and ears. Darrell shook his head, but it did no good. The rifle was even slicker, coated now with rain and mud, making it more difficult for Darrell to maintain any grip on it. He realized he was running out of time. His strength was fading, and holding on was getting harder. But he knew it had to be the same with Harrington. The man was twenty years older, and Darrell could hear him wheezing and gasping for air.

Darrell had to do something to change the stalemate. He shot a glance at the wet mud. His compulsion made him squirm, but he didn't know what else to do. With his free hand, he reached down and grabbed a fistful of wet mud. He stuffed the clod into the owner's face. He pushed hard, smashing the wet dirt into the man's eyes.

Harrington cried out, shaking his head hard back

and forth. When that didn't do any good, the owner released one hand to try to wipe the mud out of his eyes. Seeing his chance, Darrell returned his second now muddy fist to the gun and, using both hands, struggled to rip it from Harrington's one-handed grasp. But the owner's single hand held on tight, even as his other arm flailed at Darrell in a blind rage. Darrell dragged his foot through the mud and braced it against Harrington's body. In one swift motion, Darrell shoved hard with one leg and ripped at the gun. It broke free of the older man's grasp. Darrell fell backward in the mud. He struggled to get one foot steady in the sloppy mess and then set a second foot down. He stood up and raised the gun at Harrington, collapsed on his back and gasping for breath. The rifle, like Darrell, was covered in mud.

Darrell's glance jerked to the side where a figure was approaching. He started to bring the gun around and saw Erin holding Helen's rifle, now aimed at Harrington as well. He looked across and saw Luis standing over the older woman, who knelt on the ground weeping.

The rain kept coming, steady and hard, though the intensity seemed to back off a bit, the wind no longer lashing the drops. It still ran down his face but was more of a steady shower than the torrential downpour of a few minutes earlier. Now the wind carried the *whoop-whoop* of a siren through the downpour, and he could see the flashing strobe of a police car. The cruiser barreled down the gravel road, pebbles and stones kicking out behind the tires. It bumped across the uneven surface of the yard and came to an abrupt stop fifty feet from where they huddled, its tires sliding in the wet mud. The driver's door opened, and Deputy Atwater jumped out, silver pistol drawn.

Water running in his eyes, Darrell looked at the cop and yelled, "Took your time getting here, Atwater."

The deputy kept his gun pointed their way and said, "Drop the rifles, and we can talk."

Darrell glanced across at Erin, her red hair dripping in the rain and her face soaked. Her green eyes shone, and she gave a tired grin. He nodded. She set her rifle down, and he followed suit. Both raised their hands. Even through the noise of the abating storm, Darrell heard a faint sound off to the side and looked. Daniel and Mia had taken up the Spanish carol again, softer this time. As he watched and listened, they smiled at him, two beautiful, innocent smiles, and then the image faded along with the strains of their Christmas song, evaporating into the rain.

Chapter 51

It ain't over till it's over

As Atwater approached, Darrell's gaze went from the officer to Harrington. The plantation owner pulled himself together and stood, his bearing erect, stiff even. He wiped the mud off the khakis and called, "Thank heaven you arrived in time, Deputy Atwater. These people broke into Tom Stickley's house, and they bashed him on the head and almost killed him." He indicated the obese figure lying several feet away. As if on cue, Tom Stickley raised his head up and groaned, his hand going to the cut at the hairline.

"Helen managed to get a call to me before they grabbed her, and I came right over," Harrington continued, heaving as he talked. "It's a good thing I did. They were planning on killing them both and burying them up there." He gestured behind him toward the top of the mound.

The rain had slowed to a steady drizzle, turning the entire scene into shades of hazy gray. Standing there, water dripping off a plastic-covered "Smokey the Bear" hat, Atwater appeared to study the group, eyes going from Darrell, Erin, and Luis, now standing together, to Harrington and finally Helen, huddled on the ground. "Everyone, over there." He pointed to the right, away from the rifles. Without waiting, Darrell, Erin, and Luis moved where the cop indicated.

Harrington didn't budge and said, "You got to believe me, Deputy. These people are dangerous. I'm not sure what all they had in mind, but it can't be good. Well…" His hands flew out wildly. "A few days ago, Savannah and I welcomed these two into our home. They were asking about some…some kids, but that was only a…a ruse. They came here to rob us." He pointed at Luis. "And *he* came along. I bet if you check you'll find he has a record." He nodded at the officer, as if they shared some secret. "You know how those people are." In the middle of the rant, Darrell caught Harrington's eyes darting toward the rifles lying only a few feet away.

Atwater's face betrayed nothing, and he kept his pistol directed at the plantation owner. "I'll sort this out in a minute. Right now, I need you two to move over there with them, sir."

Harrington opened his mouth to argue but stopped. He trudged deliberately across the ground, his shoes making sucking sounds in the thick mud.

Helen didn't move though. She still knelt and bent over, hands pounding the ground over and over, even as the rain continued dripping on her.

The cop called, "Mrs. Stickley?" When she didn't respond and didn't even raise her head, he must have decided she was no threat. He stooped down and used his free hand to collect the mud-caked rifles. One after the other, he tossed them away from the group and next to the cruiser, all the while keeping his pistol aimed at the four people standing to the side. Opening the front door, he reached inside and grabbed the mic. He barked a few words and returned it to its stand. Then, without ever taking his eyes off the group, he popped the trunk, placed both rifles on the floor, and shut the lid.

When he came back, he turned toward Darrell. "What about it, Darrell? You have anything to say to Mr. Harrington's accusations?"

Darrell glanced at Erin. "Deputy, if we could have a look at the hole we dug up there"—he pointed back up the mound—"I think it will answer all your questions."

"Lead the way." Atwater gestured with his gun.

Darrell climbed up the incline, the cop a few feet behind.

"Don't go up there!" screamed Helen Stickley. Both Darrell and Atwater turned, and the cop came over to Helen. She had risen partway up, now facing them. A trembling finger pointed toward the gaping hole. "Don't disturb them graves no more."

"What graves, Mrs. Stickley?" the deputy asked. "Who's buried there?"

"The kids. Those poor children. Daniel and Mia Sanchez."

Harrington leaned across woman and whispered loudly, "Quiet, Helen." Then he straightened and tried again. "Don't listen to her. She's a little—" He pointed to her head.

The deputy leaned down next to the woman.

Helen stared at the officer and said, "And some other migrants, some really mean wetbacks. I'll tell you everything, the whole horrible story. But Tom didn't want to hurt them kids. Harrington made him."

"Shut your trap or I'll kill you *and* Tom!" screamed Sterling Harrington.

Atwater stepped next to Harrington and raised his

pistol. "I've had about enough from you. Sir." Then, after a moment, he added, "I listened to what you said. Now, I'd advise you to invoke your right to silence." Atwater stared at him, rain dripping slowly off the rim of his hat.

The owner collapsed to the ground again, kneeling in the mud.

Tom Stickley rolled over and sat up slowly, holding his head. His finger probed the small gash on the side of his skull. He glanced around at the group, and his eyes settled on the deputy. "What happened?" he asked, his voice groggy and slurred.

Atwater turned toward the injured man. "Just sit still. I've called, and someone is on the way to check you out."

In the distance, two more emergency strobes cut through the waning rain along with the waling sirens as the group watched. A second black-and-white barreled down the gravel drive and pulled to a halt, another uniformed officer getting out. Thirty seconds later, an ambulance followed, pulling around the gravel circle, and stopped. Two EMT's bolted from the doors, and Atwater directed them over to Tom Stickley.

It was over then, though it took hours to sort everything out.

Atwater had the second cop, a deputy named Goldrich, keep a gun on everyone else while he accompanied Darrell to the hole, now quickly filling with water. Darrell knelt next to the opening, and his fingers pushed aside the mud to reveal the bones so the deputy could get a good look at the skull. Atwater's revulsion was similar to Darrell's, though he didn't have to retch. The cop had seen enough, and they rejoined the others.

After checking everyone else and bandaging the burns on Darrell's hands, the EMT's took Tom to the hospital in Dixon to have him examined. Twenty minutes later, the medical examiner's team arrived, and he conferred with Atwater. The coroner and his assistant started to work, preserving the site as best they could in the rain, erecting a tent over the open grave.

While the lab-coated men toiled on their gruesome tasks, the officers transported everyone else back to the sheriff's office, Darrell, Erin, and Luis in Atwater's car, and Helen and Harrington in the second cruiser. From the lost and found, the cops managed to scrounge some dry clothes that almost fit everyone, though the shirt and sweats barely hung on Helen's thin frame.

Darrell held the stained tee shirt and worn jeans he'd been given at an arm's length. Who knows who had worn these before? He glanced down at his own damp and mud-caked khakis and his once-yellow polo shirt, now various shades of brown. Then it struck him. He'd been in so deep, his anger, fear, and loathing for what happened to the kids must've suppressed his OCD. Now, standing there in the ugly police station restroom, staring at the cracked mirror, it all came flooding back. He was covered with mud. He couldn't get the filthy clothes off fast enough. As he pulled the fresh shirt over his head, he thought, at least these looked clean.

As typical with police work, it took hours for Atwater and his fellow officers to get statements from everyone. Well, everyone except Harrington. The owner refused to say any more and was still waiting for his lawyer to arrive from Orlando when Atwater drove

Darrell, Erin, and Luis back to their car in the dark. By the time they arrived back at the Stickleys' close to midnight, the storm had passed. Darrell was surprised to see the team from the medical examiner's office still at work, their bright halogen lights igniting the tableau like a macabre movie set. He saw a few more workers than the two he'd met earlier. As he got out of the cop car, he turned a questioning glance toward Atwater.

The officer must have read Darrell's unspoken question and nodded at the lighted work site. "Our coroner brought in the state boys. It turns out they found a good bit more than the bones of those two poor kids."

Darrell shook his head, not saying anything, and remembered the other sensations he'd picked up along with the kids'. Spirits of malevolence and despair. He lifted his eyes toward the site and sensed nothing now. Relieved, he mumbled, "Thanks," and led the way toward their waiting rental.

Chapter 52

Every holiday must end

They slept in together, the fog of slumber so deep neither stirred as morning light bounced off the water into the bedroom. Darrell was surprised when he finally forced his eyes open and saw the clock read ten twenty.

They spent time shuffling around the vacation house, collecting items and getting things ready for their trip back home, all the while exchanging contented, domestic glances at the ordinariness of things. Rather than go out, they finished off most of the food in the fridge and remembered to leave a nice thank you note for Luis and Bonnie. Darrell planned to take Erin for one last seafood dinner in the charming little town, and then they'd end their trip with some quiet time on the Simmons' patio.

But a call from the real estate agent changed all that. Around two o'clock, the phone rang with Bonnie Bradford on the other end. "Good, you guys are still there. When do you fly out?"

Darrell said, "Tomorrow midday."

"Good," she repeated. "Then you still have time for one last hurrah."

He turned toward Erin who had come over to the phone. "Bonnie, we appreciate the offer, but we're still recovering. The last few days have been exhausting. I think we're going to have one last quiet night here—"

"Sorry, I can't let you do that. I want you to ring in the millennium with us and some friends. Bob and I are having a New Year's Eve party tonight, and I want you to be our guests of honor."

"Guests of honor? Us?" Darrell repeated for Erin's sake.

"Sure. I got a few details of your exploits from Luis and read the piece in the paper. Not much, but enough to catch most of what happened. We don't often get to celebrate real-life heroes. Besides, Doc Simmons and his wife come every year, and he'd never forgive me if I didn't have you join us. Please?"

In the end, they didn't want to upset their host and gave in.

When they arrived at the Bradford house that evening, located a few miles outside of town, they found a sprawling, two-story mansion surrounded by a lush green lawn, all set on a peninsula that jutted out into Kings Bay. The festivities were already in full swing, and they were greeted by several couples, all dressed in unusual attire.

Glancing around at the party guests, Darrell said, "You didn't tell us it was a costume party." With the last-minute invitation, he'd put on what he was going to wear to dinner, a navy-blue polo with the Plantation on Crystal River logo above the pocket and a pair of white slacks. Erin wore another crop top, this one pale blue pulled off the shoulders and with ribbing that hugged her midriff, showing off her flat stomach. Two rows of white stitching ran in vertical lines down the front of the blouse with matching stitching on the puffy sleeves. The stylish blouse sat above white capri pants.

Bonnie laughed. "Not for our local heroes. Besides, you two look great. Erin, I love that top."

Darrell eyed their hostess. The real estate agent was draped in a heavy green fabric with gold tassels running down the center, an odd combination of the green and gold piled on her head. Across her shoulders, a curtain rod protruded through the entire outfit. She twirled and almost hit Darrell with one end of the rod. "The theme tonight is comedians. You get it?"

Erin laughed and said, "Carol Burnett...well, Carol as Scarlet O'Hara. I love that bit."

The two women leaned in and intoned together, "I saw it in the window, and I *just* had to have it," and then burst into a fit of giggles.

Once they settled down, Bonnie introduced them to the other guests, though Darrell forgot most names as soon as the agent said them. It was easier to remember the costumes. One guy was a dead ringer for Groucho Marx, complete with drawn up eyebrows, formal black tux, and exaggerated walk. His partner was Betty White, with a round wig of blonde hair, a broad, guilty smirk, and a flaunty, tight dress of blue so shimmering it was almost sheer. Erin's favorite was the young guy dressed as Robin Williams' Mork, wearing the red bodysuit with the silver triangle and the pristine white gloves. When she smiled at him, he said, "Na Nu. Na Nu."

Bonnie gave them a brief tour of the large house with high-end, modern furnishings, lots of chrome and glass. The entire place was spotless, with tasteful holiday touches sprinkled throughout—a tall toy soldier guarding at the front door, a set of small rocking horses adorning one dresser, and even a miniature sleigh and reindeer resting on the polished wood top of the buffet in the dining room. In one hallway they passed, Darrell saw a painting slightly askew on the wall. On reflex, he reached up to straighten it and noticed the subject. It was a portrait of another pair of children, two smiling, smudged, brown faces done in broad strokes, very similar to their hidden painting. When he read the signature, he made Erin stop.

Bonnie looked behind and saw them admiring the painting. "You like the piece? Bob got it for me at a local gallery in town for Christmas. It's from this young artist, Jared Emerson," she said. "He was impressed with the style and thought I'd like it. He was wrong. I love it."

"So do we," Darrell said, glancing at Erin, who grinned back in silent agreement. He was simply glad no jolt streaked down his arm when he touched the painting. That was all they'd need.

A few minutes later, they ended up in the kitchen, spacious with high-end, stainless steel appliances and a large gas stovetop. The long granite counter was covered with the most extensive display of appetizers and other food specialties Darrell had ever seen. He and Erin dug in.

Not anxious to talk yet, they mingled with the guests, eavesdropping on conversations. Mork was pontificating on who he thought would win the New Hampshire primary in one month, betting on George Bush and Al Gore, and a few others joined in the lively discussion.

Then Betty White said, "Only if the entire internet doesn't crash before then. Is everyone ready for all the computers in the world to shut down at midnight tonight?"

Not a topic Darrell wanted to concentrate on. He glanced around to assess the others' anxiety levels, but the "comedians" in the room merely shrugged.

White added, "When I was little girl, we didn't have any dang computers. Besides, who wants to meet someone online when you can have the real thing in person?" She grinned and paraded around the room, planting a dramatic kiss on several male "comedians."

When she came to Darrell, Erin did a theatrical shove and declared, "Not with my man." Then Erin planted the loudest kiss on Darrell she'd ever delivered. Everyone applauded, and Betty White laughed.

Another guest bore a striking resemblance to Steve Martin, complete with full head of hair, white suit, black tie, and fake arrow through his head. He pointed to his arrow and then Darrell's bandaged hands and Erin's dressing, barely sticking out below the sleeve of her top. "Another hunting accident?" he asked.

"I wouldn't call it an accident," Darrell said.

With that opening, Mork asked about what *really* happened in Meridian County. As the group crowded around them in the huge, high-ceilinged great room, Darrell and Erin stood in front of a beautifully decorated Christmas tree and shared most of the narrative—leaving out any details about the ghosts.

"What a discovery. How did you hear about what happened to those two kids?" Groucho asked, fingers waggling a cigar.

Exchanging a glance with Erin, Darrell said, "Well—"

"I tell Mr. and Mrs. Henshaw about missing kids. I learn from someone at Settlement," cut in Ricky

Ricardo, who had just stepped into the room. Next to him stood a young, red-haired Lucille Ball. He said, "Isn't that right, Lucy?" Lucy nodded.

Luis, aka Ricky, wore a green blazer and pink bowtie over a white shirt, and a silly grin to match. Juanita, aka Lucy, sported a stylish black dress with a tight necklace of fake pearls, her hair up in curls upon her head.

Erin moved in and gave Lucy a hug. "Good to see you again, Juanita. You look great in that getup."

"You too." The young girl beamed, crinkling the fake freckles on her face.

Luis did a half turn. "You like the outfits. Miss Bonnie arrange."

Darrell and Erin nodded.

Betty White spoke up. "I think it's great what you did. However long they throw that Harrington fellow in prison, it won't be long enough."

Darrell said, "I only hope his fancy lawyer isn't able to let him wiggle out of it."

A beer in one hand and a fake Emmy in the other, Bonnie joined the group. "I doubt it. I heard on CNN both Stickleys turned state and have given pretty damning evidence against their boss."

Bonnie's husband Bob, dressed as Tim Conway, complete with an Einstein wig of silver hair, came over. He carried three beers and gave one each to Darrell and Erin. They both nodded their thanks.

The host took a sip of his and joined the conversation. "Yeah, and I saw earlier tonight on the news they also discovered the remains of three men in that makeshift grave at the supervisor's place. According to the reports, the Stickleys claim they were a couple of illegals running drugs among the farm workers, and Harrington had them executed as an example. That plantation owner must've thought he was some kind of dictator."

Darrell realized now where the malevolent sensations emanated from and breathed a sigh of relief he hadn't had to deal with them. He leaned over and whispered to Erin, "Maybe it was all worth it then."

She whispered back, "You're worth it."

They clicked bottles and drank. Their exploits were the talk of the evening, and although they were a bit embarrassed, they appreciated the recognition. Still, Darrell was glad when the group broke up to get ready to watch the ball drop in Times Square.

Steering Erin away from the TV, he convinced her to wander out to the patio to watch the promised light show in the Florida sky. The spectacular fireworks display, which started at one minute past midnight and continued nonstop for more than thirty minutes, did not disappoint. The explosions of reds and blues, yellows and greens, and blinding whites skyrocketed across the sky, creating mirror images on the water of the bay. As the blasts and booms echoed in the air, he held Erin tight in his arms. It was an incredible experience, the colorful explosions in the sky matched with shimmering imitations across the water, all accompanied by the booming sounds. Most important, they got to savor it together, a thunderous conclusion to their exciting honeymoon vacation.

By the time the last of the sparkle died away in the sky, leaving only lingering gray smoke that settled over the water like a heavy cloud and the whiff of gunpower drifting in with the breeze, the patio was crammed with every partygoer.

A crack behind them made Darrell and Erin jump. They turned and saw Tim Conway pouring champagne flutes. Carol Burnette delivered theirs, and they all clinked. "Happy 2000!" Bonnie said.

"Happy 2000!" Darrell and Erin echoed.

Bonnie said, "I'm so glad you came. I hope you can stick around. We have plenty more food."

Darrell and Erin exchanged a look, and she said, "Thanks so much for the invite. It was a wonderful party, and we're stuffed. Couldn't eat anything more."

Bonnie tried, "Oh, yeah, and we have some great, fun games we're going to play."

Darrell saw Erin give him a sly smile. He said, "We need to get home and finish, um...packing."

Twenty minutes later, they pulled into the Simmons' circular driveway for the final time, and he held the expensive glass and wood front door open for Erin with one hand and a food container in the other. Bonnie insisted they take a few treats for the road and had packed them up.

Erin laid a hand on his arm. "Why don't you put that away?" Then she whispered, "And then you can help me with some, uh...packing. In the bedroom." She flashed him a sexy smile, as if he needed it.

He hurried to the kitchen, opened the commercial fridge, and stored the food he wasn't sure they'd ever eat. He turned to head to the master bedroom. Before he closed the large door of the refrigerator, the light from inside spilled across the island. The painting of the sailboat sat in the precise center of the granite top. Before closing the door and extinguishing the light, he reached for the piece. No shock. He turned the framed work over and stared. The two kids were still there, brown hair, caramel eyes, and dirty clothes, captured in the broad strokes. Only now they both wore wide smiles. A *real* Christmas miracle. Darrell smiled too.

He closed the door, shutting off the light, and whistled as he headed down the hall to the bedroom.

A word about the author…

Dr. Randy Overbeck is an award-winning educator, author, and speaker, capturing state and national accolades for his work, first in education and later in writing. As an educator, he served children for more than three decades in a range of roles captured in his novels, from teacher and coach to principal and superintendent. His thriller, *Leave No Child Behind* (2012) and his recent mysteries, *Blood on the Chesapeake* (2019) and *Crimson at Cape May* (2020) have earned more than a dozen five-star reviews and garnered national awards and recognition from such professional sites as Literary Titan, ReadersFavorite.com, ReaderViews.com and N. N. Lights Bookheaven. As a member of the Mystery Writers of America, Dr. Overbeck is an active member of the literary community, contributing to a writers' critique group, serving as a mentor to emerging writers, and participating in writing conferences such as Sleuthfest, Killer Nashville, and the Midwest Writers Workshop.

When he's not writing or researching his next exciting novel or on the road sharing his latest presentation called "More Things That Go Bump in the Night," he's spending time with his incredible family of wife (Cathy), three children and their spouses, and seven wonderful grandchildren.

Read a few of his incredible reviews, check out where Dr. Overbeck will be speaking next, or catch up on his popular blog at his website, www.authorrandyoverbeck.com. Or you can email him at randyoverbeck@authorrandyoverbeck.com, send him a tweet @OverbeckRandy or friend him on Facebook at Author Randy Overbeck.

A bit about the artist featured in this novel
Jared Emerson

One central feature of this story is the portrait of two young Latino children, which to Darrell appears to have special powers and helps lead him to seek justice for the kids. The character I used for the artist who created that special painting is based on a very real artist who does indeed paint with his hands—as well as in more conventional ways. He heralds from South Carolina, where he has a flourishing studio. While I attempted to capture him as a young man extending his artistic wings in northern Florida, the episodes I wrote into the narrative are wholly the fabric of my imagination, though I hope I did justice to his talent and character.

In reality, Jared Emerson is today a world renowned and recognized artist who is perhaps most famous for his live painting of individuals, objects, and even the Face of God. Jared has taken his charcoal, oils, acrylic, and graphite to locations all over the world to perform and create. He is blessed and empowered by his strong Christian faith and brings an intensity to his creations not often seen in an artist. Millions have witnessed and awed, in person and on television, as his creations emerge on canvas from his inspiration, talent, and faith.

Using careful, meticulous brushing or rapid, fluid motions of his fingers and hands, he has captured on canvas such memorable individuals as Mohammed Ali, Dr. Martin Luther King Jr., and Albert Einstein as well as many athletes and celebrities. Because of his incredible talent, he has been asked to perform his live paintings at fundraisers for such organizations as the Ronald McDonald House, Make-A-Wish Foundation, and Big Brothers and Big Sisters. The venues where he has been asked to create his unique, artistic magic are many and varied, from cruise ships and major sporting events to small family gatherings and intimate wedding receptions. In fact, our paths crossed several years ago on board a Royal Caribbean cruise ship where he was doing a special event with Pittsburgh Steeler fans to raise money for charity.

For Jared Emerson, his faith and talent are intertwined and interconnected. His own words capture it best: "My faith guides me. The focus of my work is to capture the essence of what I create, whether it's a person, an object, or anything you can envision. Christ has given me the strength to provide a level of intensity that pours onto the canvas at every event. With every stroke and every detail, I let my heart pour onto the canvas."

Check out more details about this incredible artist and view some of his remarkable pieces on his website: https://jaredemerson.com. You, too, will be impressed.

Author's Notes

This novel is a work of fiction. With the exception of the artist, Jared Emerson, (please see accompanying page for his info) all the characters are products of the author's imagination. However, the town of Crystal River, Florida, is quite real and just as remarkable as represented. This small resort town, located a little more than an hour north of Tampa and nestled into the quiet Gulf Coast, is a real gem of a find. Crystal River is, in fact, the only place in the world people can swim alongside eight-hundred-pound manatees, perhaps the most graceful of sea creatures.

Scarlet at Crystal River is set in December 1999, and I've attempted to recreate this wonderful town in that recent past. The businesses, tourist spots, and restaurants Darrell and Erin visit in the narrative were operating in 1999 (and thankfully still are, even through the 2020-21 pandemic) with one notable exception. Natives and frequent visitors to Crystal River will recognize that the National Wildlife Refuge of Three Sisters' Springs was not developed and opened until several years after this story takes place. But when I visited the Springs and spent some quiet time with these gentle giants, I decided to use a little literary license to include this now iconic stop in my fictional tribute to Crystal River.

The second location of the novel, Meridian County, is however quite fictional. Though the description of this agricultural part of the state is, I think, fairly accurate, I did not want to link the heinous crime depicted herein to any real place. Many of the large farms and plantations in this part of the state do employ a major number of migrants, sometimes in conditions quite similar as depicted in these pages (like the Harrington Plantation) but I did not want to lay this particular tale at the foot of any actual county or town. The plight of the immigrant children at the heart of this story is sadly not unique. And the issue of immigration and migrant workers continues to this day to be a complicated, political, and very human issue. After having completed the research regarding migrant workers for this endeavor, I believe we could all benefit from more extensive and thorough understanding of the issue. I certainly did. To that end, I've included some references that readers might find helpful in educating themselves about this issue at the conclusion of this novel.

The Plight of Migrant Workers in the U.S.

In this country, we are fortunate to have access to the widest assortment ever of fresh produce in our grocery stores and supermarkets. The shelves in the produce aisle sparkle with overflowing selections of healthy fruits and vegetables of every shape and color. Almost any time of the year, shoppers can select from rows and rows of fresh strawberries and crisp broccoli, from green beans and flavorful blueberries, from plump grapes and brussels sprouts. But we should be aware these choices come at quite a price.

Much of this rich harvest of fresh, healthy produce comes to grocery stores through the toil, sweat, and hard work of farm workers across the southern United States, a great many of them migrant workers, an estimated three million, at last count. Their work of harvesting almost-ripe strawberries or picking green beans can be back-breaking labor, and their compensation is among the lowest of all American industries. According to agricultural statistics, their work is among the most dangerous in the country, with a fatality rate for agricultural workers five times the national average. Because of the harsh working conditions and low pay, ranchers and farmers often have to look to undocumented workers to fill their ranks, and that draws illegal immigrants from other countries to the U.S. This need for migrant workers and the desire to provide fresh produce at attractive prices—which translates to low pay to workers—is the push-pull situation that fosters the migration of illegal immigrants from Central America.

Through my research for this novel, I learned that

immigration is a very complex issue, one, I believe few people have a good understanding of. Below, I've listed a few current sources I discovered about migrant workers, both native and undocumented, as merely examples of the information available to educate us on this important issue, if we are willing to search out this knowledge. Readers will have no trouble finding other sources to confirm the basic information provided in the sources below.

Those of us whose families have been in this country for generations sometimes forget we *all* came to this country as immigrants—unless we happen to be Native Americans. As we consider the fate of "illegal" immigrants and how they should be treated, we might do well to remember our own history. Like many of our ancestors, these migrants left their homes and their families to come to America in search of a better future. Perhaps, the next time we bite into a juicy strawberry—like the ones Daniel and Mia's parents were harvesting in my story—we might pause a second to ponder what struggles it took to get that fruit from the sunbaked fields of Florida to our breakfast table.

A Few Sources:
https://www.migrantclinician.org/issues/migrant-info/migrant.html
https://brandongaille.com/28-remarkable-migrant-worker-statistics/
https://www.peoplesworld.org/article/the-true-conditions-of-farm-workers-today/
https://copdei.extension.org/migrant-farm-workers-our-nations-invisible-population/